DAMNED
TO
SUCCESS

By HANS HELLMUT KIRST

Revolt of Gunner Asch

Gunner Asch Goes to War

Return of Gunner Asch

The Officer Factory

The Night of the Generals

What Became of Gunner Asch?

Soldier's Revolt

The Last Card

Brothers in Arms

The Wolves

Last Stop Camp 7

No Fatherland

The Adventures of Private Faust

Hero in the Tower

Damned to Success

DAMNED TO SUCCESS

HANS HELLMUT KIRST

TRANSLATED FROM THE GERMAN
BY J. MAXWELL BROWNJOHN

Coward, McCann & Geoghegan
New York

First American Edition 1973

First published in German under the title VERDAMMT ZUM ERFOLG
Copyright ©1972 by Verlag Kurt Desch GmbH, Munchen
English translation copyright ©1973 by Wm. Collins & Co., Ltd.

SBN: 698-10522-2

Library of Congress Catalog Card Number: 72-94118

Printed in the United States of America

This is a novel. Its plot and characters are fictitious. Any apparent resemblance to or correspondence with real events is unintended. The same applies to my portrayal of public figures in the city which serves as my backdrop. They are merely fictional and symbolic characters, not reconstructions of reality.

The book that follows is dedicated to my first dog, Anton the Newfoundland, and to Muckel the poodle, fellow-creatures to whom I am indebted for moments of unadulterated joy.

The truth — or what we imagine it to be —
is like a swing that recedes and advances, swoops and soars.
It all depends when you climb on.

The attempted destruction of Harald Fein began one evening in late summer. Within a few weeks his downfall seemed complete, but this proved to be a fatal misconception.

Full details of the affair remained largely unknown to the general public. Assumptions, suppositions and conjectures – various and all grossly conflicting – broke surface and quickly submerged again. Many of our fellow-citizens have deplorably short memories, and many others gamble on their forgetfulness.

One unknown factor was the existence of some notes kept by a CID officer named Keller. Few could have foreseen what the result would be.

Keller was bold enough to seek justice and obtain it by methods which were notable for their consistency and dangerous in their temerity.

Chapter One

She had buttocks like a horse. A thoroughbred, naturally. Smooth, firm and rounded, mobile and mettlesome. There was a seductive, stupefying scent about her – or so he guessed.

In short, a first-rate filly capable of winning any class of race for her owner of the moment. No doubt she had her price. Whatever it was, Harald Fein could pay it. As things stood.

For the moment he seemed content to survey the lovely female specimen from a distance, meditatively. It was the third time he had kept watch in two weeks – or was it the fourth time in three weeks? He couldn't remember.

She emerged from her usual haunt, the bar on the corner, and sauntered towards the apartment house. Her heels tapped out a slow but purposeful rhythm on the sidewalk. She must be expecting a visitor, perhaps a succession of visitors. Harald Fein wondered who would be first in line this time. He already knew several of her regulars by sight and one in particular.

It was the sort of late summer evening which is only possible in Munich, with opalescent shades of blue that merged with the gathering gloom but threw everything into focus. Sharply silhouetted buildings, human figures like cardboard cut-outs, the streets a blue-grey wash applied with a loaded brush.

There was little movement at this hour – a few cars, a few pedestrians, scarcely a dog in sight. It was time for the simultaneous ingestion of supper and TV news broadcasts, a habit which was boosting the incidence of unwonted gastric disorders in an age noted for its multitude of strange new ailments.

Harald Fein, sitting in his parked car beside the kerb, looked watchful and faintly amused. He smiled to himself as he registered what went on around him. His patience seemed inexhaustible.

Harald Fein, some days later, while being interrogated by the CID, otherwise termed 'assisting the police with their inquiries':

I was driving home from the office as usual. I pulled up near an

9

apartment house in V-Strasse. Quite by chance. I suppose there happened to be a parking space.

I was exhausted – who wouldn't be, after twenty years in a job like mine? So I parked and turned on the radio. It was news time.

DETECTIVE: V-Strasse isn't on your direct route home.

FEIN: I must have made a detour. I often try out new ways of dodging the rush-hour traffic. That was it, probably – I don't remember for certain.

Paul Plattner, chairman and majority shareholder of the respected, efficient and influential Plattner Construction Company, was leafing through the daily report that had been submitted to him after closing time. He eyed it with mounting indignation.

'This,' he declared, 'is a monumental fuck-up. Site 14 has been starved of material for days.'

Facing him at a deferential distance stood Gottfried Wamsler, the office messenger, a conscientious individual of proven reliability. His face conveyed commiseration. If Plattner called something a fuck-up, it was one.

'Get me Herr Fein,' Plattner commanded.

Wamsler cleared his throat discreetly. 'Your son-in-law has already . . .'

'In this office,' Plattner corrected him, 'Herr Fein isn't my son-in-law, he's my managing director. There's a subtle but important difference, Wamsler. Kindly remember that.'

'Yessir,' barked Wamsler.

'So what the hell are you waiting for? Tell the managing director I want him.'

'But he already left. On the dot, as usual. Said he was driving home.'

'In that case, call him. Tell him to get back here, and tell him I said so.'

Harald Fein leant back in the driver's seat. His car was a Mercedes 280SL, a luxury vehicle designed for the upper middle-class market and one his father-in-law insisted he maintain for prestige reasons. After all, Harald was a somebody.

Made months ago, this statement had vanished into limbo – as if Harald were a somebody no longer. Heads rolled quickly in Munich's social and commercial jungle. Harald sat back and stretched his legs, outwardly preoccupied with the astonishing figure of the blonde.

Behind him on the back seat crouched an alert but long-suffering creature, a stunted heraldic beast in the shape of a dog named Anton. Not well-groomed like a poodle nor decoratively unkempt like an old English sheep-dog – more of a mini-New-foundland with traces of dachshund. A wholly indeterminate mix-ture, a canine challenge to the geneticist's imagination. Anton squatted there blinking, not entirely without hope of diversion.

Harald Fein seemed to accept Anton's presence as a matter of course. Anton, he believed, was the only creature in the world which made no demands on him, and Anton did nothing to destroy that belief. He never intruded, least of all on an occasion like this.

'Where's Daddy?' asked Helga Fein. 'I have to speak to him, urgently.'

'He isn't home yet.' Her mother, Hilde Fein, was poised over her dressing-table applying eye-shadow. The desired shade of blue refused to materialize, a failure which threatened to fray her nerves. 'What do you want him for?'

'I've got a problem.' Helga stared at her mother from the doorway, trying to hide her repugnance at the sight of so much window-dressing. 'What's up tonight – the usual? A gala occasion, or something more intimate, like a small party for sixty?'

'What sort of problem?' said her mother.

'You wouldn't understand. Daddy would.'

'Would he?' Hilde Fein raised her head and stared into the mirror, first at her own reflection, then at her daughter's: in her view, a sad contrast between careful grooming and slovenly neglect. 'You overestimate him.'

'I asked where he was, I didn't ask for your opinion of him. Everyone knows that.'

'Listen,' said Hilde, 'couldn't we at least try . . .'

'No.' There was no rancour in the girl's voice, just regret. 'We both have our own ideas about Daddy.'

Wamsler clicked his heels. 'Your son-in-law – I mean, the managing director – left here at the usual time, just after six, but he hasn't reached home yet.'

Paul Plattner, still at his desk, frowned. 'Any idea where he could be? Well? Out with it, if you know.'

'Knowing is one thing,' Wamsler said cautiously, 'suspecting's another.'

'Any suspicions, then?'

'Well, there may be a woman. It's just possible.'

'What woman?'

'I don't know, sir. Not yet.'

'Try and find out, Wamsler. It could pay off – need I say more? Now get me Herr Jonas. Dig him out, wherever he is. Office hours mean nothing in this place.'

Excerpts from preliminary CID notes relating to the apartment house at No. 33 V-Strasse:

The usual picture, at first sight. Tenants in the middle to upper-middle income bracket. Downstairs two doctors: one ear-nose-and-throat specialist, one dermatologist. Some senior executives: three company directors, two bank employees. A retired professor, the wife of an impressionist painter, widowed for half a century, and a married couple who write poetry for kicks.

Finally, the woman on the sixth (top) floor. Official occupation: model. Vital statistics: 39-24-39. She would have been thirty in ten days' time.

First sighted by Harald Fein three or four weeks earlier, the woman had begun to preoccupy him more and more, and not only because he found her an alluring prospect, something which promised to make all his secret hankerings come true.

Dashed hopes and an agonizing lack of fulfilment had failed to blunt his recurrent pangs of desire. This superbly primitive body seemed to hold promise of release or, at worst, relief. Not for him alone, but he didn't care.

He had meanwhile discovered a few things about her. With a fair degree of regularity, as though faithful to her own fixed working hours, she emerged from the apartment house just before 8 p.m. and sauntered over to the bar on the next corner, the *El Dorado*.

There, like someone taking a break between shifts, she consumed three fried eggs on a slice of ham and washed them down with a glass of German champagne. Clearly, she was fortifying herself for further social activities.

Anton propped his head on the back of the passenger seat. His brown eyes were watchful, not that Harald turned to look. The dog's gaze was fixed on the entrance to the apartment house. Someone was standing inside the glass doors, avoiding the hall light. Just standing. He had been there a long time.

Harald turned up the radio in quest of information and, if possible, entertainment. It was time for news and comments on world affairs.

The newscaster announced:
'The President – ' presumably that of the United States – 'is deeply concerned . . .'

'The President – ' presumably another one, Arab or Central African – 'has proclaimed his determination to safeguard the rights, honour and freedom of his people . . .'

'The President – ' yet another, this time of some organization connected with the forthcoming Munich Olympics – 'wishes to stress with all the force at his command that the additional expenditure of forty-eight million marks in no way represents a deviation from original estimates. On the contrary . . . unforeseen circumstances . . . economic conditions . . . factors beyond our control . . .'

'What a world!' Harald chuckled and switched off the radio. 'Full of liars and idiots who not only believe anything that takes their fancy but are ready to die for it. Pay for it, too.'

He had often caught himself talking aloud in recent weeks, but only when he was alone with Anton, his captive audience. Anton pricked his ears and registered total comprehension.

'Money and lust,' Fein said to Anton, peering up at the sixth floor. Her light was a subdued glow now, tinged with red, softly fused with the surrounding darkness. 'Lust for money and money for the gratification of lust – it's a vicious circle. Few people break out and few ever want to, but I do. I'm ready at last, understand?'

Anton had stretched out on the back seat. He shook his head vigorously, either in affirmation or because his ears itched. After a

13

desultory lick at his forepaws he resumed his watch on the man in the shadowy hall.

Paul Plattner eyed the assistant managing director of his construction company with a hint of indulgence. 'You're a sharp dresser, Jonas.'

'If I am,' Jonas assured him gravely, 'it's only for the firm's sake.' He stood confronting his employer in a rust-red dinner-jacket tailored by Pierre Cardin. 'Your daughter asked me to escort her this evening. The London Pub is celebrating its third anniversary.'

'Very important, I'm sure.' Plattner's voice softened at the mention of his daughter. 'On the other hand, so is Site 14, and Site 14 is a shambles. Someone's been sabotaging the whole operation – there's no other word for it.'

'Not guilty, Herr Plattner.'

'Who is, then? Fein?'

'Not me, that's all I know. It's not my department. What's more – if you don't mind my saying so – it wouldn't have happened if I'd been in charge. I pull my weight.'

'From my daughter's angle?'

'From *every* angle.'

'Good, then you can assume responsibility for Site 14. Everything else can wait, including my daughter.'

Hilde Fein smiled down at her friend Melanie Weber. 'I've fixed a Martini, extra dry. Just the way you like it.'

Melanie sank back in her chair and stretched luxuriously. She was a brunette with a low, husky voice and a habit of laying dramatic stress on every other word. 'I like anything that's *in*, darling – anything that suits my mood, anything that belongs to *our* kind of world. A pity about Harald, by the way. Have you really written the poor man off for good?'

'If there's one person who doesn't belong in our kind of world, it's him,' Hilde said briskly. 'I thought we saw eye to eye on that subject.'

'But is it *final*?'

'Any reason why not? Don't tell me you're taking a fresh interest in him.'

'I wonder why you married him in the first place, that's all.'

'You're talking about nearly twenty years ago, for God's sake. Think of all that's happened since then.'

'What, for instance?'

'Must we discuss it?' Hilde downed her Martini. 'We never have so far. Let's leave it that way. What matters is the two of us and all that's ours – exclusively ours.'

'Too true, darling.' Melanie pressed her friend's hand tenderly – she had joined her on the sofa. 'Worry plays *havoc* with a woman's appearance, and no man's worth *that*, Harald included. The same goes for Joachim Jonas, doesn't it? Or *does* it?'

The man standing in the shadows in the hallway of No. 33 V-Strasse was tall and scraggy. His pallid face seemed to emit a faint glow in the dimness, but his features were indistinguishable.

He stood there staring out for minutes on end. If footsteps approached he retreated; if someone entered he vanished in the direction of the basement. Soundlessly, on rubber soles.

Alone once more, he would resume his post near the door and glance at his watch, self-absorbed, then hurriedly scribble something in a notebook. Two or three words at most. Or figures. A name, perhaps no more than a code-word.

Then the shadows swallowed him again.

One thing was certain: No. 33 V-Strasse did not lie anywhere on Harald Fein's direct route home.

Furthermore, his presence there could not be explained by any form of traffic diversion or the desire to take a short cut. His house, or, to be more precise, his wife's house, lay in the Grünwald direction. His office, or, to be strictly accurate, that of his father-in-law's firm, was situated in the Marienplatz immediately facing the Rathaus, or City Hall. Plattner Construction occupied an eight-room suite on the fifth floor.

Munich, demonstrably the most expensive city in the affluent Federal Republic, 'Germany's secret capital', 'Gateway to the Balkans', home of breweries, beer-tents and the Oktoberfest, Hitler's stamping-ground, Germany's answer to Chelsea and Greenwich Village, famous for café society, student riots, intimate review and theatre workshopism . . .

Plenty of room for everyone and everything, from super-capitalists to social misfits, from displays of genitalia alias cinematic art to mind-blowing perversions of every kind. A place where mumbo-jumbo passed for mysticism, obscenity for wit, self-interest for philanthropy, social polish for culture. The place where Sigi Sommer wrote his humorously splenetic pieces, where Ernst Maria Lang's disconcertingly apt and mordant drawings first saw the light, where Erich Kästner raised his gentle but persistent voice in admonition.

It was also a city in which sections of the younger generation – small sections – indulged in noisy protest. If not with any great stamina, always with enthusiasm. Only, so it seemed, to relapse into pleasures of an entirely different kind: the deafening uproar of the student den, the cloying aroma of a sick world. Pot.

In this city and its immediate environs alone, the police confiscated five hundred pounds of drugs in a single year. 'Probably just a small percentage of the goods available,' commented a CID narcotics expert. Even schoolchildren had started to smoke pot in the outer suburbs. Urbanization through vice.

The fact that this cauldron neither boiled over nor exploded seemed primarily due to one man, His Honour the Mayor of Munich, though even he had his hands full with the Fein affair. And this, no doubt, was just what his political and other opponents had been praying for. Munich has never been short of churches.

A CID officer named Feldmann, some days later, during one of the first official interrogation sessions:

Herr Fein, how long does it take you to drive to the office from your home, or vice versa?

FEIN: About fifteen minutes, but only under normal traffic conditions. In rush-hour – which is normal enough, I suppose – half-an-hour or more.

FELDMANN: We have several statements to the effect that you start work at 9 a.m. When do you quit?

FEIN: As soon as I can. Officially, about 5 p.m., but it can easily be later – a lot later. Sometimes I don't get home till midnight.

FELDMANN: Even when you've left the office at 6 p.m.?

FEIN: Why not? My time's my own, isn't it? Well, isn't it?

FELDMANN: Quite so, generally speaking. It all depends.

FEIN: On what?

FELDMANN: Well, on what you do with it.

From personal notes kept by Detective-Superintendent Keller. His first entry concerning the present case:

A succession of monotonously similar days, like peas in a pod – like the corpses I encounter on the job.

Corpses in every conceivable position – lying full length, bent double, crouching, hanging, sprawled on their bellies. Corpses in every conceivable location – on beds, beside them, under them, dangling from transoms, on landings, in lavatories, in cars, in the middle of the street, drifting in rivers. Corpses injured or mutilated in every conceivable way – amputation, decapitation, evisceration, strangulation, etcetera. All in a day's work to us. We have printed forms designed for every eventuality. I fill out upwards of a thousand every year.

Just occasionally, though, something different comes along – something which promises to shatter the usual routine. E.g. this morning, when Superintendent Braun gave an excited yelp and announced that he'd hooked a big one.

He was referring to a man named Harald Fein.

Assertions, explanations and conjectures voiced by Gottfried Wamsler, an employee of the Plattner Construction Company, while chatting confidentially with a detective assigned to pump him:

What happened on the evening of 15 September, at head office in the Marienplatz? I remember perfectly. Why? Because it was my wife's birthday, that's why. You should see the woman – a belly on her like a Japanese wrestler and haunches so fat she can hardly hoist herself out of a chair. I wasn't in any hurry to get home. Particularly since I was expecting Herr Plattner, the boss. I'm close to the old man – have been for years. I'd do anything for him and he knows it. He trusts me, and plenty of people resent the fact.

Anyway, the fat was really in the fire that evening. Plattner turned up first, after office hours. He'd been out somewhere. The place was deserted except for me. It was all Fein's fault. If the old man isn't around his son-in-law quits on the dot and the rest of the office staff pack up a few minutes later.

It takes a lot to rattle the old man, but this time he blew up.

17

Told me to get hold of Fein but I couldn't reach him. Jonas was next in line for a chewing-out – and what a chewing-out!

Then he asked to see Fräulein Wagnersberger, his personal secretary. She was out on the town, and that pretty little assistant of hers, Lulu, didn't answer her phone either. I tell you, he nearly blew his top!

Then he asked for his granddaughter, Helga – he's always had a soft spot for her – but she wasn't at home.

'Things can't go on this way!' he yelled, and slammed his fist on the desk. Plenty of muscle, the old man has. Built like a bull, but a proper gentleman – they shouldn't have treated him that way. Like I said, it was all Fein's fault.

That was only the start, though. The real fireworks came later.

Hilde Fein replaced the receiver with an exasperated expression. 'Harald's being irresponsible again,' she said. 'He's vanished into the blue and left Joachim to do his work for him.'

Melanie Weber stretched her legs. 'At least it gives us some time to *ourselves*, darling. We've had little enough of that in the past few months, not to say years.'

They were sitting side by side in the drawing-room of the Fein villa in Munich-Harlaching, busy with their third Martini, extra dry. Their expertly painted faces were developing a slight bloom.

'What shall we do if Joachim can't make it?' This, for the moment, appeared to be Hilde's most urgent problem.

'We can go to the party without him, if you really insist. You won't go unescorted, though, not if I know you. For your father's sake. He likes everything to be just so, however squalid.'

'Father knows what he wants and so do I. After all, I am his daughter.'

'And Harald's wife.' Melanie stared searchingly at her friend. 'Aren't you two getting on any better?'

'Worse and worse,' Hilde confessed. 'I've reached the stage where I hardly know how it happened. Youthful irresponsibility, perhaps, or a first crazy infatuation. He kept badgering me. He overwhelmed me – it was like a volcanic eruption . . .'

'So the warmth of a man's body drove me from your mind!' Melanie's style was on the purple side.

'You'd been out of town for weeks. I was feeling lonely and he took advantage of it. It all started in a café on Feilitschplatz. We'd been drinking – cheap liquor, of course. He systematically worked on me until I agreed to go back to his room. That's how it happened. He got me pregnant.'

Statements made by the gossip columnist of the Morgenzeitung, *popularly known as the MZ. Pseudonym: 'Argus'. 'Argus' on the subject of Hilde Fein:*

A prominent member of Munich society. Her couturier: Maison Létrange of Paris. Her hairdresser: Robert, also of Paris. Supplements her wardrobe at Arabella's of Beauchamp Place, London, and occasionally at Bessie Becker's, Munich.

Present at all the smartest functions in our warm-hearted city. For instance, at the opening of the Atlantic Bar, where savage sharks cruise behind plate glass. Also at Nero's, whose marble floors, imported from Italy, are sprinkled with genuine Tiber water flown in twice weekly, and whose powder-room boasts rolls of toilet paper threaded with gold.

A prominent socialite, as I say. Very rarely escorted by her husband in recent months but almost always arm-in-arm with Melanie Weber. Recently, too, with Joachim Jonas, a close business associate of her husband's.

All in all, not a woman to be ignored. Even Sybille, social columnist of the *Stern* and one of Munich's journalistic image-makers, is reputed to have given her a meaningful smile. At a function of some importance, too – a party held to celebrate a Munich team's triumph in the German Football Cup.

Still, as I implied, there's been a soupçon of melancholy about her lately.

A man lurched across the darkened street, a small bent figure in a baggy raincoat. He came to a halt just beside the Mercedes in which Harald Fein was sitting, swayed for a moment and then seemed to stare intently into the gutter.

A splashing sound was heard.

'Do you mind!' Harald called through the open window. 'Can't you do it somewhere else?'

'Screw off!' countered the bent figure, retreating crabwise. 'I suppose you get a kick out of watching. One of those, are you?'

Anton barked furiously. He enjoyed barking defiance, especially from a safe position behind his master. Anton was anything but stupid.

Harald chuckled. 'As far as I'm concerned,' he said, 'you can relieve yourself anywhere you like, just as long as you don't do it on my car.'

From a subsequent interview between Detective-Superintendent Braun and a man named Franz Baumholder:

BRAUN: All right, Franz, start talking and make it snappy. Bullshit won't get you anywhere – you know me from way back.

BAUMHOLDER: What am I supposed to tell you, Super?

BRAUN: One of our prowl cars picked you up in V-Strasse late on the evening of 15 September. What were you doing, trying car doors? Fancied a ride in a nice shiny Mercedes, did you?

BAUMHOLDER: I've turned over a new leaf, Super, honest. Stealing cars is out. I'm part of the protest movement now. Nothing illegal about free speech – it says so in the Federal Constitution. Some folks'll pay you good money for carrying a banner. So who cares what's written on it? Everybody's got a right to sound off. Anyway, last Saturday it was 'Hands off Hanoi!' – I toted that one all round the city centre. The same evening it was 'Marco's for the Nudest Show in Town!'

BRAUN: I told you, Franz, no bullshit. What about the Mercedes?

BAUMHOLDER: Okay, so I pissed on it. It was a sort of protest. That's to say, I didn't actually piss on it, just in front of it. I did it to rile the guy inside. He was one of those.

BRAUN: One of which?

BAUMHOLDER: You know, the kind that hang around after dark, spying on people – a guy taking a quiet piss or couples pawing each other. They get a kick out of it.

BRAUN: Okay, Franz, let's go into your story in a little more detail.

Further comments on the present case taken from the personal notes of Detective-Superintendent Keller:

I share an office with Braun. Not in the interests of closer co-operation, mind you, only for lack of space. Convicted criminals get more elbow-room than the poor bastards who have to catch them.

We all belong to the Capital Crimes Division, popularly known as the murder squad. Our precinct, which extends from Stachus to Marienplatz, can set up eight CID teams at any one time. One of them is headed by Braun. I don't belong to any particular team and haven't for several years. My job is PECD, or Preliminary Establishment of the Cause of Death.

In practice, that means I take a couple of subordinates and turn up whenever a dead body comes to light. Washed up on the river bank, asphyxiated in a garage, beaten to death in a back alley – you name it, I've seen it. In the long run, you get bored and exhausted by it all.

PECD amounts to a sort of non-medical autopsy. We examine all bodies in cases where there's a possibility that death may not have been due to natural causes, i.e. diseases and doctors' attempts to cure them. We then record our provisional findings: accident, suicide, natural causes or putative manslaughter, if not murder. In the latter instance the case is taken over by one of our teams – the Chief Superintendent decides which one. Meanwhile, we move on to the next cadaver.

It's a soul-destroying job, and distractions are always welcome. Especially when they're provided by my colleague Det.-Supt. Braun. A busy bee, Braun. He thinks any case he handles must be top priority because *he's* handling it.

The results can be pretty spectacular. Braun's a great one for seeing things in black and white. The Harald Fein case was no exception.

Information supplied by Detective Chief Superintendent Dürrenmaier to a reporter from the newspaper München am Mittag, *or* MAM *for short, and recorded in shorthand:*

Our officers are over-extended and underpaid. Most of the time they're juggling half a dozen cases at once. Hardly surprising if someone makes the occasional boob, is it? It doesn't happen very often, God knows.

All right, since you're so interested, let's talk about Superintendent Keller. A top man in his field. He's headed scores of special investigations and homicides over the years – chalked up scores of successes, too.

He's still our best man – one of the best, anyway. This division isn't short of first-rate officers. It's a question of assigning them where they'll get the best results. Keller has specialized in PECD – preliminary establishment of the cause of death. He never misses a trick. As far as expert knowledge goes, I'd back him against plenty of forensic scientists.

Of course I've heard the rumour. Some people say Keller overstepped the mark when he was still in charge of a homicide squad – i.e. when he suspected a government minister of criminal conspiracy. These things happen, but evidence has to be watertight before you act on it. If it is watertight, an officer has every right to pursue such a line of inquiry. Unfortunately for Keller, it wasn't.

No, he wasn't demoted – take my word for it. I simply assigned him to a job more in keeping with his qualifications. Obviously, somebody had to take over his team. It happened to be Superintendent Braun.

Harald Fein, lounging in his Mercedes, smoked his fifty-third cigarette of the day. He only admitted to forty, and that was thirty more than his doctor allowed.

His doctor, and also his wife's doctor. It was inevitable that he treated Harald precisely as Hilde deemed appropriate. Deliberate and universal abstinence – half a pack of cigarettes, a low-calorie diet and no alcohol.

A doctor who realized what was expected of him. He ministered not only to Harald, his wife and children, but also to Harald's father-in-law, Paul Plattner. Plattner paid his fees, which were no doubt fatter than the diet he prescribed.

He appeared promptly whenever a child coughed, whenever Hilde felt unwell or complained of migraine, whenever Plattner demanded hormone injections or Harald lay slumped in a corner, drunk. No family function was complete without him.

And one day he came, saw and declared: 'Herr Fein, you're killing yourself.'

As if Harald needed to be told!

Information about the Plattner Construction Company, Harald Fein and circumstances relating to Site 14, supplied by Alfred Rosenegger, a civil engineer employed by the firm:

The site in question – we always give them a number for identification purposes – is some distance outside Munich. The project was a new bridge over the Isar. Very handsome lines, too. Harald Fein had designed it.

I'd been appointed site engineer. As usual in such cases, the head office was responsible for technical supervision, appointment of personnel and supplies of material. In this particular instance the chain of command got snarled up. Fein was in over-all charge but Jonas bore immediate responsibility.

Every construction project has its ups and downs, but this time the problems were out of all proportion. Jonas assigned me a labour force which was second-rate, to put it mildly. Professional loafers, drunks and drifters. What's more, when I requisitioned material from Depot No. 2, which was responsible for keeping the site supplied, I didn't get what I wanted and I didn't get it on time.

It may have been the fault of Pollock, the Depot No. 2 gateman, who took receipt of all requisitions and passed them on. Ours went to the bottom of the pile. The strange thing was, I knew Pollock had been picked for the job by Jonas – or Jonas's department.

Not just to make trouble for Fein – or not so you could prove it, but the outcome was the same. Fein didn't suspect a thing, I'd swear. He went on tinkering with his designs. Brilliant, they were. At least, I thought so.

Unfortunately, the firm seemed to have it in for him. I spotted that even before the Site 14 business. The snake-pit – that's what a lot of us used to call head office. Fein wasn't snake-pit material. He didn't have enough natural venom.

. . . as Hilde Fein, 38, remarked to her friend Melanie Weber, also 38, in the course of their heart-to-heart chat:
    . . . systematically taking advantage of me. I couldn't fail to realize it as time went by. No one can blame me. I'm at the end of my tether, Melanie – if anyone understands that, you do.

MELANIE WEBER: I'm *devastated* for you – both of you. We made such a *harmonious* trio, the three of us, at least for a while. I imagine you're asking me to choose. Much as it hurts me, darling, I won't duck the issue. You see, I'm still fond of you – *very* fond.

HILDE FEIN: Yet I can remember a time when Harald was torn between us.

MELANIE WEBER: Yes, and he chose you. You got yourself pregnant and that clinched it. That is, it did until now.

23

Do I know Melly – pardon me – Frau Weber? Have for over
twenty years, bless her. She used to model for me. A bewitching
figure – boyish, somehow. I still design most of her wardrobe.
Casual, slightly butch sportswear. Plain flowing evening gowns,
ultra-sophisticated but demure.

Melanie always was very reserved – at least in public. Comes of
good Munich stock, but no money in the family. If I remember
rightly, her father was a university lecturer or something of the
kind. All she ever wanted was the good life. She married very
young, when she was just over twenty. He was thirty years her
senior, but what a catch!

He was one of the Weber brothers. One was a banker, the other
an art collector and big-time stock-market speculator. She married
the second and had a child by him. Not long afterwards he was
struck down by some kind of stroke. Very few people have set eyes
on him since then.

Melly fulfils their social obligations singlehanded. She's a
thoroughbred, take it from me.

Harald Fein continued to stare at the warm red glow of the
windows on the sixth floor of No. 33 V-Strasse. He pictured the
girl with the fabulous behind and tried to imagine what she was
doing up there.

She must be very different from the women he'd known to date,
hot-blooded, thrusting and passionate. He could feel her yielding
body, hear her cries . . .

Anton emitted a growl.

'You're illegally parked,' said a crisp voice, inches from his ear.

It was a policeman with a smooth rubbery face, round as a full
moon and almost as featureless. A balloon-man. 'Licence and
papers,' he added.

'I'm not parked,' Harald said. 'I just pulled in for a couple of
minutes.'

'Are you looking for trouble?' The policeman sounded genuinely
surprised. 'If you are, you're going the right way about it.'

Harald politely indicated the string of cars parked ahead of his
own. There were several lining the kerb and several more in the
parking-space outside 33 V-Strasse: two Volkswagens, a Ford,

three Opels, two other Mercedes from lower down the price-range, and a Jaguar with silver-grey or gun-metal paintwork.

'What about them?' he demanded.

'All in good time. You're first in line, so let's see your papers.'

Pocketbook entry made on the night in question by Police Constable Gustav Penzold:

Fein, Harald, born 15 March 1925, Heiligenblut near Rosenheim. Resident Munich-Harlaching.

Examined driver's licence: number, date of issue, licensing authority. Ditto insurance certificate.

Cautionary fine of DM10 summarily imposed and paid by the person cautioned. Receipt issued in the said amount.

Melanie Weber with her husband, about an hour before midnight on the same day:

'The whole situation has become so *complicated*. Hilde seems to be prepared for the worst – I sensed that almost *physically*. She's so mixed up she can't see straight any more – at least, that's my impression. Perhaps it's all an act.'

'Keep out of it,' advised her invalid husband. He was lying on his back, legs extended, arms close to his sides, head supported by pillows. He breathed with difficulty, trying to smile.

'All I ever wanted was to see you happy,' he wheezed tenderly. 'Never mind who or what it is that brings you happiness – I don't begrudge you a thing.'

She bent over him, her lips brushing his forehead.

He was swathed in silk. The Chinese rug on the floor of his bedroom had a silken sheen, as did the chair covers. Double doors stood open to reveal his bathroom. Carrara marble, Venetian mirrors and gold taps. He spent nearly twenty-three hours out of every twenty-four in these two rooms.

'I hear the London Pub party was fabulous,' she reported. 'James gave one of his *wittiest* speeches, Marianne interviewed Julian de Montrésor – you know, the designer – and Alex was well away before the second Martini. He demonstrated a new dance – the Pelvic Polka. Hilde was *sick* not to be there. So was I. And all because of Harald . . .'

'Melanie,' Weber said, his eyes half-closed, 'you can do what you like with Hilde – whatever she'll let you do. Do what you like with Harald too, if there's anything to be done with him. But watch out for Paul Plattner. Crossing Plattner's a luxury not even we can afford, I regret to say.'

'Argus', gossip columnist of the Morgenzeitung, *commenting on Paul Plattner:*

Plattner's a big wheel in any language. He's one of the Top Hundred, one of the few dozen men who are reputed to have the city and half the province in their pockets – *pace* our Mayor. Bankers, property tycoons, import-export kings, oil barons, brewery-owners, chain store moguls and other big shots in the same category. None of them worth less than thirty million marks – private capital, of course.

Plattner, who must be over sixty, owns one of the three really big construction companies in Munich, the others being Duhr & Sons and the Moll Corporation. Plattner's speciality: roads, bridges and subways. Nobody to touch him in that field. He occasionally builds high-rise blocks too.

A solid citizen, Plattner. Son of a builder, Munich-born. Joined the business as a boy and soon made his mark. Took over the firm in 1945, his father being an ex-member of the Party. Made a killing during the postwar building boom.

Plattner is one of our most respected citizens. Cultivates a dignified social image and fends off excessive publicity, but no genuine Munich function is complete without him – Oktoberfest, Fasching, etcetera. Honorary member of half a dozen clubs, guilds and associations.

A City Hall representative, speaking at a recent reception, called him an ornament to Munich and the entire province.

'How about it, darling?' asked a studiously seductive voice. 'You're just my type.'

'Don't judge a man by the car he drives – you could be disappointed.' Not without curiosity, Harald looked up at the girl who had accosted him while Anton gave another low growl.

His curiosity vanished. The face that peered back at him was sharp-featured and rapacious. Even in the dim light, premature wrinkles showed up at the corners of her mouth, and the garishly painted lips were coarse. The breast that jutted against his elbow might have been pure silicone.

Politely, he indicated No. 33 V-Strasse. 'Do you live there too?'

'Can't afford it,' the girl said ruefully. 'Don't make enough. I'm too good at my job – over-eager, that's me. Why not see for yourself?'

Harald shook his head. She obviously didn't catch the gesture, so he said, still politely: 'No, thanks. I won't pretend I couldn't use some. It's just that I don't like to make things too easy for myself.'

'You can have it as complicated as you want,' she assured him. 'You only have to tell me how you like it.'

Harald squinted into the gathering darkness. The sky had lost none of its purple splendour. The air seemed even more limpid and had become considerably cooler. It must have been ten p.m.

'I'm very obliging, really I am,' she persisted. Her voice took on a wheedling note, a blend of eagerness and resignation. He felt sorry for her. 'You ought to try me. I always give value for money.'

'Another time, perhaps.'

He reached into his trouser pocket and pulled out a wad of notes, peeled one off and gave it to her. Fifty marks. 'Here, take it. Call it a down payment.'

From personal notes kept by Detective-Superintendent Keller:

15 September. A quiet day – only three bodies turned up. Two of them were routine. I was only assigned to the third case – probably murder, possibly a *crime passionnel* – because there was no police surgeon on tap.

One of my specialities is the detection and evaluation of blood stains. I know them all – drips, splashes, jets, smears. Then there's the varied coloration of blood, which isn't necessarily bright red, the way they show it in films. It can also look grey, brown, greenish or bluish, depending on subsoil, temperature, murder weapon, prior conditions, lapse of time, etc.

Routine points, all of them. They called me in because I was available, so I picked up my tool-bag, which I always keep handy, and hurried over to No. 33 V-Strasse, sixth floor. The girl's body was still warm to the touch, but I was eager to try out my new post-mortem thermometer. Range: 0–50 degrees Centigrade. Accurate to within 0.1°–0.5°. It worked like a dream.

But to proceed chronologically:

Cadaver No. 1: a boy in a swimming pool. I accompanied the father, who was working in the garden of a villa. Owner absent. The boy was eventually found at the bottom of the dirty pool. Resuscitation attempted without success. Police informed promptly. Accidental death – no doubt about it.

Cadaver No. 2: a woman aged 41, living with her sister. Ostensibly a heart attack, already confirmed by the family doctor. No external peculiarities. When the upper part of the body was raised, however, mucus seeped from mouth and nose – greenish-yellow, acrid-smelling. Ingestion of toxic substance indicated. Probably suicide.

Cadaver No. 3: female, aged 30 or thereabouts, probably a call-girl. The particulars appended are taken from PECD records, most of them completed by me.

Melanie Weber, confiding in her diary the same night:
As poor sweet Hilde told me herself:

'You can't imagine what I've been through, Melanie, my dearest. The boy arrived shortly after we were married and the girl a bare two years later. After that, everything went dead between us.

'He never understood me – never tried to, just pursued his own selfish interests. My friends left him cold and he made it devastatingly clear. He had no feeling for beauty, no aesthetic sense, no culture. First nights bored him, concerts put him to sleep, receptions made him want to puke, as he so delicately put it – and not only to me.

'He prowled around, used impossible language, got drunk at the first opportunity – often before lunch, treated respectable society women like potential whores. For a while he became a complete alcoholic.

'Even then I refused to abandon him. I didn't want to break up our home, if only for the children's sake. Last but not least, for Father's sake. Father had invested so much in us. His love, his hopes for the future – even his business interests, because he had such implicit faith in me. That weighed very heavily, of course.'

MELANIE: How often have you been unfaithful to Harald?
HILDE: How can you even ask such a thing?

MELANIE: I know you pretty well, darling.

HILDE: I know you do – better than any other living soul with the possible exception of Father. But a marriage like mine entails duties and obligations. Especially in Father's world . . .

MELANIE: What about temptations – men, I mean? They're hard to dodge, sometimes.

HILDE: Well, yes, naturally there was the occasional temptation, but I never fell. I couldn't do it for lots of reasons, one of them being *us*. Which is something totally different, of course.

Particulars taken from PECD records relating to the V-Strasse case and subsequently incorporated in Detective-Superintendent Keller's notes:

A. Position of body: lying diagonally across bed, full-length, supine. Feet pointing towards window, arms and hands at chest-level, as if parrying a blow. Clothing: a black silk négligé, open, collar and sleeves torn.

B. Physical injuries: wound at base of skull caused by single impact with left outer edge of bed frame. No splashes of blood, subsequent oozing only. Primary cause of death: strangulation. Severe bruising in region of carotid, less severe on larynx.

C. Traces on body and in immediate vicinity: semen, sweat stains, saliva. Killer presumed to have spat at his victim – traces of spittle detected, specimens preserved for examination. Also traces of urine. The killer apparently relieved himself over his victim after the act. Not an uncommon feature in itself.

Plenty of evidence, sufficient to keep several lab technicians busy for days. Numerous other clues present, all susceptible of chemical and physical analysis. The lab boys started work on their scene-of-the-crime picture.

The semen, sweat and saliva specimens were crucial, provided it was possible to classify them accurately enough to point the finger at one particular suspect. The general public aren't aware that a man's blood can be typed from secretions like semen, sweat and saliva. As for urine, that can be almost as damning as a fingerprint. Advice to killers: hold your water.

Harald lit another cigarette from the butt of its predecessor. His expenditure on matches had hit a new low recently. Still, he hadn't touched a drop of liquor for months.

Eighteen months, to be precise. He didn't want to go off the wagon – couldn't and mustn't. He'd come to terms with the idea. Not that he didn't get the urge sometimes – say for a large brandy when he was in conference with his father-in-law. Or, as now, staring up at the warm glow of the girl's bedroom, for a glass of champagne.

He groped in his jacket pocket and took out a box of pills, collected some saliva in his mouth and gulped two of them. They were tasteless but he wagged his head and grimaced with disgust. Behind him, Anton gave a sympathetic shake.

The flow of traffic in V-Strasse had dwindled. Television sets flickered behind innumerable windows as the German consumer settled down to an evening of predigested entertainment as insipid as the prepacked fare that accompanied it.

And still the sky above Munich preserved its dusky blue magnificence. Assailing it came the full-throated electronic roar of the city's hundred discothèques: in Goethestrasse, in Schwabing, and round the Hofbräuhaus.

Harald inspected his face in the rear-view mirror. He saw a forehead scored with lines, few but deeply incised, one bisecting his brow like an exclamation mark which ran vertically to the bridge of his nose.

There was a hint of mournful amusement in the grey-blue eyes. The nose was prominent; the mouth, with its harmoniously curving upper lip, seemed frozen in a set smile.

The smile widened as he studied his reflection. A pitiable face, he thought, but not altogether unfunny. It was probably the hint of helplessness that made it comic. The realization that you were a figure of fun didn't prevent you from being amused. Harald despised himself. He didn't fit in, and there were times when he regretted it – and regretted the fact that he regretted it.

Harald restarted the car and drove home.

From Detective-Superintendent Braun's preliminary notes on the V-Strasse case, with special reference to Harald Fein:

Mercedes 280SL parked in vicinity of block, duration two to three hours, licence number ascertained, owner: Fein, Harald.

Preliminary information concerning Fein, Harald: married to Hilde, née Plattner, father-in-law Chairman of Plattner Construction Company, two children, boy 18, girl 16. Senior executive on

30

Plattner's pay-roll, annual income approx. DM50,000 plus expenses. One-time alcoholic, obviously unstable.

Statements about Detective-Superintendent Braun compiled subsequently by Counsellor Henri Messer, attorney-at-law. Among those interviewed:

1. Hermine Kohl, proprietress of The Raised Elbow, *a stand-up bar off Elisabethenplatz:*

I know Herr Braun from way back. We first met in Berlin during the war, when he was working with the vice squad. His job was to check on our income. The Nazis planned to tax us, the swine. Well, he found out that quite a few of us better-class girls could earn up to two hundred marks a day. Braun was only pulling in five hundred – a month. If that wasn't bound to cause ill-feeling, what was?

2. Siegfried Wolf, formerly a practising physician, now a scholar of independent means and one of the few Jews living in the Federal Republic:

Yes, I knew Braun. Came across him in 1938. He usually turned up the day before an arrest was due and dropped a few hints. That's why there are still a few of us alive to testify in his favour.

Anyone who ignored his warning was detained next day, usually by a mixed squad of Gestapo and uniformed police. Braun was one of those in charge. He carried out his orders to the letter. I'm sure he knew what would happen to the people he arrested, but he did his job with disconcerting thoroughness.

3. Valentin Fischer, former detective chief superintendent, Berlin-Wiesbaden-Munich, expert on finger- and palm-prints, versed in every major system; now retired:

Hearing you mention Braun's name puts me in mind of his daughter Erika. His wife left him in spring 1945, when the child was only five. She abandoned the little girl as well, you see. Braun looked after her to the best of his ability.

Erika grew up with him and his mother, who died in 1957. When Erika was nearly twenty she fell in with the so-called jet set.

To cut a long story short, she got pregnant and had a messy abortion. After that she disappeared, no one knows where to. They say she's been seen in Hamburg and Rome. As for Braun, I sometimes had the impression that he was looking for her. Everywhere – whatever case he was engaged on.

Hilde Fein glared at her husband. 'Where have you been?' she snapped. 'Talent-spotting, I suppose.'

'Call it what you like,' Harald said, flopping into a chair. Anton promptly leapt on to the chair beside it and made himself at home. 'Where are the children?'

'Out,' she retorted belligerently. 'Must that mongrel of yours spread itself all over my furniture?'

'Anton? He can if he wants. I asked about the children.'

'They're just like their father – unstable. Heinz is probably dreaming up revolutionary slogans with those bearded friends of his. As for Helga, knowing how she is, I wouldn't be surprised to find her dumped on our doorstep one night, pumped full of some drug or other.'

Harald shook his head wearily. 'You're imagining things, Hilde. What on earth's the matter with us?'

'Whatever it is,' she said, with an accusing stare, 'it isn't my fault, any of it.'

'You really believe that?'

'Absolutely, but all that interests me at the moment is that you left the office just after five and didn't get home till ten.'

'So you've been checking on my movements.' Harald's tone was almost indulgent. 'Not for the first time, I imagine. What do you hope to achieve?'

'You planned to eat at home – I ordered dinner for you specially. After that I had a date with Melanie. We were invited to a party but you didn't show up, so we had to cancel at the last minute. And all because of you. Where have you been?'

'I haven't seen Melanie for ages,' he mused. 'You really mean it's possible for a sane person to lead her kind of life for twenty years without dying of boredom?'

Hilde frowned. 'Don't change the subject. I refuse to be treated like a piece of your property. I'm still your wife, remember.'

'And your father's daughter.'

'Of course.'

'An unusually intimate relationship, don't you agree? One that's intrigued me ever since the day I got to know you properly.' For

32

once, Harald succumbed to temptation. 'A remarkable relationship. I've always found it rather grotesque.'

'Leave Father out of this,' she said, even more curtly than before. 'Don't meddle in things you don't understand. You'd do better to control that mongrel of yours – it's slobbering all over my cushions.'

'Who's changing the subject now? You dropped a few hints once, in an unguarded moment. You told me you used to creep into his bed every Sunday morning when you were a little girl. Nothing wrong with that, except that you continued the custom into adolescence – and beyond, no doubt. Here in Munich and down at the Tegernsee villa. How long did it go on? Be honest.'

'Harald,' she said coldly, 'don't provoke me. And don't involve Father. He'd never forgive you. It could be bad – bad for you.'

'Really? What could be worse than the current set-up?'

'This time,' she hissed, rising to her feet and staring down at him with contempt, 'you've gone too far. What's more, you'll regret it.'

Chapter Two

*Remarks exchanged during one of the routine 9 a.m. briefing sessions
held daily at HQ No. 1 Precinct. Division: Capital Crimes. Presiding
officer: Detective Chief Superintendent Dürrenmaier, divisional chief.*

DET. CHIEF SUPT DÜRRENMAIER: In other words, nothing
special to report?

DET.-SUPT BRAUN: Nothing that I know of.

DÜRRENMAIER: Not even on the V-Strasse front?

BRAUN: No problem there.

DÜRRENMAIER (visibly relieved but preserving the air of
shrewd suspicion which was one of his main professional assets):
Really not?

BRAUN: Everything's going according to plan, sir. As far as I
can tell.

From Detective-Superintendent Keller's notes:

It was the standard 9 a.m. performance. The Chief Super took
care to cover himself, as usual. He had every right to. He also had
every reason to, at least where Braun was concerned.

Braun's views and methods were no secret to those in the know.
He was a straightforward law-and-order man, all in favour of
drawing a line and making people toe it, heartily opposed to
anything and anyone that threatened his own ideas of what an
ordered society should be.

He despised bar girls and big businessmen equally. He had very
little sympathy for homosexuals and exhibitionists, perverts and
prostitutes. Given a free hand, he'd probably have put the entire
jet set behind bars, along with the gossip columnists who boost
their public image.

Lying on Braun's desk, always within arm's reach, was a typed
card bearing a pronouncement he had once heard. It was attributed
to the retiring chief of the Federal Crime Bureau, who apparently
gave vent to the following remarks, off the cuff and off the record:

'We can handle a few hundred thousand criminals. The people
who really give us trouble are the thousand-odd self-styled

intellectuals who try to impose their peculiar standards on the rest of us.'

Braun was tickled by that sort of thing. So was I, except that the conclusions I drew were different from his.

Braun had the bit between his teeth this time. In view of that, Dürrenmaier was smart enough to assign him a detective-inspector named Feldmann, a stolid, down-to-earth officer without any dangerous personal ambitions. A man like a card index. Nothing carried any weight with Feldmann unless it could be reduced to words of one syllable. He was an old pupil of mine.

DÜRRENMAIER: The victim of the V-Strasse killing was a prostitute?

BRAUN: Yes, but not officially registered. I'd rate her B-Plus to A-Minus. Almost in the luxury class.

DÜRRENMAIER: And you say she had an extensive clientele? We'd better tread carefully or there could be trouble.

BRAUN: I see no signs of any, so far.

DÜRRENMAIER: If you do, notify me at once. That is not a suggestion, it's an order. Investigating human aberrations is one thing, serving them up for public consumption is another. If you know what's good for you, Braun, play it cool.

BRAUN: Of course, sir.

From Detective-Superintendent Keller's notes:

I pricked up my ears at that. Braun was all sweetness and light. His act wasn't lost on Dürrenmaier, either, but the Chief Super took care not to show how far he could see through it. I distinctly got the impression that Braun was defusing all the more explosive features of the case, presumably so as not to alert his chief too soon. If Dürrenmaier had got wind of any complications he'd have taken Braun off the case and dropped it in someone else's lap.

But that was just what Braun seemed determined to avoid. He could obviously smell something that fitted nicely into his plans.

The situation promised to provide me with a certain amount of secret entertainment. I was becoming quite curious to see how it developed.

Points extracted from CID reports, still of a preliminary nature:

The presence of a variety of fingerprints was only to be expected in an apartment frequented by so many people. They were identified and recorded by Det.-Insp. Feldmann, who favoured the Magna Brush System, using four different kinds of dust: soot, manganese dioxide, argentorate and graphite.

It turned out in this case that someone had deliberately covered his tracks by obliterating them on a considerable scale. The smears extended from the front door, via the passage, to the murdered woman's bed.

The inescapable inference was that the murderer must be an experienced criminal or a person blessed with imagination and intelligence.

'It's time you were up.' The Feins' maid addressed Harald with mock severity.

'Don't feel like it,' he mumbled with his mouth buried in the pillow. He heaved himself laboriously on to his side, presenting his rear end in the process. He heard the girl giggle, which mildly amused him but brought an irritable growl from Anton, who was stretched out under the bed.

The bedroom curtains were flung wide. Harsh morning sunlight dazzled him. He clamped his hands over his face. 'Must you?' he said plaintively.

'Why, aren't you feeling well?' The maid, whose name was Maria Trübner, eyed him – and his rear end in particular – with interest. 'Like me to wake you up?'

Harald struggled into a sitting position. He might have been seeing her for the first time. A buxom creature, exuding stable warmth and an aroma of fresh milk. She planted her legs apart and smiled at him. The thighs under the short dirndl were like smooth slipways.

'Wake me up? You?'

'Why not?' asked Maria, bending over him. 'Give me a chance and I'll show you how. I'm the willing type, Herr Fein – your wife says so too.'

Maria Trübner's current boy-friend, Peter Palitschek, enlightening her on his philosophy of life:

Love you? Of course I love you, but bed isn't everything, even when two people click the way we do. Peace of mind is what really matters, sweetheart, and that's where money comes in. I mean, I want to offer you a decent home.

I work like a slave, you know that, but I'm always short. I don't get paid by results, worse luck, and I'm not the only one. It's a lousy world. The whole system's gone haywire, so we have to adjust it – each in our own way, get me?

You mean you still haven't caught on? Don't act dumber than you are, baby! Okay, I'll spell it out for you: we're short and other people are flush – the Feins, for instance. That's one of the things that needs adjusting, right? So get to work on him. After all, bed isn't . . .

Harald stared at Maria, feeling slightly more cheerful. 'Do you enjoy seeing me nude?'

'You're a good-looking man,' Maria declared. She continued to eye him while Anton extended his forepaws and stretched mightily, thrusting his haunches into the air.

'Very flattering,' Harald said drily. He stood up and reached for his bathrobe. She helped him into it. 'I might take that as an invitation. Aren't you worried?'

'Not about you.'

'What about my wife?'

'She left half-an-hour ago. All she said was, wake him at the usual time and ask if he needs anything.'

'What do you mean, she left?'

'She took a suitcase and two fur coats and drove off.'

'Where to?'

'How should I know? She didn't say. She was in a terrible mood, if that means anything to you.'

'Turn Anton loose in the garden,' Harald said eventually. 'He's dying to cock a leg.'

Instructions issued by Detective-Superintendent Braun to Detective-Inspector Feldmann, the new member of his team:

Kindly bear this in mind at all times: our job is to investigate criminal acts. Doctors can provide any medical evidence we require and the courts are there to pass judgement on offenders. Those things don't concern us.

Which means, in practice, that underpaid government dicks like you and me aren't employed to draw distinctions between criminals

37

and the mentally disturbed. We're the drudges of the legal system, Feldmann. All we do is dig up the facts. It doesn't matter who gets mixed up in the works. They all get the same treatment. No special consideration for any particular person – or personality. All men are equal before the law, right? Well they're twice as equal before the CID, so get cracking!

'I understand you,' Helga assured her father in a conspiratorial whisper. She caught hold of Anton and clasped the dog fiercely to her breast. Anton tried to wriggle free. 'I've always understood you.'

'Really?' said Harald. 'Hey, please don't hug the poor fellow like that. Anton hates being smothered. He's an individualist, and individualists appreciate tactful treatment. Thanks for the kind words, though. What have I done to deserve all this sympathy and understanding?'

'You're so – so *noble!*' Helga blurted out.

Harald studied her as she sat facing him at the breakfast table. He experienced a faint but agreeable pang of surprise, an emotion which seldom overcame him these days.

Helga Fein was sixteen, a graceful girl with coltish legs. Strong white teeth could be glimpsed between her slightly parted lips. She had a quiet beauty which was unspoiled by her rather neglected appearance, but Harald noted it with mixed feelings. He was dominated by the thought that his daughter looked much as her mother must have looked at the same age.

'You're far too good for her.'

'Her?'

'Your wife.'

'Are you by any chance referring to your mother?'

'I'm referring to a woman who doesn't have a spark of feeling for you.'

Extracts from Helga Fein's diary:

. . . I heard Mother saying 'No!', over and over again. It must have been in the small hours. I couldn't sleep because of a film on TV. There was a grave in it, an open grave which magically attracted me. And then I heard her cry out 'No!' in a choked sort of voice.

Again:

38

. . . Daddy never looks at the screen when we sit watching TV. He keeps his eyes fixed on her – Mother. His expression is the saddest thing. It breaks my heart.

'Go easy, Helga,' Harald said earnestly. 'Nobody's a saint, my dear girl, least of all in other people's eyes. My guess is, there's hardly a family in the world that lives in perfect harmony. We have to coexist, which means showing a little consideration for each other.'

'But that's just what she's *never* done, not with you. You're far too good for us – too good for her, anyway.'

Harald felt touched and concerned. 'Try not to see the world in black and white, darling. Believe me, I'm no saint and your mother's no sinner. Everything's relative – there are two sides to most problems.'

'How tolerant you are!'

'Perhaps you're confusing tolerance with weakness or calculation.' Harald smiled to himself. 'No one lives for himself alone, however lonely he seems. Even the most solitary man can indulge in sins of commission or omission which hurt a fellow-creature.'

'Why doesn't Mother understand you?'

Harald sighed. 'Who really understands anyone? But we have to live together just the same.'

Paul Plattner, building contractor, on the subject of his son-in-law Harald Fein. Excerpts compiled from several taped sessions, most of them monologues:

I've got my principles and I act on them. Principles based on experience. Expert knowledge is the first essential if you want to go places, that's my motto. Next come energy, efficiency, initiative and a sense of purpose. Every man deserves at least one chance, I always say. As long as he looks like a paying proposition, of course.

I gave Harald Fein a chance.

I admit I was worried when Hilde introduced the man she'd got involved with – a little prematurely. Likeable enough, but no drive, that was my first impression.

However, the two young people had produced a *fait accompli* and that settled it. I need hardly tell you that I didn't for a moment consider the possibility of an abortion. It would have been easy

39

enough for a man with my contacts and resources to arrange one, but my religious convictions forbade it.

Make the best of a bad job, I told myself. After all, my sole concern was Hilde's happiness.

As it happened, I hadn't cast my bread on the waters in vain. For safety's sake, I made some inquiries about my prospective son-in-law's background. He turned out to be a qualified civil engineer and architect, currently employed as a technical draughts-man by a construction company – a third-rate concern. I assure you, it never for an instant occurred to me that Harald Fein might have got my daughter pregnant because she was the only child of a big contractor . . .

Being optimistic by nature – optimistic but never rash – I did my best to concentrate on Harald's more positive aspects. One of them was his only friend Hermann Abendroth, with whom he was evidently on very close terms. Abendroth worked in the urban planning department at City Hall. He was very young, but the Mayor had sponsored him personally and he looked like a man to watch.

To cut a long story short, I decided to give Harald his chance, not only with Hilde but also in my firm, which was just beginning to make its mark. Mind you, I had my reservations.

From one of the early exchanges between Detective-Inspector Feld-mann and Detective-Superintendent Braun:

FELDMANN: Lab tests are in progress on all the stuff we picked up at the scene. We should get some preliminary results in a couple of days. I've passed on your instructions about speeding things up. Meantime, standard procedure: routine checks and interviews handled by me and my team, working in close con-sultation with the uniformed police from the local precinct.

BRAUN: You don't have to plug your skill as an interdepart-mental co-ordinator, Feldmann, not to me. I take that for granted. Any leads yet – anything to get our teeth into?

FELDMANN: Nothing very solid so far, but we've turned up three characters who may be worth a closer look.

First, the dead girl had a pimp, a man named Kordes. Where-abouts still unknown, but we're trying to trace him.

Next, a fellow-resident named Stenzenbach. He made a lot of noise during routine questioning – sounded off about 'that degenerate bitch on the sixth floor' and so on. His wife, who was present during the interview, blew her top – and I quote: 'You're a fine one to talk. You used to patronize her yourself, and a hell of a lot of money it must have cost you. No wonder I'm still waiting for that fur coat you promised me.'

BRAUN: Great. Who else?

FELDMANN: Finally there's Harald Fein, the man you drew my attention to. His presence near the scene of the crime at the time in question seems to be established beyond doubt, but we can't prove he actually entered the building. That is, we haven't so far.

BRAUN: Fein sounds promising to me. Big earner, unstable, ex-alcoholic – if there *is* such an animal . . . I wouldn't put anything past a moral cripple like him. Look, Feldmann, I'm not telling you to concentrate on Fein to the exclusion of the rest. All I say is, keep a damn close eye on him.

'I don't have anything against you, Father – personally, I mean.' Heinz Fein sat down at the breakfast table. 'You try, I'll grant you that.'

'How nice,' Harald said drily. 'Fancy making allowances, even for me. I call that downright generous of you.'

Heinz didn't look at his father. He ignored his sister and leant back to busy himself with Anton, who had curled up on the couch behind his chair. Anton's back was scratched and his ears tugged. He stretched gratefully.

'What about you, you gorgeous beast? No problems, eh? You're the only one around here with the right to lie back and let it happen – you don't have any option, lucky dog.'

Heinz turned a boundlessly indifferent, almost contemptuous eye on all that the breakfast table had to offer. 'What a sight!' he sneered. 'Anyone'd think we were running a delicatessen. Over half the world's inhabitants are starving, or hadn't you heard? There are millions of undernourished Indians, millions of under-privileged blacks in America . . .'

'Don't forget Biafra,' Harald said, without a trace of sarcasm, 'or Bangladesh, or the Palestinian refugees, or Latin America – etcetera, etcetera . . .'

'You know all that, yet you feel at home here.' Heinz surveyed his surroundings. All glass, chrome and lacquer, glossy surfaces, leather and plastic. A hundred sheep had contributed their fleece to carpet the floor. 'I suppose it's all the same to you whether running water comes out of gold taps or streams down the walls of a mud hut.'

'Stop picking on Daddy!' Helga turned on him. 'Grandfather chose the décor personally – and paid for it, too – and Mother's responsible for the housekeeping. As for breakfast, *your* appetite seems healthy enough.'

'Yes, because I'm politically immature.'

'Mentally retarded, you mean.'

'I'm the son of my parents.'

'I don't think you're being quite fair,' Harald said deliberately.

'I know, I know – you're so infinitely tolerant, patient, understanding, sympathetic. I've heard that one before, Father – it's the parental Top of the Pops. What about giving us the flip side, the way Mother would if she were here? Heinz, my darling, you don't have any consideration for us, you've no sense of responsibility, you're giving the family a bad name. *Me* giving the family a bad name? What a laugh!'

'Who else?' Helga demanded furiously.

'Why not ask Father?' the boy retorted with casual truculence. He tossed Anton a slice of Westphalian ham.

From Detective-Superintendent Keller's notes:

It's common practice in police and legal circles to give every case a name, e.g. Mariotti, Sacco-Vanzetti, Crippen. The trouble is, names can have an emotive or suggestive effect. I think I was the first man in the service to introduce a neutral system of code letters. That was when I still headed a murder team.

Braun adopted the bare bones of my method and developed it when he took over from me. Less, I suspect, in order to avoid the problems names can present than because it helped to dissuade worried superiors like Chief Supt Dürrenmaier from breathing down his neck.

Braun certainly deserved his nickname, which was 'Foxy'. Even I found it hard to make out exactly who he was after at any given time. He didn't mind making a detour, however circuitous. One thing you could bank on: Braun would never let anything slip. Anything or anyone.

Another extract from the exchange between Detective-Superintendent Braun and Detective-Inspector Feldmann:

BRAUN: I hope it won't prejudice you to know that the dead woman was a prostitute?

FELDMANN: Of course not, sir.

BRAUN: Or that this man Harald Fein is a member of the so-called upper crust – the marble shit-house brigade? Are you influenced by that sort of thing?

FELDMANN: Certainly not, sir. Anyway, we haven't dug up any firm evidence to connect him with the killing.

BRAUN: Dig faster, then, and dig in the right place. Apply yourself, Feldmann. A slob like Fein sits there for hours in his Mercedes, doing sweet fuck-all – so he says. That's perverted to begin with, isn't it?

FELDMANN: Maybe it's like he says – maybe he felt like a breather. He can afford it.

BRAUN: His kind can afford more than a breather, my friend. They think their money can buy them anything – respectable married women, schoolgirls, whores – the lot. They're bound to overstep the mark sooner or later.

FELDMANN: Just the same, the preliminary results of our inquiries . . .

BRAUN: Are preliminary, period. Let's get back to Fein. What kind of man would sit there in his car for hours on end, twiddling his thumbs? Maybe he had to get out for a pee. Maybe he went and had a beer – maybe he felt like a bit of the other and picked up a tart. Carry on, but bear those possibilities in mind.

Harald eyed his son quizzically. 'May I ask what you meant by that dig – the one about giving the family a bad name?'

'Why ask me? Why not ask Mother? She's far more competent to answer.'

'But she isn't here.'

'Precisely,' Heinz retorted. 'You said it. She packed her jewellery, slung a couple of mink coats into the car, and split. If that isn't family harmony, what is?'

'You've no consideration for Daddy's feelings,' Helga told him. 'You ought to be ashamed of yourself.'

'Bullshit! I see things the way they are. I see two pathetic products of the capitalist system, two ageing members of the affluent society, forty-plus and too old to know better, cavorting like circus-horses just to show how mobile they still are.'

Harald smiled faintly. 'So in your view, has-beens in their mid-forties are past redemption. They're selfish, rapacious and soulless.'

'That's it, more or less.' Heinz shrugged. 'What puzzles me is, how do they get that way?'

Helga was furious. 'You're awful, Heinz!'

'At least he's honest,' Harald said quietly.

'Not only honest but on target.' Heinz spoke without exultation or regret. He might have been reading the weather forecast.

'Oh, you!' Helga exclaimed with a mixture of sorrow and belligerence. 'Know what I think you are?'

'Yes,' Heinz said obligingly. 'Ungrateful.'

Helga gazed at her father, tenderly and with boundless affection, begging forgiveness for her brother, but Harald avoided her eye.

Information given by one Sebastian Berner, a medical student at Munich University, now in his sixth year:

Who were you asking about? Helga? Oh sure, I knew Helga. Very uptight. She reminded me of a puppy that doesn't know whether to widdle or where.

To top it all, there was this brother of hers. He stormed in one day – called us a bunch of social parasites and started throwing punches.

Where was this? A disco in Schwabing where they're liberal enough to let the youngsters share an occasional joint. *Goldfinger's*, it's called. Anyway, this character Heinz dragged his sister out by the hair. She didn't object – in fact she seemed more relieved than anything else.

Harald glanced first at Anton, who was still sprawled on the couch, and then at the window. It was a glorious day, as it almost always was when the Bavarian summer yielded to autumn. Now more than at any other time of year, the city was flooded with radiance. A gentle sun simulated comforting warmth, the air-borne contagions of the modern metropolis were unimaginable as well as invisible, and the sky looked infinitely high and wide – a pleasure-tent of vast dimensions. The Oktoberfest was less than a week away.

'Day-dreaming?' Heinz's tone was impatient. 'The favourite

refuge of people who accept the status quo: a snug world, modest pleasures, the brotherhood of man . . . It makes me want to puke!'

'I see what you're driving at,' Harald said. 'You obviously feel that you're the victim of incessant demands. From your sister, from me, from the world at large. Here in this house, you think you're constantly being presented with a bill for love vouchsafed or services rendered. For eighteen years' supply of food, clothing and accommodation, for toys, school fees and medical attention. For everything that can possibly be expressed in numerical terms.'

'You put your finger on it, Father,' Heinz said defiantly. He didn't look at his sister. 'That's the whole point. I mean, what are we supposed to be? A miniature welfare state with benefits geared to contributions – or a family? You tell me.'

'We're human beings,' Harald said simply and helplessly.

Extracts from a conversation between some press correspondents and Hermann Abendroth, head of Munich's urban planning department. The occasion: an informal dinner-table press conference. The subject: preparations for the 1972 Olympics. It is not long before the name Harald Fein crops up in connection with the Plattner Construction Company. Special focus of interest: the approach roads to the Olympic site.

ABENDROTH: Of course I know Herr Fein – have done for years. We were students together.

QUESTION: Would it be true to say that you know him intimately?

ABENDROTH: Well, yes, I suppose so. But then, who knows anyone when you come down to it?

QUESTION: Does that mean you're anxious to dissociate yourself from Harald Fein? No one could blame you, in view of all that seems to have happened lately.

ABENDROTH: What have recent developments to do with a youthful friendship?

QUESTION: Is it true that this youthful friendship of yours persisted, even when you were employed in quite a senior capacity by the urban planning department of this city?

ABENDROTH: You're not, I take it, implying that our friendship matured into a mutual back-scratching society? Good, in that case we can approach the subject with due candour.

Harald Fein was an extremely likeable person, always cheerful, always obliging, not in the least bit hard to get along with. Extremely talented, too. Even as a very young man he designed buildings that wouldn't have disgraced Wright or Ponti. However, our once close relationship deteriorated. For some years now, we've only met at government and municipal functions, official receptions, the opening of a bridge he designed – that sort of thing. We say hello, shake hands, and go our separate ways.

Life's like that.

The Marienplatz offices of the Plattner Construction Company, where Harald was condemned to spend his working day, affected him like a nagging toothache.

For one thing, the whole emphasis was on functionalism. No distractions were permitted, no flowers, no forms of embellishment. Diagrams, production schedules and architects' drawings stood proxy for paintings. This applied to three of the eight rooms in the head office, as well as the typing pool.

The two central offices occupied by Plattner's immediate subordinates, Fein and Jonas, managing and assistant managing director respectively, each contained a carpet, pseudo-oriental, twelve-by-fifteen, and one oil painting. Harald's depicted a Bavarian lake scene, Jonas's a Bavarian mountainscape. The furniture was emphatically regional.

Between these two offices lay that of the chairman's private secretary. Décor: old Viennese with functional overtones. The mistress of this domain was Eva-Maria Wagnersberger, sometimes called the lynch-pin of the whole organization, sometimes referred to as 'the Dragon'. Her absolute reliability was famed throughout the firm and beyond.

Fräulein Wagnersberger, with almost two decades of company service behind her, was still a very attractive woman, fashionably dressed at all times, always fragrant if sometimes excessively so, ever aware of her undisputed value to the firm.

'Anything special?' inquired Harald.

'Depends on your point of view,' said Eva-Maria. 'Herr Plattner seems upset this morning.'

'Company trouble?'

'Possibly, but I doubt it. If it were, Herr Jonas would have let me know – he keeps his ear to the ground.' She produced a private secretary's omniscient smile. 'I assume it must be something personal. *You* should know if anyone.'

Harald shrugged. 'Whatever it is, I suppose I'd better get moving. Yet again,' he added resignedly, as though to himself.

Dr Barthel, Public Prosecutor, destined immediately after these events to become – in quick succession – Senior Public Prosecutor and State Secretary at the Bavarian Ministry of Justice, here expressing his personal views on certain matters of fundamental significance:

. . . absolutely no intention of criticizing, let alone challenging, the present set-up in Federal Germany or the Western world . . .

. . . cannot, however, refrain from worrying about a number of undesirable features in our society. We live in an age devoid of calm and reassuring moderation. We've swung from one extreme to the other. Duty, discipline and good order have given way to permissiveness, unbridled individualism and freedom of self-expression.

This is clearly discernible in the criminal depths to which our once so warm and congenial city has sunk. Concentrated immorality and unrelieved demoralization – a virtually unrestricted market in all the world's vices. In addition, we're treated to the spectacle of orgies – often acclaimed by the press as 'social functions' – attended by prostitutes posing as grandes dames, pimps as talent scouts, sexual predators as purveyors of entertainment, or 'showbiz', as I believe it is called.

Daily occurrences, so it seems, and beyond the reach of the law – after all, we subscribe to *habeas corpus* and a man's right to ruin himself. Freedom of self-expression is guaranteed down to the ultimate perversion.

As long as such things remain confined to their natural environment, no great danger arises. These people have their own code, unwritten but binding – a code which outsiders can ignore or take for granted. What complicates the situation and renders it downright dangerous is when someone breaks out – in other words, sets himself against his social class or deliberately defies it.

Which brings me to the subject of Harald Fein . . .

Harald reported to his father-in-law's office, nerve-centre of the Plattner Construction Company and a dozen major building projects employing between five and seven thousand men. Paul Plattner's harsh voice assailed him as soon as he entered the room.

'There you are at last. Nearly an hour late. Hardly an example to the staff, eh? I'm a tolerant and understanding man, God knows, but things can't go on this way.'

Harald nodded. 'You took the words out of my mouth.'

'Thanks to your mismanagement of Site 14, we're in danger of losing a lot of money.'

'Why should I care about Site 14? Any pleasure I had in the project was destroyed long ago.'

'My dear Harald,' Plattner said ominously, 'we're not in business to give you pleasure. We're here to make profits. Because of this bottleneck, the men sat around playing cards and we're two weeks behind schedule. What have you got to say for yourself?'

'Nothing.'

'What the hell do you mean, nothing?' Plattner was furious. 'How dare you give me an answer like that! I demand an explanation.'

'Very well,' Harald said, unimpressed. 'As far as Site 14 goes, I handled the design and planning. I also supervised the preliminary phase. The Organization and Methods department took over from there, so it doesn't concern me any longer. Why not check?'

'I will, and if I find you're to blame I'll hold you liable.'

'Anything else?'

Paul Plattner, head of an enterprise whose current market value was conservatively assessed at one hundred and fifty million marks, looked small but far from frail. He had incongruously large hands which he always tried to conceal. He stuffed them in his pockets, clasped them behind his back or hid them, as now, under the lip of his massive desk.

Two reports on Paul Plattner.

1. Horst Huber, 61, foreman:

Known him close on forty years, I have, and I won't hear a word against him. Plattner's still got time for the likes of us. Puts in a personal appearance at every anniversary celebration and never comes empty-handed. A couple of bottles of schnapps, maybe, or a case of beer. Clinks glasses with us like one of the boys. A decent sort, Plattner is.

48

Tough, too. I've seen him turn up at the site, city suit and all, and hoist a sack of cement on his shoulder – a hundred pounds of the stuff – without turning a hair. You'd hardly believe it, would you?

2. Thea Samtner, 24, for three months deputy private secretary to the chairman:

What a man! At his age, too – I ask you!

I hadn't been with the firm two weeks before it dawned on me, but I got married soon afterwards.

Don't get me wrong. Nothing improper happened. Except that I came to like and admire him – tremendously!

Paul Plattner raised his big hands and fitted the knuckles together like cogs. 'Harald,' he said, 'what are you trying to do to me? I'm not talking about Site 14 now – we'll worry about that later. What I find far more disturbing is your personal attitude to those who are close to me.'

'What do you mean, exactly?'

'My dear fellow, I could try to discuss things with you – our future as a family, for instance – but I know it would be a pure waste of time. However, I suppose even you are aware that I've invested a great deal in you – a lot of hopes, a lot of faith in your co-operation. Well, every investment ought to bring some kind of return.'

'And I'm a bad investment, is that what you're implying?'

Plattner parried the remark with a sweeping gesture and stared out of the window. The mechanical figures set high in the façade of the Rathaus began to gyrate as the clock struck ten.

What a city Munich was, and what vicissitudes it had undergone, Plattner reflected. A royal capital till 1918, it had experienced beer-hall democracy, a few days of Soviet republicanism, the Beerhall Putsch, the rise of Nazism, the growth of clandestine resistance to the régime, American occupation, the benefits of West German affluence – and all in the space of little more than half a century . . .

'In this place,' Plattner mused, 'almost anything is possible. The sky's the limit. You, Harald, are a mere grain of sand, but sand can cause friction. I refuse to let you clog the works. My firm, in which I was generous enough to give you an interest, is one of the most successful in the country. It could have been the most successful bar none. If only . . .'

'If only I'd sold my soul to you. If only I'd done everything you demanded of me, everything you hoped and expected . . .'

Preliminary notes on potential suspects in the V-Strasse case, based on the findings of Detective-Inspector Feldmann and his team:

1. Kordes. Long-time 'financial adviser' of the murdered woman. Seems to have left Munich some days earlier, destination unknown. Can probably be ruled out, but 'Wanted' notice circulated, also to Interpol.

2. Stenzenbach. Resident in same block. Acquaintanceship with deceased divulged by wife. Claims to have spent relevant evening with business associates, bowling at a suburban roadhouse. Alibi seems to check.

3. Fein. Still no directly incriminating evidence. Equally, nothing which definitely eliminates him.

Investigation proceeding.

'Let's forget all that for the moment.' Plattner made another dismissive gesture. 'I'm talking about realities, unfortunately, not day-dreams. The fact of the matter is, you've consistently let me down, at least in recent years.'

'I may even have got a kick out of it,' observed Harald.

'Well I'm not going to tolerate it. I've made up my mind, and there are only two alternatives: either you co-operate from now on, or I kick you out. It's one or the other. I owe it to the firm – to my daughter, your wife. You won't get a second warning.'

'What does that amount to, in practice?'

'First, you'll apologize to Hilde for your behaviour. And make it convincing. I can't stand to see her suffer, least of all because of you.'

'What else?'

'From now on you'll devote a lot more time and thought to your family, which includes this firm. No more stepping out of line, no more bumming around . . . in other words, lead a normal life. Be sociable. Get on with the right people – Abendroth, for instance.'

'What if I don't? What if I don't want to?'

'Then,' Plattner said, smiling genially, 'I'll ruin you. You and your best friend – the only friend you ever had. I don't make idle threats. Surely you wouldn't want to push me that far?'

'This,' Hermann Abendroth had said, several years before, 'is probably the most challenging assignment I've ever been offered. Designs for the Olympic complex plus approach roads – I doubt if I'll ever get another chance like it.'

'I'm delighted for you,' said Harald. They were closeted in Abendroth's study over a bottle of spicy Palatinate wine, swapping ideas, enjoying each other's company. 'What exactly do you have in mind?'

'Something really bold and sweeping.' Abendroth reached for a map of Munich and outlined the Oberwiesenfeld in grease pencil. 'Here's where we'll locate the main Olympic buildings. The site lends itself perfectly to maximum concentration.'

'What about road links?'

'The approach roads will have to be planned on just as grand a scale.' Abendroth's thick pencil began to move again. He drew a smallish circle. 'Here's the city centre.' Two more concentric circles took shape. 'Here are the inner and outer ring-roads.' Now the pencil seemed to slice across the map. 'And this is the main approach road. It's the best and most effective solution – the simplest one, too.'

'All brilliant ideas are simple,' Harald said. 'I like your basic design, Hermann. It's a winner.'

Not that he realized it at the time, Harald was committing the lay-out to memory. Endowed with the keen and retentive eye of the trained architect, he could have reproduced it in every detail. And he did.

Further exchange between Detective-Superintendent Braun and Detective-Inspector Feldmann on the subject of inquiries in progress:

FELDMANN: The first lab reports have come in. Preliminary results: saliva, semen and urine specimens from the dead woman's body display almost identical characteristics. Blood type A, probably A1. They think we can rule out A2.

BRAUN: That's something at least. Anything else?

FELDMANN: Kordes, the girl's pimp, was seen in Zürich two days before the murder. We're still trying to trace him. Stenzenbach's alibi checks, so he drops out. However, we've turned up another possibility, a character named Lenbach. He's a major paper manufacturer – toilet tissue, mainly.

BRAUN: What's his claim to fame?

FELDMANN: Lenbach was one of the deceased's most enthusiastic customers. An awkward customer too, from her angle. He lives in Offenburg, but whenever he visited Munich he acted as if he owned her. Used to raise hell if she wasn't available, one such occasion being the night in question.

BRAUN: Right, put the screws on him. What about Fein?

FELDMANN: We've checked and double-checked every detail of his story, also the statements of three witnesses: PC Penzold, the car-thief Baumholder, and a prostitute who says he gave her fifty marks for doing nothing. There's a suspicious smell about the man, Super, but nothing that would stand up in court.

BRAUN: In that case, maybe it's time I took a hand – personally.

The same day witnessed the inauguration of a new boutique in an arcade off Theatinerstrasse. Present at the opening: 'Tout Munich'. The following details taken from Argus's column in the MZ:

Our host, Günther, presided in a pale lilac burnous cut from material specially woven in Lyons. Hetty wore an ivory toga, slashed at the nipples. Hannelore, who has deserted pop-singing for ceramics and is now a baroness, favoured a skin-tight pants-suit in green which contrasted effectively with her blue Afro wig.

I also caught a glimpse of Soraya, once an empress but now a simple unspoilt girl, very demure in a little black Balmain. Her voice sounded a bit hoarse. My diagnosis: too much nocturnal wandering in the gardens of her Roman villa . . .

Cocktails at four, cold buffet at five, this time from Dallmayr's, not Käfer's. Pâtisserie from Kreutzkamm's, canapés from the Residenzcafé. Drinks, notable for their profusion, from the Nymphenburg Sektkellerei.

Fashion show from five-fifteen onwards. Everything for the woman who has everything. Average price-tag: just a soupçon over three thousand marks. A mere bagatelle – Günther is simply *giving* the stuff away.

Argus's verdict: A successful and much-applauded display of up-to-the-minute chic.

(Obliquely mentioned in the 'Argus' column: an incident which raised a few eyebrows but was generally considered to have made the evening.

Joachim Jonas, who was escorting Plattner's daughter plus Melanie Weber, stepped up to Johannes-Eduard Duhr, youngest son of Plattner's keenest competitor in the construction industry, and hurled a glass of champagne – brand: Fürst Ferdinand – into his face.

Accompanying remark: 'Keep your filthy insinuations to yourself, okay?')

More discussions at Police HQ. Detective-Superintendent Braun and Detective-Inspector Feldmann:

FELDMANN: I've taken a closer look at our friend Lenbach, the toilet paper man from Offenburg.

BRAUN: Well?

FELDMANN: He's a very successful businessman. He invented the Lenbach Maxi-Roll. Made millions out of it. Even bought himself a Rembrandt with the proceeds – a fake one.

BRAUN: And no better than he deserves for blotting a million assholes a day. Let's have your notes on the interview, please.

Detective-Inspector Feldmann's notes on his interview with Otto Lenbach, company director, concerning the V-Strasse case:

Herr Lenbach, temporarily staying at the Bayerischer Hof Hotel, volunteered a statement. The gist was that he had visited the deceased on the evening of 15 September, which seems to check. At 10 p.m. Lenbach met a business associate for dinner at Humplmayr's and remained there until just before midnight.

Under intensive questioning, Herr Lenbach stated that no sexual intercourse had occurred between him and the deceased. On the contrary, he had – and I quote – 'roughed her up a bit' because she asked a higher price than last time.

BRAUN: What about Lenbach's prices? Haven't *they* gone up?

FELDMANN: Fifty per cent in the last five years – I should know, my wife buys his stuff.

BRAUN: I hope you didn't leave it at that.

FELDMANN: No, I questioned him for a good half-hour, particularly about his blood type. It was down there in black and white, on a certificate pinned to his driver's licence: type O. That puts Lenbach in the clear.

BRAUN: Which leaves Harald Fein. Right, Feldmann, I plan to tackle him tomorrow morning. I can hardly wait.

'I have an apology to make,' Harald informed his wife, who had returned to the family home at her father's behest. 'I'm not quite sure why, but perhaps you'll tell me. I want to do a convincing job.'

'You – you get on my nerves!' Hilde said explosively.

'I sympathize,' Harald replied. He bowed his head. 'I get on my own nerves. My hair's going grey, I smile for no good reason – I've even taken to shedding the odd tear in private. I'm growing older, that's all.'

'But no wiser!'

'You're wrong,' Harald assured her. 'I learn something new every day. Every day I'm obliged to live through increases my interest in nature, my love of animals, my sympathy for human beings. Even for you.'

'Kindly spare me your lectures on animal psychology,' she snapped. 'My name isn't Anton.'

'True,' he said.

'I'm married to you!' she screamed at him. 'Married to you and I can't stand the sight of you!'

'But you came back.'

'Only because Father asked me to. It's the last time – he promised me. Just until you step out of line again, and I won't have long to wait.'

They were sitting in the big drawing-room of the Fein villa, several yards apart. Heinz and Helga were out, the maid had gone shopping and Anton was rooting around in the garden, so there was nothing to prevent them from speaking their minds or raising their voices. Hilde took full advantage.

She had recently favoured the Murillo Madonna look. Flowing gowns, predominantly blue, eyes skilfully made up to accentuate their size, also in blue, lightly waved hair with Spanish chignon, colour of hair – for some time now – ash-blonde with discreet lights. The voice that went with this new image was gentle, subdued and virginally seductive. She was not using it on this occasion.

54

'Obviously,' Harald said, not looking at her, 'all your father wants is a glossy façade.'

'Isn't that the least he can expect of you? Father has his reputation to consider.'

'His pocket, you mean.'

'Kindly refrain from such insinuations in the future, even at home. That's another of Father's provisos. He's very worried. Business hasn't simply been stagnating recently – it's falling off, and he says it's your fault. Carry on this way and you'll ruin his image.'

'I know,' Harald said wearily. 'Your beloved father threatened to ruin *me*.'

'He would, too.'

'Except that you're my wife and the mother of my children. Heinz may take over the firm one day – he's tough enough. I'm pretty certain your father's banking on that.'

'Don't overrate yourself,' she sneered. 'Heinz is *my* son. I gave birth to him – your contribution was over in ten seconds flat. Besides, Father's the only one who counts. I'm his daughter – I'm not expendable like you. Finding a replacement for you would be child's play.'

'What do you mean?'

'Well, I can think of at least one man who'd suit me and be acceptable to Father.'

Harald looked faintly amused. 'Who is this paragon? Not Joachim Jonas, surely?'

'Why not?'

'Good God, Hilde, I brought him into the firm. He's indebted to me, he works with me – he's a *friend* of mine.'

'So what? That means nothing at all – only that you're pathetically unsophisticated.'

Joachim Jonas knocked discreetly at the chairman's door. It was long after office hours.

'I've something to tell you, sir. I'm afraid it can't wait.'

'I'm listening,' said Plattner. He camouflaged the latest issue of *Playboy* with a large file labelled 'Site 14' and propped his elbows on the huge desk.

'An unpleasant business, Herr Plattner, but I accept full responsibility. The name of the firm was at stake. To cut a long story short, I threw a glass of champagne in someone's face tonight.'

'Whose?'

'The youngest of the Duhr boys, Johannes-Eduard.'

'Why?'

'He had the nerve to make derogatory remarks about our business methods in front of several important people. He left the party at once, so that was the end of it – otherwise I'd have taken him apart. However, there's a chance that Herr Duhr senior will get in touch with you and . . .'

'He already did,' Plattner said airily. 'He phoned me a few minutes ago.'

'And?'

'Duhr and I are competitors when circumstances leave us no option. At other times we co-operate. We have an unwritten rule: we iron out our differences in private, never publicly. Duhr junior broke that rule. His father called to apologize on his behalf.'

'Phew!' Jonas looked highly relieved. 'Then I did the right thing – or rather, I didn't do the wrong thing.'

'You're coming along, Jonas,' Plattner assured him benevolently. 'Keep up the good work.'

Further exchanges between Hermann Abendroth of the Urban Planning Department and journalists present at an 'informative working dinner':

ABENDROTH: Certainly. I also know Herr Jonas. He worked in my department at City Hall for four or five months, several years ago. A first-rate man, particularly in the administrative field. Professionally ambitious, too, in the best sense of the word.

QUESTION: He switched jobs – deserted you for private enterprise. Why?

ABENDROTH: To better himself financially, I imagine. Herr Jonas wasn't an established civil servant. He took advantage of a favourable opportunity, that's all.

QUESTION: Did you encourage him?

ABENDROTH: To do what?

QUESTION: He joined the Plattner Construction Company. Was that a coincidence, or were you in some way responsible?

ABENDROTH: Not directly, I assure you. I merely knew that Herr Jonas wanted to move on. Herr Fein happened to be looking

56

for an able man who could take some of the weight off his shoulders. I introduced them. It seemed the natural thing to do. I believe in giving people a helping hand, don't you?

QUESTION: Did Herr Jonas personally collaborate with you on preliminary designs for the Olympic complex, including the approach roads?

ABENDROTH: He did not.

QUESTION: Did he have access to such plans – files, records and so on?

ABENDROTH (after a moment's hesitation): 'No.'

'Are you telling me,' Harald said, still smiling, 'that you've slept with Joachim?'

'What if I said yes? What business is it of yours?'

Harald leant back in his black leather arm-chair. 'So you have – is that what you're driving at?'

'Why should I feel any obligation to be frank with you? It's years since you've been my husband in anything but name.'

'Even so, what if your father hears about this alleged affair of yours?'

'Who'd tell him? Just you try it and see what happens. I'd dismiss it as a malicious lie – and you know which one of us Father would believe.'

'All right, have it your own way,' Harald said bitterly. 'We'll carry on as we are. The question is, how much longer can we stick it out?'

Urban Planning Supervisor Abendroth in conference with his immediate superior, the Director of Public Works, early next morning:

ABENDROTH: I don't like the way things are shaping. To be honest, I'm worried.

DIRECTOR OF PUBLIC WORKS: We've all got good reason to worry, considering the amount of public money we're juggling with. The closer we get to the Olympics the less I sleep. Every week seems to inflate the cost by another million.

ABENDROTH: Yes, and that's just why they'll try and pin the responsibility on some convenient scapegoat. I head the field with you running a close second and the Mayor in third place. There's a witch-hunt on. Who started it, that's what I'd like to know?

DIRECTOR OF PUBLIC WORKS: What exactly are you scared of?

ABENDROTH: To put it bluntly, an attempt to prove corruption – to prove that my department's been involved in the manipulation of contracts. Somebody seems bent on fabricating direct links between our planning staff and various civil engineering firms, notably Plattner Construction.

DIRECTOR OF PUBLIC WORKS: That's bad. I must notify the Mayor immediately.

'There are two men outside,' reported Maria Trübner. She looked awestruck. 'They're asking for the master.'

Hilde went to the door. She found herself confronted by a short stocky man with a pear-shaped, amiable face, and behind him a more indeterminate figure in a belted raincoat. Plainclothesmen, every inch.

'Frau Fein?'

Hilde nodded.

'Where can we find your husband?'

'In bed. He's still asleep.'

'We'd appreciate a word with him,' said the pear-faced man. 'Allow me to introduce myself. Feldmann's the name, Detective-Inspector, CID. May we come in?'

'If you insist,' Hilde replied ungraciously.

'But I don't.' Feldmann gave her a winning smile. 'You can send us away if you wish – if you think it's in your best interests, which I doubt.'

'What do you want with my husband?'

'We'd like him to accompany us to Headquarters. Pure routine, of course – no question of compulsion. Just an invitation to assist us, that's all. A pressing invitation, you might call it.'

Interview between the Director of Public Works and His Honour the Mayor. After a general and exhaustive review of current problems, mostly to do with increases in the cost of Olympic installations, special misgivings are voiced in regard to Fein, Plattner, Jonas and Abendroth.

DIRECTOR OF PUBLIC WORKS: In my view, Your Honour, a most alarming state of affairs. What do you suggest we do?

MAYOR: Stand firm – not budge an inch. We mustn't make the slightest attempt at concealment. It's the only way.

DIRECTOR OF PUBLIC WORKS: With respect, sir, wouldn't it

58

be better to take evasive action – nip any possible scandal in the bud?

MAYOR: No. If certain of our fellow-citizens insist on charging like mad bulls, we'll provide them with a matador. Rather an amusing prospect, don't you think? After all, why shouldn't I have an occasional bit of fun?

Chapter Three

Detective-Superintendent Braun positively radiated cordiality as he greeted his reluctant visitor.

'Delighted to meet you at last, Herr Fein.'

Harald stared round the superintendent's office without enthusiasm. 'What am I supposed to be doing here?'

'Let's put it this way: we'd appreciate your help.'

'How can I help you?'

'We think you may be able to assist us in our investigation.' Braun smiled ingratiatingly and drew up a chair. 'A case of murder,' he added.

Harald looked wholly unmoved. 'I still don't see why you had to drag me down here.'

'Oh come, Herr Fein! Nobody dragged you – you were invited.'

'And if I hadn't accepted?'

'I could, of course, have exerted a little pressure. The police are entitled to pull in any citizen for questioning, blood tests, fingerprinting or photographic identification. They can insist, if necessary. Were you aware of that?'

'No. There seem to be a few gaps in my education, I'm afraid.'

'We can soon rectify that, sir,' Braun said with bluff good humour. 'It'll be a pleasure to take you in hand.'

HILDE FEIN TO HER FATHER: What's going on, Father? Harald was hauled off by two detectives. That means he must be mixed up in something unsavoury. What are you going to do about it?

PAUL PLATTNER TO HIS DAUGHTER: My dearest girl, you have a habit of dramatizing things. Keep calm and rely on me to do what's best for us all. Perhaps they simply want to question him about a highway accident or something. They may even need him as an expert witness – the authorities could be planning to prosecute some fifth-rate building contractor for criminal negligence.

HILDE: But what if it turns out to be something serious?

PLATTNER: Stop trying to force my hand. You know how devoted to you I am. I'd do almost anything for you – I might even fix you up with Joachim Jonas.

HILDE: You know, then?

PLATTNER: That you've been having an affair with the man? I've known for the past year.

HILDE: I'm in love with him.

PLATTNER: If you say so. There's nothing more human than human nature, I realize that, but Munich is still an ultra-Catholic city in spite of all this talk of a permissive society. It may be a nuisance, but there it is.

HILDE: But Joachim would make a perfect successor – business-wise, I mean, not just from my own selfish point of view. He's efficient, isn't he?

PLATTNER: On the face of it. He certainly makes an effort – he's even prepared to earn my goodwill by taking an occasional risk. What's more, he's trying to demonstrate the sort of ruthlessness this business needs. For the moment, however, he's neither your husband nor my son-in-law. The name of my managing director is still Harald Fein.

HILDE: Yes, but for how much longer?

Detective-Superintendent Braun, still smiling, extracted a photo-graph from the folder in front of him and pushed it across to Harald. 'Do you know this woman – or lady, whichever you prefer?'

Harald looked at the photograph and nodded. It showed a voluptuous female with dazzling blonde hair and lips carefully pouted in a display of pin-up sensuality, her breasts jutting camerawards.

'I know her,' he said. 'Or rather, I've seen her a few times in the distance. I've never spoken to her.'

'When we found her,' Braun said, 'she looked different.'

'How different?'

'Don't you know? I thought you might be able to throw some light on the subject.'

'Me? What makes you think so?'

'Very well,' said Braun, 'I'll make a note of that. You claim complete ignorance of this woman's present condition.'

'How do you mean, condition?'

'Her skull has been battered and her throat shows distinct signs of strangulation. In other words, she's dead.'

Harald stared at the superintendent. 'I'm sorry to hear that,' he said, and looked away.

'Really?' Braun eyed his visitor with a mixture of curiosity and expectancy. 'Are you sorry for her or sorry for what happened to her?'

'I don't follow, Superintendent.'

There was a lengthy pause.

'You don't seriously think,' Harald said suddenly, ' – you don't believe I could have had anything to do with . . .'

'I don't believe anything, Herr Fein. I've got out of the habit of believing things – and people. I'm simply trying to establish the facts.'

'And they are?'

'I don't know yet. I only know you're nervous – it's written all over you. You don't look at me – you avoid my eye the whole time. Ten to one you're trying to hide something. The question is, what?'

From Detective-Superintendent Keller's notes:

They eyed each other like a couple of poker players. Both of them knew how to bluff – even Fein, which surprised me as much as it did Braun. Looking at the pair, I smelt trouble.

I happened to be in the office during that preliminary interview. My desk is in the far corner, beside one of the two windows. It gives me a view of the central courtyard, which is packed with prowl cars and police jeeps, some of them ripe for the scrap heap. I was supposed to be running through the daily PECD reports.

Case 1: unidentified infant, three weeks old. First strangled, then brained, probably against a tree. Four separate fractures recorded. Body recovered from river. Actual cause of death: drowning. Public Prosecutor's department notified.

Case 2: a girl aged thirteen, six months pregnant. Killed after falling from a third-floor window, probably with assistance from her mother, whose second husband may have been the prospective father. Passed to Homicide.

Case 3: a fifty-year-old man, found dead on his feet – a real rarity. Most bodies are found in a recumbent position, some hanging, others floating. This one, discovered in a suburban tenement, was standing wedged between some shelves and a cupboard. Death due to alcohol poisoning aggravated by severe diabetes. Body released for burial.

Death, in all its varied forms, has long been a commonplace to me, though I took a long time to get used to it. Getting used to the methods favoured by my colleague Det.-Supt Braun was an even harder job, I'm happy to say.

The 'it's written all over you' gambit was just a trick of the trade, a legitimate weapon in the interrogator's armoury. However, even though I had no direct connection with the case, something about Fein's manner alerted my professional instincts as well as Braun's.

I too felt that Fein knew something he didn't want to mention.

'So you *did* know the woman, Herr Fein. You're prepared to admit that much.'

'I'm not admitting anything, I'm simply telling you what I know.' Harald remained studiously polite. 'I assume I haven't been brought here for cross-examination.'

'What else do you assume?'

'That you want some information.'

'Put it any way you like.' Braun strolled to the far end of the office and leant against a filing cabinet. Keller sat hunched over some papers at his elbow, outwardly so engrossed that he might have been alone in the room.

'So you saw the woman,' Braun said, 'a number of times. You say you never spoke to her, but you do know where she lives – lived, rather. Do you admit that?'

'I admit nothing, Superintendent, I told you already. If you're trying to establish a link between me and this unfortunate business, I decline to say another word.'

'You misjudge me,' Braun growled. 'You also misjudge the position you're in.'

'Appearances can be misleading, Superintendent. I merely parked my car in V-Strasse and sat there. I smoked several cigarettes and listened to the radio. Is that a crime?'

'Not in itself.' Braun scowled irritably. Defiance always got under his skin.

'In that case I can go. Someone's waiting for me.'

'Who?'

'My dog. He's all alone in the car and I don't like leaving him too long.'

'Your dog?' Braun raised his eyebrows.

'Yes, any objection?'

'Your dog can wait.'

'This one can't.' Harald noted Keller's seated figure for the first time. The man seemed to be grinning sympathetically, but Harald, who was concentrating on Braun, dismissed the impression as false. 'Anton – that's his name – was with me the last time I parked in V-Strasse.'

'Are you planning to subpoena a dog?'

'There are several witnesses I could call. A loiterer, a prostitute – even a policeman.'

'I know all that,' Braun said, pouncing. 'We've already got statements from all three. What makes you think they'd testify for you and not against you?'

'Don't overreach yourself, Superintendent.' Harald still sounded calm and relaxed. 'You may think I'm a push-over but I'm not – not from your angle or any other.'

Peter Palitschek, part-time insurance agent, to Maria Trübner, his current girl-friend:

Okay, sweetheart, do your stuff. No time like the present. Let's get it straight. Fein has made improper advances to you, the filthy brute. More than once – in fact whenever he gets the chance. On the stairs, say, and in the bathroom, and in his bedroom when you bring his breakfast up on a tray. He's always making passes, especially when you're alone in the house, because when his wife's at home he's another man entirely. He even makes a point of bawling you out in front of her – calling you a stupid bitch and so on. Right so far?

Right. It all began when he started leering at you. Next thing you knew, he grabbed your hand. Before long he was squeezing your tits and sliding his hand up your legs. Is that the way it was?

MARIA TRÜBNER (wistfully): It'd have been nice.

PETER PALITSCHEK (doggedly): That's the way it was, and you hated every minute of it, understand? You were shocked and disgusted – he revolted you. Innocent young girl versus dirty old man – it's an old story but it always goes over big. You didn't

64

want to lose a good job and you were fond of Frau Fein and the kids – you didn't want to hurt them. So you fought him off tooth and nail, and he offered you money.

MARIA TRÜBNER: How much? A thousand marks?

PETER PALITSCHEK: You must be joking! You aren't worth a thousand. I mean, not to a man like Fein. His kind are in the market for anything available, but they know what the going rate is. Let's say he offered you two hundred – three hundred, if it makes you feel happier.

Anyway, you turned him down flat. He upped the ante to five hundred, but you weren't having any. You were outraged. You decided to confide in your boy-friend, i.e. yours truly.

I'll take it from there.

'My dear boy,' Plattner said, wagging his head, 'what's all this I hear?'

He waved Harald into the chair immediately in front of his desk, a French chair, guaranteed genuine Louis Quinze.

'Tell me, is it really true you're having trouble with the police?'

'I wouldn't call it trouble.'

Plattner circled Harald and laid two granite hands proprietorially on his shoulders. 'I'm told,' he said, lowering his voice, 'that you've been questioned at police headquarters in connection with a murder. I can't believe it.'

'Then don't,' Harald said lightly.

'Pardon me, but you're still my daughter's husband. If you're in deep water, Harald, I can't help feeling concerned – it's my duty. Come on, what's it all about?'

'You really want me to tell you?'

'I'm a seeker after truth, Harald, you ought to know that by now.'

Exchange between Detective-Superintendent Braun and Detective-Inspector Feldmann:

FELDMANN: Your interview with Harald Fein – does it put him in the clear?

BRAUN: Like hell it does. What's the matter with you, got a crush on him or something? The man's abnormal – a complete misfit.

FELDMANN: Maybe he's simply trying to save his neck.

65

BRAUN: Don't give me that! Stick to what we've got and stop theorizing. How about the woman's address-book – any luck?

FELDMANN: Records are checking it right now. It's a hard job, with telephone numbers being changed from one day to the next. Also, she wasn't exactly a neat writer. Lots of the numbers she noted are hell to decipher – her sevens could be ones and her fives look like threes, and vice versa.

BRAUN: But you've turned up one number in particular?

FELDMANN: Yes, the number of the firm Fein works for – if the figures have been identified correctly. All the same, Plattner's employ six or seven thousand people. Are we supposed to check them all?

BRAUN: You should know better than to ask me that. Six or seven thousand? Don't make me laugh! There can't be more than a couple of dozen employees who could afford her prices. Directors, senior executives, site engineers – the managing director. Concentrate your inquiries on that area.

'All right, whatever you mean by the truth, here it is.' Harald eyed his father-in-law with a trace of pity. 'I was near the place in question at the time in question, but I had nothing to do with the crime in question.'

Plattner stared at him with raised eyebrows. 'Was it really murder?'

'So I gather. She was a call-girl. I happened to be in the neighbourhood, but I wasn't the only one. The address is 33 V-Strasse, sixth floor. Does it ring a bell?'

'And you were there at the time?' Plattner paused for some moments before continuing, with an ominous undercurrent in his voice: 'Harald, my boy, I hope you haven't started drinking again.'

'You needn't have bothered to ask that question, certainly not in the present context. If you're hinting I murdered someone in a drunken frenzy and lost my memory afterwards, forget it. You know perfectly well your daughter would have told you if I'd hit the bottle again. She's only waiting for the happy day.'

'Don't talk like that, Harald. You do Hilde an injustice. What's more, you misjudge me. The very fact that you're sitting here now ought to convince you I'm always at your service.'

'And always ready to remind me of my duty to you and the firm.'

66

'Why not? Mutual obligations are a good thing, Harald – a fine thing. They're worth money in the bank.'

'Does Abendroth realize what he's taken on?' Plattner had asked Harald several years earlier, during a midnight conversation at the Fein villa. 'Won't it prove too much for him, this Olympic assignment of his?'

Harald shook his head. 'Some people might fold under the pressure, but not Hermann.'

Plattner was sipping mineral water. Harald had just embarked on his second bottle of champagne.

'The Oberwiesenfeld is a perfect site for the Olympic complex,' mused Plattner. 'Compact, self-contained, almost wholly owned by the province and municipality. What about communication by road, though?'

'A bold and sweeping solution – it's the only possible way. Hermann thinks so too.' Harald poured himself some more champagne. 'His plan is brilliantly simple.' He reached for the map Plattner pushed towards him and took out a pencil. 'No system of by-passes, no attempt to extend the present ring-roads.' Red lines took shape on the map as he spoke. 'Here's the city centre and here are the inner and central ring-roads. And here,' he said triumphantly, 'running straight from the city centre, is the main approach road. It cuts across an exhibition site, some waste land, two sports arenas and the Sunset Estate, which is largely inhabited by old age pensioners. In other words, no major problems of any kind.'

'None at first sight,' Plattner agreed, promptly tweaking the map towards him. 'We should be able to make something out of this. I'm much obliged to you, my boy.'

'You've got me wrong. I didn't mean to . . .'

'Don't be so modest. You've justified your place in the company at last. I won't forget this in a hurry.'

Harald shook his head with finality. 'I can't breathe the air in your capitalistic swamp, not any more.'

'Marxist balderdash, Harald! Leave that kind of hot air to your son. Heinz can afford to indulge in such stupidities – he's still in his teens. You've been part of this firm for nearly twenty years, and on one vital occasion you performed an important service – a very important service, I admit. Then you stopped pulling your weight. Worse, you became a positive liability.'

Plattner frowned. 'And now? Now you seem hell-bent on exposing me. Why, Harald? It would be suicide, even you must realize that. Start a scandal and you'll be risking your personal future.'

Harald shrugged. 'What's that worth? Nothing, so I've got nothing to lose.'

Plattner rose, looking genuinely agitated, his hands gripping the edge of the desk.

'By all means despise me and my daughter,' he said. 'Despise yourself too – self-contempt comes naturally to your kind – but get this straight: in my book, you're a complete zero from every angle bar one. You fathered a son, and I've earmarked him to take over the firm. Heinz has got drive. He'll make a worthy successor once he gets all that revolutionary crap out of his system – and experience tells me it won't be long. Are you planning to bitch up his life for good?'

'Is that supposed to be my incentive for swallowing everything that happens from now on? Is that the price of silence?'

'Yes,' Plattner said, breathing heavily, 'and you'll pay it. You'll pay it if you really love the boy, which you do because he's your flesh and blood.' A thought struck him. 'He is, I suppose?'

From Detective-Superintendent Keller's notes:
Harald Fein began to interest me, even preoccupy me. There was something about him – a strange blend of gaiety and melancholy. Most things seemed to make him smile without really amusing him. He had a peculiarly sad expression. The only time his eyes lit up was when he spoke about his dog, Anton. I became very curious to meet him – Anton, I mean.

'Herr Fein?' said the stranger who had called on Harald at the Marienplatz offices of the Plattner Construction Company, a thin rat-faced young man with a wary expression. 'I'm Peter Palitschek.'

'Please sit down,' Harald said. 'I think I've heard your name before. Aren't you a friend of Fräulein Trübner, who keeps house for us?'

68

Palitschek nodded mournfully. 'Maria and I are engaged, or as good as.'

As though on cue, Anton rose from his sheepskin rug and trotted over to Palitschek, sniffed him briefly and withdrew at speed, backwards. He began to shake himself vigorously, head first, then shoulders, then back and flanks, then tail. Finally he resumed his place on the rug.

Palitschek looked a trifle disconcerted. 'What was all that about?'

'It's only my dog. Don't let him put you off – you were talking about Fräulein Trübner.'

'A girl in a million,' Palitschek proclaimed.

'I'm sure she is. My wife thinks very highly of her.'

'But too sensitive for her own good, though you might not suspect it at first sight. Maria's got a lovely nature. She's a decent girl from a good home, not a tart.' Palitschek paused. 'Maybe you wouldn't agree.'

'Why shouldn't I? Anyway, what are you driving at?'

'Only that I'm an ordinary, decent, respectable person, and so's my fiancée. All we want is an ordinary, decent, respectable future together – plus financial security, of course.'

Harald smiled faintly. 'Are you planning to blackmail me?'

Palitschek fended off the suggestion with both hands. 'Who said anything about blackmail?'

'All right, just what are you driving at?'

'It's simple. You're a broadminded man, Herr Fein. So am I. We all slip up occasionally, but nobody minds as long as we put things right.'

'And what's the best way of doing that, in your expert opinion?'

'Compensation,' Palitschek said briskly. 'Look at it this way, Herr Fein. From what I hear, you badgered Maria into going to bed with you. I don't blame you, but she's never had a fair return – not so far. There's such a thing as conscience money . . .'

'You're knocking at the wrong door, Herr Palitschek. In the first place, I never asked Maria to extend me the services you mention. Secondly, I couldn't pay for them even if I'd had them. I own next to nothing. I live in a big house but it belongs to my wife – or rather, her father. Plattner's pay me forty or fifty thousand marks a year, but all that goes on living expenses – food, clothing, heating, telephone, electricity, garbage disposal, school fees, doctors' bills, taxes, car repairs, insurance, road tax, gas, and so on. How much do you think that leaves for me, let alone you?'

'Try scraping the barrel, Herr Fein. I don't suppose you want to break up the happy home.'

'Wrong again, Herr Palitschek. I'm beyond caring, and it's a wonderful sensation. You've no idea what a relief it is to know you don't have anything to lose. I told you, you've come to the wrong place.'

'In that case,' snarled Palitschek, 'I'd better try somewhere else.'

'Go ahead,' Harald said coolly. 'Why not apply to Herr Plattner direct, if you're so determined? I'll be fascinated to see how far you get.'

The crime at 33 V-Strasse was noted by all the Bavarian capital's leading dailies, only two days after the event.

The Münchner Allgemeine, *studiously earnest, deliberately aloof from party politics and internationally oriented, printed a small paragraph at the foot of page 7, under the heading 'Local Police Reports':*

. . . a person of the female sex found dead in her apartment. The cause of death has yet to be definitely established. Inquiries are proceeding.

The Münchner Nachrichten, *equally earnest in tone but far more politically committed and aimed at the solid citizens of Bavaria, included the murder in its 'Local Reports' section on page 3:*

. . . a scantily clad woman of dubious occupation found dead in her apartment with severe injuries which suggest that she was strangled. The murderer is still at large, but a CID spokesman last night claimed that investigation has yielded some important leads and expressed confidence that it can only be a matter of time before . . .

The Morgenzeitung, *noted for its joie de vivre, ebullience and predilection for pop and pot, proclaimed under an eye-catching head-line on page 1:*

Battered and strangled – corpse in luxury apartment. Slain call-girl's address-book yields list of well-heeled clients from Munich's upper crust. Sensational revelations imminent.

München am Mittag, *characteristically jaunty and bent on hitting the public where it hurts, announced, likewise on page 1:*

70

Top call-girl slain in love-nest. Strangler at large?

CID baffled. Scores of suspects. Panic mounts as crime wave grows. Citizens' action committee asks police chief: 'Are we living in Munich or Chicago?' For his reply, also detailed reports and comments, see 'Murder rate hits new peak' on page 3.

Finally, Bild, *as starkly pictorial and harshly clamorous as ever:*

Murder in high places. Bid to shield socialite strangler? *Bild* demands a full-scale inquiry – *now!*

'Well?' Detective-Superintendent Braun jerked a thumb at the mountain of newsprint on his desk. 'What do you make of that?'

Detective-Inspector Feldmann shrugged. 'Freedom of the press has its advantages, even from our angle. There isn't a downright mis-statement in any of those reports.'

'Nor a single statement that's strictly accurate.'

'Hardly surprising, sir. The papers don't know what we know – or rather, suspect.' Feldmann glanced at Superintendent Keller, who was sitting in his usual corner near the window thumbing through a book on dogs.

'I've nothing against our smart young Turks from the press,' Braun said. 'They can be useful at times. Plenty of major criminals have been traced and convicted with press assistance.'

'What about "CID baffled"? Doesn't that get your goat?'

Braun laughed. 'Far from it. I've got a hide like a rhino. Criticism's a good thing in the long run. This city used to have three dailies controlled by the same press tycoon. They all followed the same line and shared the market between them. Now we've got five independents, which makes for competition.'

'How does that help us?'

'Easy. Five independent papers can't afford to express the same view on every subject. That means there'll always be at least one for, one against and one neutral. A perfect set-up from our point of view. It doesn't matter what we do – one of the five is bound to back us.'

Routine report from Detective-Inspector Feldmann to Detective-Superintendent Braun:

About three hundred leads followed to date, in and around V-Strasse. No positive results so far.

Businesses checked include restaurants, shops, a hairdresser's, a bar, a chemist's and a delicatessen which also sells champagne. The murdered woman's favourite was Veuve Clicquot, which she obviously reserved for special customers. She was well known in the neighbourhood, but nobody has come up with any information of value.

Then there's the address-book. Plenty of phone numbers but hard to decipher. Regular customers so far identified: five members of parliament, three provincial, two federal; a senior civil servant; an actor, a TV producer, and two big industrialists. Also three lawyers: two attorneys, both from Munich, and a federal judge from Karlsruhe.

BRAUN: Good work, Feldmann. Plenty to chew on there, but Harald Fein remains our No.1 suspect. Just what I was hoping for.

'Focus', the München am Mittag *legal correspondent, commenting on the case next day:*

. . . that no one, not even our police force, has the right to trespass on the private lives of our fellow-citizens, let alone publicize details of an intimate and personal nature . . .

. . . not in any way criticizing the investigation of criminal acts, which should, in our view, be vigorously and relentlessly pursued . . .

. . . are bound, however, to view with alarm the precipitate disclosure of names which may have only a tenuous connection with such cases, let alone the identification of innocent persons mistakenly suspected of . . .

. . . take this opportunity to utter a solemn warning . . .

This time it was Feldmann who sought Braun's views.

'What do you make of that, Super?'

'Great stuff,' Braun purred delightedly. 'Just what I expected, Feldmann. We're on the right track.'

'You mean it's slanted?'

'This article was bought and paid for – either that or deliberately inspired. Obviously the lobbyists have gone to work. Somebody's pulling strings – somebody with political or business interests at stake. Don't forget the circulation war, Feldmann. I wouldn't be surprised if we get some covering fire from a different quarter, and soon.' He paused. 'Maybe tomorrow, even.'

72

Melanie Weber, friend of Hilde Fein, in conversation with her protégée of the moment, a young person selected with her husband's assistance and approval. The girl's name is immaterial. A would-be actress, she is paying her way through drama school by acting as Melanie's day-and-night companion.

MELANIE: You've no idea how *cruel* life can be, darling – how absolutely merciless and unpredictable. Poor dear Hilde is a *perfect* illustration.

She positively *sacrificed* herself for years, and all for a man who's utterly unstable.

He pursued me *madly*, my dear, but I always turned him down – no one could call me disloyal to my friends. Perhaps that's why he took to the bottle. He turned into an absolute *wreck*.

Just the same, there were moments when I wondered if anyone had ever *understood* him properly or given him the right sort of *strength*. He may have been looking for someone to understand and *love* him, both at once.

A woman might do worse than make that her *mission* in life, I sometimes think. Come over here, darling – no, *closer*. Let's forget about men and be *cosy*.

Subsequent comments by Detective-Inspector – by then Chief Inspector – Feldmann on preliminary results obtained from Interviewee No. 38 in the V-Strasse case, Adolf Penatsch by name:

Detective-Superintendent Braun's team were working on five cases simultaneously. One of them showed signs of getting bogged down and another was making routine progress. The other three were:

Case 1. Hotel Ederer. Bolivian diplomat found stabbed in his room. Presumed motive: political. Routine inquiries conducted by Inspector Zengelberner.

Case 2. Plauscher Fur Company. The proprietors, a man and wife, shot dead on premises. Safe forced and ransacked. Probable culprit: the dead couple's son, who vanished with one of the sales girls.

Case 3. V-Strasse. Murder of a prostitute. Investigated by me in close consultation with Det.-Supt Braun, who compiled and sifted all available information, supervised inquiries and reinforced or reduced the various squads as necessary – a taxing job requiring a lot of co-ordination. We should have had at least three times as many men on the case.

Adolf Penatsch, the informant in question, was a quiet individual, very polite and reserved. He needed careful handling. Preliminary interviews yielded little. Employed as janitor at 33 V-Strasse, Penatsch answered all my questions readily but non-committally. He had a good memory and was well informed about his tenants' personal affairs.

It wasn't until my third late-night session with Penatsch that he mentioned a name I'd heard before. Apparently, he'd seen the man several times in recent weeks, not only near 33 V-Strasse but inside the building itself.

Braun guessed it was Harold Fein even before I'd uttered the name. He decided to question Penatsch personally and told me to assemble all available information about the man.

Hilde Fein, escorted by Joachim Jonas, is present at the opening of Orgasm 2001, *Munich's latest attraction, a cross between cocktail bar and sex emporium.*

HILDE: I'm terribly worried.

JONAS: You look it, but why? Because Melanie isn't here, or is it Harald? Don't worry, everything's going like clockwork.

Nearly all Munich's top people are present, as ever on such occasions. Also, at least six topless beauties of assorted pigmentation, an ex-Carnival Prince, two fashion designers, three youthful film directors complete with attendant starlets, four boutique owners, five TV personalities, a scattering of business tycoons' sons, from sportswear to optics, a radio announcer, two revue artistes and a sculptor in scrap-metal.

HILDE: It's all very well saying that, but things are getting me down.

JONAS: Sit back and enjoy yourself, darling. The party's only just begun.

HILDE: I can't help thinking of Father and all that's in store for him, thanks to Harald. He needs all the support we can give him.

JONAS: And he'll get it, certainly from me – for your sake. You can tell him so.

'Thank you for coming, Chief Superintendent.' Paul Plattner

spoke with elaborate courtesy. 'What can I offer you – a little apéritif, perhaps? I suggest champagne, Dom Perignon 1959.'

Chief Superintendent Dürrenmaier, head of the Capital Crimes Division, declined with equal courtesy. 'Perhaps a beer or some mineral water.'

Dürrenmaier was feeling uneasy. It was no new sensation. He had felt almost invariably uneasy ever since his promotion to CID chief, and the present set-up made his collar feel even tighter.

He had been politely but urgently requested by a provincial member of parliament – a member of the committee on industrial development, building projects included – to grant Plattner a private interview. 'It might just prove useful, not least from your department's point of view.'

Still Dürrenmaier had hesitated. He took the precaution of consulting the Commissioner of Police, whose sole response was: 'One can't entirely avoid cultivating contacts with influential members of the local community. It can be even advisable in certain circumstances – but only, as I say, in certain circumstances.'

Dürrenmaier's hesitation persisted until he received a phone call from Dr Abendroth of the Urban Planning Department. And Abendroth, as connoisseurs of local politics were aware, had the ear of the much admired and universally respected Mayor – half an ear only, so to speak, but still . . .

Abendroth on the phone to Dürrenmaier: 'I'm not trying to pressure you in any way, Chief Superintendent. If I venture to intervene at all, it's only because my old friend Harald Fein deserves all the help and support he can get. In other words, I'm simply asking you to weigh very carefully the consequences of any steps you may take.'

And so it came about that CID chief and building magnate sat smiling politely at each other over a snow-white tablecloth in the Schwarzwälder, a reputable and efficiently run restaurant situated between the luxury Bayerischer Hof Hotel and the impressive bulk of the cathedral whose twin domes loomed above Munich like asymmetrical breasts.

Surrounding them, deep in subdued conversation, were some of the city's most prestigious backroom boys: Fabian of Fabian Investments, Merker of Merker Refineries, Biermann of Biermann Transport, a group of stock-brokers and real estate dealers, a couple of chain store magnates, and several representatives from the automobile industry.

Almost everyone knew everyone else, but greetings were few and limited to an exchange of nods or glances. Each table in the restaurant was like an enclave, an extension of its occupants' private offices.

'Nice place,' the Chief Superintendent observed. 'Better grub than a police canteen, that's for sure.'

Plattner nodded. 'What's more, it's almost as private as one's own four walls. Reporters steer clear of the place – they'd only bump into their employers, and newspaper proprietors are off-limits to gossip columnists.'

It wasn't until the saddle of venison, or long after the smoked salmon, that they began talking freely, Plattner about the decline of law and order, Dürrenmaier about the difference between personal freedom and anarchy. Not, however, until the Apfel-strudel Viennese-style, or before the coffee, did Plattner begin to home in on his target.

'Chief Superintendent,' he said, 'far be it from me to put pressure on you, still less coax you into committing an indiscretion. I simply want some information, in confidence. Unless I'm completely off the track, my son-in-law is involved in a police investigation.'

'True, Herr Plattner,' Dürrenmaier said cautiously. 'There's no official secret about that. As you probably know, my officers have asked Herr Fein for certain particulars. I'm not, of course, in a position to divulge any detailed information about an inquiry which is still in progress.'

'Of course not, Chief Superintendent. I wouldn't dream of asking you to do such a thing.'

'Splendid, Herr Plattner. You've no idea how delighted I am to hear you say that – delighted and relieved. I can assume, then, that you wish to communicate some information which may help to clear Herr Fein. If so, I'll be only too happy to follow it up. After all, exonerating innocent parties is part of our job.'

'Well said, Chief Superintendent.' Plattner sniffed his brandy appreciatively – his current favourite was a mellow Otard. 'However, that's not what I was driving at.'

'No?' Dürrenmaier frowned into his coffee-cup and looked a little perplexed. 'In that case, how can I help you?'

76

Plattner stared into space with hooded eyes. 'It's like this. I'd never ask you to take sides either way – I mean, for me or against someone else. I simply want to know the worst. Is he implicated or not? Is he under suspicion or not? Do the CID intend to arrest him or don't they? I'm merely trying to prepare for any eventuality.'

'Well,' Dürrenmaier said slowly, 'let me put it this way. Our investigation is far from complete. No definite picture has emerged. As for the person you mentioned, his position may be summed up as follows: he doesn't seem to have been wholly eliminated from our investigation. In other words, the possibility of future proceedings can't be entirely ruled out.'

'That's good enough,' Plattner said. He drew a deep breath. 'Quite good enough.'

From Detective-Superintendent Keller's notes:

Corpses get you down in the long run. Dealing with hundreds of them in the course of a single year makes you long for a bit of distraction – something to offset the boredom. Most PECD officers are heavy smokers, and not by chance.

I'm a non-smoker, myself, and I seldom touch hard liquor. One beer a week is about my average, and a double shot of schnapps to go with it. I use Japanese face-masks to cut down the smell of putrefaction, or, in extreme cases, a gas-mask from the last war. It's hard on the olfactory nerves, my job.

My predecessor was retired early to make room for me, fortunately for him. His predecessor did a stint in a funny farm before they transferred him to outdoor duties in the depths of the country.

As for me, I've found another outlet. I take an interest in the living – or rather, in creatures who are still in the condition that separates birth from death. Harald Fein was one.

I duly opened a confidential file on him in addition to my routine PECD reports. It was marked 'For Personal Use Only', and it wasn't the first of its kind.

I find myself becoming more and more fascinated, these days, by what members of my profession refer to as 'victimology'. The theory – much quoted but still largely unexplored – that there is an obscure but significant relationship between a murderer and his victim.

Sheep positively throw themselves to the wolves. The defence-less tempt the predatory and sometimes provoke them. In certain cases, guilt or complicity in a murder can extend to the victim as well as the murderer.

Fein's predicament struck me as a case in point, or did until I discovered more about him.

Harald surveyed his assembled family across the breakfast table. 'I asked you to join me because I want to tell you something.'

'What is it now?' Heinz demanded rudely. 'There's no point in going over old ground.'

Helga frowned at her brother. Then she turned an affectionate and encouraging smile on her father.

'Well,' Hilde said, 'what's the trouble this time?'

'Somebody's trying to blackmail me,' Harald said. 'I'm supposed to have assaulted Maria. Indecently.'

'Who'd dare to say such a thing?' Hilde's eyes narrowed as she watched her husband intently. 'Is it true?'

'Why shouldn't it be?' Heinz chuckled. 'Maria seems to regard it as part of her normal duties. I speak from personal experience.'

They all stared at him, his sister incredulously, his mother in alarm, his father with a faintly astonished smile.

'You and Maria?'

'Why not? She offered her services and I accepted. It was a dull night on TV, as far as I can remember.'

'Here in this house?' Hilde's tone was accusing.

'Where else?' Heinz retorted cheerfully. 'This is the house I'm obliged to live in. It's your house, Mother dear. We're only tenants. What's more, you were the one who hired the girl – it's your fault if she opens her legs on the premises. Anyway, she isn't worth her wages, as I hope Father will confirm. Why all the fuss?'

From the stenographic record of an interview with Maria Trübner some days later:

. . . taken advantage of time and again, whenever there was a chance. First by the son of the house . . .

. . . brought the boy some herb tea one morning when he had a cold, or pretended he had. Just as I was bending over the bed he put his hand up my skirt. I only stood still so as not to spill the cup. Disgraceful, it was . . .

78

... Herr Fein was next. Not having a cup in my hand that time, I fought him off. I screamed, too, but it was no use, me being alone in the house with him. He held me down and tore off my panties. Then he tried to square things by offering me a couple of hundred marks. I turned him down flat, I don't mind telling you . . .

And that was only the beginning!

'It's a transparent blackmail scheme,' Harald said.

'Of course it is, Daddy,' Helga declared vehemently. 'I believe you.'

Heinz grinned. 'I don't. These things happen in the best regulated families, so why not in the worst? Maria's clever. She tried to wheedle my monthly allowance out of me, and God knows it's little enough. She soon shut up when I lodged a counter-claim for services rendered.'

'I wish your grandfather were here,' Harald said. 'He'd appreciate your business acumen.'

'Don't change the subject,' Hilde told him sternly. 'If you've really been having an affair with this girl, Heinz, I regret and deplore your conduct more than I can say. But if the same thing applies to my husband, and I can't discount the possibility, it's not only outrageous – it's downright unforgivable.'

'What are you talking about?' Harald's voice rose. 'I take the trouble to confide in my family, hoping for a little friendly advice and sympathy, hoping we can work out a solution together, and what happens? You believe the worst of me!'

'I don't, Daddy,' cried Helga.

'No, not you, my dear girl. You weren't included in that remark.'

'But I was!' snapped Hilde. 'I'm your main target, aren't I? You try to evade your responsibilities by making accusations.'

'With good reason,' Heinz said amiably.

Anton, shut out in the hall, barked and scratched at the door, but nobody paid any attention.

'Be that as it may,' Harald said, 'my problems don't end there. I'm obviously thought capable of much more serious aberrations, in a word – murder.'

'Oh no!' Helga gasped.

'You mean it?' Heinz's eyes sparkled. 'Congratulations,

I'd never have thought it of you. Who dreamed up that idea, one of Grandfather's competitors?'

'No, the CID.'

'This is too much,' said Hilde. 'I must let Father know at once.'

The following day saw the publication of an article in the Morgenzeitung, *heralded on page 1 and printed on page 3, by Mathias Engelmacher, journalist, criminologist and member of the League for Human Rights. It appeared under the headline: 'Have you got the guts, Commissioner?'*

. . . used to be claimed by our country's one-time fascist rulers that national expediency is the only law. On the contrary, law is what protects the citizen, safeguards and guarantees his liberties.

Tolerance ends where the vested interests of intolerance begin.

It is to be hoped that the police realize this. They must not shirk their responsibilities, however prominent the persons involved . . .

. . . which is why we now say to the Commissioner of Police: 'Have you got the guts? If so, give us some names.'

'Just what the doctor ordered,' Braun said, visibly heartened. 'Now we can really go to town.'

'How do you mean, Super?' Feldmann indicated the newspapers spread out on the desk between them. 'What do they expect us to do?'

'Join in the usual parlour game, of course.' Braun shuffled pleasurably in his creaky wooden chair. 'We have to play dumb and make it convincing, just so we can get on with our job in a semi-intelligent fashion, undisturbed. And we have to give the press something to sink its teeth into.'

'If you're talking about Fein, sir, I honestly wouldn't advise . . .'

'I'm not a complete fool, Feldmann.' Braun frowned resentfully. 'You really think I'd throw the press a piece of prime steak like Fein, right away? No, no, dish it out gradually. A little bit of practice and you'll have the reporters eating out of your hand.'

'Who, me?'

'Yes, you've got to learn sometime. Have them in one at a time, the bastards, and give them a quick peek at our information board. Don't spill anything about that man Penatsch, though. I want to question him personally first.'

'What about Fein?'

'Don't even mention his name. If someone raises the subject, hedge. Don't commit yourself either way – leave the whole thing vague.'

'Superintendent,' said Feldmann, 'my last job was in the lab, working on fingerprints. Can't I go back there? I'm not cut out for this kind of assignment.'

'You're here now,' Braun said tersely, 'and that's where you'll stay. If you fall down on the job you can always transfer out. You'd look lovely in uniform, directing traffic in the city centre. How does that sound?'

Hilde Fein turned to look at her daughter, who was standing in the doorway of her dressing-room.

'Missing something?' she asked. 'I borrowed a lipstick of yours – the pale red one with a bluish tinge.'

'It doesn't suit older people,' Helga said.

Hilde gave a rather pained laugh. 'You think of me as old?'

'It isn't a question of age. For instance, Daddy's even older than you are, but none of my friends can hold a candle to him. He's so different. So much more relaxed and dignified – so much more worthy of respect.'

'Is that why you came, to tell me that? My dear girl, you're old enough to know better. It's time you took off your rose-tinted spectacles, especially where he's concerned.'

'I love him!' cried Helga.

'All right, you love him,' Hilde said impatiently. She was due to meet Joachim Jonas and didn't want to be late. 'Anything else?'

'There are some things Daddy would never do.'

'For instance?'

'Well, take the opening of that new sex-shop I just read about in the paper. Daddy detests things like that and so do I. A superficial, self-satisfied bunch of social parasites . . .'

'Now see here, Helga! Whether or not one likes these people, they're part of local society. One can't simply ignore them so one has to tolerate them. One of us has to make an effort for the family's sake – for the firm's sake. In this case it's me.'

'Escorted by that man Jonas!' Helga snapped.

Hilde closed her eyes for a moment and lowered the lipstick. It was as if she couldn't face her own reflection in the big mirror.

Coldly she said: 'A woman can't go to these functions unescorted. Your father never attends them and our friend Frau Weber was otherwise engaged. Herr Jonas works for the firm. He also enjoys your grandfather's confidence.'

'Mother,' Helga said, almost inaudibly, 'are you planning to leave us?'

'What on earth gives you that idea?'

'It's true, isn't it?'

'Nonsense, Helga. I don't plan to leave anyone, certainly not my own children. My God, why can't you take a realistic view of things for once? What about that beloved father of yours? Weren't there days, weeks and months when it looked as if he'd deserted us for good – all of us, including you?'

'He was a sick man.'

'What does that make him now? Will he ever be completely cured? Has he ever shown you even a fraction of the love you squander on him, Helga? Think about *that* sometime.'

'Oh God,' moaned Helga, 'the whole situation's a nightmare!' She rushed out and slammed the door.

'This gentleman,' announced Detective-Inspector Feldmann, 'is Herr Adolf Penatsch, janitor of No. 33 V-Strasse.'

'Have a seat,' said Braun. He scrutinized his visitor's gaunt frame and pale face, so careworn that it might almost have been eroded with worry, and said: 'You look like a promising witness, Herr Penatsch.'

'It's in my nature to be helpful,' Penatsch assured him quietly.

'Herr Penatsch is more than helpful,' Feldmann amplified. 'He's a man of many parts. He handles almost all the repairs at 33 V-Strasse by himself. He also acts as a baby-sitter if required, and in his spare time he makes models. He's doing the cathedral at the moment, in matches. A thousand hours so far.'

'One thousand two hundred and twenty-four,' Penatsch amended softly.

'Remarkable,' purred Braun. 'So you're thorough, conscientious and persevering. You've given my officers some useful leads, one of them concerning a man called Harald Fein. How do you happen to know his name?'

'Well,' said Penatsch, 'I've seen the gentleman you mention several times lately, near the apartment. I usually see him sitting in his car when I'm doing my evening rounds, checking for unlocked doors, open windows and so on. You can't be too careful these days, with all the robberies you read about . . .'

'The Superintendent,' Feldmann cut in, 'is mainly interested in knowing how you discovered the identity of the said person.'

'He caught my eye. I had a feeling I recognized him from somewhere. And then I remembered. I'd seen a photograph of him in the *MZ*, at the opening of a new bridge over the Isar. I fished out the old copy and there he was, standing right next to the Mayor. The caption said: Harald Fein, architect.'

Braun stared thoughtfully, first at Penatsch and then at Feldmann. 'I see,' he drawled. 'First you see a man, presumably in semi-darkness. Then you recall seeing a photograph which reminds you of him. Finally, you think you identify him as a man named Harald Fein. A little far-fetched, isn't it?'

'I wouldn't venture an opinion on that,' Penatsch said with quiet dignity.

At a glance from Braun, Feldmann intervened again. 'Perhaps I should mention that, on his own submission, Herr Penatsch got a good look at Herr Fein on at least two occasions, once directly under a street lamp and another time on a well-lit landing inside the building itself. There's another point. Herr Fein has a sort of distinguishing feature – isn't that right, Herr Penatsch?'

'You can say that again,' Penatsch confirmed. Dull red blotches started to gather on his bloodless face, near the cheek-bones. 'There was this animal – this dog of his. A mongrel, always making a nuisance of itself. It even tried to foul the front steps, but I chased it off.'

Braun grimaced. 'Dogs don't make good evidence.'

'This one would,' Penatsch assured him. 'I'd recognize it anywhere. I didn't only see it in V-Strasse, either – it figured in that picture of the opening ceremony. It was squatting there between Fein and the Mayor, the filthy beast, just as if it was the guest of honour. I'd be bound to notice a thing like that, wouldn't I?'

Braun heaved a sigh. 'We'd better get it all down in writing. Any objections, Herr Penatsch? Good. You handle it, Feldmann – you know the points I'm interested in.'

From Detective-Superintendent Keller's notes:
Instinct is an absolute must in CID work. The other essentials

83

are an active imagination and a suspicious mind, quite apart from professional know-how, practical experience and a talent for deduction.

But there's another cardinal virtue that forms part of the detective's basic equipment, or ought to, and that's the comparatively rare ability to bide one's time.

Like other people, a detective often comes under varying degrees of pressure – pressure from above, outside pressure, pressure from below. He has to produce 'results'. In the old days his activities were noted in a so-called day-book. Now they're carefully entered in daily and weekly reports, checked and evaluated by superior officers, and assigned a performance rating. Added to that, the general public expect convincing progress reports, especially from the homicide and vice squads. All these things combine to make up the detective's daily round, which is anything but an unbroken series of real-life adventures – not that everyone accepts the fact. Quite a few policemen seem to take their cue from gangster films and paperbacks. I'm not necessarily saying that Braun was one of them. The source of his mistakes lay a good deal deeper, I suspect. It was clear that he lacked the last and probably supreme virtue proper to a good policeman: a dogged determination to be utterly objective, at least on duty. He has to try, even if he never quite succeeds.

Braun was passionately committed to his own personal views. He chipped away at the world like a sculptor with a private vision of how it should look. Braun's concept of law and order – one of his pet phrases – wasn't wholly innocuous. Not for a man in Fein's position.

Heinz Fein perched on his sister's bed, unsmiling.

'Much as I love you, Helga, you're as dumb as they come.'

'What does that make you?' she retorted.

'Anything you like,' he said, lying back with his hands clasped behind his head. 'With one exception – I'm not a raving romantic.'

'You mean you're soulless. You don't have any genuine feelings.'

'I'm a realist. I see things the way they are, especially in this house. You ought to take off your blinkers sometime.'

'You're incapable of love,' Helga told him gravely.

'Not at all. I can think of at least two people I love. You're one and I'm the other.'

84

'You're crazy,' she said, staring at him. 'Speaking for myself, I love Daddy.'

'Big deal. Anyway, I came to tell you something. I'm not going to have you mixing with a crowd of junkies just because you need to work off your misplaced love of humanity.'

'What if I tell you to mind your own business?'

'Please yourself – I always do. But if I catch you hanging around one of those drug-infested Schwabing dives just one more time, I'll make you regret it.'

Text of a carefully prepared official statement issued by Dr Hermann Abendroth, head of the Urban Planning Department:

Our development plans are not secret in themselves. We do, however, ensure that only a few trustworthy individuals have access to details of any preparatory measures which may cause substantial changes in the structure of the city, one of our principal motives being to preclude speculation based on unintentional leaks.

This was precisely the procedure adopted in the case of our plans for the Olympic approach roads. I must therefore reject, firmly and unequivocally, any suggestion that outsiders – building contractors, brokers or real estate agents – could have been prematurely apprised of the contents of these documents and so enabled to make speculative purchases in advance of publication.

JOURNALIST'S QUESTION: You wouldn't admit the possibility of an exception?

ABENDROTH: Certainly not.

THE SAME JOURNALIST: If my information is correct, you are – or, at least, were – on friendly terms with Herr Harald Fein, managing director of a firm which appears to have anticipated the official publication of your plans by buying up land which was then comparatively cheap but has since skyrocketed in value. If so, was this a coincidence?

ABENDROTH: Construction companies frequently make speculative land purchases. My department – in other words, City Hall – has never been involved in any such transaction.

'Joachim, my boy,' Plattner said portentously, 'this could be your

85

big moment.' He sat back in the black leather sofa which adorned one wall of his office. 'I sent for you because I want to iron out a few matters – important matters.'

Joachim Jonas gave a slight bow. He was thirty-four years old, athletically-built, firm-jawed and cold-eyed. 'You can count on me, Herr Plattner. All the way.'

'So I gather from my daughter. It only confirms my previous estimate of you.'

'Glad to hear that, Herr Plattner.'

'Of course, you've still to demonstrate the full extent of your loyalty.'

'Tell me what to do and I'll do it.'

'There speaks an enlightened spirit – and that's what you'll have to be if you're going to marry into my family and play a bigger role in the company's affairs. And that, in turn, presupposes an iron determination on your part, as your predecessor's successor, to neutralize him. In every way.'

'I'm ready,' Jonas assured him. It sounded like an oath of allegiance.

Statements made by Joachim Jonas, some considerable time later:
It's quite absurd to suggest that I was ever a friend of Harald Fein. We were far too dissimilar to become friends. For one thing, he's more than ten years older. For another, I've always been a practical man whereas he fancied himself artistic – and showed it.

It's equally absurd to say that he picked me for the job, gave me my chance at Plattner's and introduced me into his family circle. The truth was, he badly needed someone to relieve him of the administrative and managerial work he detested so much.

Thanks largely to his subsequent flirtation with the bottle, more and more of his duties in the Plattner Construction Company devolved on me.

Memorandum from the chairman of Plattner Construction, Paul Plattner, to his then managing director, Harald Fein:
. . . painful duty to inform you that we have no option but to relieve you of your responsibilities immediately, in other words, that we are obliged to terminate your contract of employment at short notice . . .

Memorandum from the chairman of Plattner Construction to senior executives of his firm, headed 'Restricted Circulation Only, Highly Confidential':

... inform you, with regret, that we have been obliged to relieve Herr Harald Fein of his duties as managing director, and, in consequence, that he ceases to wield any further authority within this organization. His place will be taken by Herr Joachim Jonas.

'I'll do all I can,' Jonas assured Plattner. 'There's only one point that worries me. What about Abendroth of the Urban Planning Department? Did your son-in-law really manage to peek at his plans in advance?'

'He did,' Plattner said casually. 'Purely by chance, though. He passed on the details without thinking twice. Not unnaturally, I bought up as much of the development zone as I could get my hands on. Abendroth's plans are always okayed because the Mayor thinks he's a genius – I knew that perfectly well, so I gambled. Why, does it offend your sensibilities?'

'Not in the slightest, Herr Plattner. All the same, what if Fein starts grasping at straws – what if he starts making wild accusations?'

'And injure his friend Abendroth? Never!'

'There shouldn't be any problem, then.'

'It's a push-over, my boy. I wrote Fein off a long time ago, but I couldn't fire him any earlier without running risks. From where I stand – speaking frankly and in strictest confidence – the man's a dead duck.'

Chapter Four

Detective-Superintendent Braun eyed Harald coldly.

'Herr Fein,' he said, 'I'm giving you a chance to amplify your earlier deposition.'

'May I draw your attention to one small point, Superintendent? I've made no deposition, merely answered a few questions.'

'And we've noted your replies in shorthand, just for the record. Standard police procedure, Herr Fein, or don't you believe me?'

'I'm in no position to judge. How should I know what's standard police procedure and what isn't?'

'Perhaps you'll have the opportunity to find out,' growled the superintendent.

Braun was sitting in his wooden arm-chair with Feldmann standing motionless behind him. Hunched over his desk in the corner beside the window, unheeded as usual, was Keller. His face wore a routine smile.

'What do you want this time?' Harald demanded.

'Everybody makes mistakes, Herr Fein. The human memory can play strange tricks on people. Nobody minds as long as they recognize their mistakes and acknowledge them.'

'Do you ever acknowledge yours?'

Braun restrained himself with some difficulty and attempted a smile. 'That, Herr Fein, is what I was going to ask you.'

'What am I supposed to admit?'

'A minor detail only. Up to now, you've claimed that you never left your car while it was parked in V-Strasse on the evening of 15 September. We have a witness who claims you did.'

'Then he's wrong.'

'He's ready to swear to it.'

'And you believe him?'

'Look,' Braun said, almost amiably now, 'that's the way it goes in our job. One person says one thing and another says something different. Which story are we to believe?'

'The one that sounds more plausible.'

'That's not strictly true,' said Braun, 'not from our angle – my angle. To us, evidence is what matters.'

Braun seemed to be feeling pretty sure of himself.

I sat in my corner, listening. Fein's manner was surprisingly cheerful. He seemed to be amused by the whole situation, except that he couldn't bring himself to laugh at it. Perhaps he was past laughing. Again, perhaps he expected to have the last laugh.

I could afford to dwell on the subject in peace. It was an uneventful day. I'd managed to wrap up two PECD reports in quick succession:

1. The body of a woman aged about forty. Death caused by an overdose of sleeping tablets, probably two days earlier. Time of death hard to establish with accuracy because of external conditions: body-temperature boosted by closed windows and hot sunny weather. Released for burial.

2. A four-year-old child with a fractured skull. Alleged to have climbed on to the kitchen table and fallen against the stove. Head-wound yielded minute splinters of glass, probably from a beer-bottle wielded by one of Mummy's boy-friends. Passed to Homicide.

In short, nothing of note to report except the interview between Fein and Braun. I didn't feel particularly sorry for Fein, not at that stage. My impression was, he could defend himself perfectly well – if he chose to.

'In that case, Herr Fein, you leave me no alternative. If you insist on a confrontation I shall have to arrange one.'

'How can I insist on something I know nothing about? Anyway, who do you propose to confront me with?'

'Someone who not only spotted you outside 33 V-Strasse, several times, but saw you inside the building itself.'

Harald shrugged. 'Very well, you'd better organize a line-up. One suspect in the middle of half a dozen guaranteed innocents, isn't that the drill?'

'Only on TV. We sometimes hold line-ups but not as a general rule. Certainly not in a case like this, when a witness knows someone's name and has a precise recollection of his appearance.'

'Isn't that begging the question?' Harald shrugged again. 'All right, do as you think fit – fit and proper, preferably.'

Braun nodded to Feldmann, who retired into the next office and left the door open. He reappeared almost at once, followed by

Penatsch. The janitor bowed politely in Braun's direction, then stood beside Feldmann in the doorway and subjected Harald to a wordless stare lasting several seconds. At length he said:

'I know this gentleman by sight. I also know his name. I could swear it was him I saw on the top landing at No. 33 V-Strasse . . .'

Harald shook his head firmly. 'And I could swear I've never seen this man before in my life.'

'That means nothing,' Braun said. 'Seeing and being seen are two different things.'

'Admittedly, but what does he think he saw?'

Braun snapped his fingers at Feldmann. 'The Penatsch file, Inspector.'

Extracts from Penatsch's first deposition:

' . . . sure I saw Herr Harald Fein at least three times in the three or four weeks preceding the crime, not only in the immediate vicinity of No. 33 V-Strasse, where I am employed as resident janitor, but actually on the premises.

The first time I saw him, he was sitting in his car smoking and listening to the radio. He seemed to be watching the entrance and the front of the building, especially the upper storeys. I couldn't fail to notice him, also the dog on the back seat.

The second time – roughly ten days before the murder, though it may have been two weeks – I caught sight of Herr Fein emerging from No. 33 in a hurry, or so it seemed to me. Once he reached the street he stopped and looked round in what I can only describe as a furtive way. Then he got back in his car, where the dog was waiting for him.

The third time – the night of the murder – I was coming up from the basement, where I'd been fixing a fuse, when I saw Herr Fein enter the building. That would have been about 10 p.m. There was something about his manner which made me suspicious – wary, he looked.

Feeling worried, I went upstairs after him and found him standing outside the murdered woman's door. He pounded on it with his fist, several times, and called her first name in a loud, threatening voice.'

'That,' said Harald, 'is complete and utter nonsense.'

'I'm afraid not, sir,' Penatsch insisted solemnly. 'It's a fact, and one I'm ready to swear to if necessary.'

90

Harald turned to Braun. 'It's either a downright lie or an acute case of hallucination. You really believe his story? No, you couldn't be that gullible.'

'I merely process and evaluate information, Herr Fein. In this instance I shall be compelled to investigate your movements even more closely than I have so far.'

'Does that mean you suspect . . .'

'It means, I'm afraid, that you can't be eliminated from our inquiries. Are you now prepared to submit to official interrogation?'

Late the same night, the first edition of the Morgenzeitung *informed its readers:*

Breakthrough in V-Strasse murder hunt. Sensational disclosures imminent. Jet-set killer? Well-informed sources last night revealed that . . .

München am Mittag, *following on the MZ's heels with its usual celerity, reported:*

V-Strasse murder keeps CID guessing. Scores of suspects interrogated. Possibility of deliberate leak not ruled out. *MAM* calls for fair play, confident that our police force . . .

We learn from well-informed sources that . . .

Detective-Superintendent Braun tossed the latest editions aside and turned to Feldmann.

'What's up? Why all the fuss? Don't tell me it's standard press reaction – ask yourself what lies behind it. Either they're clairvoyant or somebody has shot his mouth off ahead of time.'

The Mayor, alluding to the same subject in conversation with the Commissioner of Police, whom he had met, quite by chance, at a local party get-together:

Want some advice? Wrap it up quick. Better an open scandal than an official smokescreen. Sneaking suspicions are political poison, take it from me.

'I can guess what you're after.' Paul Plattner studied his visitor through eyes narrowed like those of a watchful cat. Palitschek had requested an appointment and was ushered in immediately. 'No need for any time-wasting preliminaries.'

'All the better,' said Palitschek, sinking into one of the silk-upholstered arm-chairs that graced the chairman's office. 'Okay, how much? I'll keep quiet and so will my fiancée – you have my personal guarantee. What's it worth to you?'

'Nothing.'

'Come again?' Palitschek stiffened. 'I could make your son-in-law's name a household word – a dirty one. You wouldn't want that, would you?'

'My dear Palitschek,' Plattner said, smiling, 'you obviously don't know who you're up against.'

'No? You tell me.'

'You're dealing with a straightforward man who refuses to dodge the facts of life.'

Palitschek's jaw dropped. 'Say that again.'

'The long and the short of it is, you're demanding money as the price of silence. I find that distasteful.'

'I still don't get it. You must take me for a fool.'

'Simmer down and listen to me instead – listen carefully. It's against my moral principles to hush things up. I'm a lover of truth, Palitschek. Does a man of your calibre really find that so hard to understand?'

'What?' Palitschek stared incredulously at his intended victim. 'You mean you actually want me to frame this Harald Fein?'

'I wish you'd be more discriminating in your choice of words. My view, quite simply, is this: the truth deserves an airing, and anyone who helps ventilate it deserves his just reward.'

'Done!' said Palitschek, who had finally grasped what was expected of him. 'How much? Fifty per cent in advance, though. Cash.'

'How would two thousand marks appeal?'

'Three thousand.'

'Very well. Fifteen hundred now and the balance as soon as you've both made convincing statements to the police – in the service of the truth, mind you. Is it a deal?'

It was.

Conversation between Hilde Fein and her friend Melanie Weber in the Carlton-Teeraum *on Briennerstrasse:*

HILDE: My God, Melanie, things are going from bad to worse.

MELANIE: I did warn you, darling, *innumerable* times.

HILDE: Oh for the old days, when it was just the two of us . . .
MELANIE: What are you driving at?
HILDE: Can't you guess, darling?

'I'm worried.' Detective-Inspector Feldmann wagged his pear-shaped head.

Braun smiled at his subordinate. 'You've got reservations. So have I. I always have, especially when I smell dirt. To me, putting degenerates behind bars is the most satisfying aspect of this job. I don't publicize my opinions, though. They might be misunderstood.'

'That's not quite what I meant. It's Penatsch – I don't feel happy about his evidence.'

'A witness is a witness. In law, that covers anybody from an imbecile to a child. We've got to make the best of what we've got.'

'Pardon me, Super, but I'm certain you think Fein's innocent. In that case, why put the screws on him? Who are you really gunning for?'

'Listen to the man!' Braun exclaimed in high good humour. 'You're beginning to understand my methods, Feldmann. That's a step in the right direction. You've realized Fein isn't my main target – he's more a springboard to bigger things. All you have to do now is find out who I'm planning to land on.'

Hilde and Melanie were drinking tea, innocent of milk or sugar but fortified with white Jamaica rum.

The tea-room, with its discreet décor – dark velvet drapes predominated – and air of solid comfort, had ties with Munich tradition. The niche in the furthest corner had once been favoured by a man named Hitler and his hangers-on.

The place was now given over to middle-class respectability. Most of the patrons at this time of day were female: the wives of company directors, bankers, industrialists, senior civil servants, business executives, major stockholders and municipal councillors.

MELANIE: Think how many heartaches you'd have saved yourself if you'd stuck with me!

HILDE: If only we could turn the clock back.

MELANIE: Make things the way they were – between us, you mean?

HILDE: I'd adore to, but there's the problem of Harald. Also, what about my father? I owe him a lot, you know.

MELANIE: I understand. Somebody has to dig you out of this mess, darling, and who better than me? Let's put our heads together. But first, how about another cup of tea?

'Here we go again,' Harald said briskly to Anton.

Anton trotted patiently along beside him. He negotiated escalators with masterly ease, leapt into lifts, crossed busy roads, and was a nonchalant traveller by air, land and sea. He also moved about the Marienplatz offices of the Plattner Construction Company as naturally as he romped in the garden of the Feins' villa.

'Know something, Anton?' said Harald. 'Even you aren't at liberty to lift a leg wherever you like. You've learnt to conform, which is more than I have.'

Harald strode through the outer office. Nobody acknowledged his arrival, but he grinned down at Anton just the same.

For once, Anton hung back and let Harald walk ahead. Harald traversed the office of the chairman's personal secretary, where Eva-Maria Wagnersberger was apparently so engrossed in her work that she failed to hear him say good morning. Still smiling, Harald walked into his own office and made for the desk.

It was already occupied by Joachim Jonas, his loyal colleague and family friend – his personal discovery.

Anton scuttled into the corner normally occupied by his sheepskin rug to discover that it had gone. He gazed reproachfully at his friend and master, but Harald had eyes only for Jonas.

'Feeling at home, Joachim?' he inquired.

'Why not?' Jonas spread his hands. 'It's a comfortable office. Comfort has always been your strong suit, Harald. I only have to sit here to feel it seeping through the seat of my pants.'

'Glad you're so cosy,' said Harald. 'However, that chair you're sitting in happens to be mine.'

'It was yours,' Jonas retorted, stressing the past tense. 'So was this office. Now it's mine. Like some written confirmation?'

Harald stared at Jonas as if he were seeing him clearly for the first time in his life.

'Unless I'm mistaken,' he said at length, 'I'm the managing director of this firm.'

94

'Wrong again,' Jonas told him. 'You *were* the managing director. Now I am.'

'Really?' said Harald. 'Are you absolutely positive?'

Comments on the subject by Eva-Maria Wagnersberger, secretary to the chairman of Plattner Construction:

I don't suppose I'm giving anything away when I tell you there's never been more than one boss in our firm, and that's Herr Plattner.

Harald Fein married into Herr Plattner's family in the early 1950s. Herr Plattner took him into the firm, not without some resistance on Fein's part, and offered him a very favourable contract – at least, it looked that way at first glance. Fein's official title was Managing Director. Herr Plattner thought he was worth the status, if only because of his personal links with Dr Abendroth of the Urban Planning Department, who looked like a man who was going places.

But Herr Plattner remained the real managing director. Nothing ever escaped him and he never relaxed his grip for an instant. His most important orders were given verbally and in confidence.

Although Fein's contract seemed generous, Herr Plattner saw it purely as an indirect means of financing his daughter's material well-being. Besides, it contained a summary dismissal clause – only three months' notice or salary in lieu. Fein had no security at all, not that he realized it. On the other hand, perhaps he didn't care.

Jonas was offered an almost identical contract. I warned him against signing, but all he said was: 'My name isn't Harald Fein. Harald was naive enough to accept it as a final settlement. To me, this is just a modest start. It gives me an official position – something to build on. With your help.'

Munich was aglow once more. The sky above the Theresienwiese, site of the Oktoberfest, shone with dazzling radiance. People ate and drank in the beer tents, peppered targets in the shooting galleries, fought or made love among the guy-ropes. By the dozen – indeed, by the hundred.

A thousand scents drifted skywards: grease and rotting garbage, candy-floss, sweating bodies. There was an aroma of barbecued

95

chicken, beer, pickled herring, pork sausage, horse-dung and women, all compounded into a bewildering amalgam.

Like the final days of Carnival, the Oktoberfest period was peak season for criminals of every persuasion, also a time of full employment for policemen, casualty departments and the fire brigade.

Crimes of violence showed a steep upward trend, as did their degree of brutality. Extremes threatened to become the norm. Anyone who was in the way had by some means to be eliminated, in politics as in business.

The modern secret of success gained popularity with disconcerting speed: attack and destroy, tear down and trample. Send the weakest to the wall for a quick profit, even if there's a would-be successor breathing down your neck.

'I've got your dismissal notice here, Harald.' Joachim Jonas tapped a sheet of paper. 'It's my sad duty to hand it over.'

'What am I supposed to do, congratulate you?'

'No one could be sorrier than I am, Harald.'

'Sorry for what? My dismissal or the fact that you're obliged to notify me of it?'

'Believe me . . .'

'I'm past believing you, Joachim. Anyway, if it's any consolation to you, I welcome the news with open arms.' Harald took the pink slip and stuffed it in his trouser pocket. 'It's a tremendous relief. I feel genuinely liberated – really free at last.'

'Free from what – free to do what?'

'Lead a semi-normal life, slough off my obligations to a double-dealing outfit that makes profits the way a cow drops dung. As far as I'm concerned, it's full speed ahead to a new existence.'

Jonas looked puzzled. 'I don't follow. Is that a threat?'

From Detective-Superintendent Keller's notes. Preliminary investigations for his file marked 'Personal Use Only'. Particulars relating to Harald Fein, his childhood and adolescence:

Born 15 March 1925. First child. A sister followed almost ten years later but became a chronic invalid as a result of an accident sustained in infancy. He always did his best to provide for her until her early death from cancer.

His father: a tax inspector, stern disciplinarian. His mother:

96

working-class background, one of ten children, hard-working, unselfish, God-fearing, devoted to her son.

Fein, given names Harald Maximilian Heinz. Sensitive and imaginative, also extremely stubborn, even as a youngster. Obviously a handful. Reserved but self-assertive. At school: remarkably versatile, occasionally brilliant, often lazy and indifferent to a degree which exasperated those who tried to teach him.

His real forte was drawing. A budding Picasso, according to one of his teachers. According to another, 'tinged with the sort of genius that never matures beyond a certain stage'.

'We've both made plenty of mistakes,' Harald said. 'Nobody's denying it.'

'Plenty?' Hilde retorted. 'That's an understatement. What's more, you made them, not me.'

She had summoned him to a formal interview in the drawing-room, where she now sat in the arm-chair favoured by Paul Plattner on his sporadic visits. Above it hung a portrait of Bismarck *après* Lenbach, Plattner's wedding present to the happy couple. Harald couldn't look at it without a slight feeling of nausea, possibly because he was a painter manqué. The pose was too heroic to be true.

'Aren't you listening?' Hilde demanded. 'Never mind, I'm used to it. You've never spared a thought for anything or anyone but yourself.'

'That may have been true at one time,' Harald said. 'I know I've failed in many ways, but I've honestly tried to be a good father and earn the children's love and respect. I hoped you'd credit me with a little unselfishness, if only from that angle. Obviously, I was expecting too much.'

'You're the ungrateful one!' Hilde snapped. 'Ungrateful to Father, after all he's done for you. Ungrateful to me, who sacrificed myself year in, year out – long before you drank yourself into a pathetic, degenerate wreck.'

'I thought we'd agreed not to reopen the subject.'

'You force me to!'

Statement made subsequently to Counsellor Henri Messer, attorney-at-law, by Dr Friedrich Wengel:

Herr Fein became a patient of mine in 1956. Automatically, as it were, because of his connection with the Plattner family, whose private physician I was and still am. He contracted no illness of note for many years, though I did warn him, very early on, against the dangers of over-indulgence in alcohol.

His breakdown occurred in 1968 – March 21st, to be precise – – on the occasion of an otherwise extremely congenial party given by Frau Fein for family friends and members of her father's firm.

Herr Fein turned up late, and in a thoroughly inebriated condition. He held forth in an embarrassingly loud voice and insulted a number of my fellow-guests. Finally he collapsed in the middle of the drawing-room rug. I carried him into an adjoining room with the help of Herr Plattner and Herr Jonas.

He was eventually admitted to a private clinic run by a friend and colleague of mine, near the Starnbergersee. There he remained for two months, stubbornly insisting that his dog should be allowed to keep him company. At the end of that time he was pronounced cured and discharged.

To the best of my knowledge, he has avoided hard liquor ever since.

'Hilde,' Harald said, 'if we're ever to have a chance of starting afresh, now could be the time.'

'It's too late.'

'It's never too late, given a little goodwill on both sides.'

'Which you've never shown a sign of! Why delude yourself at this stage?'

'Because I don't believe twenty years of marriage can sink without a trace. So much has happened in that time, Hilde. It's bound to have created a bond between us.'

'It doesn't have to be a permanent one, not after the way you've treated me. I refuse to let you alienate my father. I won't tolerate any more of these constant humiliations. We're through, Harald. I simply can't take you any longer.'

'Is that what you wanted to tell me?'

'Yes, and it's my final word on the subject.'

Comments by the ex-headmistress of a girls' boarding-school near Lausanne, Switzerland, concerning Hilde Plattner, later Hilde Fein:

Yes, I remember Hilde well. She was with us for several years. Her father, a most distinguished and generous man who had lost his wife in a tragic accident, shortly after their marriage, escorted Hilde to the school in person. He looked after her during the holidays with a love and devotion which touched us all profoundly.

Hilde was a bright and adaptable child, but she had a certain tendency towards individualism. To quote a little incident which illustrates this perfectly, she once threw a stone at a fellow-pupil who had, in her opinion, provoked her. The girl sustained a severe head-wound, but Hilde refused to apologize. Nothing would persuade her that she was wrong.

'My God,' Hilde blurted out, 'how you made my skin crawl!'

Harald rose. For a moment he seemed to sway. Then, breathing heavily, he felt for the back of his chair and steadied himself.

Hilde walked quickly to the liquor cabinet. She produced a bottle of brandy and a tumbler, filled the glass and held it out.

He took it.

'It's over and done with,' she said in a harsh voice. 'I've already filed a petition for divorce, so kindly leave my house. Get out and stay out.'

He raised the glass and stared at it with dark, troubled eyes. Then he drained it.

Memorandum No. 204/70 from Detective Chief Superintendent Dürrenmaier to the Commissioner of Police:

. . . studied a progress report on the V-Strasse case submitted to me by Det.-Supt Braun. I was forced to conclude that several items of circumstantial evidence (summary appended) pointed in the direction of a man named Harald Fein. Det.-Supt Braun clearly considered this evidence sufficient to justify our application for a warrant for his arrest.

Careful examination of these particulars did, however, raise certain doubts. Our application for a warrant in the name of Harald Fein was, therefore, provisionally refused by the competent authority.

I advised Det.-Supt Braun to reinforce and extend his chain of evidence. I further stressed that premature release of information, however vague, must be avoided at all costs.

'This is an unexpected paternal pleasure.' Harald eyed his son curiously. 'What brings you here?'

'I wanted to see Anton,' Heinz said. 'Where is the Gorgeous Beast?'

'Lying in the empty bath. It's the one comparatively cool place in this overheated egg-box.'

Heinz disappeared into the bathroom to say hello to Anton, who gave a succession of joyful barks. Leisurely, Heinz smoothed Anton's unruly coat, stroked the hair out of his eyes and caressed the handsome moustache.

That done, he rejoined his father and flopped into an arm-chair.

'What did you really come for?' asked Harald. 'To revel in the sight of a broken man?'

Heinz grinned. 'You said it. I couldn't pass up a chance like this, could I?'

They were on the fifth floor of the Royal Hotel, a not uncomfortable four-star establishment where Plattner Construction usually entertained visiting senior executives from associate companies. Harald sat on the bed with a half-empty bottle of brandy beside him.

'Hitting the bottle again?' asked Heinz. 'You ought to lay off. It's a lousy example to the younger generation.'

Heinz rose and returned to the bathroom, taking the bottle with him. He held it to Anton's nose, and Anton sneezed and shook himself. Then he poured the contents down the pan and flushed vigorously.

Harald stared at his son with dawning interest. 'Don't tell me you're worried about me?'

'Worried?' Heinz laughed. 'A man can kill himself any way he likes as far as I'm concerned, provided it gives him a kick. This is a free country, so they say. However, you're making a spectacle of yourself and I plan to enjoy it for a while longer. Stick around, Father. It's the least you can do for your devoted son.'

From the diary of Sabine Faber, 17, high school student, currently on intimate terms with Heinz Fein:

He's in love with me, but he seems to hate me the way he loves and hates everything and everyone close to him. He refuses to let go and lose himself in someone else.

He's terribly unhappy – I can sense it. It's almost as if he expects me to release him from something, redeem him in some way. But how? My love doesn't seem to be enough on its own.

He clung to me the other day, like a baby. 'Why do they all lie?' he moaned. 'Why do they spend the whole time deceiving each other – and themselves?'

Only a few years earlier, Hilde Fein had told her husband that Plattner wanted Heinz educated with a view to taking over the firm. 'It doesn't matter how, as long as he qualifies in something – business management, law, architecture, engineering . . .'

'If it's all right with Heinz,' Harald said. 'Otherwise not.'

'What if he resists the idea? What will you do then?'

'Everything in my power to save him from a fate like mine.'

'You mean you'd thwart Father's wishes?'

'Why not? It's Heinz's future we're discussing, and he's my son.'

'He's my son too, and that makes him Father's grandson!'

Harald smiled wryly. 'I know, my boy. I'm hardly a model parent – not in your eyes.'

'To me you're the inevitable end-product of your environment – the complaisant husband of a self-centred woman, the reluctant business associate of a demanding father-in-law. And all for the sake of money – for firm and family in that order. In short, a typical representative of our profit-hungry age.'

'If that's the impression my life has made on you, I'm sorry, but I've left it all behind me.'

'I don't believe that, and neither will anybody who knows you. You've been feeding happily at the capitalist trough for nearly twenty years – you couldn't make a living any other way.'

'Is that what you think?' Wearily, Harald drew the back of his hand across his cracked lips. 'All I can think of is that bottle of brandy on its way to the sewer. Get me another.'

'Like hell I will! Stick to mineral water – it's better for you.'

'You mean you're really concerned about me?'

'I only came because I was sent by the family.'

'Do they want to know how I am?'

'My God, Father, you haven't learnt much in twenty years. Do you really think anybody gives two hoots for you – not counting dear, silly little Helga? You've been amortized, written off as a bad debt. You don't figure in the family balance sheet any more.'

'Is that why you came, to tell me that? You despise me, I suppose.'

'It's worse than that, Father. I'm beginning to feel sorry for you.'

'Don't bother.'

'But that isn't why I came either. There's another reason. I'm here as a sort of courier. Just after you left the house this afternoon, Grandfather turned up. He was very worried – not about you, of course. All that was eating him was a missing key. The spare key to his safe.'

'I completely forgot about it.'

'Well, I was deputed to extract it from you. Mother wouldn't and Helga couldn't – she's been in a state of collapse ever since you moved out. That left me.'

'Here,' Harald said quickly. He produced a key from his pocket and tossed it on the table. 'The spare key to your grandfather's office safe. Tell him I renounce all access to his dirty secrets. From now on he can soil his hands in splendid isolation.'

'So you not only cheat people but keep fat files on the subject. That's what I call method.'

There was no reply. Harald continued to sit on the bed, yearning for sleep and not caring if he never woke up.

'Know what you remind me of?' Heinz said quietly. 'A blind man blundering across a busy intersection.'

'You can get run over any time, even with your eyes open, if someone chooses to violate the highway code. Thousands of innocent people get mown down every day.'

'Innocent maybe, but it doesn't make them any less dead.'

Page 1 of the Morgenzeitung *announced, in banner headlines:*
Suspicion mounts. V-Strasse arrest imminent. Socialite killer? (For editorial comment, see 'Truth will out' on p. 3.)

. . . the police seem finally determined to proceed without fear or favour, a natural assumption which does not, unfortunately, hold good in every case . . . pressure from certain influential parties whose contacts apparently extend to the higher reaches of City Hall itself . . .

Whereupon, a few hours later, München am Mittag *blazoned the following across its front page, likewise in banner headlines:*
Irresponsible witch-hunt. Innocent man's reputation in

jeopardy. Suspicion used as instrument of political pressure? (For editorial comment, see 'Fair play and the police'.)

MAM's call to arms had been preceded by a telephone conversation between Detective Chief Superintendent Dürrenmaier and Karlheinz Kahler, the paper's regional editor.

KAHLER: It's obvious that vital information has been withheld from my paper. Considering how well we've worked together in the past, I think it's highly unfortunate.

DÜRRENMAIER: My dear Herr Kahler, we've made no official statement whatsoever. It can only have been a regrettable indiscretion, a slip of the tongue, and you can hardly blame a rival paper for taking advantage . . .

KAHLER: I know all that, Chief Superintendent. I know something else too. We've since discovered who the *Morgenzeitung* was referring to when it talked about an imminent arrest. The name is Harald Fein. Any comment?

DÜRRENMAIER: There's no question of any prime suspect, Kahler, still less of the murderer having been definitely identified. Herr Fein happens to be one of the many people we've questioned in the course of our investigation, but that means nothing – so far. You can take that as an official statement. Print it if you like.

KAHLER: Thanks for nothing. If there's any change in the situation, I hope you'll give me a call.

Detective Chief Superintendent Dürrenmaier to Detective-Superintendent Braun:

DÜRRENMAIER: Somebody shot his mouth off, Braun. The press obviously know Fein is one of your chief suspects.

BRAUN: Which he is, sir, but they didn't get it from me. I know the ropes. I never sound off till I can play the whole tune. It won't be long now.

Teletype message from Interpol, via Federal Crime Bureau, Foreign Department, to Police Headquarters, Munich. Addressed to Capital Crimes Division and passed for immediate attention to Detective-Inspector Feldmann. Originator: Ministry of the Interior, Madrid. Text:

Reference Kordes, Karl Johannes. Second passport found in name of Karges, Erich Ernst, but personal description tallies.

Hair black, eyes dark brown, face oval, own teeth, scar on tip of right index finger, height 172 cm., weight 73.5 kg. Date and place of birth identical on both passports: 20 April 1933, Unna, Westphalia.

Photographs and fingerprints follow.

Kordes/Karges claims not to have been in Munich on 15 September last but declines to give further details.

Madrid authorities unlikely to grant any request for extradition pending charges against Kordes/Karges under Spanish law.

Feldmann laid the teletype message on Keller's desk.

'The pimp,' he said.

Keller glanced through it and nodded before returning to his book on animal – notably canine – behaviour. The chapter which seemed to interest him most of all was entitled: 'Unpredictability in Mongrels'.

Feldmann initialled the message and, in Braun's absence, inserted it in a folder.

In response to journalists' inquiries, the following Xeroxed statement was issued by the office of Joachim Jonas, managing director of the Plattner Construction Company:

Herr Plattner, who is currently abroad, profoundly deplores the tone of certain irresponsible rumours and conjectures that have recently been voiced in the press, and would regret it still more if he were compelled to take legal proceedings in this connection.

The following confidential information may serve to clarify matters:

1. Herr Harald Fein is no longer employed by the Plattner Construction Company.

2. Any personal ties that used to exist between Herr Plattner and Herr Fein have now been severed. Frau Hilde Fein, née Plattner, has already filed a petition for divorce on purely personal grounds which have no bearing on the present issue.

'May I join you?' asked the small grey-suited man. His face was hawklike but cheerful, his voice amiable.

Harald shrugged. 'This is a public place. On the other hand, I can still see a few empty tables.'

'But I'd appreciate a word with you. Subject to your consent, of course.'

Harald was sitting in a restaurant in the centre of the city, near the Marienplatz and not far from the Royal Hotel. He couldn't stand his hotel room any longer. The telephone buzzed incessantly but he hadn't answered. Instead, he'd taken refuge in the far corner of Schneider's, a solid middle-class establishment which served beer as well as wine. Now his seclusion had been shattered by this smiling stranger.

'I know you,' Harald said suddenly. He surveyed the grey-clad figure with growing attention. 'I'm sure I've seen you somewhere before, but where?'

'I'm inconspicuous,' said the little man. 'A fact I've come to appreciate. Overlooked and underrated, that's me. If you're interested, Herr Fein, my name's Keller.'

'You know me?'

'I wouldn't put it as strongly as that. I know you by sight.'

'Got it!' said Harald. 'You were sitting in Superintendent Braun's office, in the corner near the window.'

'Correct.' Keller's smile verged on gratitude. 'So you noticed me after all. May I ask why?'

'Because you seemed to be the only one there who wasn't interested in me – who wasn't trying to pin something on me.'

Keller shook his head. 'A false assumption, Herr Fein.'

'You mean you do want to pin something on me?'

'You're wrong only in assuming a lack of interest on my part.'

Harald gestured impatiently. 'Why don't you sit down?'

Keller did so. He ordered some beef marrow on toast and a quarter of Franconian wine. At length he said:

'Perhaps I should tell you something, Herr Fein. My connection with your so-called case is nil.'

'So why are you here?'

'For that very reason. My presence here is purely fortuitous. I make a habit of strolling through the city centre after duty hours, killing time, window-shopping, observing people. I happened to see you emerge from the Royal Hotel with your dog, so I followed you.'

'What's your angle?'

'No special angle. Let's say I'm interested in your dog. A magnificent specimen.'

'You think so?' Harald's manner warmed perceptibly.

'Like something out of a fairy-tale – a mythical beast.'

'That's more or less what my son says.'

Anton, recumbent beneath the table, crawled out and sniffed Keller's feet and hands, in that order. To judge by the purr-cum-growl that issued from his throat, he was satisfied with the result of his inspection.

'Anton likes you,' Harald said. He sounded surprised.

'It's mutual,' Keller assured him earnestly.

Anton resumed his place under the table and stretched out comfortably with his hindquarters on Keller's shoes and his muzzle on Harald's. It was clear he felt thoroughly at ease.

'Anton's very particular,' Harald explained. 'There aren't many people he takes to on sight, but you appear to be one of them. I'm glad.'

'Anything else I can do, apart from endear myself to your dog?'

'As a policeman?'

'You didn't say that with rancour, Herr Fein – you sounded more amused than anything else. I listened to you very carefully, down at Headquarters. You seem to greet everything that happens to you with the same sense of comedy.'

'Little do you know, Herr Keller.'

'Little indeed, Herr Fein.' Keller glanced at Harald's king-sized snort of brandy. 'Who can really tell what goes on inside another human being, let alone himself? I've seldom met anyone who has even the vaguest idea what he's capable of.'

From Detective-Superintendent Keller's notes. Further research into Harald Fein, his youth, student days and choice of profession:

Everyone who came into contact with him found him extremely volatile. Flashes of brilliance were followed by total failure, hours of exuberance interspersed with spells of deep depression.

A few unimportant love-affairs. Very few friends – in fact Hermann Abendroth was probably his only real confidant. Their youthful ideas and dreams were similar, no doubt, but they differed in one essential respect. Abendroth brimmed with vigour and determination, whereas Fein was given to sporadic bursts of fierce creative activity.

They were inseparable for many years. Then, something must have happened to estrange them. Neither man volunteered an explanation when questioned on the subject.

They both sailed through their qualifying examinations in

architecture and civil engineering between 1947 and 1949. Even at
that stage, Abendroth's ambition – to quote a letter of his – was
'urban planning – coming to grips with the future'.

Compare Harald Fein: 'I want to build houses like dreams come
true, transform concrete into poetry, help to create an environment
that can bring happiness to this technological age!'

And then he married Hilde Plattner.

'I admit I know almost nothing about you, Herr Fein,' Keller said.
'Apart from a couple of minor details.'

'Which are?'

'Well, first there's Anton. He's a point in your favour. Dogs are
virtually unbribable except with love and affection. What's more,
they don't lend themselves to business, funny or otherwise. They
can't count and they aren't calculating. If they were, you probably
wouldn't be in the mess you're in now.'

'Perhaps not,' Harald conceded a little reluctantly. 'Anything
else?'

'Just this. Generally speaking, your resistance is low. You don't
have the will to defend yourself.'

'Against the CID, you mean?'

'Against anyone or anything. Either you don't recognize
danger when you see it or you don't want to, whatever the source –
police, members of your family, even the bottle.'

Harald nodded. 'I suppose you're right. I'm amused by your
colleagues' ludicrous attempts to make a murderer of me. The
reactions of my family remind me of a French farce. As for hard
liquor, my system is still rebelling against the stuff. I expect I'll
get used to it again before long.'

Keller picked up Harald's glass and tipped the contents on
the floor, taking care not to splash Anton. Then he turned to
Harald.

'I'm telling you, man – defend yourself.'

Harald laughed aloud. 'Against whom? I'm planning to live my
own life at last, be myself and no one else.'

'Listen,' Keller said drily, 'I'm here as a dog-lover. Don't
expect me to play the philanthropist as well.'

'No, you listen, Herr Keller, and you can pass this on to your
department. I plan to move out of the Royal as soon as possible
and rent a place for me and my dog. Then I'm going to design

houses, the way I always wanted to. There are people who've been clamouring for my services for years.'

'Always pipe-dreaming, aren't you?' Keller spoke with deliberate asperity. 'Some day, someone's going to come along who understands and appreciates me, someone I can trust wholeheartedly – is that what you're hoping? Believe me, you're tempting Providence.'

'Rash I may be, Herr Keller, but it's a nice thought.'

'In this world? It's not only unrealistic – it's suicidal. I'm not telling you to conform, I'm merely advising you to be careful. Take out some insurance. Get yourself a good lawyer, and fast.'

Harald smiled. 'You obviously have no faith in the automatic triumph of justice.'

'Justice can triumph even in this day and age, but it needs help. You've no option, Herr Fein. Either defend yourself or they'll destroy you. I'd regret that, if only for Anton's sake.'

Chapter Five

'I had quite a job running you to earth.' Joachim Jonas stared round Harald's apartment like a prospective buyer. 'You picked yourself a pretty classy place, I see.'

'Fair to middling,' Harald said casually. 'It does have a balcony, though, and that means a lot to Anton. Anyway, the Royal has a note of my new address. It can't have been that hard to find me. Did you think I was hiding from someone – you, for instance?'

'Of course not.' Jonas kneaded his hands together. 'Look, Harald, you know what things are like in the firm. I hope you don't bear me a grudge for handing you that pink slip.'

'Oh no, you were acting under duress.' Harald laughed and leant back in the arm-chair from which he hadn't bothered to rise when his visitor walked in. 'It hurt you to do it, I'm sure.'

'You misjudge me, Harald.'

'Not any longer, but that doesn't mean I've got you completely figured, even now.'

Jonas, who had paused in the middle of the room, smiled ingratiatingly. 'I'm fully aware of my debt to you, Harald. You brought me into the firm and took me under your wing. In return, I willingly took a big load off your shoulders – all the staff problems, all the labour disputes on the building sites, all the red tape and paperwork. There's an obligation on your side too, wouldn't you agree?'

'Why the flattery, Joachim? Trying to soften me up?'

'No, simply trying to stop you from making matters worse.'

'Why didn't you say so right away? Don't be shy, said the spider to the fly – lie back and enjoy it. I like your nerve!'

Memorandum 'For Official Use Only' from Detective-Inspector Feldmann to Detective-Superintendent Braun:

No more incriminating evidence against Fein. Other leads are being followed up. Additional lab reports appended. Request for Kordes's extradition transmitted via Interpol.

Fein under constant surveillance, as instructed. Detective-Constables Gutmann, Jahrisch and Ramsch operating in eight-hour shifts. Summary of reports to date:

Fein has left the Royal Hotel and rented an apartment in Torremolinos Towers. Two rooms, third floor left. Monthly rent: DM500.

Only two visitors so far: his son Heinz, twenty minutes, and Joachim Jonas of Plattner's, twenty-five minutes. Fein is working on some plans for private houses.

Consignment of drawing materials delivered by Kaut-Bullinger & Co. Food sent up by the Torremolinos Grill, in the same block: open sandwiches, roast chicken, steak (presumably for his dog), mineral water, brandy, wine (mainly Franconian). No incoming or outgoing telephone calls noted by the building's switchboard.

Fein regularly leaves the block at nightfall to walk his dog. Extended strolls, taking in Karlsplatz, Odeonsplatz and Marienplatz. He usually stops off at Schneider's or the Hofbräuhaus, both of which admit dogs. The new Hofbräuhaus manager not only admits them but puts on a special menu for their benefit.

Fein's financial resources relatively limited. Current account in credit at just over DM8000. A further DM3000 – his final salary cheque – should be payable by Plattner Construction in due course. His Mercedes is already up for sale. It ought to bring DM4–5000.

At the present time, Fein has no legal representative.

'Harald,' said Jonas, 'if a man makes a mistake he ought to put it right, agreed? Especially if the whole thing can be settled quietly – and we're quite prepared to stretch a point.'

'I'm mystified. What are you so generously prepared to settle quietly?'

'Don't play dumb,' Jonas said. 'You know perfectly well what I'm driving at.'

'Go on, amaze me.'

'I'm talking about that red folder in the chairman's safe.'

'What about it?'

'It's missing.'

'Really?' Harald's initial surprise swiftly yielded to a surge of hilarity.

Harald Fein, some time later, in conversation with his lawyer, Henri Messer:

It amounted to about forty sheets of paper clipped inside a red plastic folder.

The documents consisted of land procurement schemes, draft contracts, surveyors' reports, receipts for ex gratia payments – alias bribes – and planning estimates. Among them, details relating to a property known as the Sunset Estate.

Value of the sites listed, surveyed, pre-planned in every detail and then purchased: a shade over one hundred and fifty million marks.

'Yes, missing!' Jonas said crisply. 'Missing from a safe to which you had access. You not only knew the combination – you had the spare key as well.'

'A key which is now in your possession, no doubt. Plattner holds the other and always has.'

'Surely Plattner's above suspicion!'

'I don't see why. He may well have hidden the folder in order to incriminate me and make trouble for you. You're next in line for the axe, Joachim. I wouldn't put anything past my father-in-law.'

'Harald,' Jonas entreated, 'be reasonable. I strongly advise you to hand it over.'

'I wouldn't give it back to Plattner even if I had it.'

'He'll destroy you, Harald. Don't underestimate him. Haven't you suffered enough as it is?'

'Not by a long shot. It only confirms how right I was. It proves what I refused to accept for years – that the wolves aren't extinct in this country. They're all around us, in the street, in offices, shops, restaurants, even in bed.'

'I warn you, Harald, you're going too far.'

'Which means, I suppose, that you're threatening me. On Plattner's behalf.'

'I only came here to save you from even bigger trouble. Of course Plattner sent me, but you'd be well advised to hand over the folder.'

'What makes you think I've got it?' Harald settled himself more comfortably in his chair, relishing the situation. 'Plattner may have it himself. Or, you may have taken it to put pressure on

Plattner, strengthen your own position and make me look even worse.'

'I'm beginning to understand what Plattner meant,' Jonas said. 'Take care, he said, the rules of civilized behaviour don't apply to that man. He's a law unto himself.'

Harald smiled. 'I never thought Plattner was a fool.'

'So you're planning to cash in!' Jonas snapped. 'Okay, how much? What do you want for the damned thing?'

'Nothing. I don't have it.'

'If Plattner gets those papers back he'll talk terms. What do you want?'

'At the moment, privacy. Shove off, Jonas, you're getting on my nerves.'

Detective Chief Superintendent Dürrenmaier shook his head with finality. 'No, Braun, you've done a good job, but in my opinion your case wouldn't stand up. There are too many holes in it.'

His subordinate frowned. 'Sir, does that mean we're supposed to give preferential treatment to particular individuals or groups of individuals? I'm not against the idea in principle, but I'd like to get things straight. If it's hands off, I need to know who you're alluding to.'

'I made no allusion of any kind,' Dürrenmaier retorted sharply. 'I'm not proposing to shield anyone. I'm not insinuating anything to anyone, least of all you. I'm simply pointing out a few facts and doing my best to see you take them into account. You ought to be grateful.'

From a courtroom address of considerably later date delivered by Henri Messer, attorney-at-law, during one of a series of hearings in which Harald Fein was either plaintiff or defendant:
. . . seems to have involved a blatant failure on the part of the CID . . . precipitate allegations . . . submission of dubious evidence . . . inescapable conclusion that an attempt was made to conceal errors of judgement . . . baseless charges heaped upon my client . . . a tidal wave of prejudice which compels one to assume that the police indirectly, and perhaps unwittingly, contributed to a potential miscarriage of justice . . .

'Sir,' said Braun, 'the fact remains that we can produce three witnesses who all agree that Fein systematically spied on the murdered woman.'

'Which proves virtually nothing. Your three witnesses merely state that Fein was sitting in his car near the scene of the crime at the time in question, not that he left the vehicle.'

'The janitor claims otherwise.'

'Who is this man – have you checked his story?'

Braun nodded. 'I have.'

Extracts from records made available by the Federal Crime Bureau, Wiesbaden:

Penatsch, Adolf Paul, aged 56, several convictions. 1953 complicity in theft; 1958 demanding money with menaces; 1959 receiving stolen goods (purchase and sale of pilfered television sets); 1960 larceny; 1963 conspiracy to burgle.

Thereafter, three years' imprisonment. Released 1966 with maximum remission for good conduct. Has shown some readiness to act as police informant. 1968 onwards, janitor at 33 V-Strasse, Munich.

Under observation by narcotics squad since 1970. Suspected middleman trading in cannabis. No definite evidence to date.

'And you honestly consider this man a fit candidate for the role of chief prosecution witness?' Dürrenmaier shook his head again.

'No one,' insisted Braun, 'is entitled to discount sworn evidence because a witness has been previously convicted, on whatever grounds.'

'I know, I know. The law says anyone can give valid evidence, even a murderer, but think what happens in practice. Any defence counsel worth his salt would blow your witness and his story sky-high. Then there's the press. If one of the papers got hold of his record it could be damned awkward.'

Braun sat there without moving. His face seemed to have turned to stone, but there was a glint in his eye. The glint became more pronounced as he saw Dürrenmaier smile.

'If you're thinking what I think you're thinking, Braun, forget it. We're both on the same side. That's just why I have to insure us against premature moves.'

'If you'd only give me a free hand, sir – if I could only detain Fein, at least temporarily, I guarantee you he'd . . .'

'No,' Dürrenmaier said firmly. 'In my view, there still aren't sufficient grounds for an arrest.'

'Am I to assume, sir, that you intend to assign another officer to this case?'

'Do you want me to?'

'No.'

'Then I won't. But take my advice and shore up your case. For instance, I don't see any record of your having questioned Penatsch in detail, preferably on the spot, about his alleged encounter with Fein inside 33 V-Strasse. How was Fein dressed? What were his exact movements? What did he say, if anything? And so on.'

'Inquiries of that kind have already been made.'

'Then be so good as to complete your records accordingly. Have you ruled out all your other suspects?'

'Of course not, sir. I never drop a lead till it peters out, but Fein's trail is by far the hottest.'

'Just by way of an exception, I'll assign you another three men. What about the pimp, Kordes?'

'Kordes is clean – he left Munich three days before the murder. They've remanded him for questioning in Madrid. Seems he's in trouble with the Spanish authorities.'

'He may not be the killer, Braun, but he could be a valuable informant. Have you applied for his extradition?'

'Yes, sir.'

From Detective-Superintendent Keller's notes:

Braun came out of Dürrenmaier's office swearing furiously. The monologue went on for five minutes, with Feldmann listening avidly.

Then, from one moment to the next, Braun buried himself in his work again, firing off orders, drawing up duty rosters, devising new-fangled surveillance methods. I remember feeling glad I wasn't in Harald Fein's shoes.

My services were in great demand that morning. Dürrenmaier called me in and asked me, without preamble, if I'd like to do another stint with the Murder Squad – for instance, take over the V-Strasse case.

I said no and asked him to speed up my retirement. I also

implied that I'd seen enough of crime and criminals to last me a lifetime. He seemed to take my point.

What I didn't tell the Chief Supt was this: the older I get, the sorrier I feel for victims of ill-treatment, human and animal. I find it impossible to react as a policeman any more, and that, I frankly admit, is a development which has its dangers.

'You must have made a mistake.' Hermann Abendroth toyed nervously with a ruler. 'Did you really say Herr Fein wanted a word with me?'

His secretary nodded. 'He's waiting in the outer office.'

Abendroth rose and peered around the door. Heinz Fein, his godson and the son of his erstwhile friend Harald, stared at him diffidently.

'Oh, it's you, Heinz!' Relief flooded into Abendroth's face. 'Good to see you again.'

'I don't suppose you can spare the time – you must be up to your ears . . .'

'Nonsense, my boy. Come in.'

The secretary cleared her throat with well-rehearsed zeal. 'You've a meeting with three city councillors in the map room in fifteen minutes' time. After that there's the Olympic Planning Committee, and you're due to report to the Mayor at midday.'

Abendroth put an arm around Heinz's shoulders and propelled him through the door. 'Keep the councillors at bay with your usual tact, Greta. I'm tied up until further notice.'

'What have I done to deserve this?' Heinz asked drily. 'Why didn't you give me the brush-off? It's what I was expecting – in fact I almost hoped you would. It might have been the best thing for both of us.'

'Sit down and stop needling me,' Abendroth said. 'I've acquired a hide like an elephant these past few years. You can hardly avoid that in a job like mine, but it doesn't prevent me from being genuinely pleased to see you. You're looking fit, Heinz.'

Heinz stared round the office. 'So you haven't deserted public service for the rat-race like my dear father, your former friend.'

'Harald isn't my former friend. He's my friend, period. Either friendship's a permanent condition or it's a fraud from the start.'

'And wasn't it?'

'I'll be frank with you, Heinz. I wasn't the one who broke off our friendship or let it lapse, it was your father. He retired into his shell and started avoiding me.'

'That was just after your biggest coup, wasn't it? What went wrong?'

'I don't understand.'

'I'm talking about the millions Plattner Construction made, aided by Harald Fein and abetted by his good friend Hermann Abendroth, who kindly let him see some development plans before publication.'

'What gives you that idea?'

'I can put two and two together. Why should Plattner's have invested in the Sunset Estate area if they didn't know it was going to be bought up to make room for the Olympic Way?'

'That's an absurd suspicion,' Abendroth said. He might have been trying to convince himself.

'So you never came to any crooked but profitable arrangement?'

'I asked you where you got this crazy theory.'

'Who cares? It *could* be correct, that's what matters. You contrived to give my father a look at some important papers. He passed the details to Grandfather, who exploited them so ruthlessly that your beautiful friendship broke up.'

'Heinz, never even suggest such a thing outside this room. I hate to think of the possible consequences.'

'Could they be worse than they are? Father's being booted around like a football by three teams at once. The police are trying to hang a murder rap on him, Mother's suing him for divorce, and the old man's doing his best to ruin him.'

'This is terrible,' Abendroth said, genuinely appalled. 'How can I help him?'

'I think he should be made to defend himself. He needs a damn good lawyer.'

'Leave it to me,' Abendroth promised. 'I can't do much but I can do that.'

Detective-Superintendent Braun turned to Penatsch.

'All right, where exactly was he when you saw him?'

'There,' the janitor replied, pointing up the stairs to the top landing. 'Herr Fein was standing right outside the woman's door. It was just about this time of night.'

'In other words, 10 p.m.' Braun checked his watch. 'And you could recognize him without difficulty? That wall-bracket doesn't shed much light.'

'Enough for me. My eyesight's good.'

'Describe him,' Braun said, glancing at Feldmann, who was busy taking notes in the background. 'What did he look like? What was he wearing? Try and remember every detail.'

'Well, he was standing there with his head lowered in a threatening sort of way. Maybe she'd just thrown him out and he was trying to get in again – I can't say. Anyway, he banged on the door several times and called her first name – that much I do know. He certainly made a lot of noise.'

'Was he wearing a hat?'

'A grey one, as far as I can recall.'

'What sort of suit was he wearing?'

'I don't remember exactly. He could have been dressed in a blue raincoat – the kind everybody wears.'

Henri Messer, legal adviser to Harald Fein, interviewing Penatsch at a later date:

Of all the nebulous evidence that has been patched together in the course of this so-called investigation, Herr Penatsch's deposition takes the cake for sheer implausibility.

Quite apart from the witness's shocking history of previous convictions, his statements are open to question on several points.

Point one: my client very seldom wears a hat. He owns three but never uses them unless it's raining or snowing. What's more, he doesn't own a grey one.

Point two: everyone acquainted with Herr Fein's wardrobe agrees that he has never owned a blue raincoat, only a brown one.

PENATSCH: Blue or brown, what's the difference? It was dark-coloured, that's all I know. Anyway, I can swear that it was Herr Fein I saw.

DETECTIVE-SUPERINTENDENT BRAUN: Alleged discrepancies in colour or errors on the subject of male fashion are irrelevant, Herr Messer. What matters is that Herr Penatsch saw your client and identified him at a later stage, also that he's prepared to repeat his statement under oath.

Detective Chief Superintendent Dürrenmaier to Detective-Superintendent Braun during a confidential exchange of views immediately subsequent to the above interview:
I admire your tactics, Braun, even if your methods don't always impress me as having the requisite lightness of touch. In this case, however, I can't help feeling that you've bitten off more than you can chew. Who are you really gunning for?'

BRAUN: With respect, sir, I think you know perfectly well but you won't admit it – you can't, not in your position. I understand. Sit back and leave the dirty work to me.

'Delighted to see you, my dearest girl!' Paul Plattner rose and went to meet his granddaughter. He put his arm round Helga's shoulders and led her to the black leather couch reserved for special visitors to the chairman's office.

'How pretty you are,' he said, sitting down beside her. 'Just like your dear mother at the same age. But you're looking sad, sweetheart – why?'

'Because of Daddy.' Helga gazed at him hopefully. 'Surely you understand . . .'

'Of course I understand, my dear, sweet, lovely child.' Plattner took Helga's submissive hands in his. 'Your worries are my worries – believe me.'

'I believe you, Grandfather.'

Statement by Frau Besenbinder, formerly housekeeper at the Plattner country residence:
. . . his daughter Hilde often spent the night there, usually at week-ends . . . sheets all rumpled and stained . . . no two ways about it . . . absolutely disgusted, so I gave notice . . .

Comments on Frau Besenbinder by Erika Haar, briefly employed as a housemaid in the same establishment:
. . . arrogant, frustrated old cow! What if Herr Plattner did make a pass at her sometimes, the way he did with me? These things happen when a man gets lonesome – and anyway, it paid off financially.

Besenbinder got uppity, though – she wanted him all to herself and kept butting in. The old man fired her, and not before time. I was glad to see her go.

Helga gave her grandfather a tearful smile. 'You will help, won't you?'

'I'll try, darling, if only for your sweet sake.' Plattner pressed her hands, lingeringly. 'I'm afraid it isn't going to be easy.'

'If you can't help Daddy, nobody can.'

'Possibly, sweetheart, but there's no point in rushing things. We must feel our way carefully, and we can't make plans here in this office atmosphere. I suggest you come down to Tegernsee this week-end. Then we can talk it over in peace.'

From Detective-Superintendent Keller's notes:
If I'm certain of one thing after forty years in the CID, it's this: human nature is a bottomless barrel full of dirty water.

'*Hello*, darling!' Melanie Weber fixed Harald with a bright stare. 'How *are* you!'

'As well as can be expected,' Harald said. 'In other words, I'm in trouble. Not that you'll lose any sleep over it.'

Melanie sighed. 'Oh, Harald, Harald, why do you always misjudge me so?'

Anton had fled on to the balcony as soon as Melanie swept through the door of Harald's apartment. She ignored his off-stage growls and sat down as though she owned the place.

'No feminine touch,' she declared after a brief inspection. 'You need a warm, *congenial* atmosphere, Harald, and I'm going to see you get it.'

'Did Hilde send you?'

'Of course not. Why should she?'

'I thought you were her best friend.'

'But I'm also a friend of *yours*.' Melanie gazed at him, doe-eyed. 'Think of all those *gorgeous* times we had together – Capri, Lake Garda, Pontresina . . . Don't tell me you've forgotten.'

From a letter written by Harald to Hermann Abendroth eight years earlier, when they were still in close touch:
. . . moments when I actually enjoy this state of affairs . . . two

extremely decorative women in tow, Hilde discreetly elegant, Melanie flamboyant, slender as a boy, dressed in vivid colours . . .

. . . often see myself as a faintly comic figure. Hilde and Melanie always talk to each other, never to me. They exchange secret smiles and whispers behind my back, and when they laugh I seldom know the reason.

'But *darling*,' Melanie insisted, 'nobody could be more desolated than I am to hear that you're splitting up. After all, your marriage has been a part of *my* life too . . .'

'Touching of you to say so.'

'All I want is to *help*, darling.'

'How nice, but in what way? You wouldn't by any chance have volunteered to help me disgorge a red plastic folder?'

Information supplied by one of three porters formerly employed at the Grand Hotel, Pontresina:

Herr Fein was a regular guest of ours for some years, and so was his wife. They occupied adjoining single rooms. A third single, also adjoining, was usually booked for Frau Melanie Weber, who seemed to be a very close friend of Herr and Frau Fein.

You could see they were on intimate terms. More than that I wouldn't like to say.

'A *folder*?' cried Melanie. 'Are you *crazy*, Harry?' Indignation sparkled in her black eyes. 'Surely you know me well enough to realize that I'm a complete dunce where papers are concerned.'

'Except cheque-books, I imagine.'

'Not even those, darling. I charge everything.'

'Well, some things aren't for sale. The red folder's one.'

Melanie shook her head bemusedly. Then, displaying her delightful inability to pursue a theme to its logical conclusion, she asked: 'Have you *really* forgotten what we meant to each other?'

'Melanie, that was nearly twenty years ago – even before my marriage to Hilde.'

'Have I changed that much?'

'No. Or if you have, not to your disadvantage. Is that what you wanted to hear?'

'Yes,' she replied, smiling at him. 'You see, this is *after* your marriage to Hilde.'

Maximilian Weber, land-owner and merchant banker, commenting on his brother Konrad Weber and the latter's wife Melanie. The following confidential remarks were transmitted to Henri Messer, attorney-at-law, by a friend of a friend:

Melanie has class. Not exactly my type, but just what the doctor ordered for my brother. After all, he has to get rid of his money somehow.

Really hot stuff, that woman. Her mother was Hungarian. The ageless type, always looks wonderful, gossips in four or five languages. She presented my brother with a son – a nice youngster.

Poor old Konrad's a human wreck. Spends most of the time in bed, but she never neglects him or the boy, let alone her duties as a hostess. Those bi-annual parties of hers are red-letter days in the social calendar.

No wonder Konrad overlooks her little peccadilloes, especially when they're easy on the eye like Hilde Fein.

'So he claims he hasn't got the folder,' said Plattner. 'Did he deny it point blank?'

'Not exactly point blank,' Jonas reported, 'but not very convincingly, either. I'm pretty sure he's revelling in the situation.'

'That,' Plattner said darkly, 'sounds typical of the man.'

Memorandum by Paul Plattner, filed for future reference:

. . . requested my former managing director, Herr Fein, to return the spare key of the firm's safe, which he did. The said key was received by my grandson Heinz and handed to Herr Jonas, who passed it to me for safekeeping. When the contents of the safe were checked the following day, a file with a red cover was found to be missing.

'It must have been him,' Jonas said.

Plattner nodded grimly. 'Who else?'

'But it didn't stop him pointing the finger at us.'

'You and me?'

'Yes. I don't know what this folder contains, or only vaguely, but Fein obviously thinks it's worth a lot to the firm. Whoever has it rules the roost – that's his idea.'

'Do you have it?' Plattner asked abruptly.

'No, but that's what he's trying to imply. He wants to play us off against each other.'

Paragraph 2 of Plattner's memorandum:
The said folder merely contains a few rough estimates, together with a description of certain development schemes. Although no secrets are involved, these documents are not intended for the eye of the general public. Irresponsibly interpreted, they might have awkward and undesirable repercussions. These must be avoided at all – repeat, all – costs.

'Let's get this straight, Joachim. You don't have the folder, nor do I. Therefore, Fein must have it. What did you offer him?'

'Precisely what you suggested. Several months' salary in excess of contract, also a lump sum – I hinted that you might go to a hundred thousand marks – also a discreet settlement of his personal problems, i.e. no publicity over the divorce. I also promised him every possible assistance in his brush with the police.'

'How did he react?'

'He laughed.'

Plattner shook his head. 'He's far deeper than I suspected. To think I trusted him all these years . . .'

'It might be an idea to prefer charges against him for stealing documents from your safe. The police are itching to hang something else on him.'

Paragraph 3 of Plattner's memorandum:
. . . contemplated preferring charges against Harald Fein for theft, then dropped the idea in view of our previous relationship and because I wanted to give the man another chance . . .

'Preferring charges,' Plattner said, stroking his jaw, 'might just conceivably backfire on us. It isn't specially important, this folder, but we must retrieve it before someone misuses his knowledge of the contents – retrieve it quickly and quietly. You understand?'

Jonas understood. He reacted swiftly. 'Does Fein have a safe-deposit box?'

'Yes, at Merker's head office in Promenadeplatz, but it's in Hilde's name as well as his. He wouldn't hide it there.'

'Well, if he hasn't rented another one yet, the folder's more or less bound to be at his apartment.'

'Excellent, Joachim. I'm glad to see I don't have to spell things out for you. Carry on, my boy. The firm will owe you an eternal debt of gratitude.'

From Detective-Superintendent Keller's notes:

Late summer tends to be high season for drownings – there were two found today, both in the Isar. Women favour death by drowning, presumably because it rates as 'clean' or non-disfiguring, and quick into the bargain.

This is a terrible misconception. You can generally assume with a fair degree of certainty that a frustrated suicide will try again. Not so people who try and drown themselves. Very few of them have a second shot.

Of course, it goes without saying that not every corpse found in water belongs to a suicide. The deceased may have been the victim of an accident. Or of a murderer.

A PECD officer's first rule is to chuck the rule-book out of the window. You must conduct your inquiries with no preconceptions whatever. This comes hard sometimes, e.g. when you're confronted by a corpse whose identity you know – when you know the dead girl's father.

'My name is Messer, Henri Messer,' announced the latest visitor to Harald's rented apartment at Torremolinos Towers. 'I'm your legal adviser.'

'Really?'

Harald smiled wearily. He had started drinking early in the day, but only champagne. Melanie Weber had left him three bottles of Pommery – vintage, naturally – and removed his entire stock of hard liquor.

He heard himself say: 'I wasn't under the impression I needed a lawyer, Herr Messer. I didn't send for you.'

'Herr Abendroth did so on your behalf. He rang and asked Seidl Partners to represent your interests.'

'But you aren't Dr Seidl.'

'Consider yourself fortunate, Herr Fein,' Messer said blandly. He was a thin man of medium height, with a shock of wiry hair and a face furrowed by the good-humoured smile that seldom deserted it. He made himself at home in Harald's best arm-chair and enthusiastically accepted a glass of champagne.

'Perhaps I should tell you,' he went on, 'that Dr Seidl is not only a lawyer of the highest repute but a man of the utmost caution. He's my senior partner. I joined the firm a short while ago.'

'Did Abendroth speak to Dr Seidl personally?'

'Yes, and retained him – or rather, his firm. Hence my presence here.'

'You mean Dr Seidl declined to handle my case?'

'Right first time.' Messer gave Harald a congratulatory nod. 'I'm sure we're going to hit it off splendidly, Herr Fein. You can rely on my complete candour.'

'Let's see how candid you can be,' Harald said. 'About Dr Seidl, for instance.'

'Discounting his legal activities, Dr Seidl is a man who maintains close contact with the dominant political, financial and industrial circles in our delightful province. His personal connections extend far beyond its borders and at least as far as Bonn. He ran a quick check on your case and promptly identified it as a hot potato. Being reluctant to turn down a retainer from a man like Abendroth, he passed it to his minions. I happened to be available – in fact to be quite honest, I dropped everything else. I wanted your case.'

'Why?'

'Because it's studded with possibilities. I didn't need a second glance at your particulars to see that. Simply place yourself in my hands, Herr Fein, and leave the rest to me.'

Extracts from a police dossier, one copy filed at the Provincial Crime Bureau, another at Police HQ, Munich. Identical entry in the M section:

Messer, Heinrich, styles himself Henri. Born 1930, only child. Father county court judge, maternal grandfather Franconian civil servant.

An able pupil, but openly anti-fascist from an early age. Trouble with school authorities on account of so-called subversive remarks about the then head of state, Adolf Hitler. Matriculated 1949, with distinction. Studied law until 1954, when he entered the public service.

1959–63, Junior Public Prosecutor, Munich. No activities of special note. Already on Ministry of Justice's list of potential state secretaries, but political allegiance still vague. From then on, involved in a series of incidents.

Examples: Messer took part in public protests, spoke at non-party debates, and was ultimately hailed by the *Morgenzeitung* as a 'liberal-minded and progressive upholder of civil liberties'. No response to reprimands from worried superiors.

Further examples: a public stand over the *Fanny Hill* trial, which he termed 'a relapse into the Middle Ages'; participation in an unauthorized protest march by rioting students, after which he narrowly escaped arrest; published pronouncements on drug addiction which ran counter to preventive laws currently in force.

In 1969, faced with a choice between discipline and dismissal, Messer decided to leave the public service and resigned his post. By virtue of his outstanding and undisputed legal expertise, obtained employment with Seidl Partners, the well-known law firm. Initially assigned to reorganize the firm's archives.

'At long last, Herr Fein, here's a case after my own heart. I'm entirely at your disposal.'

'How do you plan to proceed?'

'First, we'll put a stop to all these insinuations you're being subjected to. Attack's the best method of defence, in law as in war.'

'Whom do you propose to counter-attack?'

'Everyone who's gunning for you. Same weapons but bigger calibre.'

Harald's eyes widened. 'You realize who you're up against?'

'Perfectly.'

'You know who Superintendent Braun is?'

'I do. A real pro, but hamstrung by the fact that he's a public servant. I'll handle Braun.'

'And Plattner?'

'Let him do his worst. I've been itching to tackle a social parasite like Plattner for years.'

'I think you underestimate him. Not many people have tangled with him and survived. Even the Mayor handles him with kid gloves, and not just because he's afraid of soiling his fingers. Believe me, I'm an expert on Plattner.'

'But not on me, Herr Fein. Here's what I suggest, just for starters. One, we declare your contract and its termination by Plattner's to be legally and ethically indefensible, claim damages on grounds of wrongful dismissal to the tune of, say, five hundred thousand marks. Two, we respond to your wife's petition for divorce by cross-petitioning that she alone was responsible for imperilling and ultimately destroying your marriage. Three, we go for the police – officially, for Braun himself. His methods are such that we demand a full and immediate inquiry. You follow me?'

'Not entirely.'

'You will. I'll explain our best course of action as each problem comes up. Leave everything to me.'

'But I don't propose to. I'm sorry, Herr Messer, but I can't accept you as my legal adviser – you or anyone else.'

'I quite understand,' Messer replied, promptly and without resentment. 'Your reaction comes as no surprise – in fact I was warned to expect it. He wants his peace and quiet, I was told, he doesn't want to be bothered. You obviously think the whole thing will blow over and leave you free to live your own life.'

'Exactly.'

'You're wrong, Herr Fein. We're dealing with wild animals who are determined to have your blood. Just how quiet do you want to be – as quiet as the grave?'

'I'll tell you what I *don't* want, Herr Messer, and that's your kind of help. You'd obviously stop at nothing. I don't wish to seem rude, but please leave.'

'Very well, I'll go.' Messer smiled. 'But I'll be back. You'll send for me when you reach the end of your tether, and you're almost there now.'

From Detective-Superintendent Keller's notes:

Today was a great day for Supt Braun, certainly in his own estimation.

He made one long-distance phone call after another: Federal Crime Bureau, Central Records Office, and Interpol, West German liaison centre. The latter confirmed the following points:

Madrid declined to extradite Kordes, the murdered woman's pimp, because he first had to answer charges under Spanish law. He was suspected of complicity in a counterfeiting operation.

Braun announced that he must have a chat with Kordes even if it meant a special trip to Madrid.

He flew there the same day.

Braun's air ticket was a waste of tax-payer's money. One question to me would have saved a lot of unnecessary bother. I knew Kordes from way back, when I was still on outside work. A shrewd cookie who'd say anything he thought you wanted to hear – as long as it didn't incriminate him personally.

From Fein's angle, Kordes couldn't have been a worse prospect. Braun would obviously give the man every opportunity to take part in his little game.

During the afternoon I went to Chief Supt Dürrenmaier and made another inquiry about my retirement date. Not through yet, I was told, but it could only be a matter of days.

Harald dined with Melanie Weber at the *Schwarzwälder* that evening, as excellently as any patron of that establishment could expect: shrimps, wild duck and Apfelstrudel washed down with sparkling Fürst Metternich and topped off with strong black coffee.

Melanie's phoned appeal: 'Please, Harald, you simply *must* come. Be my guest. Don't you know what today is? I'm sure you don't, you *unromantic* creature! Exactly twenty years ago tonight we went back to your apartment and I stayed for breakfast.'

Harald couldn't remember. He'd always thought it had been spring-time, not autumn, but perhaps he was wrong. He was getting less and less certain of anything these days.

It had been a relatively gay evening, with Melanie resolutely at her best. She radiated warmth, chatted brightly and avoided all reference to his recent troubles.

'Thanks, Melanie,' Harald said as he escorted her to her car. The chauffeur-driven Rolls was waiting near the cathedral. 'It was a pleasant evening.'

'The first of many, I hope.' She embraced him in the playfully affectionate après-ski manner cultivated by Munich's high society: reciprocal pressure on the upper arms accompanied by two quick pecks, one on each cheek.

Then she got in. Harald stared after her thoughtfully, Anton with relief.

127

Information about Helga, daughter of Harald Fein.

1. Hilde Fein, her mother:

She didn't come home that night. I checked next morning and her bed was untouched.

She'd been in a highly emotional state those last few days. I did my best to calm her down, but she avoided me. As if that man didn't have enough on his conscience already!

2. Constance Bergold, a friend:

The day before – that's to say, Friday – Helga asked if she could borrow my Mini for a couple of days. I didn't ask her where she was going.

Two days later the car was back outside our house with a full tank. The keys had been posted through the letter-box as arranged. As far as I could judge, there were about 150 kilometres on the clock.

3. Ludwig Breitwieser, janitor of Torremolinos Towers:

Yes, I recognize the girl in the photo. She drove up in a red Mini and parked near the entrance. She hung around for quite a time. About half-an-hour, I'd say.

Then Herr Fein came out with his dog, accompanied by a lady. They all climbed into a Rolls-Royce and drove off.

The girl in the photograph stared after them. She'd got out by this time and was standing in the shadows as if she didn't want to be seen. Then she drove off too.

'Anton,' Harald said as they rode the lift to the third floor, 'I feel like a night-cap. Let's make ourselves comfortable.'

With Anton trotting contentedly behind him, he made for his apartment. Light flooded to meet him through the door, which was wide open.

All the lamps were burning. They shone with harsh clarity on rifled drawers, cleared shelves, gutted cushions, up-ended furniture, ransacked cupboards.

Harald slumped into the nearest chair, watched with consternation by Anton. For some moments he incredulously surveyed the chaos around him.

Then he jumped up, hurried to the ice-box and took out one of Melanie's bottles of champagne. He uncorked it and filled a large tumbler till the foam cascaded over his hand, then drank it at a gulp.

Anton threw back his head and howled.

Almost simultaneously, Superintendent Braun renewed his application for a warrant in the name of Harald Fein.

Three days later a body was found in the Nymphenburg Canal. Superintendent Keller, acting in his official capacity as PECD officer, noted the dead girl's name without comment and turned away.

It soon became apparent that Harald was almost certain to be parted from Anton as well. This completed his dispossession of all that he had ever – in any sense – owned.

Chapter Six

'We've got him!' announced Detective-Superintendent Braun.

Detective Chief Superintendent Dürrenmaier knew who he meant. 'Are you sure?'

'Absolutely,' Braun assured him. 'The case is a hundred per cent complete.'

'I hope so,' Dürrenmaier said. 'The CID has a fine reputation in this city. Let's try and keep it that way.'

'It paid off,' Braun told his chief, almost vivaciously. 'The trip to Madrid, I mean.'

Permission to interview Kordes had been granted after only twenty-four hours' delay. Braun had been obliged to give a written assurance that Kordes was not wanted by the Federal German authorities on political, racial or religious grounds. The interview was restricted to thirty minutes and supervised by an official from the Spanish Ministry of the Interior.

'Well, Braun,' Dürrenmaier asked drily, 'and how did your little chat go?'

From shorthand notes of the interview with Kordes:

The first ten minutes were devoted to explaining the purpose of the interview and assuring Kordes that his statements would be treated as confidential.

KORDES: Okay, what do you want to know and why?

The next ten minutes were devoted to a full account of recent developments.

KORDES: But that's terrible! The poor bitch certainly didn't deserve to go that way. You think I killed her?

BRAUN: No, we know you were abroad at the time in question.

KORDES: If I agree to co-operate, will you do me a favour?

BRAUN: Depends what you're selling.

KORDES: You want evidence, right? Okay, I can supply some on condition you don't get me extradited. Is it a deal? Right, here goes. The one thing I insist on with my girls is a businesslike approach. On my advice, she kept a record of current earnings, complete with names and dates. You'll find all the dope in a safe-deposit box at the Deutsche Bank in Munich.

'These particulars,' said Chief Superintendent Dürrenmaier. 'Did you find them?'

'I did.' Braun could hardly conceal his exultation. 'The safe-deposit box contained share certificates to the value of roughly eighty thousand marks, a foreign exchange pass-book worth over a hundred thousand, and a set of engagement diaries covering her activities up to a few days before she was killed. The lady kept a daily record of all her visitors, complete with times and takings. Her fee varied between a hundred and three hundred marks.'

'And one of the names she noted was Fein's?'

'No less than three entries, sir, each marked DM 200. Three weeks, twelve days and seven days before the murder.'

'No possibility of a mistake?'

'It's all down there in black and white. In other words, Fein's a dead duck – as good as convicted, I mean. With this evidence under our belt we can prove he's been lying from start to finish. I formally request that we take out a warrant for his arrest.'

'In that case I'd better apply to the public prosecutor's department. On your advice, Braun.'

'On my head be it, sir.'

'So it's you again,' said Harald. He eyed Keller quizzically. 'What brings you here this time, accident or design?'

'Take your pick,' Keller said. 'Which do you prefer?'

'Perhaps you didn't come to see me at all.' Harald's tone was elaborately off-hand.

'Anything's possible,' Keller said. 'Let's assume I dropped in to see your dog.'

Anton, who was already on his feet, looked up at Keller and wagged his tail delightedly.

Keller knelt down and scratched the dog's head. No one in the little café near the Viktualienmarkt looked twice. The White and Blue not only took its name from Bavaria's old national colours but was more Bavarian than a pair of leather shorts. It was small, cosy, slightly scruffy, and innocent of foreign tourists. Scrubbed wooden chairs and tables, pinewood panelling, and straw mats for the greater comfort of visiting dogs. To the people of Munich, dogs were an integral part of life. There were four canine customers apart from Anton. They lay at their ease, exchanging peaceable glances.

Almost before Keller sat down at Harald's table, a stone mug of dark beer appeared in front of him. He nodded to the waitress, who evidently knew him, and drank with reverence.

'If you want to know how I am,' Harald said at length, 'the answer is, I'm still alive and kicking.'

'But not for much longer, the way you're acting.'

'What do you mean?' Harald protested. 'I'm simply waiting for the dust to settle, then I'll relax. It's worth being patient. After all, who cares about a few sticks of furniture?'

'Furniture?' Keller inquired sharply.

'Yes, somebody ransacked my apartment.'

'When?'

'Last night, while I was out having dinner with an old girl-friend. When I got back the place looked as if it had been hit by a bomb.'

Keller drained his stoneware mug, lost in thought, and ordered a refill with a Danish schnapps on the side. Then he asked: 'Did you notify the police?'

'There didn't seem to be any point.'

'Someone takes your home apart and you don't call the police? You really are a glutton for punishment, aren't you!'

'Oh, go on, what can the police do in a case like that? I'll tell you – put it all down in a little black book and forget about it.'

Keller shook his head ruefully. 'I'm sorry to say it, Herr Fein, but you're an unfair temptation to the criminal fraternity.'

Confidential remarks voiced by Detective Chief Superintendent Dürrenmaier to Assistant Commissioner Schulz of the Administration and Operations Department and noted by the latter in writing:

Det. Chief Supt Dürrenmaier drew my attention to unofficial inquiries undertaken by Det.-Supt Keller on the basis of all statistics available to him. The following points seem to emerge:

The years 1968–9 represented a turning-point in the field of West German crime detection, but one which passed virtually unacknowledged because the inescapable inferences were too unwelcome.

In short, the number of offences continued to climb steadily whereas the detection rate began to stagnate in 1968–9 and has remained almost constant since then.

Which means, in effect, that the CID's efficiency – or effectiveness – is decreasing.

Keller spotted this and I couldn't deny it.

'Mind if I ask you a few questions?' said Keller, patting Anton. 'For instance, where was this dog when your place was ransacked?'

'With me, as usual.'

'According to my information, you've been spending almost the entire day in your apartment. You take Anton for a fifteen-minute walk at about 9 a.m. and don't emerge again until nightfall, when you exercise him for an hour or so.'

'Correct.'

'So your only regular outings are these two daily strolls with Anton. The dinner date you mentioned – was it an exception?'

'Well, yes, if you want to put it that way.'

'Who was the lady?'

'A friend of many years' standing. Melanie Weber – she's a friend of my wife's too.'

'Who suggested the night out – Frau Weber?'

'What are you hinting at, Superintendent?'

'Never mind that for the moment. Tell me, what would you consider the most valuable thing in your possession at the present time – cash?'

'No. I don't keep much, and that I carry around with me.'

'Documents of some kind?'

'No, but what makes you ask?'

'Don't give it another thought. I'm merely running through the sort of routine questions we're trained to ask. To repeat, what do you own that's valuable – apart from Anton?'

'Well, there are my new architectural designs. They're worth something to me, if not to anyone else.'

'Where were they when the apartment was ransacked?'

'Lying spread out on my desk.'

'A proven method of concealment, but your visitors may not have been looking for them at all. Whatever they were after, you're going to be in big trouble unless you get yourself an efficient lawyer.'

Harald laughed. 'Funny you should say that. I already had one volunteer but I turned him down. He was all for charging the whole of contemporary society like a run-away tank – at my expense.'

'What was his name?'

'Henri Messer. Do you know him?'

'I certainly do.'

'Well, what do you think of him?'

'Professionally speaking, not much. Humanly, a great deal. There's a difference.' Keller winked at Anton, who was contentedly chewing a hunk of sausage. 'I can tell you one thing. There was a time in my life when I really admired Henri Messer.'

'And you think he's a man to be trusted?'

'Put it this way,' Keller said. 'Henri Messer never does anything for free, and I'm not talking about money. He's a human computer plus imagination. He knows the score.'

'So you think I ought to put myself in his hands?'

'Do you have any option? Drowning men clutch at straws, Herr Fein, but Messer isn't a man of straw. He could turn out to be a lifebelt. You're in deep water. Whether or not he'll extricate you I wouldn't like to say, but if I were you I'd take a gamble.'

Detective-Inspector Feldmann addressing Harald Fein at the latter's apartment in Torremolinos Towers:

I must ask you to accompany me to Headquarters, sir. Detective-Superintendent Braun would appreciate a word with you. I've a car waiting downstairs.

HARALD: By all means. There's just one problem, though. I can't leave the dog, so I'll have to take my own car. Anton feels at home in it – he'll sit there for hours on end without kicking up a fuss. I hope you understand.

FELDMANN: We always do our best to be accommodating, sir. I should make it clear that you're not under an obligation to accompany me at all.

HARALD: But I will if I'm wise?

FELDMANN: Not wise, sir, public-spirited. An innocent man has nothing to fear. Very well, use your own car.

Paul Plattner frowned at his new managing director. 'Still no trace of that folder? What the devil's he doing – holding out for a higher price?'

Joachim Jonas looked equally worried. 'There wasn't a sign of it. The men I hired really took the place apart . . .'

'Men? What men?'

'It's all right, they're a hundred per cent reliable. One of them's a foreman who owes me a few favours . . .'

'I disapprove of such methods,' Plattner declared virtuously. 'I utterly condemn them – is that clear?'

It was clear enough. Jonas realized at once that the new broom was his alone to wield. Plattner wanted a prospective son-in-law who would clean up the mess by himself.

From an ale-house monologue delivered by Roderich Rogalski, a Plattner foreman specializing in ferro-concrete construction:

Jonas? I won't hear a word against him. His heart's in the right place, take it from me. Like the other day, down at Site 14. I fell asleep on the job after half a dozen beers. Man, did that s.o.b. of a site engineer chew my balls off! He really went to town, sounding off about negligence, safety regulations, etcetera. I told him – I said, quite quietly: Shut your fucking trap or I'll shut it for you.

The bastard reported me to head office and I was hauled in front of Jonas. All he said was: Had a bit of trouble, eh? I said: These things happen, and he said: Yes, but they've happened a couple of times before, haven't they?

It was true, but only an old woman like the site engineer would have made a big deal out of it. Jonas didn't. He just laughed and said: Okay, forget it. Herr Jonas, I said, you're a real gentleman, and he said: We've all got to pull together – that's what they call team spirit.

Well, I said, if there's ever anything I can do for you, you only have to let me know.

I may take you up on that sometime, he said.

'Where can the folder be?' Plattner asked sharply.

'Not in his apartment – that we know – but not locked away in a safe either. He's taken to carrying a briefcase around with him these last few days. I suspect he keeps it in there.'

'So how do you intend to proceed?'

'I've got a few cards up my sleeve. There's Melanie Weber, for one. She might help.'

Plattner shut his eyes. 'Melanie Weber's a mischief-maker,' he said with some asperity. 'She came between me and my daughter, many years ago.'

'I'm sure she didn't do it intentionally,' Jonas said discreetly. 'Some people are born without arms and legs. Melanie was born without morals, which is just why she could be useful. Hilde thinks so too.'

'Very well, very well. I don't see why we should go easy on Fein – he doesn't deserve it. I don't care what happens as long as I get that folder back.'

Harald Fein was escorted into Police Headquarters by Feldmann, shepherded into Braun's office and, after a brief delay, taken to see Detective Chief Superintendent Dürrenmaier.

'Herr Fein,' said Dürrenmaier, with his usual mixture of briskness and courtesy, 'kindly take a seat.'

Harald did so. Dürrenmaier was sitting behind his desk with Braun at his elbow and Feldmann hovering in the background, near the door.

'I'm bound to inform you, Herr Fein, that certain documents have come to light which seem to cast a heavy burden of suspicion on you – so much so that the possibility of your arrest can no longer be discounted.'

'Correct me if I'm wrong,' Harald said politely, 'but wouldn't that depend on the public prosecutor's department?'

'Your information is correct,' Dürrenmaier agreed, just as politely. 'However, such a decision may soon be forthcoming. The Public Prosecutor, Dr Barthel, should be here at any moment.'

Dr Barthel, then Public Prosecutor and soon afterwards Senior Public Prosecutor, conversing with a close friend:

Generally speaking, our department can rely on the findings of the CID in ninety-nine cases out of a hundred. The evidence they supply is nearly always watertight, which is why few applications for arrest or search warrants are ever turned down.

Where exceptions do occur, one learns to smell them. Take the case of Harald Fein. Quite instinctively, I felt a reluctance to give the CID carte blanche and decided to intervene before things went too far. It was Detective-Superintendent Braun who gave me food for thought.

An admirable man, Braun, but subject to pressure from various quarters and afflicted with a sort of persecution mania in reverse. He was obsessed with the idea of finding a murderer – one particular murderer – and felt convinced that he'd done so. The trouble was, he proceeded to produce two more in quick succession.

And that was going a bit far.

'It's also my duty to inform you, Herr Fein,' Dürrenmaier pursued, 'that you have a right to decline to make any statement, volunteer information or submit to questioning without legal representation. The police have no power or authority to compel any such disclosures on your part.'

'So I gather,' said Harald. 'Inspector Feldmann was kind enough to brief me in advance.'

Braun glared at Feldmann and snorted, but Dürrenmaier went on: 'I'd like to point out, Herr Fein, that I would consider it advisable for you to nominate a lawyer to represent your interests. I can recommend someone if you like.'

'But I already have a lawyer,' Harald heard himself say, 'Counsellor Messer of Seidl Partners.'

The reactions to this announcement were varied. Braun shook his bullet-head incredulously, Feldmann's full moon face creased in a covert smile, and Dürrenmaier registered polite surprise.

'In that case,' said the chief superintendent, 'we'll await the arrival of Dr Barthel and invite Counsellor Messer to join us.'

From a conversation between Hilde Fein and her son:

HILDE: You ought to keep an eye on that sister of yours. God knows what she's up to!

HEINZ: Wherever she is, it's better than being forced to listen to your eternal nagging, Mother – and that takes strong nerves. It's almost too much for me, let alone a shrinking violet like Helga.

HILDE: Don't be impertinent. And while we're on the subject of impertinence, kindly keep out of my affairs.

HEINZ: Affairs is the word. They may be yours but they affect me and Helga. I can't stand what you're doing to Father – it's been dragging on for too long.

HILDE: What do you expect me to do?

HEINZ: Give him the coup de grâce. He's like a maimed animal hobbling along on three legs. The least you can do is finish him off.

137

HILDE (shaking her head sadly): I've never understood what goes on inside you, Heinz.

HEINZ: You've never tried. Some day soon you'll find out, but by then it'll be too late.

'Remember me?' asked Henri Messer. 'Or are you going to plead amnesia?'

'Not in your case,' Keller said cheerfully. 'You're the unforgettable kind.'

Messer had been summoned to Police Headquarters by Chief Superintendent Dürrenmaier, speaking on Harald's behalf. The desk sergeant had asked him to wait on arrival, but waiting was alien to him. He made his way to Superintendent Braun's office, only to discover that Braun was with Chief Superintendent Dürrenmaier, likewise Inspector Feldmann. There was no one in the room but Keller, who clearly welcomed an excuse to shelve his paperwork.

'What brings you here?' Keller demanded. 'You did me a favour once. I hope you aren't planning to collect.'

From Detective-Superintendent Keller's notes:

It was back in 1968, during the student riots. They assigned every available man to cover them. I was heading a team which specialized in muggings. We didn't have any major case on hand so they naturally roped us in. Our job was to keep tabs on a café called *The Little Bell* and its regular customers, who included some of the leading student rebels.

The café was pleasant enough, and I enjoyed my visits. I got to know most of the regulars, a lot of whom used to argue with me for fun. They probably thought I was an old ass but I didn't mind. I'm partial to donkeys.

Several arrests were made on the day of the big demonstration, in which two people died. My own café was raided by officers who knew me but had instructions to act as if they didn't. They would have detained Messer too, if I hadn't given them the sign. Imperceptibly, or so I thought, but Messer spotted it.

Some days later, when the rebels had got over the shock of all those carefully planned arrests, they started moaning about Gestapo tactics. Attempts were made to reconstruct the chain of events, and this led to allegations that a number of police spies had infiltrated various student meeting-places.

My name wasn't mentioned in this connection. Messer went to some lengths to keep me out of it – considerable lengths, as I later discovered.

Messer smiled. 'I came to assist a client of mine – Harald Fein. Do you know him?'

'Only slightly. I know his dog better. Anton's a prize specimen.'

'Really?'

Keller nodded. 'I'm beginning to think I know more about dogs than people. Still, I know enough about Fein to feel sorry for him.'

'So you're familiar with his case?'

'Don't jump to conclusions,' Keller said with a laugh. 'I haven't headed a murder investigation for years – not since our last meeting, in fact. You were the kiss of death, Messer. My present duties are limited to writing PECD reports.'

'But you share an office with Braun.'

'Shortage of space, that's all.'

'Whatever the reason, you've got keen eyes and sharp ears. If you sit here in the same room as Braun there can't be much you don't know about Harald Fein and his troubles.'

'In your place,' Keller said cautiously, 'I wouldn't pin too many hopes on the man. He behaves like a born loser.'

'I know,' said Messer. 'He thinks he's a sacrificial lamb, but he isn't – he's a golden calf, and I'm not going to have him slaughtered. Golden calves are rare beasts. They deserve to survive.'

'With everyone's help including mine?'

'Do you always have to come straight to the point?' Messer chuckled. 'All I meant was, if you could just drop the occasional hint . . .'

'You've bitten off a man-sized mouthful and you know it.' Keller regarded Messer with a lingering smile.

'Why, is his position as hopeless as all that?'

'Not necessarily. Not if you're good at reading between the lines.'

'Go on.'

'Well, take the murdered woman's notes on her regular customers and current earnings. I managed to sneak a look at them

139

– accidentally, of course. A really damning piece of evidence against Fein, at first glance.'

'And on closer inspection?'

'On closer inspection it becomes apparent that the lady had a habit of abbreviating her boy-friends' names. For instance, it's been proved that one of her best customers was Friedrich Benzinger, the big haulage contractor, but she listed him simply as Benz – just Benz, with a note of how much he paid for her services.'

Messer's eyes narrowed. 'What's the inference?'

'Work it out for yourself.'

'Can't you be more specific?'

'Think about abbreviations and their possible applications. I've given you one example. She wrote Benz but she meant Benzinger, get it?'

'Got it,' said Messer. 'Thanks a lot.'

Hermann Abendroth, head of the Urban Planning Department, in conclave with the Mayor:

ABENDROTH: I'm afraid I've put my foot in it. Harald Fein needed a lawyer and I recommended one.

MAYOR: Nothing wrong with that. Who's paying?

ABENDROTH: I don't think it's been definitely settled yet, but if Fein can't afford it I'll foot the bill myself.

MAYOR: As a favour to an old friend, eh? Very noble of you – at least, I think so, but who else will? It wouldn't take much imagination on the part of certain mean-minded people to put a sinister construction on your kindness. Who's representing him?

ABENDROTH: Seidl Partners.

MAYOR: Excellent choice. Dr Seidl's a first-class lawyer with a reputation for strict political neutrality. The composition of his firm makes that very plain. On the one hand he employs die-hard conservatives like old Dr Süssmeier. On the other, he gives house-room to radicals like Henri Messer. Messer probably specializes in representing the delinquent children of Seidl's wealthier clients.

ABENDROTH: It's Messer I'm talking about. I don't know how it happened, but Harald's case was passed to him, of all people.

MAYOR: On Seidl's instructions?

ABENDROTH: Probably – I don't know.

MAYOR: And you're getting cold feet?

ABENDROTH: Yes. Either Seidl deliberately assigned Messer to the case or Messer grabbed it on his own initiative. Either way, there could be complications – and conjectures. Try this one for size: Abendroth plus Fein plus Plattner equals huge profits at public expense. I tell you, the stink won't stop at my door – it'll drift under yours.

MAYOR: What do you suggest?

ABENDROTH: That I formally resign and announce that I'm doing so at your request. At least that gets you off the hook.

MAYOR: But I don't want an easy way out, Hermann. The Fein case had to blow up sooner or later. You've no idea how much I enjoy these public rows. No, kick off with the 'no comment from City Hall' gambit. That way you won't spoil my fun.

'Argus' of the Morgenzeitung (*guaranteed salary DM 5000 a month, plus expenses, plus repayments in respect of disbursements to informants, plus tokens of appreciation from publicity-seekers, allegedly payable in kind by younger aspirants of the female sex), commenting on a stand-up buffet held in the main salon of the Weber residence:*

. . . found myself standing between Uta and Hanna. Uta chatted about her psychiatrist while Hanna fed me caviare on toast. The indispensable Petra, decorative as ever . . .

. . . virtually everyone who's anyone – in fact you could have counted the absentees on the fingers of one hand. Günther was missing, reportedly injured while riding (quite what, nobody seemed to know), also James, who was in the thick of preparations for the next Grand Prix. Marianne was detained at the studio – she's currently starring in a series of deodorant ads. Another missing face was Mitzi, who's making a new film with Roy, promisingly entitled *Miss Permissive 1972* . . .

Melanie Weber to her dear friend Hilde Fein, escorted by Joachim Jonas:

You're looking positively pale, darling. Is it that dress? Well, it is a bit on the *sombre* side. Perhaps it's that husband of yours. If so, leave him to me. Helga's gadding around, you say? But *darling*, we did the same at her age, and *she's* got the pill to fall back on. Don't begrudge her a little fun. Have some yourself!

Still at the same party. Hilde Fein, escorted by Joachim Jonas, to her dear friend Melanie Weber:

Don't overdo it, darling. You'll get creases around your mouth, smiling like that. Keep us company for a minute or two. Joachim wants to tell you how grateful he is for your offer of help.

Information given by Karl Bockelmann, law student and friend of Heinz Fein:

Friendship's a fine thing, sure, but it can also be a drag. I certainly thought so when Heinz roped me in for a tour of all the dives in Munich. When I asked him why, he said it was on account of his sister. She'd gone missing, apparently.

Helga was a nice kid. Inhibited and over-emotional, but you couldn't help liking her.

I tagged along, but we never found her.

From Detective-Superintendent Keller's notes:

There were three fatalities in my area that day.

1. A forty-five-year-old woman found lying in bed. The family doctor had already signed a death certificate. Chronic respiratory disorder, he called it, but I noticed some red blotches on her face. She'd gassed herself and the family had covered up for her. Accidental death virtually ruled out.

2. A man aged twenty-five turned up at a suburban police station and reported that he'd inadvertently shot his wife with a small-bore rifle. The local inspector transmitted the details to Headquarters, so I had to make an examination. Body left in situ. The woman was lying in their double bed, eyes closed and hands folded. She must have been shot in her sleep. Intensity of powder-burns cast doubt on husband's story. Passed to Homicide.

3. A drowning, female, late teens. Fished out of the Nymphenburg Canal. Immersion time provisionally estimated at two days, minimum.

It's very difficult to gauge how long a body has been under water. Contributory factors include physical condition, also the temperature of the water and its organic content. Generally speaking, the fingers acquire a 'wash-day' appearance after about three hours. After two days, pronounced swelling of the palms develops, and five days of immersion turns them chalky-white.

It's equally hard to tell on first inspection whether the deceased was dead or alive when immersed. It takes an autopsy to discover whether the lungs contain water, sand or minute particles of vegetable matter (you can't inhale when you're dead!).

This one seemed to be a case of suicide. Clothing intact, no marks of violence. Deceased immediately identifiable from papers found on her person.

It was Helga Fein.

'Gentlemen,' said Detective Chief Superintendent Dürrenmaier, 'the purpose of this meeting is to clarify certain matters of common interest.'

Those present, apart from Dürrenmaier himself, comprised the Public Prosecutor, Dr Barthel, CID officers Braun and Feldmann, and Harald Fein, with the latter's legal representative, Counsellor Henri Messer, in attendance. They were sitting round a circular table in one corner of the office, near the window. The chairs were hard and rather shabby.

'My client,' Messer hastened to point out, 'has no intention of exposing himself to unfounded allegations of any kind. His presence here merely signifies a readiness to contribute, where possible, to the clarification of specific points. He was not involved in the events at No. 33 V-Strasse. If you are prepared to proceed on that understanding, you may rest assured of our co-operation. If not, we reserve our position.'

'Counsellor Messer,' said the Public Prosecutor, with an amiable expression on his lean and puckered face, 'I suppose I may assume that you wish to be as fully briefed as possible?'

'Your assumption is correct,' Messer said.

Barthel glanced at Chief Superintendent Dürrenmaier, who nodded encouragingly at Superintendent Braun. Braun cleared his throat.

'First, we have conclusive proof of Herr Fein's presence in the immediate vicinity of No. 33 V-Strasse on various occasions, one of them being the night of the murder.

'Second, the janitor of No. 33 V-Strasse, Herr Penatsch, states that he saw Herr Fein standing outside the murdered women's door in a highly agitated condition, at or about the time of the murder.

'Third, Herr Fein's name occurs several times in the murdered woman's diary.'

'First,' retorted Messer, 'all the other police witnesses state simply that my client parked in the said street. They do not claim that he ever left his car.

'Second, in view of Herr Penatsch's previous record, I suggest that little credence can be given to any statements made by that gentleman.

'Third, I deny that my client ever visited or patronized the deceased.'

Barthel looked almost hurt. 'But that, Counsellor, is precisely the point on which evidence now appears to be forthcoming.' He turned to the police officers. 'Am I right?'

Feldmann smiled and Dürrenmaier preserved an air of official discretion. Braun removed a slim black book from his briefcase and plunked it down in the middle of the table.

'A daily record of her takings,' he said. 'She listed the name Fein as a source of income. It occurs several times, opposite considerable sums of money.'

'But that's crazy!' Harald blurted out.

Messer gave him a warning look and he relapsed into silence.

Picking up the diary with a studiously casual air, Messer thumbed through. He took his time. Finally he laughed. 'Just as I thought,' he said, striving hard to supress his relief and exultation.

'What do you mean?' demanded Braun.

Messer's smile broadened. 'One of the lady's most assiduous patrons was a man named Benzinger. A wheeler-dealer whose reputation extends far beyond this city and one whose business dealings would, in my view, repay closer study by the Public Prosecutor.'

Barthel gave a noncommittal shrug. 'But not in the present context.'

'Quite apart from that,' Braun put in pityingly, 'Benzinger's a non-runner. He was down on the French Riviera with his family when the murder took place – at Antibes.'

'Who cares?' Messer was unimpressed. 'All that interests me is the fact that his name occurs repeatedly in the lady's log-book, but not in full – not as Benzinger. She shortened it to Benz.'

'Well?' drawled Braun. 'What does that signify?'

Messer paused for effect before replying. 'Only that if your chief exhibit contains the name Benzinger consistently abbreviated to Benz, the same may apply to the name Fein. Fein could be short for Feininger.'

Silence fell. The Public Prosecutor inspected his fingernails. The Chief Superintendent turned a searching gaze on his two subordinates, who avoided his eye. Messer smiled at Harald, and Harald, with something of an effort, smiled back.

Dürrenmaier addressed himself to Braun. 'Well, Superintendent, can the possibility be ruled out?'

'No, sir,' Braun replied, wincing a little, 'I suppose it can't.'

Barthel rose abruptly. 'Application for a warrant in the name of Harald Fein refused.'

Telephone conversation between Dr Barthel and Wilhelm Feininger, Member of the Federal Parliament, deputy chairman of the Finance and General Purposes Committee, joint deputy chairman of his parliamentary party, board member of the Olympic Consortium, director of several banks, Lufthansa, the South German Automobile Works and Air Bus International. After some introductory courtesies on both sides, the following exchange took place:

BARTHEL: My real reason for phoning you was to request some information. Your name has cropped up in the course of a police inquiry – just the name Feininger, without any closer identification.

FEININGER: In what context?

BARTHEL: That's the tricky part. It's to do with the murder of a lady who used to change partners with some frequency – for business reasons. She operated from 33 V-Strasse.

FEININGER: Are you saying I was involved with her?

BARTHEL: Not necessarily you – perhaps a namesake. There must be plenty of Feiningers in existence. This is a precautionary move, nothing more.

FEININGER: (after a lengthy pause, hoarsely but with dignity): Look, Barthel, you know a man in my position has enemies. Some of them are itching for a chance to frame me, and they'd probably succeed tomorrow if I didn't have friends I could rely on. Can I count on you in this instance?

BARTHEL: Need you ask? Just to be on the safe side, though, may I assume that you had nothing to do with what happened at 33 V-Strasse?

FEININGER: Nothing whatever. That doesn't preclude the

145

possibility that someone might try and incriminate me, but I'm sure you'd do your utmost to prevent it. I'm more than grateful.

Manfred Hirzinger, one of the seven or eight prominent Young Socialists on the Munich executive of the SPD, speaking about the Mayor:
. . . still enjoys our confidence but has forfeited our unqualified approval . . .
. . . questionable dealings in respect of the forthcoming Olympics . . . irresponsible distribution of vast sums to private business interests . . . at bottom, nothing less than the encouragement, if not actual promotion, of greed and profiteering in the purely capitalist sense . . .

From Detective-Superintendent Keller's notes:
I'm a PECD officer, not a bearer of evil tidings, but sometimes I take it upon myself to act as both. I did so in the case of Helga Fein's suicide.
My pet principle is this: don't break it to the next of kin direct – instead, make a careful detour, preferably by way of close relatives. In this instance I decided to approach Paul Plattner.
He kept me waiting for quite a while. When I was eventually shown in, he said something about pressure of work. His time was very limited, so would I kindly be brief.
I obliged. I said: 'Your granddaughter Helga Fein has been recovered from the Nymphenburg Canal. She's dead. Everything points to suicide.'
It was the first time I'd seen Paul Plattner and – I found myself hoping – the last. He was a model of his kind. Blue-jowled, self-assured, well-nourished, arrogant – in short, a challenge to the likes of me.
He did a double-take to begin with, so I said it again: 'She's dead.'
He stared at me after this revelation, then quailed and averted his head in silence for some moments.
'Not Helga too!' were his first words. 'As if he didn't have enough on his conscience already!'
'Who?' I asked.
Plattner didn't give me a straight answer. All he said was: 'He'll pay for this, damn him! The things that man has done to me . . .'

146

'What man?' I persisted.

'What's it to you?' he yelled. 'What do you want, anyway?'

'A little information, if you don't mind.'

'I've none to give, not to you or anyone. Clear out – leave me alone, blast you!'

He waved me to the door. I noticed that his hand was trembling.

Henri Messer patted his client gaily on the back as they emerged from Police Headquarters.

'Well, my friend, that disposes of one hurdle. A difficult one, too.'

'I'm tired,' Harald said. 'Besides, my dog's waiting for me.'

The lawyer didn't react. 'What's more, we're going to win. It's simply a question of agreeing on tactics.'

He steered Harald to a café in Theatinerstrasse five minutes from Police Headquarters. Messer asked for a black coffee, a double cognac and a bottle of mineral water. Harald ordered a half-bottle of champagne. 'Granted,' said the lawyer. 'As long as you're paying.'

'Talking about expense,' Harald said patiently, 'I don't care what it costs, but I'm not prepared to wash my family's dirty linen in public – not under any circumstances.'

'A noble sentiment,' Messer observed. 'By all means preserve your nobility of mind, Herr Fein. If there's any laundering to be done, I'll do it. After all, that's what I'm paid for.'

'You obviously see things from the legal angle. The human element doesn't seem to interest you.'

'The human element doesn't win cases, or not in general. Plattner knows that. He's declared war and we've got to fight back.'

'But that's precisely what I don't want. I can't resort to his methods. As for my divorce, when a marriage fails the responsibility isn't all on one side.'

'True,' Messer said. 'But the law deals in right or wrong, guilt or innocence, simple affirmatives or straightforward negatives. Shades of grey only blur the issue.'

'Look, Counsellor, my marriage may have been an unhappy one, but twenty years is a long time . . .'

'Litigation and sentimentality don't mix,' Messer said sternly.

'You'd stop at nothing, from the sound of it.'

'And you'd better give me a free hand if you want to come out of this with a shirt on your back.'

Harald massaged his forehead wearily. 'You mean I'll be beggared whatever happens?'

'Not at all. With my help you ought to emerge from this affair a rich man – in fact I'm counting on it. For a start, however, I'll need five thousand marks.'

'I might still raise it – just.'

'We'll use the money to buy off Maria Trübner, that maid of yours, and her boy-friend. That should persuade them to supply all the testimony we need – and that, in turn, will plug another leak in your hull.'

'What a repulsive idea!'

'Repulsive but customary. Also, I've taken the precaution of dropping a few hints to your former colleague Herr Jonas.'

'Why him?'

'Because he's the obvious candidate to succeed you. In every capacity.'

'If that's an aspersion on my wife, Herr Messer, I cannot and will not . . .'

'God Almighty!' The lawyer flung his arms in the air. 'Sentimental, naive, and a gentleman into the bargain. I wonder you've survived as long as you have. You're a born scapegoat, Herr Fein, but I'll save you in spite of yourself.'

Paul Plattner calls on his daughter Hilde Fein. His manner is grave, solemn and preoccupied.

PLATTNER: Get a grip on yourself, Hilde. I've some bad news for you.

HILDE: About Harald? Don't tell me it's all off! If you're asking me to take him back, Father, I can't bear it!

PLATTNER: It has nothing to do with him, not directly. It's Helga.

HILDE: What's she been up to this time? Harald has systematically ruined the child. She's capable of anything, and it's all his fault.

PLATTNER: I'm bound to agree. With a heavy heart, I need hardly add.

HILDE: Why, what's the matter?

148

PLATTNER: She's dead. She killed herself. As you say, it's all his fault. God help the man.

'I've been waiting for hours,' Jonas said. He was sprawled in the most comfortable chair in Harald's apartment, smiling in a patent endeavour to sweeten the atmosphere.

'What do you want?' Harald asked resentfully, leading Anton to his new sheepskin rug.

'I don't blame you for sounding fed up,' boomed Jonas. 'You're tired, you want some peace and quiet – a chance to recharge your batteries, fulfil your life's ambition and satisfy your creative urge. And what happens? People pursue you and make trouble for you – they even smash up your apartment.'

'How did you know?'

'I know more than you suspect, that's why I sympathize. Anyway, I'm ready to help.'

'At what price?' Harald paused in the middle of the room and stared at his visitor.

Jonas ignored Anton's growls. 'If you're prepared to be reasonable,' he said, 'we can kill two birds with one stone. You'd save yourself a hell of a lot of unpleasantness.'

'Come to the point.'

'Very well. You hand over the red folder. In return we guarantee you a lump sum – two years' salary, say – and a quick, painless divorce with no distasteful publicity. Equal apportionment of blame, no financial obligations on your side, equal access to the children.'

'Equal apportionment of blame, you said.'

'I did.'

'But that implies an admission of guilt on Hilde's part, which is absurd.'

'I'd volunteer to act as co-respondent.' Jonas closed his cold grey eyes for a few seconds, then continued: 'After all, why not? You were the one who encouraged me to become friendly with your family. Stranger things have happened.'

'You mean that you and my wife . . .'

'I could testify to that effect – only to save you a disagreeable session in court, naturally. Let's say I'm ready to sacrifice myself, but only if that red folder turns up. Otherwise . . .'

'What a conniving bastard you are,' Harald said levelly.

149

'Better that than a fool. And now listen carefully. I'll give you an hour to mull it over. You know my number. If you haven't called me by six I'll assume you're turning me down. Whatever happens then, you've only yourself to blame. However, I don't suppose it'll come to that.'

Detective-Superintendent Braun and Detective-Inspector Feldmann in conference at Police Headquarters:

BRAUN: The Fein case is getting hot. We'd better be prepared.

FELDMANN: But what about that tip of Messer's – the Fein-Feininger theory?

BRAUN: Just a red herring. Clever, mind you. I wouldn't have given him credit for it, but who cares? Facts are all we go by. Did you compare those times with Fein's movements, the way I told you?

FELDMANN: The 'Fein' entries in the murdered woman's diary have been checked against Harald Fein's desk diary at Plattner Construction. There's no obvious discrepancy. Fein was in Munich on all the days in question, not that it proves anything.

BRAUN: Your job is to collect information, Feldmann. I evaluate it, understand? All right, go on. Does he carry much money around with him?

FELDMANN: Up to a thousand marks. Five hundreds and ten fifties. It's a habit of his.

BRAUN: Gamblers, blackmailers and whores don't take cheques, they insist on cash. You see? We're getting somewhere at last. The next step is to concentrate even harder on anyone who's ever been connected with Fein. Colleagues, business associates, his doctor, his domestic servants – anyone he came into personal contact with. Draw up a list, and make sure it's complete.

FELDMANN: I'm already working on it. What about his next of kin?

BRAUN: I'll handle them.

FELDMANN: Whatever grounds for suspicion there are against Fein, some of them may point to other people as well. Pardon me for asking, Super, but is he our only target from now on?

BRAUN: Stop crowding me, Feldmann! Fein's like the first crack in a dam. If we want to bust the whole thing wide open we've got to concentrate on the weakest point.

'Everyone I meet wants something out of me,' Harald said. He stared suspiciously at Keller, who had sat down beside him. 'Now it's your turn.'

'How's Anton?' asked Keller. It was an unnecessary question, because the dog crawled from under the table, scrambled on to his lap and sat there, wagging his tail happily.

Harald smiled. 'Looks as if he was expecting you. Anton doesn't often fall for people.'

'Maybe it's more than I deserve,' Keller said, fondling the dog's ears.

They were sitting in a small restaurant in a side street between the Bayerischer Hof Hotel and the cathedral, a homely and respectable establishment with clean floors, scrubbed tables and a modestly priced menu. Excellent *Weisswürste* were served there eighteen hours a day. Anton's normal ration was a trio of these pallid but succulent sausages.

'Mind if we talk?' said Keller. 'About your family, if it wouldn't annoy you.'

'My family?' Harald reached for his glass. 'I'll tell you what a family is. It's a financial syndicate based on expediency. As soon as family ties lose their usefulness, you're struck off the register.'

'You're wrong,' Keller said. 'Everything leaves its mark. The woman you've lived with, the children who've entered your life and stayed – never long enough, unfortunately . . .'

'What would you know about the joys of parenthood? Do you have any children?'

'I did have – three of them. Two boys and a girl aged five, four and two. They were killed in one of the last air raids on Germany. My wife died too, Just four charred bodies, clinging tightly together. I identified them.'

'I'm sorry,' said Harald. 'I couldn't have known that.'

'My dear Herr Fein, how much do we really know about the people we live with or come into contact with every day? For that matter, how much do we really know about ourselves?'

Harald Fein's last birthday party, a celebration arranged by his wife Hilde and held in the restaurant of the Hotel Vier Jahreszeiten, Maximilianstrasse. Present: twelve people, including relatives and acquaintances close enough to pass for friends, among them Paul Plattner and Joachim Jonas. Several speeches were made.

PLATTNER: . . . sustained by mutual trust . . . all the sincerity in the world . . . gathered here in perfect harmony . . .

JONAS: Friendship is everything!

Toasts, embraces, kisses on both cheeks, displays of boundless esteem and affection.

But that was almost a year ago.

Keller looked down at the dog on his lap. 'If it isn't an impertinent question, are you fond of your daughter?'

'Helga? I'm devoted to her,' Harald said. 'What's more, if there's one person alive who's genuinely and sincerely devoted to me – not counting Anton – it's her.'

'Tell me,' Keller said, combing Anton's coat with his fingers, 'when did you last hear from her?'

'A few days ago, but why do you ask?' Harald was overcome by a mounting sense of unease. 'What are you driving at?'

Routine notes made by Werner Freudenfeld, senior assistant PECD officer at Police Headquarters, Munich. Subject: cadaver, female, found in the Nymphenburg Canal.

Hair pale blonde. Eyes hazel. Nose small and straight. Lips normal, lightly made up. Complexion fresh. Face oval. Ears of medium size.

Upper part of body moderately well developed. Breasts still immature, abdomen flat, thighs firm, legs smooth and lightly muscled. Feet slender, nails well tended.

Clothing: underpants, nylon, white, no soiling or staining of any kind. No bra. Trouser-suit, corded velvet, brown. Pullover, thin man-made fibre, matching trouser-suit. Leather boots marked Jourdain, Paris.

Preliminary assessment: putative suicide. Some bruises and abrasions on neck, back and legs (details appended), possibly sustained while jumping into the canal or drifting in same. Death estimated to have occurred roughly forty-eight hours prior to retrieval.

Keller raised his head and looked straight at Harald. 'My impression of you, Herr Fein, is that you're developing Job-like qualities. Are you prepared for a shock?'

'Not Helga!' Harald said in a choking voice. He buried his head in his hands.

'Your daughter's death was officially recorded eight hours ago. Your wife has been notified by your father-in-law. Didn't either of them think to tell you?'

Harald clasped the black briefcase tightly to his chest. Seeing nothing, hearing nothing, he staggered out of the restaurant with Anton, visibly bewildered, at his heels.

Outside in the narrow alleyway between Promenadeplatz and the cathedral, he tripped over an extended leg and fell headlong. As he lay there almost unconscious, with his face against the paving-stones, something struck the base of his skull.

Blood spurted from his neck, trickled through his hair and down his face, blinding him. He heard Anton bark. The barking dwindled to a series of whines and yelps and was swallowed up in the darkness.

The last thing Harald knew before he passed out was that someone grabbed his briefcase. His dog was no longer at his side. Boots thudded into his chest and stomach, and he lost consciousness.

Chapter Seven

From Detective-Superintendent Keller's notes:

Harald Fein tottered out, beside himself. Breathing hard, hands clasped over his briefcase, face pale and expressionless. Anton bounded after him excitedly.

I sat there, glass in hand, digesting the incident for thirty seconds – thirty seconds too long, as it turned out. Fein's reaction disturbed me, so I hurried after him.

Nearly a hundred yards away down the narrow side street I saw a figure lying on the ground. I knew it was Fein – it had to be. Two men were bending over him, kicking and beating his motionless form – in total silence, so it seemed – while a third stood watching.

I shouted 'Police! Halt or I fire!' It was only bluff, of course – I wasn't carrying a gun.

A moment later the alley was deserted except for Harald Fein, who lay spreadeagled on the sidewalk. I ran towards him.

Almost simultaneously, Anton scampered out of the gloom and leapt at me. He was limping, growling and trembling all over. I knelt down and gave him a reassuring hug. He nestled against me, his small body still shaking.

I bent over Fein and felt for his carotid. He was still alive. His mouth was wide open, almost as if he were screaming, but no sound emerged. Very gingerly, I rolled him over on his side so that he wouldn't choke on the blood flowing out of his mouth.

Then I sent for an ambulance and alerted the Emergency Squad. Harald Fein was admitted to the Right Bank Infirmary. I accompanied him as far as Emergency. So did Anton.

The same night:

Two new establishments opened, one restaurant with international cuisine, one private club. Also, at the Hermaphrodite, the first 'total striptease' ever presented in Munich – complete nudity with intimate views, frontal and posterior, illuminated by flesh-pink spotlights.

All the big names were there. The usual crowd, well-heeled and in high good humour, eager to see and be seen.

The new nightclub, entitled Black Flair, opened with a particular flourish. The mood was set by Alice, Monika and Rosemarie, who turned up in black hot-pants and nothing else. Günther, too, dressed entirely in black (slacks and turtle-neck). He had just come from the funeral of his uncle Franz – a fortunate coincidence which absolved him from the need to change.

'A night to end all nights!' wrote 'Argus'.

Meanwhile, at Police Headquarters:

Twelve muggings so far reported. Also, eight motor vehicles stolen, four break-ins, one resulting in a fatality, three persons seriously injured in eighteen road accidents of varying severity, two probable murders and five putative suicides. Average frequency of ambulance and patrol car calls: one every three minutes.

'A fairly quiet night,' commented the duty officer at Police Headquarters.

That night, one of Munich's buildings went up in flames, almost certainly as a result of arson.

The building in question 'happened' to be a Jewish old folks' home. Seven inmates, – i.e. Jews – were incinerated. Thirty years late, so to speak.

Official indignation was widespread. The most diligent inquiries were set in motion but came to nothing, and this despite rewards for information and a massive deployment of CID manpower. Final comment by one Munich newspaper: 'The motive behind this crime remains a mystery.'

Harald Fein, his head, chest and stomach heavily bandaged, recovered consciousness. The pain that engulfed him was dull, insistent, almost audible. He opened his eyes with an effort. The daylight seemed agonizingly bright, even though it was muted by greenish curtains.

It took him some time to realize where he was. He saw a magnolia-white hospital-room, curtained windows, an expanse of brown parquet floor and, near the door, a white-garbed figure regarding him intently.

'I must phone,' he said. The words were barely audible, but he felt as if he had shouted them.

'You'll do nothing of the kind,' said the nurse. 'No talking, no moving, no excitement. You've been through a bad time.'

'I have to telephone,' Harald said doggedly.

'I'll phone for you, if you insist. I was asked to contact two people when you came round, a Counsellor Messer and a Herr Keller. You can decide which one you want to call first.'

'I demand to be given a telephone!' Harald's voice rose to a shout and he tried to sit up.

The nurse forced him back on to the pillows. He hardly felt the brief stab of pain as the needle punctured his right arm. Almost instantly, he sank into a deep and lasting sleep, a world of darkness threaded with quivering strands of light.

Detective-Inspector Feldmann and Detective-Superintendent Keller, off the record:

FELDMANN: Fein's in hospital. They say he was beaten to a pulp.

KELLER: I know, but why come to me?

FELDMANN: Because you were there, or almost. I'm not badgering you on instructions from Superintendent Braun, sir. I want to know for my own satisfaction. Why was he beaten up and who did it?

KELLER: How should I know, my friend? There are several possibilities. He may have been a chance victim. On the other hand, he may have been set on deliberately.

FELDMANN: I'm beginning to feel sorry for the man.

KELLER: So am I, but emotions don't count in our trade. It's safer to stick to facts.

FELDMANN: Right, but which ones?

When Harald came round again several hours later there was a telephone on the small table beside his bed.

Panting with the effort, he picked up the receiver and asked the hospital switchboard to give him a number. He waited a few moments with his eyes closed. An unfamiliar voice answered, high-pitched, almost shrill. 'Fein residence.'

'Harald Fein here. I'd like to speak to my wife.'

Half a minute dragged by before the shrill voice made itself heard again. 'Frau Fein isn't available.' Then the line went dead.

Harald sank back against the pillows, still holding the receiver. He lay there exhausted until he heard the brisk voice of the switchboard operator.

'Are you still speaking?'

'No, please re-connect me.'

Another half-minute passed before the unfamiliar woman uttered her strident, impersonal 'Fein residence!'

When Harald again asked to speak to his wife, the response was gabbled so hurriedly it might have been memorized: 'Frau Fein instructs me to tell you not to pester her any more. She also instructs me to say that an application for an unlisted number has already been made, and that she's taken the precaution of changing all the outside locks.'

The woman hung up. Harald waited for the switchboard to come through. He asked to be connected yet again.

'Harald Fein here,' he said, almost gagging with fury. 'Shut up, whoever you are, and don't you dare hang up on me again. I demand to talk to my wife. Or, if she still refuses, my son Heinz. And tell her this: I'll force her to talk to me sooner or later – in court, if necessary!'

There was no answer, but the line did not go dead. A gentle humming sound drifted down the line, mingled with footsteps and a subdued murmur of voices. Harald felt the sweat erupt on his forehead.

Detective-Inspector Feldmann and Detective-Superintendent Braun:

FELDMANN: He was beaten up. Persons unknown, according to this report from the local station. The third such incident this week, and all in the same area. Why Fein, though?

BRAUN: I can't say I'm unduly surprised. That man is a victimologist's dream – he attracts trouble like a magnet. For the time being, we can safely leave the local boys to handle things. Simply note the incident and call it a day. There's plenty of time to sort out the implications, if any.

'So you're still alive.' The voice on the telephone was overlaid with mild sarcasm and not noticeably friendly. It belonged to Harald's son. 'To what do we owe the honour of your sudden interest, which Mother – your beloved wife – chooses to describe as harassment?'

'What exactly happened to Helga?' Harald asked.

'Your guess is as good as mine.' The boy's tone was suddenly hostile. 'Anyway, why bother to ask now? What happened to Helga happened three or four days ago – it's been in the papers for twenty-four hours. You're late with your condolences.'

'I couldn't get through any earlier. I'm in hospital.'

'Where, in the alcoholics' ward?'

'The night before last, just after I'd been told of Helga's death, I was attacked and beaten up – Anton too. I only came round this afternoon.'

Heinz sounded quite serious now. 'Are you sure you aren't imagining the whole thing? Mother says you're drinking again.'

'I'm in the Right Bank Infirmary. The ward sister can give you details of my injuries. So can the local police. Ask anyone you like, if you don't believe me.'

'But who attacked you and why? Did they steal anything? What were they after, your money or your life – or your brief-case?'

'That's unimportant, Heinz. Tell me about Helga.'

'They found her in the Nymphenburg Canal. She couldn't swim, as you know. You never taught her – or me, for that matter. They think it was suicide.'

'But why, Heinz? Why did she do it?'

'Mother's theory is that it was a sort of mental blackout caused by unrequited affection and loneliness – and all brought on by you. Grandfather puts it even more bluntly. He says you systematically drove Helga to kill herself by your coldness and lack of affection. Mental cruelty, he calls it.'

'No!' Harald could barely breathe. 'That's an infamous suggestion.'

'Then do something about it,' Heinz said brutally, and hung up.

From notes made by Henri Messer, attorney-at-law, after his first visit to Harald Fein at the Right Bank Infirmary:

I'm tempted to cut my losses and drop the case. Fein's stubborn silence baffles me.

For instance, he simply says he was attacked. He refuses to

speculate on who attacked him and why, though he does admit that his briefcase was taken.

QUERY: What was in the briefcase?

RESPONSE: How's Anton?

That's the way it goes. I told him that Anton was staying with Keller, which seemed to relieve him immensely. Next, he wanted to know if Anton had been hurt. I told him no, although Keller hadn't let me know. He merely sent word he was looking after the animal.

'He's quite fit,' I said.

'That's wonderful news,' Fein said happily.

QUESTION: I took the liberty of asking what your briefcase contained. I'm still waiting for an answer.

ANSWER: Blueprints for privately commissioned houses, or rather, rough designs and preliminary estimates. Three projects in all.

QUESTION: Why should anyone want those?

ANSWER: Perhaps they expected to find something different in the briefcase – a red folder, for example. I don't have it, but no one believes me.

QUESTION: Herr Fein, how much are you concealing from me?

ANSWER: A good deal, I'm afraid. How soon can I see Anton?

That just about did it. I was on the verge of abandoning the case altogether, but I resolved to defer my final decision until I'd spoken to Keller.

Dürrenmaier regarded Anton with surprise. 'What have you got there,' he asked Keller, 'a new recruit?'

'This dog,' Keller explained politely, 'answers to the name Anton. He's my guest, Chief Superintendent. I'm looking after him for a few days. I hope you don't mind. There's nothing in regulations which specifically bars dogs from police premises.'

'That's all right.' Anton, who seemed to have found favour with the chief superintendent, spotted the fact at once and began to wag his tail. 'What's his forte, tracking, drugs, or what?'

'Companionship,' Keller replied simply.

Dürrenmaier, courteous as ever, offered the PECD officer, plus dog, a privileged place beside his desk. 'My dear Keller,' he said,

'I hope you realize what a high regard I have for your professional ability.'

Keller gave a wry smile. 'I do indeed, sir. Such a high regard that you took me off Homicide and saved me from getting ulcers. Examining corpses is a nice peaceful occupation.'

'But Keller, old friend, you were just about to arrest a government minister.'

'And his deputy.'

'A rash step, however justified your suspicions were – but let's not dwell on that. As I already told you, you can take over a murder investigation any time you like. A very important one.'

'Braun's, you mean?'

Dürrenmaier gave a portentous nod. 'Braun's an outstanding detective in many ways, but he has his blind spots. Prejudice is one of them.'

'Are you asking me to keep an eye on his activities?' Keller asked, suddenly alert.

Dürrenmaier lost none of his courteous and confidential air. 'Let's put it this way. A man of your experience should find it easy to spot any undesirable developments early. And – in consultation with me – nip them in the bud.'

The chief superintendent looked first at Keller, then at Anton, who was lying snuggled against Keller's feet. It was an idyllic picture.

'What exactly do you propose, sir?'

'It's quite simple. You've already provided the opening we need.'

Dürrenmaier tapped a file on the desk in front of him. 'This is your PECD report on Helga Fein.'

'The seven-hundredth-and-sixteenth report this year, if my memory serves me. You've initialled all the others without a murmur. What's wrong with this one?'

'I was startled when I read the name Fein, so I studied it more closely than usual. It contains a couple of points that worry me a little. You too, judging by the way you stress them – or am I wrong?'

'You've always been good at reading between the lines, sir.'

'So I was right.' Dürrenmaier smiled. 'At first glance your report is perfectly consistent with suicide. However, one of the injuries you list is a wound on the back of the head.'

'Possibly caused by striking a blunt object when she jumped into the canal – a stone or a piece of timber.'

'But we can't entirely rule out the possibility that she was stunned by a blow before she entered the water?'

Keller eyed his superior officer with growing admiration. 'Nothing can be ruled out in our profession.'

'Quite so, and that's why you're going to do what you so obviously want to do.' Dürrenmaier's expression became sternly official. 'Superintendent, I authorize you to re-examine this case in even greater detail. You can have an entirely free hand, but report to me direct every day.'

'Isn't there a possibility that my investigation may overlap with Superintendent Braun's?'

'I'm counting on it.'

'Wouldn't it be wiser to send me on leave, preferably until my retirement date?'

'We'll discuss that later. For the time being you're indispensable. Remember, the CID's reputation may be at stake.'

Munich had always been the home of diametrical opposites: solid civic responsibility and a mania for destruction, beer-garden *Gemütlichkeit* and savage belligerence, staid traditionalism and revolutionary insurgence.

Radicalism, often at any price, was fostered by a massive display of late capitalist phenomena. The same firms' names leapt to the eye, clamorously obtrusive, wherever self-styled human achievements took shape – in the suburbs, in the city centre, on the Olympic site.

Chain stores and supermarkets, drug companies and airlines, automobile manufacturers and breweries – all competed for media attention with the consent of the city fathers, who were bound by their ordinances and had little choice but to rubber-stamp this plethora of commercial pollution. The social revolutionaries raised vociferous protests. They also demanded free transport, electricity, water and gas, expropriation of privately owned land, and communes on a district, street and house basis.

The Mayor called these ideas impracticable and claimed that their cost would exceed the city's revenue many times over. His opponents inside the party promptly declared that a man so devoid of consistent socialist thinking ought to resign immediately.

Voiced by a bare dozen branch representatives, these demands had been framed by two hundred delegates out of Munich's twelve thousand registered Social Democrats – yet the Mayor had been directly elected by almost eighty per cent of the voting population.

His enemies, both inside and outside his own party, yearned for a scandal big enough to rock the foundations of City Hall. Their wish was on the point of fulfilment.

'My God, Harald, how *ghastly* you look!' Melanie Weber hurried to Harald's bedside. 'What on *earth* have you been doing to yourself?'

'Nothing. Someone else did it.'

'But they've bandaged you up like a *mummy*, darling. They might at least have made you look *presentable*. I'll speak to the nurse.'

'If the sight of me offends you, Melanie, you only have to shut your eyes. Or go away.'

'Don't be flippant, darling,' she said indulgently. 'I've a feeling you've changed. It isn't just the bandages – you've changed *inside*, I mean.'

'Sorry to disappoint you.'

'Disappoint me? You?' Every gun in her arsenal of cosmetic beauty opened fire. 'You don't know me, darling, but you will – at last!'

Melanie Weber to her dear friend Hilde Fein, an hour later:

. . . wouldn't believe how he's changed. From every point of view – *physically*, apart from anything else. Face like a balloon, bloodshot eyes, forehead simply *bristling* with stitches. They say he's bruised all over . . .

. . . obviously drinking again, I could tell from the way his hands shook. He probably got involved in a brawl after leaving some bar or other, and they robbed him – it happens all the time . . .

. . . but these changes in his character, darling . . . it's *too* depressing . . . always used to have his own brand of humour, but *now* . . . so much of what he says sounds cynical and aggressive . . .

Did he ask about Helga? Not a *word*, darling – not even about his dog. Nor about you, naturally.

'What happened to Helga?' asked Harald.
    'I don't know, not in detail.' Melanie studied her hands.
    'Tell me what you've heard.'
    'I only know what it says in the papers.'
    'How about Hilde – what did she tell you?'
    'Nothing, darling. Our links are virtually severed. Because of you.'
    Harald ignored the last remark. 'Look, if you genuinely want to do something for me, find out what really happened to Helga. Get the details from Hilde.'
    'Would you like me to look after your dog too?'
    'No need, thanks, he's in good hands.'
    'How *nice*.'

Information supplied by Dr Huber of the Right Bank Infirmary, some weeks later:
    Harald Fein was a typical product of late-night violence. I examined and treated him. No surgery was required, though his injuries were quite severe. His powers of resistance seemed strangely low in a man of his age and physical constitution.
    He was the sort of patient who immediately arouses one's personal sympathy – resigned and uncomplaining. He made no demands on the staff and followed our instructions to the letter.
    His patience was all the more remarkable considering the stream of visitors who forced themselves on him. One of them was Messer, his lawyer. I also recall a woman named Weber, who was rather eccentric and tried to lecture me on cosmetic surgery. Finally, there was a man with an extraordinary-looking mongrel.
    I made it clear to Herr Fein that he needn't have any visitors at all if he didn't choose to, but he merely replied that some people had to be faced sooner or later, so why not now?

'We must get you out of here,' Melanie said in a voice of loving concern. 'Otherwise you'll miss the boat.'
    'What boat?'
    'You must get back to work, darling, tackle your legal problems,

spend more time with me. I could nurse you far better in your apartment.'

'All I need is rest, the doctor says. I'm only interested in knowing what happened to Helga – and how Anton is. Oh yes, and I'd like a word with Heinz. Other than that, I'm terribly tired. I could sleep forever.'

'You'll soon get over that, darling, with me around. I'll engage a private nurse for you. Also, I'll try and contact that son of yours. Anton can come and visit you when you're back in your own apartment – the hospital won't admit him.'

Harald sat up. 'That,' he said, 'is a point.'

'You mustn't be so *lethargic*, darling. Here, I've brought you a couple of letters. They may be important.'

First letter, from Max Emanuel Wagner, owner of a large brewery and two four-star hotels, president of various civic associations, member of the Olympic Tourist Committee:

. . . regretfully point out that I have not entered into any firm commitment with you regarding the design of a new house . . . preliminary discussions of an informative nature only . . . as such, no binding force whatsoever . . . particularly as I do not, in the foreseeable future, intend . . .

Harald's comment:

Max Wagner, a prominent and universally respected figure, has close business links with Plattner Construction.

Second letter, from Mehlinger & Kolbe, specialists in tax accountancy:

. . . regret to advise you, pursuant to a letter just received from Plattner Construction (copy to the appropriate Inland Revenue authority) that your liability in respect of income tax has substantially increased.

. . . are informed that you have, in the past year, drawn DM60,000 in director's fees, not DM30,000 as at first stated . . . entails not only the full and immediate discharge of your indebtedness to Plattner Construction, but also an additional tax liability in the sum of DM18,520.53, payable within fourteen days . . .

Harald's comment:

Mehlinger & Kolbe, a large and reputable firm of tax account-

164

ants, have handled Plattner's business and family tax problems for almost twenty years, working on a fat retainer.

Keller shook his head reprovingly. 'This is hardly standard procedure, Herr Messer. I don't like being bearded in my den.'

'Forgive me, Superintendent,' Messer said politely. 'I'm quite aware that policemen's homes are off-limits to the general public, lawyers included.'

'Then why are you here?'

'Let's say I came to inquire about Anton's welfare.'

'He's fine, all things considered.' Keller gestured to the sofa, where the dog lay full length.

There was a pause. Then Keller said: 'Why did you really come?'

Messer glanced round the policeman's small sitting-room before replying. The shelves that occupied most of the wall space were overcrowded with books, mainly of a technical nature.

'I came to ask your help.'

'I see,' Keller said with a smile. 'So we're back on the subject of Harald Fein.'

'Precisely. To tell the truth, I'm getting nowhere.'

'Who's stopping you?'

'A lot of people, among them Superintendent Braun.'

'That's understandable – your minds don't work the same way. You're a first-class defence lawyer, Herr Messer, but how much do you know about routine detection?'

'I'm learning all the time. I've even ploughed my way through the manual of criminal investigation published by the Federal Crime Bureau. I believe you contributed to it.'

'Not a bad book in spite of the gaps. I'm working on a PECD manual now. It should become a standard work, with luck.'

'I'm sure it will, but pardon me for reverting to my main worry of the moment. The fact is, my client virtually refuses to work with me.'

'Yes, he's a complicated customer.'

'I'd prefer to call him suicidally unco-operative. If you can't suggest a way of handling him, no one can.'

Gist of a psychiatrist's report provided by Professor Geisenberger:
   . . . several opportunities to conduct in-depth conversations

with Harald Fein . . . initial reserve yielded to a growing acceptance of my good intentions . . . ultimately spoke with complete candour, or almost . . .

. . . transpired that, due probably to a series of grave personal disappointments, he tended to be extremely withdrawn and reticent, at least where his private life was concerned . . .

. . . had once trusted everyone around him, almost unhesitatingly, and expected his faith to be returned with an equal lack of hesitation . . . hoped in this way to be able to live his own life, secure and undisturbed . . .

. . . not what might generally be termed a sociable type . . . extremely sensitive and diffident, most reluctant to make pronouncements, favourable or unfavourable . . . easily hurt, rather naive and unsophisticated . . . bound to be disillusioned sooner or later . . .

'Fein's relationship with his dog is pretty well all I know about him,' Keller said. 'It's a distinct point in his favour.'

'The man's a human seismograph – he reacts to every little tremor. I've no idea how to help him, have you?'

'Come now, Herr Messer, don't pretend you've given up. You're only half-way through the case, and I suspect that your present requirement is an experienced detective. You're trying to rope me in, aren't you?'

'Let's say, for the sake of someone whose dog you've taken a fancy to.'

Anton had jumped on to Keller's lap. 'If you want to get anywhere with a man like Braun,' he mused, 'you'll have to beat him at his own game.'

'How?'

'Try and arrange an on-the-spot confrontation with Penatsch at 33 V-Strasse, having first talked Fein into making himself available. I'm sure Braun will play ball.'

'You bet he will,' said Messer. 'He's holding a fistful of trumps, that's why. His pet witness knows the building like the back of his hand. Fein has never set foot inside the place. Braun will naturally take advantage of the fact.'

Keller smiled to himself as he scratched Anton behind the ears. 'You're missing the point. What matters is, you'll have a chance to inspect Penatsch at close range. With your courtroom experience you may be able to shake his story by using what you know about him.'

'Which isn't much.'

'Which is plenty, Herr Messer, including a few items Braun himself may be ignorant of. I doubt if he thought it was worth rummaging through the files.' Keller savoured the lawyer's sudden look of surprise. 'Here, take a look at this.'

Messer took the closely typewritten sheet of paper which Keller held out to him, a semi-official document headed 'Penatsch, Adolf'. Messer marvelled at the thorough but concise way in which it summarized the fruits of Keller's inquiries.

'Great stuff,' he said at length. 'Am I at liberty to use it?'

'You are, Herr Messer. That's to say, memorize all the points you think useful. You can even make notes, but don't forget – I never gave you a written document of any kind.'

'So I'm privy to official information but forbidden to say where it came from? All right, I agree, but is it a hundred per cent reliable?'

'As reliable as police records ever are. It's a digest of reports from stoolies and undercover men. But remember, it's only background material – it wouldn't carry much weight in a court of law.'

'I follow,' Messer said gleefully. 'A mixed hand, you mean. It all depends how I play it.'

Keller smiled. 'You're learning fast.'

'With a teacher like you? Who could fail?'

Excerpts from a tape-recorded telephone conversation between Dr Barthel, Public Prosecutor, and Detective-Superintendent Braun:

BARTHEL: This is only a general investigation, Superintendent. How far have you got with the V-Strasse case?

BRAUN: Not much further, sir. Harald Fein is still our best bet.

BARTHEL: Anyone else in view?

BRAUN: No one definite.

BARTHEL: I'm rather relieved to hear that, Superintendent. However, should you by any remote chance find it necessary to delve into the movements and activities of a public figure, – from the world of politics, for example – please notify me at once.

'You refused to see me several times.' There was no hint of

reproach in Hermann Abendroth's voice. 'Knowing you, I'm sure you only did it out of consideration for me.'

'You know me,' Harald said. 'A pity you didn't know me better.'

Abendroth lowered himself into the visitor's chair beside Harald's bed. He had a lean, narrow face threaded with a fine tracery of wrinkles, but his high-domed forehead looked blandly smooth by contrast. He was forty-six, and an almost exact contemporary of Harald's.

'Two or three years ago,' he said slowly, 'you let our friendship cool off. I could guess your motives but I wasn't in a position to discuss them, not then.'

'And now you want to make up for lost time?'

'Pretty late in the day, you mean? Well, I'm hoping it isn't too late.'

'So you know the truth.' Harald closed his eyes.

Abendroth nodded. 'Your side of it, but you obviously don't know mine.'

'I'm grateful to you for coming, Hermann, but I can't accept your help. It's time I told you why we reached the parting of the ways – why there was no alternative.'

'Let me say it for you,' Abendroth urged. 'It may come easier from me.'

'No, Hermann, it's my job.' Harald's voice shook slightly as he went on: 'Plattner kept prodding me to find out about your advance plans for Olympic subways and approach roads. I refused at first. Then I gave in – anything to escape being pressured by Plattner, nagged by my wife, badgered by people like Jonas.

'During that last private encounter of ours you let me see your plans. In confidence, between friends. Like a lot of architects, I'm blessed with an almost photographic memory.'

'Yes, Harald. It didn't take me long to realize that.'

'But you never thought I'd be capable of doing what I did. I reconstructed your lay-out from memory for Plattner, who evaluated it in his own way. Afterwards, I couldn't look you in the eye any more. No friend would have done what I did.'

'No,' Abendroth protested, 'it wasn't the way you think.'

'You trusted me and I betrayed you.'

'No, you're wrong.'

'Thanks to me, Plattner became party to your plans ahead of

time and made millions as a result. It's a fact, Hermann. You can'
wish it out of existence.'

'Your version of the truth isn't the whole truth, Harald. The
plans Plattner extracted from you weren't my final plans. I
modified them.'

'After my last visit to you?'

'Shortly after. I altered them – drastically – because I lost faith
in their merits. The details you gave Plattner didn't correspond
with my original lay-out.'

'But they did!'

'That was coincidental. The details you supplied may genuinely
have matched the official scheme which was published later on,
but the lay-out wasn't mine. It was the work of two urban-
planning experts brought in from Frankfurt and Berlin.'

Harald shook his head. 'It's the intention that matters. I didn't
realize till now the full extent of what I did to you – of my guilt.'

'Forget it. You've got enough on your mind without brooding
about that.'

'It's dogged me for years, Hermann. I was sickened by the
thought that I'd betrayed a friend, and not only betrayed him but
jeopardized his career. I couldn't concentrate any more, I started
to drink. I despised myself.'

'Good God, a word of explanation between friends would have
been enough.'

'It wasn't as simple as that. You're forgetting Plattner. My
reconstruction of your plans for the Olympic approach roads
became his trump card. He threatened to break you if I made
trouble for him.'

'He couldn't do that.'

'But he could try. He could fling plenty of mud and some of it
would stick.'

'Let him.'

'No, it's my responsibility. There's something else on my
conscience now. I forced you to give up your original plans, and
they were good ones. They were the best things you'd ever done,
and you had to hand them over to others. You gave them up
because you had to, for both our sakes.'

Abendroth shook his head. 'You're overcomplicating things.'

'Nothing can undo what I did,' Harald said. 'You were my
friend – the only real friend I ever had,' he added quietly.

'I still am your friend, that's why I'm here now. Tell me how I can help.'

'I only know how I can help you.' Harald spoke with grim determination. 'I'm not going to stir up a hornets' nest. I refuse to jeopardize your reputation, so please let me do what I have to do.'

A government reception held in honour of 'personalities from the world of commerce and industry'. 'Argus' of the Morgenzeitung, *commenting thereon:*

. . . the great hall, dazzlingly illuminated by crystal chandeliers and dominated by the Bavarian coat of arms . . . a number of prominent figures . . .

There followed the usual list, complete with ranks and titles. It included, apart from the provincial premier himself, two ministers, four state secretaries, two dozen members of the lower house, five senators, a deputy mayor, some merchant bankers, and senior executives representing insurance companies, an automobile works, an electronics and weapons development group, two oil refineries, three trucking firms, five major construction companies, etcetera. Roughly two hundred and fifty persons in all.

Two of the five big-time building contractors were sharing the same table, to wit, Paul Plattner and Clemens Duhr of Duhr Concrete, Duhr Haulage, Duhr Construction, Duhr Civil Engineering, Duhr Earthmoving Machinery Inc. They appeared to be enjoying their night out.

PLATTNER: Strictly between you and me, I've got the East-Exit West-Access project pretty well buttoned up. It just so happens that I own most of the proposed route.

DUHR: Congratulations.

PLATTNER: Save some congratulations for yourself, Clem. I need a firm of your calibre to split the action with.

DUHR: Why not? We've always worked well together in the past.

PLATTNER: We certainly have, but there's a proviso. They tell me you're planning to build yourself a new house – three million marks' worth, so the rumour runs. I'd be sorry if the commission went to Harald Fein.

DUHR: But he's your son-in-law.

PLATTNER: He used to be. First he abused my trust and now he's in trouble with with police.

DUHR: In that case, rest easy. I wouldn't think of having a man like that design my house. You can count on me.

Lights burned on the landing of No. 33 V-Strasse, although it was broad daylight. Adolf Penatsch, the janitor, had seen to that.

Henri Messer looked more than usually cheerful, unlike his client, who had been allowed to leave his sick-bed for two hours and was standing around forlornly. Penatsch was the focus of attention. Detective-Superintendent Braun, accompanied by Detective-Inspector Feldmann, seemed to have high hopes of his star witness.

'Right, Penatsch,' said Braun. 'Where were you when you saw this man?'

'Four or five steps down. He was standing outside the girl's door, pounding on it and yelling.'

Braun turned to Harald. 'Kindly take up your position, Herr Fein.'

Harald had put on his raincoat, as instructed, also a brown hat. He went and stood immediately in front of the door but made no move to knock.

'That settles it,' Messer exclaimed. 'Anyone standing outside the door must have had his back to the landing light. The witness couldn't have seen his face.'

'But I did,' Penatsch said quietly. 'He swung around, perhaps because he heard me coming. I'm positive it was Herr Fein.'

'Take it easy,' Messer told him. 'There are three factors involved here, Herr Penatsch. The stairs, the door and the light source.'

Penatsch frowned. 'What's that supposed to mean?'

'Don't let them fool you,' Braun interposed quickly. 'They're trying to confuse you, and here's how. If Herr Fein was standing outside the door, you couldn't have seen his face. If he heard you coming and turned round, he'd have looked down the stairs but not into the light, get it?'

'In that case,' Penatsch said, 'I can't have expressed myself correctly. The fact is, he looked all round – and the light shone on his face.'

Braun gave a vigorous nod and glared at Messer. 'Any more questions, Herr Messer?'

'Yes, one more. Tell me, Herr Penatsch, are you absolutely positive you haven't made a mistake?'

'Absolutely. I've already made several statements to these gentlemen. It's all down in writing.'

'Yes, but mistakes do happen, don't they?' Messer edged closer to Penatsch and bared his teeth in an amiable smile.

'Plenty of times.' Penatsch sounded almost flippant. 'We were always saying it.'

Messer pounced. 'Where, in prison?'

'That's enough,' Braun said. 'Kindly keep your insinuations to yourself, Herr Messer. Far be it from me to teach you the law, but a witness's previous convictions don't detract from the validity of his evidence, so stop trying to browbeat this man.'

Messer's smile persisted. 'Wherever you heard the saying, Herr Penatsch, wouldn't you agree that a person's visual impressions needn't necessarily accord with reality – just as he may be mistaken about what he hears?'

'Perhaps, Herr Messer,' Braun said superciliously, 'you'd be good enough to translate your question into plain language.'

'With pleasure. I can quote you a case I heard of recently. Just over three years ago, a convict in a penitentiary swore that a fellow-prisoner – his cell-mate – had admitted being an accessory to murder.'

The relevant entry in Detective-Superintendent Keller's notes, to which Henri Messer had access:

Penatsch, Adolf Paul, October–November 1968, serving a term in Stadelheim prison. Recruited to spy on his fellow-prisoner Rudolf Bleichert, who was remanded on suspicion of complicity in the murder of a dentist, a charge which he consistently denied.

Bleichert alleged to have admitted in Penatsch's presence that he had become infatuated with a woman named Gruhner and been used by her. Penatsch made a sworn statement to this effect.

'A statement,' Messer continued patiently, 'which later turned out to be demonstrably false. The man alleged to have confessed was entirely innocent and could not have been involved in the

172

crime. His fellow-prisoner eventually conceded that he must have misheard. Now do you see what I mean about mistakes?'

Penatsch had shrunk away from his inquisitor with an air of dismay and was looking anywhere but at Braun, who stiffened like a beast about to spring. Harald sat down on the top step with Feldmann hovering over him.

'What are you getting at, Herr Messer?' asked Braun.

'Nothing specific – as yet.' The lawyer continued to gaze searchingly at Penatsch. 'I'm simply pointing out a couple of things to your witness. I hope he's beginning to take them in. Are you, Herr Penatsch?'

'Well, yes, if you want a straight answer. Nothing's a hundred per cent guaranteed, naturally.' Penatsch was still looking at no one in particular. 'All I can say is, I acted in good faith – always have. It may have been Herr Fein. Then again, it may not. I couldn't be absolutely sure . . .'

'Shut up!' Braun snapped. 'We won't get anywhere like this. The show's over for today.'

Detective-Superintendent Braun and Detective Chief Superintendent Dürrenmaier, immediately after the foregoing episode:

BRAUN: Things can't go on this way, sir.

DÜRRENMAIER: Things go on whether we like it or not, Braun. What's worrying you now?

BRAUN: It's my star witness in the Fein case . . .

DÜRRENMAIER: Permit me to correct you – there isn't any Fein case. You're investigating a murder – still unsolved, I regret to say – so kindly refrain from prejudging the issue. And now tell me, what's the matter with this so-called star witness of yours?

BRAUN: It's that lawyer, Messer. What annoys me is, he's operating with information obtained from police files.

DÜRRENMAIER: Ah, files, files! There must be millions of them tucked away in scores of places – the Federal Crime Bureau, the provincial crime bureaux, regional Police Headquarters, and heaven knows where else. Anyone can get hold of files – real estate agents, property developers, finance companies – so why not a lawyer?

BRAUN: But the facts he's quoting can only have been lifted from confidential police records.

DÜRRENMAIER: Do you have any definite proof?

BRAUN (reluctantly): No.

DÜRRENMAIER: In that case, Braun, don't jump to conclusions.

Helga Fein was buried on a day charged with the mellow beauty of early autumn. Munich had awoken to yet another radiant dawn, and its cemeteries were flooded with sunlight.

The cemeteries of Munich had once, only a few decades earlier, been situated on the fringes of the city, where houses were low and gardens small. Now, the metropolis had not only sprawled to meet the cemeteries but extended beyond them, engulfing and slowly constricting them between slab-like buildings of increasing height. Graveyards had been metamorphosed into city centres of the dead. Economically speaking, interment was becoming a luxury.

Today's tally of funerals was considerable, especially at the East Crematorium, where business was brisk. No less than two dozen clients were neatly incinerated there between 9 a.m. and 4 p.m.

Even now, all Munich's citizens were guaranteed a grave. One of the freshly dug holes was reserved for Helga Fein.

From Detective-Superintendent Keller's notes:

Helga Fein's funeral was preceded by a certain amount of official, administrative and ecclesiastical desk-warfare, and most of the débris landed on me.

It all boiled down to this. My PECD report, duly approved by the police surgeon, contained the word 'suicide', which created technical problems and brought discreet objections from the church authorities. Plattner had planned an unostentatious but suitable Catholic ceremony, and the reference to suicide was a fly in the ointment.

Thanks to some officious manipulator of red tape, the whole matter was again referred to Police HQ – and to me, as the officer responsible – via the municipal authorities, the medical council and the archiepiscopal secretariat. And I, without a murmur, added the following rider to my original report: 'The possibility of accidental death cannot be ruled out. Signed: Keller, Detective-Superintendent.'

174

I couldn't have known it at the time, of course, but it was my last official act as a serving police officer.

Helga Fein's body, encased by an oak coffin trimmed with silver, lay in the cemetery chapel.

Paul Plattner, as head of the family, had decreed: 'Next of kin only. Public expressions of sympathy declined with thanks. Obituary notice and funeral announcement to be published subsequently.'

At 1.45 p.m. – the ceremony was scheduled to start at 2 p.m. – Herr Plattner and his immediate relatives, Hilde and Heinz, were chauffered to the cemetery in Plattner's Mercedes 600. The only outsider to attend was Joachim Jonas, who arrived in his own car, a scarlet Porsche.

Jonas had reached the scene a few minutes before Plattner and was waiting for him at the main entrance. Plattner leant forward and spoke out of the car window.

'Have you made sure no one will interrupt the proceedings – the funeral, I mean?'

Jonas nodded. 'It's all taken care of.'

Matthäus Palmbrecher, senior administrator of the cemetery:
It wasn't one of your run-of-the-mill interments – I distinctly recall a number of unusual features. For one, there was a mass of paperwork. Suicide or accidental death, family plot or individual grave, etcetera. It took up a lot of my time, I can tell you.

The burial registration number was 71/364.

The day before the funeral I was presented with a rather odd request by someone called Jonas, who turned out to be acting on behalf of Herr Plattner. He asked me if there were any plans to cordon off the graveyard, and, if so, who was responsible – cemetery attendants, security guards or the police.

I was taken aback, to put it mildly. This is a garden of rest, I told him. What was he afraid of?

Forcible intrusion by undesirable elements, he replied. Being members of one of Munich's most prominent and influential families, the deceased's next of kin were anxious to avoid an embarrassing scene.

It turned out that Herr Jonas was referring to the 'nominal father' of the dead girl, as he put it. The presence of Herr Harald

Fein would be unwelcome, so he must be denied access to the cemetery. I naturally refused to entertain such an idea.

A number of problems arose in consequence, especially when the man with the mongrel turned up.

Plattner gestured to his daughter and grandson to walk on ahead. His eyes narrowed as he gazed around the cemetery before turning back to Jonas.

'So you've taken precautions,' he said. 'Good. I couldn't stand the sight of him, not at a time like this.'

'I've posted two reliable men just outside the main entrance, the No. 2 Depot gateman and a foreman who has the firm's interests at heart. If Fein tries to inflict his presence on us they know what to do.'

Plattner nodded gravely. 'I want this to be a simple, dignified, reverent occasion.'

So saying, he followed his daughter and grandson to the door of Chapel No. 1, where he doffed his hat. It was as though he had worn it solely to be able to remove it.

Meanwhile, at the cemetery's main gate, a man had appeared. He looked like an old age pensioner exercising his dog. It was Keller, closely escorted by Anton.

Keller paused and took stock of his surroundings. Anton sat, his head brushing the policeman's right leg. They both looked expectant.

From the gate, which afforded a good view, Keller inspected the cemetery, the chapel, the Plattner family plot and its mound of newly turned soil. Everything looked appropriately funereal with the exception of one small point which struck him as unusual. Two men were standing just outside the gate, like sentries. Anton caught their scent and started to growl.

Alerted by the sound, the men stared at Keller. They were a tough, resolute-looking pair. Keller had a feeling he'd seen them before somewhere, if only for a fleeting moment.

A taxi drove up and Harald got out. Anton rushed to meet him, whining, yelping, squirming, wagging his entire body.

Harald knelt in the dust beside the cemetery gate and hugged Anton, wincing because the effort hurt him. His doctor had reluctantly granted him another two hours' leave of absence.

176

Keller watched the ecstatic reunion with a smile. Most of the dogs that crossed his path seemed to suffer from unrequited affection.

'Anton's fond of you,' he said.

As he spoke, the dog detached itself from Harald and trotted back, paused at Keller's feet, sat, and gazed up at him.

Harald shook hands with Keller. 'He's fond of you too. I can't tell you what a relief it is to know you're looking after him.'

'It's been a pleasure,' Keller said. 'You'd better hurry – there isn't much time. I'll wait for you here with Anton.'

'Thanks,' said Harald, and headed for the entrance.

The two men barred his path. One of them, the foreman, said: 'Shove off, you. No admittance.' He said it quite politely.

Harald stared at him in disbelief. 'What did you say?'

'You're not wanted,' the foreman amplified. 'Herr Plattner's orders.'

Harald shook his head. He glanced back at Keller and saw that the policeman was already on his way to join him. Anton, growling again, had bared his teeth and was straining at his collar.

Keller shortened Anton's leash and approached the two sentries. He studied them closely while Anton lunged furiously at them. 'Steady, old fellow,' he said to the dog, and to the two men: 'Don't be foolish. Stand aside.'

'You keep out of this!' said the foreman. His voice rose abruptly. 'We don't like people butting in, so watch out.'

Keller turned to Harald, barely restraining Anton. 'Herr Fein, do you by any chance know these two muscle-men?'

Harald nodded. 'This one's Rogalski, a foreman with Plattner Construction. The other's Pollock, gateman at a supply depot, also employed by the company.'

'So we work for Herr Plattner,' said Rogalski, hands on hips. 'So what?'

'I work for the law,' Keller announced in a growl that rivalled Anton's. He produced his credentials and thrust them at each man in turn. Three seconds later he snapped his wallet shut and pocketed it. 'Keller's the name. Detective-Superintendent Keller.'

Rogalski and Pollock looked impressed. 'We weren't to know that.'

'Well you do now. And kindly note this: any person who

without due authority seeks forcibly to deny another person access to a public place, such as a cemetery, is guilty of threatening behaviour and liable, on conviction, to a minimum of six months' imprisonment.'

'I don't know what you're talking about,' Rogalski said, edging away from the entrance. Pollock followed close behind. 'We were only advising Herr Fein not to make trouble, the way Herr Jonas asked us to. That's all there was to it.'

'You're forgetting something,' Keller told them, with a glance at Anton. 'Our dog doesn't like you. I wonder why.'

Sylvester Nebunzahl, Catholic priest:
I don't know why I should have been chosen to officiate at that particular funeral, but I was assured that was an honour – that Herr Plattner was a practising Catholic and a highly respected man. My task was to say a prayer over the coffin and accompany it to the graveside. Another prayer, this time silent, then a benediction.

After I'd said my piece in the chapel and invited the next of kin to pay their last respects, both doors were opened and our little procession moved off. That was when the first incident occurred. Herr Plattner shouted 'Halt!' and nodded grimly at one of his fellow-mourners.

The latter – a Herr Jonas, as I later discovered – sprang to life while the rest of us stood there in shocked silence. He hurried up to a man who was barring our route – his face was covered with bandages – and addressed him in a fierce whisper. Eventually the man stood aside to let us pass. 'Carry on!' shouted Herr Plattner.

That was the first distressing incident, but there were more to come – as, for instance, when one of the mourners – a young man – ostentatiously left the family circle at the very moment of burial.

Heinz Fein turned his back as Helga's coffin was lowered into the grave. His worried mother laid a restraining hand on his sleeve, but he threw it off and went to join his father.

Harald, standing among the gravestones some distance away, said nothing at first, merely nodded. Heinz walked up to him and stared for some moments, also in silence. Then he stationed himself beside Harald as though waiting, willing him to do something.

'I had to come,' Harald murmured, looking across at his daughter's grave.

Heinz gave him a quick sidelong glance. 'Well, that's a step in the right direction. You weren't invited but you came – you wouldn't be stopped. Why aren't you over there at the graveside?'

Harald ignored the question. 'I loved her, you know that.'

'I believe you, Father. The trouble is, you never got to know her well enough.'

'I didn't want to intrude. I wanted her to live her own life.'

'And it ended here.'

'You're always making veiled accusations, Heinz. It's a waste of breath. I've been accusing myself for years, far more bitterly than you ever could.' Harald's eyes never left his daughter's grave. He gazed at it with a sort of longing. 'These last few days have been a torment. I've been asking myself over and over again, how could it have come to this? Whatever my failings, she shouldn't have done it – it's too cruel.'

'But it's a fact,' Heinz said firmly. 'She's being buried over there, and that's where you ought to be standing right now. Instead, you're waiting on the sidelines. As usual.'

A surprisingly harsh note entered Harald's voice. 'Do you know something? Just now I felt a crazy impulse to chase those people away and take their place at the graveside. If anyone belongs there, I do.'

'That's just what you should have done. I'd have backed you up. Why didn't you?'

'At Helga's grave – on this day of all days?' Harald shook his head. 'This is a cemetery, Heinz, not a boxing ring.'

'But it's time you fought back. You'll have to sooner or later.'

'I will,' Harald said, almost inaudibly, 'but not over Helga's grave.'

From Detective-Superintendent Keller's notes:

Not all dead bodies are dead in every sense of the word. Sometimes it takes a death to galvanize people and release their pent-up emotions. It certainly did in Helga Fein's case.

Her funeral was quite a performance, and I had a seat in the dress circle. Leaning against one of the gate posts with Anton beside me, I saw Heinz Fein confront his father. Harald Fein, who was still rocky from his beating, seemed to shrink as they talked.

But the climax came a few minutes later.

Plattner sprinkled three handfuls of earth on the open grave. A brief nod to Jonas accorded him the same privilege.

Then Plattner offered the bereaved mother his arm and escorted her back to the waiting Mercedes 600. His recalcitrant grandson was already sitting inside, next to the chauffeur. Joachim Jonas flanked Hilde on the left – protectively, because Harald was standing in the middle of the path again.

Jonas started to advance on Harald but Hilde gripped his arm and held him back. Plattner came to a halt. Staring into space, he said crisply and distinctly: 'The impertinence of the man!'

Harald's fury did not prevent him from minutely observing the spectacle that confronted him: his wife, who studiously avoided his eye; Jonas, his ex-friend and colleague, who was making admonitory gestures; and Plattner, for whom he, Harald, might have been no more than a troublesome insect.

'Why are you treating me like this?' Harald heard himself ask. He took one step, then another, towards the official mourners. 'Haven't you done enough as it is?'

'This man,' Plattner snarled, controlling himself with an effort, 'has a human life on his conscience . . .'

'Don't say that, I warn you!' Harald said.

But Plattner deliberately ignored him. Still staring into space, he added implacably: 'One human life, if not more.'

'Plattner,' Harald said in a low voice which trembled with suppressed emotion, 'even my patience has its limits.'

'What in God's name does he want?' Plattner's fury erupted like a sudden storm, but still he refused to favour his son-in-law with a single glance. What he said seemed to be directed at his two companions alone. 'The man has no shame, even now.'

After a brief pause which he clearly considered effective, Plattner added ponderously: 'The world is an iniquitous place.'

'You're right,' Harald retorted. 'It's a sink of iniquity, and some people wallow in it.'

'Out of my way!' bellowed Plattner, bearing down on his son-in-law.

And Harald stepped aside.

Those who witnessed the scene, apart from the immediate participants, included Father Nebunzahl, who had lingered at the graveside, two cemetery attendants and three visitors, also the man with the mongrel.

'My God,' the priest muttered to himself. 'It doesn't matter what happens, people never change.'

Harald returned to the cemetery gate to find Keller and Anton waiting for him. They watched him intently, patiently. Man and dog alike.

Harald gave them a wan smile. 'I think I overdid it,' he said wearily. 'I started something just now, and I'm not sure how it'll end.'

'You finally let your emotions get the better of you,' Keller said.

'I couldn't help it.'

'Your son seemed delighted.'

'In that case it was a good thing.'

'Not good enough for him, I suspect. How many fathers have an inkling of what goes on inside these youngsters' heads? You foresee trouble? Multiply it by two and you'll be nearer the mark.'

'You may be right.' Harald stooped to fondle Anton, who happily accepted his caresses. 'But I want to know the whole truth now – all of it. Does that surprise you?'

'No,' Keller replied with a meditative smile, 'I'm past being surprised, but watch out for your son.'

'I know – he doesn't like me.'

'On the contrary.' Keller's tone was commiserating. 'I have a nasty feeling he's devoted to you, and that could be awkward. Better prepare for the worst. All fathers have to, especially fathers with sons like yours.'

Readers of the Morgenzeitung *had their attention effectively drawn to an article on page 3 by the eye-catching front-page headline:* HOW TO PRINT YOUR OWN MONEY.

Preamble: The *MZ*, which, as everyone knew, had consistently and impartially championed the cause of freedom and democracy for years, was in possession of a photocopied document whose repercussions might well be far-reaching, and whose authenticity – to judge from preliminary investigations – was virtually beyond doubt. If the paper entertained any initial hesitation about publishing the document, this was only because, being aware of its responsibilities, it had debated whether the public interest would best be served, etcetera.

Follow-up: a half-page blow-up of one sheet of the document in question. This listed properties to be purchased in and around the Sunset Estate area, obviously with an eye to the Olympic development zone and, more especially, its main approach road. The said purchases had been effected by a real estate company named Huber, Huber & Leitmann, acting on behalf of the Plattner Construction Company.

Editorial comment: We have yet to verify every detail, but preliminary checks conducted by our editorial staff have only reinforced our belief in the document's authenticity. Worried citizens have long suspected that something was gravely amiss, as witness the many unpublished letters in our files, but no convincing evidence was forthcoming. It now seems that this chapter in the recent history of our city, perhaps the darkest chapter of all, is at last nearing publication.

We therefore request the Mayor . . .

'Chief Superintendent,' Keller said, 'may I take some time off?'

'You've got some coming.' Dürrenmaier's manner towards his PECD officer was as affable as it had been for days now. 'To the best of my knowledge, you haven't had a holiday in the past three years.'

'Five years, sir. I didn't know how to pass the time.'

Dürrenmaier raised his eyebrows inquiringly. 'And now you do?'

'Yes, I've finally discovered someone to spend my leave with.'

'Would it be tactless to inquire who?'

'You've made his acquaintance, sir. It's Anton.'

'The dog?' Dürrenmaier massaged his eyes as though to soothe a headache. With studious calm, he asked: 'And where do you and Anton propose to spend your leave?'

'Here in Munich.'

Dürrenmaier heaved an audible sigh of relief. 'So I can still count on your help?'

'Of course, sir.'

'In that case, carry on. Take as long as you like – four weeks, eight weeks . . .'

'Five days ought to be enough.'

'Very well. And if there's anything I can do for you in the meantime, my dear Keller, you only have to phone.'

Chapter Eight

'This case is getting to be too much of a good thing.' Henri Messer surveyed each of his three visitors – Harald, Keller and Anton – with sovereign calm. He didn't look like a man at the end of his tether. 'The plot thickens daily.'

Keller grinned. 'No need to pretend for our benefit, Messer. You're revelling in the situation. You smell a monumental scandal – one that'll earn you some welcome publicity.'

The lawyer grinned back. 'It had crossed my mind, though I haven't managed to fit all the pieces into place. That's where you come in, Superintendent.'

'I'm only here in my capacity as a dog-handler,' Keller told him. He looked down at Anton, who was busy licking his forepaws precisely mid-way between him and Harald. Harald and Keller exchanged a smile.

'You're here, anyway,' Messer said, 'and I plan to make the most of your presence. I could use a professional detective.'

'Our services aren't available to individual members of the public, Herr Messer. We serve the cause of justice in general.'

'In that case, serve the cause of justice by enlightening me on a couple of points. This story in the *Morgenzeitung* – what does it really mean? Who leaked the information and why?'

Peter Wardeiner, Local News editor of the Morgenzeitung, *questioned by the CID at a later stage:*
The photocopy of the first document came to us through the post, like the two that followed. Judging by the postmark, all were mailed from the main-line station. The sender didn't give his name and address.

The envelopes were mass-produced articles – the kind you can buy at any cheap stationer's. The copies had been run off on the kind of duplicating machine that plenty of offices have these days. The accompanying letters were typewritten on sheets of paper torn from a writing-pad – smooth, white, medium quality, unwatermarked.

184

The text of the first covering letter, typed in lower case and unpunctuated throughout, was as follows:

enclosed is a copy of a document whose contents can easily be verified special attention should be paid to the dates because they anticipate publication of official plans for development of the olympic site.

As soon as the document's importance dawned on us we set up a special team by arrangement with the editor-in-chief.

First, we ran thorough checks on all the details. It was no trouble, thanks to the excellent co-operation we received from various municipal authorities. It eventually turned out that everything – land register entries, dates of purchase, purchase prices – was entirely accurate.

There was a postscript to the first covering letter. It read:

should the significance of the enclosed escape you the same information will be made available to a rival newspaper but if you give suitable prominence to these disclosures similar material of equal importance may be forwarded to you in due course.

'I've got to find out who's behind the operation,' Messer said. 'Who made it possible and who carried it out?'

Keller registered amusement. 'I'll give you three guesses.'

The lawyer ignored his sally and turned to Harald. 'Forgive me, Herr Fein, but I'm reluctantly compelled to ask you a question which I urge you to answer with the utmost candour. Have you anything to do with this?'

'No, unfortunately.'

'In future,' Keller said, 'either don't answer questions like that or, if you must, don't be so definite. You may think your connection with the story is nil, but you can't be sure.'

Messer raised his eyebrows. 'What are you driving at, Super-intendent? Or, to be more precise, where are you trying to steer my client? I'm still his lawyer – you're the expert on criminal investigation.'

'And as such, Herr Messer, I strongly advise you to stop thinking in black and white. Shades of grey can be far more illuminating.'

'I'm only interested in knowing who was responsible for

Helga's death,' Harald said stubbornly. 'Anyway, Keller, I don't understand a word you're saying.'

'That makes two of us,' said Messer, but his eyes shone. 'You've been dropping some pretty vague hints, Superintendent. I'm tempted to wonder if you're at the bottom of this. Are you?'

Keller chuckled. 'There are plenty of candidates. Theoretically, one of them is Herr Fein. Then there's Jonas, a calculating type who could be trying to feather his nest at Plattner's expense. Even Plattner qualifies. He may have plans to incriminate Herr Fein through his friend Abendroth and damn the personal consequences – I wouldn't put anything past him after that scene at the cemetery. Then there are Plattner's business rivals. If Plattner's star sets, their prospects improve. Last but by no means least, Herr Messer, there's you. Any *cause célèbre* is grist to your mill.'

'What about you?'

'I'm probably the only person who doesn't qualify as a potential stool pigeon.'

'Why not?'

'Because I'm an old pro. I'd have tackled the job far more subtly. With all due deference to his undoubted talents, this was the work of an amateur. And I know his identity.'

'You know?' exclaimed Messer.

Keller nodded. 'It wasn't too hard to figure out – not for someone with a touch of imagination.'

'All right,' Messer said, 'who?'

'I'm on leave,' the policeman said mildly. 'My job is to look after your client's dog while he's under medical supervision.'

Messer stared at his two visitors, plus dog, with mounting irritation and anxiety. 'My God,' he said, 'I suppose you get a kick out of hinting darkly. Can't you see the dangers of this press campaign?'

'What's so dangerous about it?' Keller demanded. 'Except to Plattner, if he doesn't react the right way, or to you, Herr Messer, if you don't watch your step.'

Next day's Morgenzeitung *carried, again on page 3, two reactions to the storm it had raised:*

1. Herr Jonas, managing director of Plattner Construction, stated in a personal interview: 'The company I represent has no

connection whatever with the allegations published by your newspaper. We reserve the right to take legal action.'

2. The City Hall press officer, speaking on behalf of the Mayor, said: 'This matter does not come within the competence of the municipal authorities and is therefore one for which the Mayor bears no responsibility. It does not concern any municipal department, nor does it bear upon the conduct of any municipal official. Any comment on our part would thus be pointless and irrelevant.'

The same day, München am Mittag *ran a headline: 'Those who sow the wind . . .'*

Exaggeration seems to have become a popular sport in certain quarters. Molehills are transformed into mountains, dead cinders fanned into a blazing inferno – and ordinary property deals represented as municipal, if not federal, finagling . . .

. . . count ourselves fortunate on living in a free country where every citizen has a perfect right to dispose of his property as he pleases. He can gamble it away, drink it away, donate it, divide it, squander it – or, what is more to the point, sell it. The conditions of sale and purchaser's identity are immaterial. But to play dubious quiz games with irrelevant details and audacious guesswork, in other words, to sow a journalistic wind in the hope of reaping a circulation manager's whirlwind . . .

Extracts from a report by Friedrich Bannholtzer, market consultant, later incorporated in the files of Henri Messer, attorney-at-law:
. . . the newspaper *München am Mittag* belongs to the Munich Print and Paper Corporation, which is controlled by Sack & Feder, which is closely associated with the banking consortium Specht, Merker & Co. Annual turnover DM60,000,000. Long-term government contracts for office stationery, printed forms, administrative leaflets. Other sources of work include the Federal Armed Forces, the Red Cross, and the Automobile Association. MPP also produces a number of house organs and magazines, ecclesiastical publications, etcetera.
Footnote by Messer:
Board member of the banking consortium: Paul Plattner. Personal friend of press tycoon Feder: Paul Plattner. Close associate of Thomas Simmerer, deputy chairman of the finance committee: Paul Plattner.

Plattner Construction's annual print and advertising bill from MPP: approximately DM400,000.

'Very well, Superintendent,' said Messer. 'May I at least count on your general support? In other words, which side are you on – my client's?'

'His dog's, you might say.'

'Look, Keller,' the lawyer said coldly, 'how much do you want?'

'For what?'

'For doing the necessary spadework – giving us the full benefit of your professional knowledge and connections. What's it worth to you? Five thousand marks – ten thousand? Name your figure.'

'Stop,' Harald said quickly. 'I couldn't afford that kind of money.'

Messer wagged his head. 'Wrong again. We can afford far more than you think.'

'Who's footing the bill?' Keller asked. 'Not Abendroth, surely?'

'No deal,' Harald said.

'Ditto,' said Keller. 'You're playing with imaginary sums. Isn't that a bit presumptuous of you?'

'Not at all,' Messer protested. 'Not with a property like ours. We should be able to parlay it into at least half a million if we handle things right.'

'And you price me at five or ten thousand?' Keller chuckled gently.

'Do a thorough job and we'll double it.'

'Now you're talking.' Keller chuckled again. 'I'm not saying I'm for hire, but if I do accept a fee it'll have to be princely.'

'What do you call princely?'

'This dog here.'

From the files of Henri Messer, attorney-at-law:
. . . willingly agreed to an interview with Herr P. Palitschek, fiancé of Maria Trübner, formerly employed as a maid in the Fein household. He assured me he had been the victim of a misconception – several misconceptions, in fact – and greatly regretted any harm done . . .
. . . that he was now prepared to make amends. He had obviously misunderstood Maria, who had been so carried away by her story that he jumped to a number of unfounded conclusions. What was

more, he had yielded to police pressure and allowed words to be put into his mouth . . .

Appended: the signature of Peter Palitschek, free-lance insurance agent.

Also appended: a signed statement by Maria Trübner to the effect that no sexual misconduct had occurred at the Fein residence. She was prepared to undergo further questioning by the police for purposes of clarification.

Enclosed in the same file: a receipt in the sum of DM5000 made out by P. Palitschek and countersigned by M. Trübner.

Also noted by Messer: Peter Palitschek's concluding remark, 'I've always said it pays to tell the truth.'

Gottfried Heinrich Wamsler, office messenger at Plattner Construction, during another session with the detective assigned to pump him:
Look, get this straight. You can forget the office messenger bit. I'm a salaried employee with special duties. I take orders direct from the chairman. It's a confidential job, get me?

Sure I do messenger work occasionally, but the rest of the time I'm responsible for Herr Plattner's office suite. Pens, stationery, hand-towels, toilet paper and so on.

My speciality's the wastepaper basket. Nobody's allowed to empty it but me. The contents are burnt by me personally. I also make the rounds every evening – check to see the windows are bolted, try the drawers of his desk, make sure the safe's locked.

I also deliver the mail and newspapers. I delivered them the day that lousy paper slung mud at the firm. It was all round the office by that time.

One look at the headline and the old man blew his top. I thought he was going to have a stroke. Then he yelled for Jonas.

Munich continued to glitter like the most prized decoration it had to bestow, a gold medal which the Mayor conferred, usually with his own hands, on deserving citizens.

'Germany's secret capital' had swelled by almost four hundred thousand inhabitants in the past few years. There was a comparable influx in the field of big business. Italian firms based in Lugano and US and Canadian firms based in Locarno were ready and eager to invest hundreds of millions of marks. Swiss banks descended from Zürich, Dutch firms bought up medium-sized industrial concerns, French aircraft and automobile firms came in quest of suitable mergers, big foreign finance houses like the First National Bank set up shop in the city.

Munich had become a prime target of international speculation. The Olympics cast a long shadow well in advance of their arrival, and the city's home-grown financial bosses were not unnaturally alarmed. They had no wish to see their golden goose lay for foreigners.

Joachim Jonas entered his employer's office to find him seated stonily behind his desk. Plattner's face was chalky. With his knotted fists planted on an open copy of the *Morgenzeitung*, he glared at his closest associate.

'It's outrageous,' Jonas said prudently, pausing just inside the door. 'A dirty, malicious, unscrupulous piece of yellow journalism – if you ask me.'

'Yes, I am asking you,' Plattner replied in funereal tones. 'Do you still believe he's entirely responsible – Fein, I mean?'

'Who else?' Jonas shrugged. 'He's getting back at you for that incident at the funeral. In my opinion, you'd have done better to say nothing.'

'I didn't ask for your opinion. Am I correct in assuming that Fein's apartment has been thoroughly searched for the red folder?'

'Twice. We ransacked the place again yesterday, at our leisure this time, but found nothing. It was the same with the briefcase my men took from him. Nothing in it but blueprints . . .'

'I know all that!' Plattner snorted. He pulled a thin green file towards him and opened it. 'This private detective you hired on my instructions – according to him, Fein has left the hospital only three times in the past few days, on each occasion for little more than two hours. He's attended a reconstruction of the V-Strasse murder, Helga's funeral, and a conference with his lawyer.'

'What's he been doing with the rest of his time?'

'What indeed? According to you he's been photocopying documents, writing letters and mailing them. Quite an achievement for a sick man, wouldn't you say?'

Further remarks made by Gottfried Heinrich Wamsler, office

190

Fräulein Wagnersberger? Don't talk to me about that bitch! I've had to put up with her for almost twenty years.

She's a first-rate secretary, I'll give her that. Takes her job seriously, too. I once saw her bent back across Herr Plattner's desk with her skirt over her head, and him doing gymnastics on top of her. They didn't even notice me.

The boss often took her with him on so-called business trips. They'd drive down to his country house down by the Tegernsee or his hunting lodge in the Black Forest, or shack up in a rented apartment in Rome or Paris.

How do I know? Because I was the only member of the firm who could be trusted with his address and phone number, in case of emergencies.

She didn't have much fun with Harald Fein, though. The boss's daughter kept him on a tight rein – or maybe Wagnersberger wasn't his type. I caught sight of her in his office once, standing there with her blouse unbuttoned. Tits like a movie star, she had, but all Fein said was: 'You'll catch cold.'

Anyway, it wasn't long before she took up with Jonas. Deserted building sites, a country inn down by the Pilzsee, a pal's apartment in Herzogstrasse, a ski lodge near Garmisch – I tell you, friend, they did it any place they could.

There wasn't much she wouldn't do for the firm, Eva-Maria. She even got to work on Herr Heinz, the chairman's grandson. He's had his hand up her skirt before now, take it from me.

'However you look at it,' Jonas said persuasively, 'Fein's the only possibility.'

'Perhaps,' said Plattner. 'You could be right, but I wouldn't bet on it. Don't forget the second key to the safe. I still have the first. Fein had the spare. Now you have it.'

'But it could have been temporarily stolen and copied.'

'Balls!' exclaimed Plattner. 'It's either me – which it isn't – or you, or him. I want this business settled once and for all. Think of something, Joachim – preferably before the *Morgenzeitung* comes out with another revelation.'

Hilde Fein to Joachim Jonas, in bed that night:
. . . you'll have to think of something. It shouldn't be difficult.

191

You mustn't let Father down – he'd never forgive you. I know him better than anyone.

Joachim Jonas to Paul Plattner, early the next day:
. . . fifty thousand marks missing from the safe when Fein handed me the spare key.

PLATTNER: Missing, you say? Have you made a written inventory of our cash reserves?

JONAS: Not yet, but I can produce one in half an hour.

PLATTNER: When it's ready send a letter to Fein, drafted and signed by you. Something along these lines: we had hoped to clear this matter up privately . . . we're still ready to do so in the interests of the firm but must insist on speedy restitution, etcetera.

Make a discreet allusion to the red folder. No threats, though – appeal to his common sense. That's the only way we'll get anywhere.

Keller sat beside Harald in the Mercedes, Harald at the wheel and Keller in the passenger seat. Anton sat behind them, seemingly asleep. The tip of his nose projected between the two seats.

'Is this more or less the spot where you used to park before the girl was murdered?' Keller asked.

Harald nodded. 'Just about. I never had any difficulty in finding a place. The street was usually half-empty. So was that private parking lot over there, outside No. 33.'

'Good,' said Keller, settling back. 'Don't do anything special. Just look around, slowly and thoroughly. Try and register everything you can see now. After that, try and visualize everything you could see then. Try and spot any differences – any changes.'

'What's the point?'

'It's a simple method, but it works. The human brain records everything the eyes transmit, however unconsciously. With a little luck, you can actually spot a needle in a haystack.'

From Detective-Superintendent Keller's notes:
The scene of the crime holds a sort of magic for detectives as well as criminals. At or near the spot itself, everything seems clearer, more distinct, more cogent. I belong to the school which contends that no one can assess a case properly unless he's conversant with the place where the crime was committed.

Every witness's statement should be checked on the spot, allowing for every conceivable factor: visibility, time of day or night, lighting, colouring, weather, traffic, acoustic background, powers of observation and so on – elementary rules of detective procedure which an experienced detective like Braun knew backwards. He wasn't too particular about the methods he used, but they generally had a very specific purpose. His dogged determination to nail Harald Fein was beginning to worry me.

An additional worry was Fein himself. He kept badgering me to tell him how Helga met her death. Everything else he dismissed as secondary.

'I don't see any particular difference,' Harald said. 'Is it so important?'

'Take your time,' Keller told him. 'Sit back quietly and digest your impressions.'

'I can see her now,' Harald mused. 'She normally came out of that bar on the corner just after eight. She used to have a snack and a couple of drinks – between shifts, I suppose.'

'Sounds as if you did more than take an idle interest in her,' said Keller. 'You made a pretty careful study of her habits. Why?'

'I don't know, it just happened that way. I felt attracted by her, somehow. She had a sort of animal vitality that was new to me. She aroused my curiosity in a strangely alluring way. Can you understand that?'

'I'm beginning to. But you never met her?'

'No.'

'Nor accosted her?'

'No.'

'So you merely kept her under observation – close observation. Just her, or her visitors as well? Anyone special you can recall?'

Remarks by the owner-cum-barman of the El Dorado, *who had been shown various photographs. The following extracts were later conveyed to Keller by Feldmann:*

Nearly all these faces ring a bell, but I couldn't say for sure. This is a one-man business, you see. Come evening, I'm rushed off my feet.

I knew the dead girl pretty well – she was a regular customer.

Terrific from every angle. The generous type, too – and I don't just mean tips. Really well stacked she was, front and back.

People were always asking me about her. She gave me permission to pass on her phone number, but only to serious prospects.

Further remarks by the proprietor of the El Dorado, *when shown a photograph of Harald Fein:*

Sure I remember him, but not just because of his face. The thing that really stuck in my mind was, he didn't touch a drop – in a bar, mind you! Never ordered anything but mineral water and paid champagne prices without a murmur.

He beat around the bush, but I guessed what he was after in two minutes flat, so I slipped him her phone number.

From Detective-Superintendent Keller's notes:

Harald Fein seemed more apathetic than usual during our visit to V-Strasse. He was day-dreaming a lot of the time, and I left him to it.

My own thoughts were preoccupied with the death of his daughter. No doubt about it being suicide, to use the standard designation which still appears on official forms. Personally, I think it's a legal and criminological misnomer.

I prefer to call it 'voluntary self-destruction', a method of dying which looms regrettably large in the life of anyone with a job like mine – especially one who's based in this city of blatant contrasts: luxury and poverty, middle-class respectability and commercialized vice.

The people who opt for voluntary self-destruction tend to be very young or fairly elderly, and male rather than female. Their favourite times are week-ends in spring and the days preceding Christmas. Methods, in order of precedence: first hanging, then poison. Drowning comes fifth.

Young people often choose drowning because their affections aren't returned, elderly people because they're plain lonely. Many of them leave a farewell letter explaining their motives. This applies particularly to those who've been in the habit of keeping a diary, like Helga Fein.

No such letter had come to light in her case. What gave me almost more food for thought was, nobody seemed curious. Not even Harald Fein had broached the subject.

Helga's farewell letter could be an important link in the chain. She *must* have written one – I was ready to bet on it.

But how, if it existed, could I get hold of it?

'Nothing,' Harald said. He leant back in the driver's seat and stretched. 'I haven't noticed a thing. It all looks the same.'

'Don't try too hard,' Keller told him patiently. 'Just sit here a while longer.'

They sat there in silence, side by side. Keller studied the image reflected in the windscreen, which had misted over slightly. Harald Fein's features were distorted into a grotesque mask. He was smiling to himself.

Keller glanced sideways at the bland cleanliness of the street, then at the smooth cold faces of the apartment buildings lining it, then up at the evening sky. It had the radiant clarity of early autumn.

'What a city,' he murmured quietly. 'I wasn't born in Munich but I've enjoyed living here. Just lately, though, I've been wondering if I want to die here.'

Anton whined and stirred uneasily.

'Call of nature,' said Keller, and opened the near-side door.

Anton scrambled over the back of his seat. Once outside, he went straight to the far corner of the driveway in front of No. 33 as though making for some definite objective. Then he paused and looked round.

'He always heads for the same spot,' Harald said. 'There seems to be something missing.'

'Like what?'

'The car that used to be parked there, I expect. He liked to lift his leg against it – first the front wheels and then the rear.'

'And you watched him while you were sitting here? How often – several times?'

Harald nodded. 'Anton was crazy about that Jaguar.'

'Are you sure it was a Jaguar?'

'Quite sure. I remember admiring it. The paintwork was something like mine – cobalt or silver-blue. Pale and metallic, anyway.'

'You didn't notice the licence number, I suppose?'

'It was a Munich plate. I seem to remember it had a C and a D in it, then a two-digit number – a low one. Is that important?'

'Apparently,' Keller said. 'To Anton, at least.'

Place: the head office of Plattner Construction. Time: next morning, just after the beginning of office hours. Those present: Joachim Jonas, managing director, and Eva-Maria Wagnersberger, private secretary to the chairman.

JONAS: You're looking gorgeous, Eva, as usual. Sorry I've been so tied up these past few weeks, but that's life. Top copy and two carbons, please.

To: Harald Fein. 'Dear Sir, you will recall that you formerly held the spare key to the firm's safe. We regret to inform you that, after its return to us, the sum of DM50,000 was found to be missing from our cash reserves . . .'

No need to raise your eyebrows, Eva, it's all right – there's no alternative. We have to make sure that all Fein's bridges are burned. The old man wants it that way, and that's good enough for me.

To continue: 'If our warnings on the subject have hitherto been verbal, although given in the presence of witnesses, this is solely in virtue of the family ties which still exist between you and the chairman of this company . . .'

But Eva, there always were large amounts of cash in the safe. You remember, don't you? Of course you do. You naturally didn't know how much, but it ran to tens of thousands, right? Right.

Okay, new para: 'We sincerely trust that you realize the extent to which our mutual interests are involved. In the event that your co-operation enables us to recover the red folder which was also missing, you may rest assured that it is our earnest desire to accommodate you in this matter . . .'

Keller walked into Messer's office looking smug. 'I've been busy collecting some old debts from friends and colleagues of mine. In other words, drumming up some inside information.'

'Any luck?' asked Messer.

'To begin with, I concentrated on Jonas. What do you make of him?'

'Nothing.'

'An apt and exhaustive summation, Herr Messer.'

'What about you? Any idea what the man's capable of – or, better still, what we can prove against him?'

196

'He's capable of almost anything, I'd say, but he's clean. No police record, no previous convictions. As a criminal, Herr Jonas defies classification. He's the kind that uses other people to do his dirty work for him. Anton has identified a couple of them.'

'The dog?' Messer said, looking mystified.

Keller nodded. 'If that animal had the gift of speech and reason as well as a good nose, he'd make a first-rate detective.'

Confidential memorandum addressed to Detective-Superintendent Keller by Detective-Inspector Salzmann of the Provincial Crime Bureau:

The two suspects you mention have been checked on the basis of information so far available. The following points have emerged:

1. Both men could have participated in the assault on Harald Fein. Neither possesses a satisfactory alibi.

2. They were assigned to guard the cemetery gate by Jonas, acting on behalf of Plattner. This was admitted by one of the suspects, Rogalski, but not confirmed by the other, Pollock. Jonas passed his instructions to Rogalski direct, with no third party present.

3. Second raid on the apartment in Torremolinos Towers during Fein's spell in hospital. A number of prints were found. One right thumb-print belonged to Rogalski, the foreman. Pollock, the gateman, left an entire palm-print on Fein's desk. Both men have a history of minor convictions for petty theft, drunkenness and assault.

'In other words,' said Messer, 'we'd have no trouble in catching the lesser fry but we couldn't touch their boss?'

'It's the usual headache,' Keller said. 'Proving things is a laborious business. Suspicions are worthless, even when they amount to a certainty. Whatever someone tells someone else in private, and whatever orders he gives, one or both of the two parties can deny it.'

'You mean you don't see any possible line of attack, Superintendent? Are you giving up?'

'Far from it. Detective work is like a jigsaw puzzle. You don't get a clear picture till you've fitted all the pieces together.'

'But can we afford to wait?' Messer sounded impatient. 'Every day and hour that goes by brings the possibility of fresh surprises. More headlines, for instance.'

Keller turned to Harald, who'd been listening in silence. 'How do you feel about the press reports, Herr Fein?'

'I don't care either way,' Harald said calmly. 'All that interests me is the reason for Helga's death. I want to know who was responsible. As far as I'm concerned, everything else is water under the bridge.'

Another confidential memorandum addressed to Detective-Superintendent Keller, this time by Dr Trübke-Marbach, Department of Graphology and Printing, an expert on chemical and mechanical reproduction techniques:

Our professional assistance was requested by the editor of the *Morgenzeitung*. We were handed, in exchange for a signed receipt, photocopies of the document in question and its covering letter. The envelope in which they had been mailed had not, apparently, been preserved.

Findings: 1. The document was produced by a Rapidex machine on paper supplied by the manufacturers. Number of such machines in use in Munich and environs: approximately two thousand. However, the machine actually used could be identified with some certainty, if located, because it leaves marginal smudges of distinctive shape.

2. Covering letter. Ordinary note-paper without any special characteristics. Mass-produced pads obtainable from many stationers, stores and office equipment suppliers. Probable manufacturer: Villingen, spring '69 making.

3. Typescript. Italian machine produced by Bernasconi under British licence in Holland. Model: Construkta Original 70. Typescript comparison: positive. Text itself: uneven impression, probably typed with one finger, though this may have been intentional. Two flaws not immediately apparent to the naked eye: a slightly off-centre 'l' and an 'A' fractionally thickened at the apex.

'It all sounds rather technical,' said Messer. 'What can we do with it?'

'Plenty, if we locate the machine in question. Is there a Construkta in your office?'

The lawyer impatiently brushed the question aside. 'I've been operating from my home these last few days. A young girl-friend of mine has been handling my correspondence in her spare time. She uses a small Olympia portable.'

'What about you, Herr Fein?'

Harald smiled. 'I don't own a typewriter and never have, nor have I dictated any letters for weeks. Does that answer your question?'

'Perfectly,' said Keller. 'Let's revert to the mysterious Jaguar.'

A third confidential memorandum addressed to Detective-Superintendent Keller. The following information supplied by Detective Chief Inspector Sämisch of the Motor Vehicle Crimes and Records Department, covering licence numbers, engine numbers, chassis numbers, accidents, thefts, drivings-away, forgery of log-books and driver's licences, lists of panel-beaters, garages, used car firms, scrap-metal dealers and breakers' yards:

Re Jaguar, cobalt, steel-blue, or blue-grey, recent model. Current list for Munich area requested from Flensburg, duly received and evaluated. Findings: only three such vehicles with said paintwork, disregarding possible resprays. Owners thereof: a hotel proprietor, an industrial salesman, and a politician. Addresses appended. Only the latter's car has a two-digit number.

'The car in question,' said Keller, 'is registered in the name of Feininger.'

'No!' Messer exclaimed. 'You must be mistaken.'

'Sämisch is a pedantic but conscientious officer,' Keller said. 'He doesn't make mistakes. The Jaguar spotted by Herr Fein can only have been Feininger's.'

'If you're right,' Messer said excitedly, 'we're in trouble. Figure it out for yourself. If we try and take the heat off my client by implicating a man in Feininger's position – because that's the way it'll be construed – well, the results could be catastrophic.'

Keller looked him straight in the eye. 'You can't back out now.'

'No,' said Messer, in command of himself once more, 'I can't and I won't. You're a dangerous man, Superintendent.'

'I've only just started,' Keller said gaily. 'May I make a suggestion? Take your information about the car and its owner to Chief

Superintendent Dürrenmaier. If I know him, it's just what he's been waiting for.'

'I've been expecting you all evening,' Melanie Weber said, beaming at Harald. 'You're here at last.'

'Only to pick up a pair of clean pyjamas.' Harald paused on the threshold of his apartment. 'I'm due back at the hospital in half an hour.'

'Just time for a teeny *riposo*. You look absolutely *drained*, darling. Anyone would think you'd been laying *three* women simultaneously.'

'Nice thought,' Harald said. He gave her a weary smile. 'One police superintendent is as much as I can cope with.'

Melanie walked over to him, embraced him tenderly and led him into the bedroom. 'Lie down for a few minutes. You need *rest*.'

Her voice was seductive. Harald subsided on the bed at her gentle prompting. Closing his eyes, he heard the clink of glass against glass. He opened them to see champagne frothing under his nose.

'Drink up,' she said, perching beside him. 'It's good for what ails you. So am I.'

Melanie Weber, a few hours later, to her bosom friend Hilde Fein:
. . . the *ghastliness* of men, with their bloated egos! I only went there to tidy that *pigsty* of an apartment, and what was my reward? I tried to fight him off but he positively *raped* me! Aren't you shocked?

HILDE: I don't believe you. He isn't like that – never was, but I'd be eternally grateful if you could prove it – if you'd swear to it in court.

MELANIE: Grateful enough to pick up where we left off?

HILDE: Perhaps . . .

Harald edged away from Melanie, who was crowding him.

'Harald,' she whispered, 'what's the matter?'

'Nothing,' he said. 'I'm not up to it, but thanks all the same. Thanks on Hilde's behalf, too.'

Paul Plattner to his daughter:

. . . better prepare yourself, I'm afraid. If that boy-friend of yours doesn't finish Harald once and for all . . .

HILDE: Melanie Weber may do the job for him.

PLATTNER: That Lesbian bitch?

HILDE: Melanie's bisexual. She'd shrink from nothing and no one. Not even Harald, if it was worth her while.

PLATTNER: What did you offer her?

HILDE: Me, by implication. Melanie still has a very soft spot for me. There's not much she wouldn't do . . .

Klaus Budenberg, member of the Munich branch of the SPD, or German Socialist Party, speaking at a closed meeting of the executive:

. . . extended our hand to the Mayor but he spurned our generous offer of support . . . called upon us instead to have 'implicit faith' in him, which is tantamount to giving him a political blank cheque and robbing ourselves of the right to criticize . . .

. . . either he finally ceases to withhold our due share of seats in the City Council and municipal committees, or we shall guarantee that he has no further opportunity to abuse his position in this high-handed manner . . .

. . . if he isn't an ally he's an enemy. Regrettable as this may seem in principle, it has now become unavoidable in practice.

I therefore move that we re-examine the question of these scandalously speculative property deals . . .

'So you're drinking again,' Melanie said softly, handing Harald his glass.

'Sorry to disappoint you and your beloved Hilde, not to mention my father-in-law.' Harald laughed silently to himself. 'I don't have an irresistible urge for alcohol, not any more, but I do enjoy an occasional drink. Just for fun, you understand. I don't get drunk.'

'I'm *delighted* for you,' she assured him devoutly. 'You mean you've really kicked the habit?'

'Apparently, so there's no need for you all to worry. My problems are somewhat different. What worries me is the border-line between murder and suicide – I'm talking about Helga. Drink doesn't bring me any closer to the answer.'

Harald to his doctor, next day:

Alcoholism's an almost incurable disease – isn't that what you told me once? Well, in my case the primary cause was psychological. I nearly drank myself insane, just for the sake of oblivion.

Then, with your active assistance, I was dried out. I didn't touch a drop for almost two years after my spell in the sanatorium.

Lately I've taken to drinking again. In moderation, without the least sign of addiction. I've regained my ability to concentrate. I don't feel that drink holds any more perils for me.

Next morning's edition of the Morgenzeitung *carried a reproduction of Document No. 2, subdivided into 2a and 2b. Both parts incorporated details from a map of Munich showing the Olympic development zone and its environs.*

2a: properties purchased in and around the Sunset Estate area, together with dates and prices.

2b: the lay-out of the Olympic approach roads. Almost all the properties acquired were situated inside the development zone selected by the Urban Planning Department.

'You don't know me,' Keller said affably, 'but I know you, and so does my faithful companion here.'

'It's Anton!' Heinz Fein stared at the dog in surprise. 'What's he doing with you?'

'He needed someone to look after him temporarily. I got the job.'

Heinz was on his way to the Black and White in Ungererstrasse, a relatively pleasant little café by contemporary standards. Not 'in' yet and no police surveillance, which made it an ideal rendezvous for planners of illegal demonstrations.

The boy was in a hurry, but he bent to pat the dog. 'How are you, Gorgeous Beast?' Anton wagged his tail, amicably but perfunctorily.

'Anton doesn't seem over-fond of you,' Keller said thoughtfully. 'Perhaps it's because you aren't over-fond of him.'

'You're wrong,' Heinz said. 'I've always had a soft spot for the animal. I wanted him all to myself, but he fell for Father. It wasn't long before he became a second son – if not an only son!'

'I see,' said Keller. He fell into step beside Heinz like an old acquaintance, with Anton trotting between them. 'You're very attached to your father, aren't you?'

'What gives you that idea?' Heinz came to a halt and stared at the little detective, who smiled at him. 'How could anyone in this high-powered society of ours feel attached to a man who doesn't know he's alive – who's thin-skinned, sentimental, indecisive . . .'

'It naturally infuriates you, and you react in your own way. I know because I read the papers. I can also put two and two together – I've had a lifetime's practice.'

'Who the hell are you, anyway?'

From Detective-Superintendent Keller's notes:

It was my first encounter with Heinz Fein. He looked exactly as I'd pictured him – like Harald Fein twenty years younger. In other words, minus twenty years' daily grind and treadmill existence, disillusionment and fatigue, self-deception and compromise. Heinz had all that ahead of him.

I told him I was a friend of Anton's, an acquaintance of his father's, and a detective – in that order. I said I wasn't acting in an official capacity, that I simply wanted to make his acquaintance too, which was true.

I asked him to listen to my advice, which would be of a purely personal nature. He needn't take it but I hoped he'd think it over because he badly needed some professional support.

Heinz was looking uneasy now. 'I don't know what you're driving at.'

'You don't have to catch on right away,' Keller told him gently. 'Take your time.'

It was late evening. They strolled through the city centre from the Hofgarten side of Odeonsplatz to Leopoldstrasse. Pedestrians were few and far between, but cars rolled past them in an endless chain of lights.

There were lights above them too, street lamps turning the asphalt bluish-grey. The sky overhead was black.

'Okay,' said Heinz, with a sidelong glance at the policeman, 'that's not bad for a start. You don't insist on my immediate comprehension and you don't claim to be entirely in sympathy with the young. Great! What else?'

'I'd like to ask you something – a favour, in a sense.'

'A favour? Don't tell me it's for the sake of my poor dear father, Herr Keller, or I'll break down and cry. Did he send you?'

'No. It has to do with Helga.'

Heinz paused in the shadow of the Siegestor. His voice sounded sombre, almost husky. 'Helga? I thought she was dead. Dead, buried and forgotten.'

'Don't take that tone with me,' Keller said, affable no longer. 'Save it for other people. I'm the last person to be sentimental, except where dogs are concerned. The only reason I buttonholed you was to discuss the possibility that your sister left a farewell letter.'

'If she did, it's news to me.' Heinz abruptly became alert and businesslike. 'What makes you think she might have?'

'Years of experience. Exceptions can't be ruled out, of course, but people who destroy themselves usually like to tell the rest of the world why.'

'In Helga's case you could be right. It's exactly what I'd have expected of her.'

Keller assumed a professional tone. 'Generally speaking, suicide notes are left in conspicuous places. In the deceased's room, stuck in a mirror frame, in the middle of a table, beside the telephone.'

'If so, someone must have taken it and kept quiet about it.'

'Quite possibly,' Keller agreed. 'Whatever their motive, the farewell letter may still be in existence. The tendency is to preserve such a thing and hide it. It ought to be found.'

'I'll find it,' Heinz said firmly. 'Even if I have to turn my mother's gin-mill inside out.'

Henri Messer devoted nearly twenty-four hours to qualms, misgivings and concentrated cogitation before he decided to call on Detective Chief Superintendent Dürrenmaier.

Dürrenmaier had him shown in at once, almost as if he'd been expecting the visit.

'Well,' said the CID chief, waving him into a chair, 'how can I help you?'

'I have some information for you. Something of a hot potato, I'm afraid.'

'From whose angle – mine, the CID's? My dear Herr Messer, distasteful problems are our daily fare.'

'In this case,' Messer said, 'the distasteful problem arises from a point your Superintendent Braun may have overlooked. May I remind you of the disputed entries in the dead woman's diary – the ones in which the name Fein figured? We agreed, I think, that Fein might be short for Feininger.'

Dürrenmaier leant back in his chair, very slowly. He made no other movement, but his voice sounded a trifle strained. 'One Feininger in particular?'

'I'm afraid so.'

Extracts from an immediately ensuing interview between Detective Chief Superintendent Dürrenmaier and Detective-Superintendent Braun:

DÜRRENMAIER: A blue-grey Jaguar observed near the scene of the crime on several occasions, including the night in question. Registered owner: Herr Wilhelm Feininger.

BRAUN: Christ, who's been nosing around? Sorry, sir. I mean, who's your informant?

DÜRRENMAIER: It doesn't matter who. Is there any truth in the story or not? Kindly check on it and report to me soonest.

Telephone conversation between Detective-Superintendent Braun and Dr Barthel, Public Prosecutor:

BRAUN: It's my duty to advise you of a new development in the V-Strasse case. Evidence just to hand leaves me no choice but to include Herr Feininger within the scope of my investigation.

BARTHEL: Incriminating evidence?

BRAUN: I don't know yet. I'll have to follow it up.

BARTHEL: Of course, but be discreet – Herr Feininger isn't just anyone. And now, Superintendent, brief me on the salient points.

Telephone conversation between Dr Barthel and Wilhelm Feininger:

BARTHEL: I thought I'd better let you know ahead of time. A policeman named Braun will be calling on you. I know you're a busy man, but you ought to see him.

FEININGER: By all means, if you consider it advisable. What does he want?

BARTHEL: The gist of it is this. A blue Jaguar was often seen parked outside 33 V-Strasse. You are believed to be the registered owner, but I ought to point out that owner isn't synonymous with user. Also, to the best of my knowledge, no one claims to have seen you personally. I'm only telling you this to save valuable time.

FEININGER: Thanks – I'm really under pressure at the moment. Incidentally, the Minister of Justice is hoping to appoint a new state secretary soon – not later than the start of the next parliamentary session. I shall recommend an able and public-spirited lawyer of my acquaintance. Thanks again.'

From the 'Focus on Crime' section of the Morgenzeitung, *p. 7:*
. . . gradually forming a picture of the way in which such property deals are effected . . . The first step is to acquire two or three sites in the desired area, initially at any price, so as to establish a bridgehead . . . followed by a ruthless campaign to depreciate the properties surrounding it . . .

Josef Donnersberg, former resident of the Sunset Estate, pictured in conversation with an MZ *reporter:*
The site next door to me was occupied by a typical old Munich house. They bought it up, demolished it and built an enormous shed in its place – temporarily, so they said. Then they installed a battery of circular saws which operated for up to ten hours a day, cutting timber. You wouldn't believe the racket – it was unbearable.

The same thing happened a little farther along. More buildings were pulled down and replaced with huts for foreign labourers. Two hundred of them packed like sardines. Come nightfall they took over the local bars, brawling and chasing the young girls – my own daughter was one. I don't have anything against these foreigners when they behave themselves, but . . .

And so it went on. Next came a fuel dump. Stacks of drums and barrels, most of them leaking. You could smell the stench for miles.

Also interviewed:
Josepha Elisabeth Grundlager, another former resident. Her late husband, owner of a newsstand at the main-line station, had brought her to the district as a bride. Three hundred square yards – a poor thing but their own. Purchased only forty years earlier for fifteen hundred marks. She was offered thirty thousand, then fifty, finally eighty.

Frau Grundlager stated:

Take care of number one, that's what I always say. You get fond of your own little patch – there's no place like home, and all that – but everything has its price.

I didn't mind the noise of the saws, myself – I'm hard of hearing. The fuel dump? I've lost my sense of smell. And as for the Italians, don't you believe all you hear about them. Gentle as lambs, they were – a lot of fuss about nothing.

I sold out. I mean, why not?

'Focus on Crime' concluded:
So that's how to print your own money!

Detective-Superintendent Braun arrived at party headquarters in Königsplatz to find he was expected. A receptionist suavely took him in tow.

'Herr Feininger has managed to fit you into his schedule – may I lead the way?'

Braun nodded, suppressing the sardonic retort which sprang to his lips at the 'schedule' routine. He followed the girl up the broad staircase, along a corridor, through two outer offices, and into the inner sanctum.

Wilhelm Feininger, grey eminence of his party, was seated behind a massive desk. He did not remain seated. On the contrary, he rose and came to meet Braun, extending a rather moist and bony right hand. The receptionist was dismissed with a curt nod.

'Please sit down, my dear Superintendent,' Feininger said affably. 'Make yourself at home.'

He gave a bright and lingering smile, offered Braun cognac – 'a gift from the French Ambassador' – and cigars – 'a birthday present from the premier, now reserved for very special visitors.'

Braun helped himself without ceremony. 'I'm here in an official capacity, Herr Feininger. May I ask you a few questions?'

'As many as you like. Fire away.'

From notes of the ensuing interview compiled by Detective-Superintendent Braun and submitted to Chief Superintendent Dürrenmaier in the form of a memorandum headed 'For Official Use Only':

QUESTION: Is it true that you own a blue Jaguar car with a two-digit Munich licence number?

ANSWER: I do, but it can't be the only blue Jag in town. I'm pretty certain I've seen a couple of similar models around.

QUESTION: Do you drive the car yourself?

ANSWER: Usually but not always. My official car is a BMW. I employ a chauffeur to drive both. His name is Wegleben – a very reliable man.

QUESTION: Do you think it possible that the Jaguar could have been parked near a building in V-Strasse – No. 33 – in the past few months? At various times and on several occasions?

ANSWER: V-Strasse? Let me think. Oh yes, it may well have been. I seem to remember that Wegleben – the chauffeur I mentioned – has some relatives in the neighbourhood. You'd better ask him.

QUESTION: Can you recall your whereabouts on the night of 15 September last?

Feininger, in the act of refilling their glasses with ambassadorial cognac, stared at Braun in some surprise. 'Good heavens, that's weeks ago.'

'So you don't remember?'

'I've an excellent memory,' Feininger said thoughtfully, 'a gift my enemies don't always appreciate – but I'm not a memory man. However, I naturally keep an engagement book with my daily schedule.'

'What would your agenda have been on 15 September?'

'Let me take a look,' Feininger replied, obliging as ever. He reached for a leather-bound pad which lay close to hand on the desk. It consisted of 365 sheets of paper, each divided into twenty-four hourly sections. Feininger riffled through the pages.

'Here we are! 15 September. Spent the day here in Munich, administrative conference in the morning, called on the Minister of Finance after lunch, then a press conference. Late afternoon, flew to Bonn and drove from there to Bad Godesberg. A get-together with some political associates at the Golden Lamb, private banqueting-room. It lasted until the small hours.'

'I suppose you can produce witnesses to confirm your presence there?'

'Any number, including a couple of government ministers. If I spent the night in Bonn I can hardly have been in Munich at the same time. Correct me if I'm wrong.'

From Detective-Superintendent Keller's notes:

I was reluctant to fly to Madrid even though I'd suggested the trip myself. The thought of leaving Anton worried me, and I didn't feel happy until Harald Fein had been discharged from hospital and was back in his apartment.

Madrid is one of my favourite places, first because of the Bosch paintings in the Prado and second because of Santos, a colleague in the Spanish CID. We worked together on a jet-set sex killing some years ago.

Santos met me at the airport and we spent most of the night talking shop. Next morning my request was granted. I found myself face to face with Kordes. Santos stood guard outside. He'd managed to get me an undisturbed two hours with the man.

Thirty minutes was all I needed.

Chief Superintendent Dürrenmaier in conversation with Jürgen T., author of several internationally acclaimed books on criminology. The following record of the interview was borrowed from the author's working notes:

DÜRRENMAIER: Policemen are human beings, with all the shortcomings, weaknesses and inadequacies of the breed. They try to be objective but they're always in danger of yielding to their own prejudices, pipe-dreams and preconceived notions of law enforcement, not to mention the pressures that are exerted on them.

JÜRGEN T.: Aren't you really saying that you accept miscarriages of justice as a matter of course?

DÜRRENMAIER: If I did I wouldn't be sitting here now, but I don't have any illusions about the human element in our profession. You have to bear it constantly in mind – it's the only way of avoiding slip-ups. Of course, I won't pretend you can eliminate them altogether. However hard-bitten a detective may be, one out of a hundred apparently routine cases may suddenly cause him to react in a humanly committed way. I can't entirely suppress such a reaction, just as I can't eradicate prejudice or even hatred for particular social classes. What I can do is to spot such tendencies early and try to head them off.

JÜRGEN T.: And you wouldn't claim immunity for anyone – not even in your own department?

DÜRRENMAIER: Not even for myself – nor for Braun, if that's who you're getting at. If there's any exception, it's Keller.

'They must have given you the wrong address, Keller.' The Munich pimp cocked a quizzical eye at his visitor. 'You didn't come all this way specially to see me, did you?'

'Specially to see you,' Keller confirmed cheerfully, and started to tour the cell like an old con. He turned on the tap, drank a little water from his cupped hand, and gave a satisfied nod. Then, having tested the mattress for comfort, he sat down. Never once, throughout this performance, did his eyes leave Kordes, who was growing more and more uneasy.

'Listen,' Kordes said fiercely, 'I don't know what you're after and I don't want to know. If it's murder, count me out – killings aren't in my line.'

'The first hint of violence and you bail out, right?'

'Damn right,' said Kordes. 'You know me.'

'We know each other,' Keller amended gently.

There had been a variety of reasons for their previous encounters, which covered a span of some years: several muggings of wealthy drunks, a case of manslaughter, and the maltreatment of a prostitute by someone armed with a razor. Kordes had never been more than a witness on each occasion, and Keller had consistently treated him as such. Remembering this, Kordes felt an obligation to show gratitude.

'Look, Keller, I'll tell you this for free. If you try and spring me I'll clam up tight, even with you. The Spaniards have got so little on me I'll be sun-bathing on the Costa Brava in six months' time. I'm not itching to see dear old Munich again, believe me. It stinks.'

'With all due deference to your sense of smell, Kordes, you're wrong if you think I came to claim you for the German authorities. My interest in you is almost entirely personal. I'd appreciate some information, that's all.'

'About the V-Strasse murder? I had nothing to do with it, Keller. I was gone by that time and you know it. Perfect timing, eh?'

The pimp's manner grew more relaxed. If the superintendent said he hadn't come to collect, he hadn't. Kordes joined Keller on the bed and gave him a confidential, encouraging nod. It was a go-ahead.

'I'd like to know some more about your late girl-friend's collection of addresses. You only gave Braun the bare essentials, but I want to know everything. I take it that the list of addresses was your idea – you got her to keep a record complete with times and prices, also the names of her satisfied customers. What you might call a long-term capital investment, am I right?'

'You're a gentleman, Keller,' Kordes said gratefully. 'You don't use words like blackmail or extortion when it's only a question of offering to keep quiet for an agreed fee. Between you and me, though, it never paid off. Some damned amateur fouled up the whole operation.'

'Harald Fein, you mean?'

'That stupid bastard!' Kordes sounded genuinely indignant. 'He tried to muscle in on the act. Thanks to him, I could still find myself hauled back to Munich, when all I'm charged with here is a couple of currency offences – an upper-class crime if ever there was one.'

'What if I guarantee you a year's holiday in Madrid?'

'You do that, Keller, and I'll tell you anything you want to know. Word of honour.'

From Detective-Superintendent Keller's notes:

Mutual trust is a very serious thing in our trade. Whether you're a policeman or a criminal, you can only abuse it once. After that, you're on your own.

The word soon gets round when there's been a breach of good faith. Kordes knew that as well as I did. We were business partners, so to speak.

With the help of my friend Santos, it took only five minutes to agree terms satisfactory to all parties. Kordes promised to give Santos a few hints on the subject of currency offences, forged passports, and so on. In return, Santos told him that inquiries would naturally take time. Kordes would be provisionally released but must remain in the Madrid area for at least twelve months.

That settled, Kordes answered every question I put, short and sweet.

1. The entry 'Fein' in his girl-friend's engagement book didn't refer to Harald Fein. The stop after it signified that it was an

abbreviation for Feininger, the big gun in Federal politics. Kordes advised me to concentrate on him – and what advice could have been more welcome?

Incidental comment by Kordes:

To be honest, Keller, we got our sums wrong. Feininger wasn't an easy nut to crack. The bastard threatened us with everything short of capital punishment. Once I saw he meant it I made tracks, first of all for Switzerland and then for Spain. After all, who can afford to tangle with a heavyweight like Feininger? Not even the police, I figure.

2. There were numerous entries against the name Paul, e.g. 'W. Paul', which referred to Wolfgang Paul, a TV actor. Then there was 'Paul W.' – Paul Wohlfahrt, sales manager of a washing-machine company. Finally – several times – plain 'Paul'.

'Who's Paul?' I asked.

'Paul is Paul,' Kordes explained. 'You know, the construction boss – Paul Plattner.'

'I see,' I said.

The same day, while searching his parental home, and far more quickly than he had expected, Heinz discovered Helga's suicide note. He found it in the bottom left-hand drawer of his mother's dressing-table.

Helga had written:

I can't take it any more. I don't want to go on. Everything's so unspeakably sordid.

I've been misjudged and taken advantage of. Nobody really loves me, everyone uses me.

You don't love me, Mother, neither do you, Daddy, nor you, Heinz.

It's almost as if you'd all conspired to expose me to this final, unimaginable act of degradation. If this is what living means, I'm happy to die.

Forgive me – especially you, darling Daddy – but I can't help myself.

Chapter Nine

'Welcome back to the big city with the big heart.' Heinz leant against the customs barrier at Munich airport with an ironical smile on his face.

Keller returned the smile, less irony. 'Good to see you.'

'Give me that bag,' Heinz said briskly. 'I'm your reception committee. I know you'd have preferred it to be Anton, but at least I've got one thing he doesn't have. A car.'

Keller surrendered his bag and they walked across the concourse to the main exit. The policeman glanced at the boy and said: 'So you found it.'

Heinz nodded. He was learning to react like Keller. 'You can read it on the trip into town.'

Heinz Fein commenting subsequently on these events to a friend:

If I ever met a born poker-player, it was Keller. No matter what happened, he never showed a trace of emotion.

He didn't then, as he sat there beside me reading Helga's note – very slowly, very carefully. He must have read it through several times. I tried to read his expression but he spotted me at once. 'Keep your eyes on the road,' he said, quite sharply.

Detective-Superintendent Braun, also subsequently, to a colleague:

. . . always thought Keller was a sly dog – I mean that as a compliment, of course.

. . . didn't prevent him from getting under our skin – Dürrenmaier's included, if I'm any judge. He was always trying to play his own little game. Fair enough, it's only what I've done myself.

. . . except that Keller was far more singleminded – more ruthless, you might say. It cost him his job. He was pensioned off after that. Voluntarily, so as to avoid compulsory retirement, get me? But not before he was upgraded to Chief Superintendent. Well, that's life.

'What do you make of it?' Heinz gestured at the letter in Keller's

213

hand. 'Something really terrible must have happened, something traumatic enough to make her want to kill herself. Father's determined to find out what it was. So am I. Will you help us?'

Keller seemed to consider the question superfluous. He merely said: 'Have you shown this to your father?'

'I thought *you* would.'

'Not immediately, if it's all right with you. Not until I think fit – maybe not at all. Do you agree?'

Heinz slowed his Volkswagen, swung right down a side road, braked to a halt and switched off. He turned to look at the little man beside him, who still sat hunched in his seat, staring at Helga's letter.

'What was that,' the boy asked, 'a suggestion, a piece of advice or an order?'

'A sort of moratorium,' Keller replied patiently. 'By mutual agreement – just for a couple of days.'

'A deal, you mean. What are you offering in return?'

'Plenty, I'd say.' Keller folded the note carefully and put it in his breast-pocket. 'As long as you keep your mouth shut, I'll do the same.'

'What about?'

'You know perfectly well. However, my silence is conditional on something else.'

'Like what?'

'I want you to do me a favour.'

'What is it this time?'

'I'd like you to pay a visit to the head office of Plattner Construction, or rather, to the office of your grandfather's private secretary. You know your way around there pretty well – in fact you're quite an expert with photocopiers and typewriters.'

'How would you know?'

'I know, that's all,' Keller said simply. You'd better resign yourself to the fact.'

Confidential memorandum specially compiled for Keller by Detective-Inspector Hohmann with the assistance of an informant employed by Plattner Construction:

9 October, 14.10–14.40. Heinz Fein alone with E. M. Wagnersberger, the chairman's secretary, in her office.

11 October, 16.05–17.00. Ditto.

13 October, 19.40–21.50. Dinner with Fräulein Wagnersberger at the *Bonne Auberge*.

Afterwards, H.F. drove the latter to her apartment in Hohen-zollernstrasse, where he remained from 22.20 until 00.10.

15 October, 18.45–19.35. Heinz Fein in Wagnersberger's office, alone. Sound of typewriter heard.

Eva-Maria Wagnersberger, private secretary to the chairman of Plattner Construction, on her relations with Heinz Fein:

Oh, come now, I'm old enough to be his – well, his elder sister. Still, he *was* the chairman's grandson and likely to step into his shoes one day. He started to take an interest in the firm – no, not me personally.

I took him under my wing for the firm's sake – it was the natural thing to do. I felt confident of Herr Plattner's approval.

Gottfried Wamsler, responsible for messenger duties at the head office, also for the chairman's personal comfort:

It was as plain as the nose on your face. If you wanted to get anywhere with the old man you had to go through Fräulein Wagnersberger – if you know what I mean. Young Herr Heinz spotted that straight off. He's got a head on his shoulders under all that long hair.

Of course he laid her, I'd bet a week's wages on it. After all, it was a sort of family tradition. I'd have been surprised if he hadn't . . .

'To recap,' Heinz said, 'you're telling me to get you a specimen sheet typed on the machine at head office – the Construkta?'

'I'm telling you nothing, simply asking.'

'Will do.'

'When, today?'

Heinz nodded. 'Anything else?'

'Yes, a specimen sheet from the Rapidex photocopier in the same office. Can you swing that?'

Heinz nodded again. 'You'll get that too, first thing tomorrow at latest. Is that all?'

'For now, yes.'

'What about Helga's note?'

'I'll come back to that. I have to make a few inquiries first, and I know where to begin. For a start, I'd like you to drop me off at your father's apartment.'

'What's the fatal attraction?'

'Anton.'

Braun and Feldmann. An off-duty monologue in the Bürgerbräu beer cellar. Subject: the Olympics.

What do you mean, international sportsmanship? It's nothing but a piece of commercial showbiz, a worldwide spectacular, like the moon landings only more profitable.

Sure the Mayor's a shrewd operator. It's his way of pumping a few hundred million marks into the city, but look what it's costing. First he says six hundred million, then a thousand. By the time that flame's lit he'll be five hundred million over the top, if not eight hundred.

The city pockets almost everything and only foots a third of the bill. The rest is split between the provincial government and Bonn, whose share has just risen to fifty per cent. But the Mayor gets his subway network, his new roads, his big squares and sports facilities – enough to keep us going till the year 2000, probably.

So far so good, but the vultures can smell blood. They want their share. They build, organize, publicize, co-ordinate and invest. Seven full-time lawyers on the Olympic Planning Committee have been selling off concessions – mustard, potato-chips, toothpaste, toilet paper, ashtrays, sausages, honey, fruit-juice, cheese, underclothes . . .

Snack bars have been springing up, the Olympic Tower beams neon advertising slogans in all directions, a thousand-plus hostesses have been engaged and four-and-a-half million tickets sold for roughly thirty million marks – in other words, less than a fiftieth of the total cost.

FELDMANN: Personally, I think a project like this ought to be credited with a little idealism as well.

BRAUN: Oh, sure. If you fleece the public you've got to anaesthetize them first, and idealism is as good a narcotic as any. However, we're policemen. Our field is crime.

FELDMANN: Where do the Olympics come in?

BRAUN: No prizes for guessing. Fein's a front for Plattner, or a giant construction company. Feininger's the tip of an iceberg consisting of various pressure groups – banks, insurance companies, haulage firms, breweries, hotel chains. Hasn't it ever struck you how the same trade names turn up wherever you go – in the traffic-free zone in the city centre, under the Stachus, on the Olympic site?

FELDMANN: That may well be, but it isn't illegal or criminal. Or is it?

BRAUN: Let's see what we dig up, shall we?

Keller heard Anton bark joyously as he neared the door of Harald's apartment. He rang the bell.

The dog rushed at him as soon as Harald opened the door. Keller picked him up, hugged him, suffered his face to be licked.

'He's been expecting you,' Harald said cordially. 'So have I. How was Madrid – any luck?'

'Maybe, maybe not, it depends on your point of view,' said Keller, tenderly preoccupied with Anton.

Harald's face fell. 'You mean it was a waste of time?'

'I certainly achieved something,' Keller told him. He scratched Anton behind the ears. 'For instance, Fein plus full point equals Feininger, and it really is the Feininger we thought it was. You give your lawyer the nod and see what he says. I'd like to take Anton for a walk – with your permission.'

Extracts from a report by Dr Rehlinger, a police consultant on typewriters and duplicating equipment, with reference to specimens obtained by Keller from Heinz Fein:

Complete identity of typescript. There is no doubt that the letter to the *Morgenzeitung* matches the specimen submitted. Both were typed on the same machine.

As to the photocopy: characteristic rhythmical smudging discernible in right-hand margin of sheet submitted. Another perfect match. In both cases, therefore, the *Morgenzeitung* and Plattner Construction specimens correspond precisely and beyond all reasonable doubt.

'Who are you?' asked Plattner. 'A policeman?'

'My name is Neumann,' said his visitor, who looked like the most solid of citizens, 'Detective-Inspector Neumann, Forensic Investigation Department, Municipal Police Headquarters.'

'Well, what do you want?'

'I came to give you some information, sir.'

'About what?'

'About a matter directly affecting you and your firm. I hasten to add that no suspicion attaches to you personally, under the circumstances. We'd simply appreciate your co-operation in clarifying a few points.'

From Detective-Superintendent Keller's notes:

I've now spent almost forty years in the police service. I've worked on thousands of cases with hundreds of fellow-detectives, and I always received help when I asked for it.

When it came to administering another jolt to Paul Plattner, however, I wavered for a considerable time before I delegated the job to a colleague. I felt an almost irresistible urge to renew my acquaintance with the man, but it seemed premature.

I eventually sent Neumann to see him – a nondescript individual at first glance, but competent. Having briefed the inspector thoroughly, I turned him loose.

Plattner glared suspiciously at Neumann. 'What do you mean, co-operation?'

'In this instance, Herr Plattner, you'd better begin by taking note of a few facts. Then you can draw your own conclusions.'

'What the devil are you talking about?'

'I'm referring to the documents that have been anonymously sent to the *Morgenzeitung*.'

'Dirty work of the first order!' Plattner snapped.

'You can say that again,' Neumann agreed. 'Especially as our technicians have established beyond doubt that all the documents were produced on these premises. The typewriter is in your private secretary's office, and so's the photocopier.'

'But that's impossible!'

'There's no mistake,' Neumann pursued matter-of-factly. 'The results of our tests correspond in every respect. Any court in the land would accept them.'

Plattner flicked a switch on his intercom. 'Get me Jonas!' he roared.

'I'm surrounded by two-timers!' Plattner snarled, when Jonas

218

was finally standing in front of him. 'All right, what have you got to say for yourself?'

Jonas stared helplessly at his chairman. 'Forgive me, Herr Plattner – I don't know what you're talking about.'

'It must have been you. You're the only possible candidate.'

'For what?'

'God Almighty, don't give me that!' Plattner bellowed. 'You know damn well what I'm talking about – that scandal-sheet and its libellous articles.'

Jonas shook his head uncomprehendingly. Plattner looked as if he were on the verge of a heart attack. So much the better. If they carried him off to hospital it would leave the chairman's seat vacant. 'Why so agitated all of a sudden?'

'Because I now have proof positive that the thing was engineered under my nose – right here in the head office.'

'No!' Jonas flinched. 'You must be wrong.'

'Wrong be damned! The CID have checked, and their findings allow of only one interpretation. *Our* typewriter, *our* photo-copier, *our* confidential information. In other.words, *you're* the culprit!'

It was Jonas's turn to lose his composure. He slumped into the nearest chair, ran a finger round the inside of his collar and stared at Plattner in dismay. 'It simply can't be true.'

'It's a solid gold certainty. I told you – you're the only possible candidate. You know your way around our files and you have the spare key to the safe – which you'll kindly hand over forthwith. Finally, you're the only person apart from me who has the run of this office.'

'No, no!' Jonas retorted fiercely. 'You can accuse me of a lot of things, Herr Plattner, but not that. I'm not a complete fool. I wouldn't shit on my own doorstep. What's more, I wouldn't jeopardize your daughter's happiness – or my own.'

Plattner had subsided. He stared into space for some moments, then said: 'If it wasn't you, who was it? Surely not Eva-Maria?'

'Who knows?' Jonas said calmly.

Eva-Maria Wagnersberger, long-time private secretary to the chairman of Plattner Construction:
The firm flourished, but it naturally suffered a few setbacks from time to time.

A bridge collapse resulting in three deaths, 1959; a law-suit for restitution of excessive charges – a put-up job inspired by one of our competitors, 1963; and a riot by foreign labourers who claimed they were being exploited and said so on TV.

Herr Plattner always managed to master these situations. As soon as he came under attack he struck back. His competitors learnt to fear him.

On this occasion, even Plattner showed signs of losing his nerve. So did Jonas. They sat facing each other like two wild beasts poised for the kill.

Plattner outlined the situation for my benefit. Jonas had the effrontery to demand my hundred-per-cent backing in the chairman's presence. That got my goat, naturally, so I said: 'I've worked here for nearly twenty years, and nobody has ever suggested that I was anything but absolutely trustworthy. Herr Plattner can confirm that. I shouldn't have to defend my good name.'

Plattner nodded. Then he said: 'Herr Jonas, you're suspended as of now. Please – your comments on the subject don't interest me. Hard facts are all that can clear the air. From now on, I shall accept nothing else.'

Which was equivalent to the axe.

Joachim Jonas, early next day, in conversation with Clemens Duhr, Plattner's only serious competitor in the Munich area:

. . . no intention of incriminating anyone or even of casting suspicion on them . . . simply anxious to clarify my own position in a way that might possibly serve your best interests, Herr Duhr.

In view of your several discreet offers of employment in the past, that's to say, hints that I might like to invest my long and varied experience in your organization, I'm now willing to consider the possibility. Provided, of course, that you're still interested enough to make me a firm offer – and believe me, you wouldn't regret it . . .

Duhr's comment to his eldest son and deputy, after Jonas's departure:

What a nerve! I'll have to let Plattner know, of course. Fair competition is one thing, disloyalty's another. You have to draw the line somewhere, especially with a close associate like Plattner.

If Jonas has finished his business career for good, he only has himself to blame.

'What nonsense!' Feininger exclaimed. He emitted a short bark of laughter and stared at Braun. 'You can't expect me to take that seriously, Superintendent. It's downright slanderous.'

'Possibly.' Braun's tone was noncommittal. 'I know it's only a conjecture, but every conjecture has to be checked.'

Feininger studied the detective-superintendent closely. He did not renew his offer of a prime ministerial cigar or an ambassadorial cognac. He missed the usual deference and readiness to co-operate. Braun made an unreceptive, unapproachable impression.

'May I therefore ask you, Herr Feininger, if you've ever visited No. 33 V-Strasse?'

'It isn't a punishable offence, is it?'

'Of course not. Moreover, any statement to that effect would be treated with the utmost discretion.'

'I know what that means. If I say yes you'll make a note of my reply – very discreetly, of course – and incorporate it in your files. Files to which a host of authorized persons have access. You expect me to run that sort of risk? Man, how stupid do you think I am?'

'In that case I shall have to note that you decline to answer.'

Feininger, an experienced verbal swordsman who had emerged victorious from many a TV duel, reacted promptly. 'I don't decline to answer. I merely decline to commit myself either way. You won't get a yes or no out of me. The Federal Constitution grants every citizen the right to resist invasions of privacy.'

'I see,' said Braun. 'You mean your private life doesn't concern us. Nor does it, unless there's a possible connection between your personal affairs and a penal offence. If there is, I'm afraid we have to check.'

'But my dear Superintendent, if you're back on the subject of 15 September, I already told you – I spent the evening with political associates at Bad Godesberg. There's even a guest list in existence.'

'May I see it?'

'By all means. Here's a photocopy, complete with agenda and programme. Please treat the contents as strictly confidential.'

Feininger picked up a sheaf of typescript which had been lying at his elbow. 'That ought to satisfy you, surely.'

Feininger's office television set was switched on in the background, ready to transmit pictures of the latest party conference. Images flashed across the screen, in colour but with the sound turned down. It was commercial time.

Feininger distracted Braun's attention by gesturing at the TV set. 'Mass hypnosis, these commercials. Positively criminal, eh?'

Braun, who was thumbing through the sheets Feininger had given him, merely said: 'The penal code determines what is criminal, Herr Feininger. There aren't any laws against mass hypnosis, as far as I'm aware.'

'Nor, I'm glad to say, against my personal way of life.'

'I'll check on that,' Braun said tersely. It was hard to tell which he meant, Feininger's way of life or the typescript which he now stuffed into his briefcase.

'I can't say I find your attitude particularly co-operative.'

'I have a job to do, that's all.'

Feininger's resentment suddenly exploded. 'Look here, Braun, I don't like this. I want to know – are you planning to make trouble for me or aren't you?'

'You may laugh, Herr Feininger, but I'm only trying to do my duty.'

'Why should I laugh, especially as I'm familiar with one or two aspects of your past career which aren't officially known to the authorities?'

Notes made by the Commissioner of Police on the occasion of an interview with Detective Chief Superintendent Dürrenmaier:

1. I was informed that Det.-Supt Braun had submitted a report on his past activities – the third in twenty years. Det. Chief Supt Dürrenmaier appended the documents previously on record. It emerged from them that:

(a) Braun has, since 1945, performed excellent detective work, first as chief inspector and then as superintendent.

(b) Braun had, prior to 1945, put his not inconsiderable talents at the service of the former régime, first as inspector and then as chief inspector.

2. Det.-Supt Braun's activities prior to 1945 have already been

investigated several times, as witness the relevant documents. First in 1946 by a de-Nazification tribunal, which declared that no criminal charges could be brought against him, and then in 1953, by a personnel screening committee at Police HQ. The result was the same.

'That needn't necessarily be the last word on the subject,' mused Feininger. 'There may be some quite different records in existence. Records of your activities in 1939 and 1940 at Mlava, a suburb of Warsaw. You remember the place?'

'I do indeed.' Braun sounded wholly unperturbed.

'People were arrested by you or your department, then tried and executed.'

'I worked on two cases where the death penalty was imposed. The men involved were straightforward criminals, a rapist with a long record of sexual offences and a murderer in the furtherance of theft.'

'So you say,' drawled Feininger. 'Other people are prepared to testify that they were Polish partisans whom Gestapo files falsely represented as criminals.'

'Even if it were true,' Braun said staunchly, 'how would that affect the present issue?'

'Work it out for yourself,' snapped Feininger. 'And be quick about it.'

Admissions, conjectures and realizations voiced by Adolf Penatsch, erstwhile janitor of No. 33 V-Strasse, to a subsequent cell-mate and police informer:

The double-crossing bastard! I'd never have thought it of a man like Braun. He was glad enough of my help to begin with. I was his star witness. Hand in glove, we were, until suddenly – bingo! – everything changed.

I was wheeled into his office at the double. No chair, no cup of coffee – not this time. He accused me of trying to frame this Harald Fein, said I'd made a lot of sworn statements which were nothing but hot air.

'And why?' he said. 'That's what I've been asking myself – why do your best to drop him in the shit with a load of fake evidence? I'll tell you why, you crafty son of a bitch. It was a smokescreen. You've been feeding me red herrings to take the heat off yourself.'

223

Detective Chief Superintendent Dürrenmaier, Counsellor Messer and Detective-Superintendent Braun, convened for what Dürrenmaier chose to term an informal exchange of views:

'Gentlemen,' the chief superintendent said urbanely, after they had taken their places in the shabby 'conference corner' of his office, 'I set up this meeting at your request, Herr Messer. Superintendent Braun raised no objection to the idea.'

'Because it's an open and shut case,' Braun insisted.

'Really?' retorted the lawyer. 'You can't have done your homework very thoroughly.'

Dürrenmaier gave him a reproving glance. 'Please, Counsellor, no unfounded assertions if you please.'

'Not so unfounded,' Messer pursued belligerently. 'With a handful of assistants, I've uncovered a whole lot more than Herr Braun and the entire city police force.'

'For instance?' sneered Braun.

'For instance, enough to exonerate my client completely. I shall expect you to issue an official statement designed to clear his name.'

'You'd just love that, wouldn't you?' Braun said, still provocatively. 'Until someone produces satisfactory evidence to the contrary, Harald Fein remains my chief suspect.'

Dürrenmaier eyed Messer with an air of courteous inquiry. 'And what, Counsellor, do you say to that?'

'I like it here.' Keller, still on indefinite leave, had commandeered one of Harald's arm-chairs – the largest and most comfortable. Anton was sharing it with him.

'You're always welcome,' Harald assured him. He surveyed the idyllic scene with a hint of resignation. Anton had stretched out beside Keller and laid his head in the policeman's lap. He appeared to be asleep. 'You make a pretty picture, the pair of you. Why spoil it by harping on the same old theme?'

Keller smiled. 'We must keep at it till we get the answer. Then we can move on, step by step, to your daughter's death. I know it's your prime concern, but we must take things in order of priority. My own first concern happens to be a question which is no doubt taxing Braun at this moment. What did you *really* see in V-Strasse on the night of 15 September? You're obviously reluctant to name names. Do you still hesitate, even with me?'

Harald looked away. 'Let's drop the subject, shall we?'

'I think I understand,' Keller said, mechanically fondling Anton's woolly head. 'In spite of all that's happened, you find it impossible to use the methods that have been employed against you.'

'I can't help it.'

'You don't make things easy for yourself. What's more, you don't do any good. Take your attempt to shield Hermann Abendroth. An admirable impulse, Herr Fein, except that all your self-sacrifice was bound to go for nothing in the world of a man like Plattner.'

'It's enough for me to feel that I've done my best to repay friendship with friendship.' Harald's voice sank to a whisper. 'What happened to my daughter? That's what keeps going round and round in my head.'

'Be patient. There are still a few links missing from the chain.'

A gala evening at the Zirkus Krone, *featuring Charlie Rivel, the world-famous clown. The audience: almost everyone of name and repute – at least, everyone with aspirations to a niche in the columns of 'Hunter', 'Argus', 'Suzanne', 'Anatol' or 'Manfred'. Also present – apart from Princess Birgitta, Archduchess Maria and Baroness Irina – Mesdames Hilde Fein and Melanie Weber escorted by Joachim Jonas. Questioned by 'Argus' on how they had enjoyed Charlie Rivel, the King of Clowns, they replied as follows:*

HILDE FEIN: As great as ever, but he left me feeling terribly sad. Perhaps that's the secret of his greatness.

JOACHIM JONAS: Like something out of the last century, which is probably why people flock to see him. He's the personification of our yearning for childish things, our hankering for traditional values, our rosy dreams of bygone days.

MELANIE WEBER: Yet another landmark in the social calendar of our beloved Munich, with its gaiety, its spontaneous charm, its sense of freedom, its . . .

'All the allegedly incriminating evidence against my client,' Messer told Dürrenmaier, 'seems to rest solely on Superintendent Braun's belief that he's the only possible suspect.'

'Suggest another,' said Braun. 'And don't tell me you're back on the Feininger tack.'

'According to my notes,' Dürrenmaier interposed cautiously, 'Herr Feininger spent the night of 15 September in Bad Godesberg.'

'Ah, yes,' said Messer. 'I took the liberty of double-checking Herr Feininger's alibi.'

Braun gave a contemptuous snort. 'What was there to check? The murder occurred about 10 p.m. Herr Feininger was seen in Bad Godesberg the same night – he even figured on a guest list.'

'Purely for your information, Superintendent, he entered his name on that list himself.'

'So what?' Braun betrayed no surprise. 'If he was there, four hundred kilometres away, which he was, how could he have been here at almost the same time? Munich to Bonn in forty minutes? There isn't a flight he could have caught at that hour.'

'Not a scheduled flight,' Messer conceded. 'No private aircraft took off during the relevant period either – I checked. You did too, no doubt.' He drew a deep breath and went on: 'However, an air force plane did take off from Fürstenfeldbrück.'

'Well?' said Braun, still undaunted. 'Are you planning to implicate the Ministry of Defence as well?'

Messer paused, relishing the superintendent's growing uneasiness. 'The air force customarily puts aircraft at the disposal of whichever government happens to be in power, and the government, in turn, offers vacant seats to ministerial officials, members of parliament, journalists, etcetera. A jet transport of this type left Fürstenfeldbrück military airfield shortly before 11 p.m. Herr Feininger was on board.'

'Do you have the passenger list?' Braun asked. 'Are there any witnesses?'

'There are,' Messer assured him. 'I can also prove that the guest list at Bad Godesberg wasn't closed until after midnight. The last name on the list was Feininger's.'

'I have to make a quick phone call,' Dürrenmaier said, and hurried out of the room.

Left alone together, Messer and Braun exchanged a slow smile. There was even a trace of mutual understanding in it.

'Well,' the lawyer asked at length, 'what do you say to that?'

Braun's smile broadened. 'What I say is, let's make the best of a bad job.'

'Meaning what?'

'My dear Herr Messer, you don't seem to grasp what criminal investigation really entails.' Braun's tone was surprisingly ingenuous. 'One of the first things a CID officer has to learn is how to deal with overnight changes in the status quo. That's why we keep several irons in the fire at once.'

'Which one do you propose to extract this time?'

Braun sat back and clasped his paunch. 'I suppose I'm right in assuming that your only concern – well, let's say your first concern – is to get your client off the hook and wash him whiter than white, correct? Well, I've no objection.'

Messer raised his head like a hound taking scent. At such moments he bore a distant resemblance to Anton. 'Who's available apart from Feininger?'

'Penatsch – the janitor,' Braun told him amiably. 'You didn't overlook him yourself. We ought to be able to make something out of Penatsch.'

'If we had something to go on, yes.'

'Run your eye over this memo.'

Memorandum 'For Official Use Only' on pale green onion skin, drafted by Detective-Superintendent Braun:
. . . thought it advisable to consult my colleague Det.-Supt Keller, PECD officer, Munich area, who shares the same office. Being aware of his contacts with the Spanish CID, I requested his assistance. Det.-Supt Keller travelled to Madrid in order to interrogate Karl Kordes, who was currently on remand there.

As a result of his inquiries, I obtained possession of a diary belonging to the dead woman, also safe-deposited with the Deutsche Bank but at another branch (2 Lenbachplatz).

It was less a diary than the outline of a novel with thinly disguised characters drawn from real life – pure porn and probably libellous. It contained a number of unmistakable references to Adolf Penatsch, the janitor. I quote:

'. . . came sniffing round me like one of those truffle-pigs you read about . . . had a pass-key to every apartment . . . burst in on me while I was in bed, entertaining . . .

. . . almost frothing at the mouth, he was. 'You bitch,' he hissed, 'I suppose you can't get enough of it, eh?' – and plenty more of the same . . .

. . . then, when he brought up my mail: 'If you don't do it with me, you Jezebel, and soon, I'll fix you for good.'

'Straightforward enough,' Braun inquired brightly, 'wouldn't you say?'

Messer stroked his jaw. 'Very promising but not absolutely conclusive. A useful foundation to build on, no more.'

Braun was swift to agree. 'I know what you mean. "I was a Teenage Tart" and all that sort of thing – these days, every call-girl in Schwabing keeps a diary with one eye on the serialization rights. If we're going to nail Penatsch properly we need to identify all the other suspects, if only so we can eliminate them. I'm convinced of one thing: Fein spotted somebody else on his visits to V-Strasse. Somebody he refuses to mention, for whatever reason. If he wants to clear himself he'll have to come clean.'

Now it was Messer's turn to rise abruptly, just as Dürrenmaier had done a few minutes earlier. 'I have to make a quick phone call.'

A statement by Paul Plattner, chairman of the Plattner Construction Company, boxed on p. 1 of the Morgenzeitung *under a reprise of the eye-catching headline 'How to print your own money (contd)':*

. . . inescapable conclusion that the whole affair is a well rehearsed attack on my company's enviable reputation, a smear campaign which has doubtless been engineered by some un-scrupulous competitor . . .

. . . deplorable and unjustified aspersions cast on the motives underlying our acquisition of properties in the Sunset Estate district . . . an entirely independent initiative on the part of my erstwhile deputy, Herr Harald Fein, while I was absent on a business trip . . .

. . . not, of course, to suggest that these transactions could in any way be linked with the long-standing friendship between my former deputy and the respected head of the Urban Planning Department, Herr Abendroth . . . still less to imply that there may be a connection between His Honour the Mayor and property deals to which there attaches even a breath of suspicion . . .

'Well,' said Keller, hugging Anton to him, 'isn't that enough for you?'

'He's wrong.' Harald re-read Plattner's statement in the *Morgenzeitung* with a satisfied smile. 'What's more, he doesn't know how wrong he is.'

'Is this part of it,' Keller asked, watching him intently, 'part of your plan?'

'I don't have one.' Harald looked Keller full in the eye. 'I sit back and let things happen. No need for me to do more, it seems. My only real concern is Helga's death, but that will sort itself out too, in due course.'

Keller gave him an appraising stare. 'I assume that your Job-like forbearance is based on the fact that you know something – something unknown to the rest of us. At least, that's what you think.'

'Why, do you know too?'

Keller nodded.

'I thank my lucky stars,' Harald said with profound sincerity, 'that I don't have you for an enemy.'

'Better thank Anton for that.'

Telephone conversation, first between Messer and Harald, then between Messer and Keller:

MESSER: Good news, Herr Fein! Don't make any more slip-ups and you're in the clear.

HARALD: Slip-ups? What sort?

MESSER: Is Superintendent Keller with you? If so, I'd like a quick word with him.

KELLER: (grabbing the phone with a pleased and expectant air): Well, is the switch complete?

MESSER: How did you know?

KELLER: I know Braun and the way he operates. If he dropped your client, or was compelled to, he must have demanded a quid pro quo. What's he after?

MESSER: Just a lead from Herr Fein. A clue to the identity of somebody he saw and recognized during his visits to the neighbourhood of 33 V-Strasse. Braun's convinced he's shielding someone.

KELLER: He could be right, but don't expect me to talk your client into making dangerous admissions. Anyway, I haven't made up my mind which way to advise him.

MESSER: I beg of you, Superintendent! This is a golden opportunity – don't knock it on the head. Tell him to talk.

KELLER: He knows the name of the game far better than we do. I'll ring you back in a few minutes – maybe a bit longer. Be patient, Counsellor. It'll do you good for a change.

Heinz had meantime entered his father's apartment without knocking, without greeting anyone except Anton, who was favoured with a friendly pat on the haunches.

He flopped into the nearest arm-chair, tossed some newspapers on the table and pushed them across to his father. Keller finished his phone conversation and joined them, looking uncharacteristically smug.

'Well,' Heinz said, indicating the newspapers, 'have you feasted your eyes on that crap?'

Harald shrugged. 'It doesn't interest me.'

'It doesn't interest him!' Heinz gave a sardonic smile and turned to Keller. 'My ever-loving father gets another load of mud slung at him, this time in company with his only friend, who happens to be my godfather and Helga's – and what's the reaction? He's not interested!'

Harald pushed the papers away and frowned. 'You're interfering, Heinz. Please keep out of this.'

'Interfering's his favourite hobby at the moment,' Keller said drily. 'You've no idea the lengths he goes to.'

'Read the *Morgenzeitung* yet?' Heinz saw Keller nod, but his father stared impassively into space. 'What about *MAM* – have you seen their version?'

Leading article in München am Mittag *written by Horst Fahne, editor-in-chief:*

. . . responsibility to the public . . . concern for our democratic system of government . . . deem it our bounden duty to call for a full and frank explanation . . .

. . . therefore address the following questions to the Mayor:

1. Is it true that close ties of friendship existed between Harald Fein, managing director of a major construction company, and Hermann Abendroth of the Urban Planning Department?

2. Is it possible that Herr Fein gained access to urban development plans prior to their publication, notably plans for road links with the Olympic site?

3. Did the Mayor become acquainted with these facts and

230

suffer them in silence, or did he simply refuse to acknowledge them? This would, to say the least, constitute a dereliction of administrative responsibility . . .

'And you're prepared to swallow that?' Heinz stared at his father incredulously.

'You don't understand,' Harald said. 'It's a long story.'

'Then let me in on it.'

'It would be better for us both if you kept out of this. You could get hurt, and I don't want that.'

'No,' Keller said firmly, one hand on Anton's head. 'Your son's part of this, Herr Fein. I know it wasn't your intention. It wasn't mine either. I didn't deliberately rope him in – he became involved of his own free will, more or less.'

'Involved?' Harald shook his head and frowned.

'Yes, for your sake.'

Heinz was quick to interrupt. 'I thought you weren't a sentimentalist, Herr Keller. Forget about personal relationships. I smelt a rat and I had to do something about it – I couldn't help myself.'

'Do something?' Harald said.

'I'll explain later,' Keller interposed swiftly. 'There's something more urgent on the agenda. Messer told me to tell you that you're almost out of the wood. Braun's prepared to cross you off his list. Permanently, subject to certain conditions.'

'What the hell does that mean?' Heinz turned on the policeman. 'What's the "almost", and what's all this about "Braun is prepared"? He plans to do some more horse-trading – I can smell it.'

'Your father,' Keller said in a slow, patient voice, 'is merely expected to help find the guilty party – come up with a name. Penatsch, perhaps.'

'Great!' Heinz exclaimed. He jumped to his feet and paced up and down the room. Suddenly he stopped in front of his father. 'It's quite simple. You only have to incriminate some poor bastard of a janitor and you've got it made. From now on you can sit back and design mansions for bloated plutocrats who don't know what to do with their millions. Frame a member of the proletariat and you're free. Free for what, from what and for whom – that's what I'd like to know.'

Keller replied for Harald, who sat hunched in his chair. 'You underrate him, he underrates you. It's fascinating to watch.'

'Who am I underrating?' Heinz demanded. 'A man who happens to be my father, and who's wondering whether to stick someone else's head in a noose – a miserable porter, a capitalist coolie who cleans up after other people.'

'Your father doesn't have to do anything he doesn't want to,' Keller said gravely. 'His problem lies elsewhere.'

'Cut it out!' Harald snapped. 'I don't want Heinz burdened with that.'

'Burdened?' Keller sounded amused. 'His shoulders are broader than you think. It's time you gave him credit for a little maturity.'

'I raised some dust,' Heinz said, 'that's all.'

'In the meantime,' the policeman continued, 'I've made a number of inquiries about Helga.'

Heinz swung round. 'Who was responsible – have you found out at last?'

'Do you really want to know?' Keller spoke very quietly, looking at Harald. 'Whatever the truth?'

'My father and I think along the same lines,' said Heinz, 'even if our ideas don't always coincide. Isn't that so?'

'It is now,' Harald said.

'Can you guess what I'm driving at?' Keller's question might have been an ultimatum. 'Are you prepared for a shock – something which may shake you even more than you suspected?'

'Yes,' Harald said resolutely. 'Whatever it is, I want to know.'

Results of inquiries made by Detective-Superintendent Keller and his colleagues into the relations between Paul Plattner and his granddaughter Helga Fein. First, Keller's introductory remarks to Harald Fein and his son Heinz:

Please believe me when I say that I've hesitated for a long time before disclosing what I can't conceal from you any longer. I should point out at once that little of it could be used in a court of law. It consists for the most part of likely inferences, suspicious features, circumstantial evidence, and so on.

You needn't accept any of our findings, but they could have an extremely important bearing on a personal decision which you'll both have to make in due course.

Like Braun, I had a definite hunch about you from the outset, Herr Fein. I felt you were trying to shield or protect someone. In the circumstances, it could only have been one of three people – your son, your daughter or your friend. Paul Plattner took an equally intense interest in all three, though for very different reasons.

Helga is dead. Abendroth has been successfully and publicly compromised. There remains your son. I presume he'll take over the firm one day – and that, Herr Fein, is what you were anxious not to prevent. Your paternal affection was too strong.

'Bugger that!' Heinz declared robustly. 'I don't mean paternal affection – I'm talking about nepotism and inherited wealth.'

'Please,' Harald said, 'think what you're saying.'

'What your father means,' Keller cut in, watching Heinz closely, 'is that you're jeopardizing a vast inheritance. It may come easy to you today, but how will you feel in a few years' time?'

Harald nodded. 'I couldn't have put it better.'

'You mean you were ready to shield the old man, just for my sake?'

Harald nodded again.

'Let me get this straight,' Heinz said. 'Were you prepared to insure my future at any price?'

'Yes,' Harald replied, looking his son full in the eyes. 'I've gone without a lot of things in my life. I've been exploited, abused and vilified, but I swallowed it all – ultimately for your sake.'

'Thanks,' Heinz retorted, 'but if I've caught the Superintendent's drift, this is carrying tolerance too far.'

'I think so too.' Harald nodded at his son and turned to Keller. 'Be absolutely frank, Superintendent. I insist on it.'

The telephone on Superintendent Braun's desk gave a discreet buzz. Inspector Feldmann picked up the receiver and briskly stated his name and rank.

The Public Prosecutor's voice, imperious as a rule, sounded almost ingratiating. Dr Barthel asked to speak to Braun, but Feldmann informed him that the superintendent was out.

'According to my notes, Inspector, you're responsible for routine inquiries in the V-Strasse case.'

Feldmann agreed that he was.

'In that case, could you come round – at once, if possible. Herr Feininger is with me. I have reason to believe that he can give you some information of major importance.'

'I'll be right over.'

Extracts from a file on Paul Plattner compiled by colleagues of Detective-Superintendent Keller and submitted by the latter to Harald Fein and his son Heinz:

1. The death of Frau Plattner, who had recently given birth to a daughter, Hilde, occurred in 1932 at St Paul de Vence, inland from the French Riviera. Ostensibly an accident. Frau Plattner died from injuries sustained after falling off a cliff. Det.-Insp. Grandier of the Nice CID considered that the odds on suicide and murder were equal. He suspected that the husband, Paul Plattner, was not the father of his wife's child. No definite proof was forthcoming on any of these points.

2. According to vague and legally inadmissible revelations on the part of domestic servants formerly employed at the Tegernsee villa, a sporadic but intimate relationship existed between Paul Plattner and Hilde, his putative daughter. These observations covered the years 1945, 1950–51 and, finally, 1964.

3. Plattner has pursued various sexual relationships inside and outside his firm. With his private secretary during the period 1950–65, also – on isolated occasions – as late as 1969. Other liaisons have involved a technical draughtswoman, an interior designer, and two junior employees from the typing pool. Also a Lufthansa stewardess, a receptionist employed by a political party which enjoys his financial backing, a hotel secretary and numerous others.

4. From the age of 50 or so onwards, he has patronized prostitutes of all categories, from street-walkers to high-priced call-girls. Among those definitely identified: Petra, Promenadeplatz, Ina, Sendlingerstrasse, Erika, Sonnenstrasse, also various random encounters at Fasching and the Oktoberfest. Addresses appended. Among his more regular haunts: Ungererstrasse, Gabelsberger-platz and 33 V-Strasse.

5. Helga Fein, daughter of Harald and Hilde Fein.

Detective-Inspector Feldmann found Barthel and Feininger awaiting him in the Public Prosecutor's office.

234

'My dear Inspector,' Barthel said, 'Herr Feininger has at last taken me into his confidence.' Feininger nodded.

'How do you mean, sir?'

Barthel smiled urbanely. 'Herr Feininger is a public figure. As such, he's governed by certain considerations – by the need for discretion.'

'And his discretion has extended to the V-Strasse case?' Feldmann inquired politely.

Now it was Feininger's turn to speak while Barthel nodded an obbligato. 'After thoroughly checking my records once more, Inspector, I cannot exclude the possibility that I was actually present on the night in question, but only for a very limited period.'

'On the sixth floor?' Feldmann asked without blinking. 'In the dead woman's apartment?'

Barthel cleared his throat. 'Herr Feininger walked in because the door was open, but – to repeat – he only stayed a few moments. There was a certain disorder about the place which aroused his misgivings.'

'In other words,' Feldmann said, addressing Feininger direct, 'the woman was dead when you got there?'

'She must have been,' Feininger replied uneasily. 'But I only saw her stretched out on the bed – I thought she was dead drunk, so I left immediately. That's all I can tell you.'

'Interesting, sir, but insufficient to put you in the clear.' Feldmann waited patiently. 'Can't you remember anything else which might give us a lead?'

Keller, Harald and Heinz. Further particulars of the fifth item on the list of findings relating to Helga Fein:

Helga's affections seem to have been centred on her father. If she cherished one genuine passion in her short life, it was for him.

All inquiries conducted in her various haunts, among friends and casual acquaintances, elicited the same answer. When it came to the pinch, Helga rejected sexual overtures and was commonly described as a 'tease'. The autopsy revealed that she was still *virgo intacta.*

She suffered a sudden trauma when she thought her father had become involved with Frau Weber, whom she regarded – to quote her diary – as a 'degenerate, destructive creature'. In evident agitation, she borrowed a friend's car and took off. Her destination was the Tegernsee.

'No,' Harald said. His voice was almost a whisper. 'It can't be true.'

'Because you refuse to believe it?' Keller demanded inexorably.

Heinz said: 'God, what a lousy world! You've got to face it – anybody's capable of anything.'

'Do I remember anything else?' Feininger mused. 'Yes, perhaps. A conversation which strikes me as curious, in retrospect.'

'With whom and about what?' Feldmann asked. 'Can you recall the precise time?'

Feininger knit his brow. 'It was a remark rather than a conversation. I left the apartment about 10 p.m. or a little after – almost as soon as I'd entered it. In the corridor I bumped into the janitor, who suddenly materialized from nowhere. He said – and I quote his actual words – "You haven't seen me and I haven't seen you." '

'He said that, did he?' Feldmann paused. 'Weren't you puzzled?'

'Not at first,' Feininger said. 'I simply thought the man must be deranged!'

Detective-Superintendent Keller, continuing his résumé of inquiries into Helga Fein's death, with special reference to Paul Plattner:

We know that Helga reached Plattner's country house overlooking the Tegernsee at about three o'clock on Saturday afternoon. The dinner engagement between Herr Fein and Frau Weber had taken place the previous evening. Helga spent the rest of the night in various Schwabing bars and slept at a third-class hotel, drunk but alone.

She had lunch in a café in Occamstrasse, still alone, before driving out to the Tegernsee, where she was warmly greeted by her grandfather, Herr Plattner. She remained with him until just after 10 p.m., when she rushed out of the house with her clothes in disarray, sobbing wildly. This has been attested by three independent witnesses.

Helga's suicide would seem to have occurred the same day,

towards midnight. She parked the borrowed car outside her friend's house and mailed the keys through the letter-box. Then she took a taxi to Schloss Nymphenburg. Not altogether by chance, because the diaries made available to me by her brother refer several times to walks with her father in the grounds there and beside the canal – happy occasions which obviously meant a great deal to her.

Her body was discovered the following Wednesday, or three days later. My department was notified and identification duly took place. I not only conducted an extremely thorough examination myself but consulted Herr Frisch-Galatis of Zürich, who happened to be visiting Munich at the time.

Frisch-Galatis, who is acknowledged to be the foremost micro-analyst in the Western world, detected some staples of grey wool on the deceased's outer clothing and undergarments. It proved possible to identify their source: a grey worsted material exported by the Scottish firm McDonald's of Edinburgh. The only tailor to stock it in Southern Germany is Wichtl's, from whom Paul Plattner customarily orders his suits.

Heinz said: 'So we've got the swine.'

Keller combed Anton's shaggy coat with his fingers. 'May I point out that you're talking about your grandfather?'

'A swine is a swine, period.'

'He could be just a helpless swine,' Keller said thoughtfully, 'a man who's spent a lifetime at the mercy of his instincts.'

'Is that the way you look at it?' Heinz asked his father.

'No. If he was responsible for Helga's death, I want him brought to book. Do you agree?'

Heinz nodded grimly.

'Don't count your chickens,' Keller said. 'Just because you know something it doesn't mean you can prove it, not by a long shot. Still, you seem to have lost your inhibitions at last. Braun will be overjoyed.'

Ensuing telephone conversation between Detective-Superintendent Keller and Counsellor Messer, the latter still at Police Headquarters:

MESSER: At last! I've been on tenterhooks. The gentlemen in charge of this case are gnawing their knuckles with impatience, especially Braun. Well?

KELLER: Your client saw a person of his acquaintance enter and leave 33 V-Strasse at about the crucial time on the night of the murder. He clearly recognized the man but he hasn't actually named him, so please treat what I'm going to say as a lead, not positive identification.

MESSER: Come on, give. Who was it?

KELLER: Paul Plattner.

'Paul Plattner,' Messer told Braun a few minutes later. The two men were alone.

'Finally!' Braun exclaimed, making no effort to disguise his triumph. 'So I was right all the time, Counsellor – my instinct didn't deceive me. Why didn't he come clean in the first place? Never mind, there's still time. I've hooked my fish at last.'

'Who do you mean?'

'Not your client, if that's what you want to hear – you're welcome to him. No, with Feininger and Plattner on the hook I'm well on the way to publicly cleaning out this rats' nest – and that, Counsellor, is something I've a yen to do. If my instinct is still functioning properly, this show could develop into a smash hit.'

'In that case,' said Messer, visibly relieved, 'have fun.'

Returning to his office, Braun discovered a note from Feldmann on his desk. It said: 'In conference with Barthel and Feininger.'

Braun promptly headed for Barthel's office, where he asked Feldmann to fill him in and then, with evident relish, took charge.

'Your readiness to co-operate is appreciated,' he told Feininger unceremoniously. 'In effect, you're a potential witness. If Penatsch comes to trial you'll have to give evidence.' Braun savoured the glance of agonized entreaty that passed between Feininger and the Public Prosecutor. 'It'll all be handled as discreetly as possible, of course, but with due attention to detail.'

'And in close consultation with me, Superintendent,' Barthel insisted.

'Of course, sir,' Braun assured him blandly. 'Let's make a start right away.' He turned to Feldmann and told him to pick up Penatsch.

The confrontation took place less than an hour later.

Feininger pointed at the janitor and said: 'That's the man. He

238

was the one who suggested that we should keep quiet about our meeting.'

Penatsch said: 'All I know is, this gentleman was a regular visitor to the dead girl's apartment. I've never spoken to him in my life.'

'Wonderful!' Braun said, rubbing his hands with glee. He assiduously ignored the Public Prosecutor's warning glances, Feininger's thunderous face and Feldmann's mounting disquiet. 'Another pair of conflicting statements. Let's see if we can iron out your little differences, shall we?'

Memorandum from Detective Chief Superintendent Dürrenmaier to the Commissioner of Police:

Harald Fein eliminated from list of suspects. Investigation still proceeding in respect of Penatsch, Feininger and Plattner. The officer in charge, Det.-Supt Braun, has again been urged to proceed with due discretion and submit daily reports on his findings.

Memorandum drafted by the Commissioner of Police and clipped to the foregoing:

I want this case listed as Item No. 1 on our agenda for next Monday's weekly conference with divisional chiefs. All divisions to be notified in advance and requested to contribute information with a possible bearing on the case. Any urgent details to be communicated at once to Det. Chief Supt Dürrenmaier.

Those to be informed of the above: first, the Public Prosecutor, via normal channels but soonest; second, His Honour the Mayor, by me personally and with equal speed.

Special note for the press officer, Police HQ: all five dailies distributed within the city limits are to be informed of these developments, but off the record. Their constructive co-operation is invited.

Further information about the case will be released exclusively by Det. Chief Supt Dürrenmaier, working in direct consultation with me.

'Well, gentlemen, that's it,' Messer declared proudly. 'We may not have won every trick, but the rubber's ours.'

He surveyed the occupants of Harald's apartment – Harald

himself, Heinz, Keller and Anton. They stared back at him with extreme scepticism, especially Anton. It dawned on Messer that he had failed to unleash a storm of enthusiasm.

'What more do you want?' he demanded. 'We've done everything humanly possible. Herr Fein is off the hook. I've managed to extricate him from the V-Strasse case and exposed his wife's divorce petition as a tissue of lies. Jonas has been neutralized too, which eliminates his evidence in any proceedings for embezzlement and tax evasion. The foreman and the gateman have talked, so he'll undoubtedly be charged with incitement to commit a burglary, not to mention robbery with violence. Last but not least, Plattner and his daughter seem privately to have dropped Jonas like a hot potato. If that isn't an achievement, what is?'

'Some achievement, Counsellor,' Heinz said scathingly. 'A family destroyed, a firm on the brink of ruin, my sister driven to her death and my father's only real friendship exploited and abused. Finally a mixed-up dog that doesn't know who he belongs to any more. I congratulate you.'

Messer shook his head, undeterred. 'All the things you mention are regrettable from the human point of view, but legally the picture's different. I know, don't tell me – mental scars hurt more than broken bones, but my province is the law. From that angle, we've won.'

'Seems to me you've only exposed the tip of an iceberg,' Keller said. 'There's another four-fifths below the surface.'

'And it isn't going to stay submerged,' Heinz said harshly. 'My father and I don't want it that way.'

Harald nodded vigorously before relapsing into pensive silence.

'Look, what more do you want?' Messer repeated the question uneasily. 'A murder charge against Plattner? We'd be tilting at windmills.'

'I'm afraid you're right,' Keller said. 'Moral certainty and solid proof are two different things. Protecting Abendroth from the worst of the muck that's being slung at him would be a good deal. The Mayor can do it if anyone can.'

Press conference in Room 208, City Hall, same day. The invitation merely let it be known that the Mayor wished to make a statement and would be pleased, at its conclusion, to answer any questions put to him. His Honour the Mayor:

240

I refer to some direct questions addressed to me by a local daily, and which I consider it only natural to answer.

You will find copies of all relevant documents, together with the full text of my previous statements, in the folders on the table in front of you – also reproductions of all documents that have so far come to light and are known to the municipal administration.

Now to the point at issue.

Friendships, whomsoever they involve, are natural and un-objectionable relationships – whether between Herr Fein and Herr Abendroth, between Herr Abendroth and myself, between the provincial premier and his party chairman, between Young Socialists and certain members of the press.

Human ties of this kind cannot be dismissed as reprehensible, let alone undesirable. All that matters is the ability to divorce private life from public office.

To continue. A start was made early in 1967 on important and confidential plans for our city's Olympic complex and, in particular, for the approach roads. Controversy has recently centred upon purchases of land and buildings, notably in the Sunset Estate district, made by Plattner Construction or a firm of brokers acting on behalf of that company. All such purchases were completed in 1967 or early 1968.

No connection exists, or can exist, between the Urban Planning Department's projected scheme and business transactions under-taken by the said company or its agents.

The lay-out designed and officially submitted by Herr Abend-roth in mid-1967 was based on the ring-road pattern, with approach roads radiating from the centre. It did not envisage the direct, broad, multi-lane highway on which Plattner Construction is alleged to have gambled.

Herr Abendroth's preliminary radial design was eventually – after lengthy discussion – adjudged not wholly satisfactory by the relevant City Hall committee, by road communication experts, and by me personally.

We therefore commissioned two more town-planning experts, one based in Frankfurt and the other in Berlin, to submit blue-prints of their own. This was at the end of 1967.

Their lay-outs were not submitted until the beginning of 1968, by which time the said company's acquisitions in the Sunset Estate district were virtually complete. The Berlin scheme was then adopted by a majority vote. It corresponded in several important respects with road development schemes which had already been launched and to some extent completed.

The inference is inescapable. No one can have known in 1967 of something which did not materialize until 1968. The allegation that a private concern gained premature access to our urban development schemes because of an indiscretion, whether deliberate or unwitting, is therefore unfounded and absurd.

So much for my statement. And now, please, your questions.

No questions were put.

'That's that!' Messer sounded thoroughly elated. 'All our clouds are melting away.'

'So are the Mayor's,' Keller said approvingly. 'They always do.'

'He's a smart operator,' Messer agreed. 'That man could teach us all a thing or two – even you, Superintendent.'

'Granted,' said Keller. 'What do you think, Herr Fein?'

Harald emerged from his reverie. 'One thing I haven't quite grasped is the function of the red folder. It isn't in my possession. Plattner or Jonas must have it.'

'You've forgotten another possibility,' Keller pointed out. 'There's your son.'

'How does Heinz come into it?'

'Somebody had to do something,' said Heinz. He sounded quite serene. 'You handed me that spare key to give to my beloved grandfather. Before I did so I peeked at the contents of the firm's safe. The red folder caught my eye, so I took it.'

'Quite so,' Messer interjected quickly. 'You mistakenly assumed that the folder belonged to your father so you took it into safe-keeping, intending to hand it over at the first opportunity. Then you forgot. No question of theft or misappropriation – it was a private family matter, not a criminal offence.'

Keller glanced at the lawyer and chuckled. 'One thing I promise. If I'm ever picked up for shop-lifting I'll ask you to defend me.'

Harald, who was visibly dismayed by the latest revelation, said: 'But Heinz, didn't it ever occur to you that you might gravely incriminate Hermann, not to mention me?'

'No. If you'd really been in cahoots, I mightn't have made the information public – mightn't have, I said – but I asked Hermann

242

come. I'll take care of Feininger myself – it'll be a pleasure. You concentrate on Plattner plus staff, in other words, Jonas, Rogalski, Pollock, the Wagnersberger woman, Wamsler and anybody else available.

Try and dig up anything that suits our case – anything at all. Feel free to employ auditors, quantity surveyors, paid informers. No need to look as if you'd bitten on a lemon, Feldmann. This whole thing's about money, and criminals need paying. Don't overlook a thing – private accounts, expenses vouchers, bonus payments, etcetera.

Don't be discouraged if you only turn up small stuff to begin with. One or two of Plattner's medium-grade or senior employees are bound to come unstuck in the process – his instructions to them may have been given in private but the rank and file had to carry them out. Maybe one of them will spill the beans.

Burrow away at Plattner's foundations until he feels the ground sinking under his feet. That's when he'll start to totter, my friend, and that's when we help him on his way with a final shove.

'I know what gets Father down,' Heinz told Keller, 'me too. It's the agonizing sensation that nothing's going to happen. Not even a partial atonement.'

'So you and your father think nothing can be proved against Plattner, that he's legally fireproof. People will merely say that he hasn't behaved like a gentleman – but then, who does? Is that what you mean?'

'Exactly. The laws of this country are made by capitalists and their henchmen to the detriment of the poor. The place is swarming with informers, errand-boys and political stooges.'

'And policemen. Why leave them off your list?'

Telephone conversation:

HARALD: I hope I'm not disturbing you . . .

ABENDROTH: Good to hear your voice, Harald. How are things?

HARALD: I must ask you to forgive me for all the trouble and unpleasantness I've caused. I can only assure you that it wasn't my intention.

ABENDROTH: Say no more – let's forget it. When are we going to see each other?

HARALD: I'm ringing to say goodbye and thank you again for everything. You've been a good friend, Hermann. Be the same to Heinz. All the best.

'No!' Hilde glared at Joachim Jonas, who stood forlornly in the middle of her drawing-room like a stranded fish. 'I wash my hands of you. You're as much of a failure as Harald.'

'Good God, Hilde, how can you even compare me with that man?'

'You're both the same, underneath. He's slipshod, you're incompetent. Apart from that, you've been deceiving me with Eva-Maria Wagnersberger.'

'A form of insurance, that's all. Look, Hilde, I want to marry you. Together we could . . .'

'Together nothing!' Hilde said implacably. 'How do you plan to keep me? Father's fired you and Duhr won't take you on – he told Father how you tried to sell him your services. You won't get another job anywhere in Munich – or anywhere else. Father will see to that.'

'In that case,' snapped Jonas, mustering the remnants of his dignity, 'there's no point in discussing it.' He walked out.

Hilde did not watch him go. She reached for the phone and dialled a number she knew by heart. It was Melanie Weber's.

Keller let Anton slide to the carpet, where he stretched out, blinking sleepily. The little policeman looked suddenly alarmed. 'What are you scared of?'

'I told you. Father seems hell-bent on forcing a decision.'

'In what way?'

'He stowed a few papers in his briefcase, also something wrapped in a raincoat – it could have been a gun. Then he had the car filled up and brought round the front. My guess is, he's heading for the Tegernsee.'

'Did you come by car?'

'Yes, a Fiat – borrowed. It's outside.'

'Come on, Anton,' said Keller, jumping to his feet.

Confidential report compiled by Detective-Inspector Feldmann for his former mentor, Detective-Superintendent Keller:

    1. Braun and Feininger. Almost total success. Feininger's

attempts at self-defence, aided by Dr Barthel and abetted by Det. Chief Supt Dürrenmaier, virtually useless. One of the big illustrateds is on the war-path. They've sent a team of top reporters to research Feininger's past career. Destruction of war-time records? Personal profits from the award of arms contracts? Shady property deals? Braun is beside himself with joy.

2. Bahr, Provincial Crime Bureau, assigned to crack Penatsch. At least seven items of circumstantial evidence: saliva, semen, urine – even fingerprints. Motive and opportunity deducible from the murdered woman's diary, various statements and comparative analyses tally closely. Bahr's verdict: thorough double-checking needed before a really watertight case can be made out, and that may take days or even weeks. Braun is delighted with this information too – it leaves him free to spin out his inquiries.

3. My own investigation of Plattner plus firm has brought to light several suspicious features ranging from padded expense accounts to tampering with the books. Plenty of obscure items. Special bonuses and ex gratia payments have been made to a number of employees for unspecified reasons. At least four members of the clerical staff are involved in illegal fiddling, and we could probably obtain sufficient evidence to nail them. Still nothing which points the finger directly at Plattner.

Braun keeps telling me to pull out all the stops and leave the rest to him.

Harald entered Plattner's Tegernsee villa by way of the french windows. Plattner was sitting at the head of a long refectory table in the pseudo-baronial hall. A bottle of Tirolean wine stood at his elbow, half full. The glass beside it was empty.

'I've come to settle things,' Harald said.

Plattner showed no particular surprise. 'Haven't you done enough already? My God, what more do you want?'

'I want to know everything.' Harald deposited his briefcase on the table. The soft leather bulged a little as though it concealed something hard and bulky. 'What really happened?'

Plattner leant back wearily with half-closed eyes. 'You mean you still don't know?' In a harsh voice, he went on: 'My daughter and I used to enjoy a happy and harmonious relationship until you destroyed it. You wormed your way into my firm and my confidence. I treated you with the utmost generosity but you unscrupulously abused my trust. The Olympic approach roads were your only contribution to the firm's prosperity. In all other respects your negative attitude proved a grave liability. You helped me to make millions but you've cost me millions more, not to mention my peace of mind.'

'How high would you rate a human life?'

'Sentimental claptrap!' sneered Plattner. 'I'm immune to your maudlin fantasies except in one respect. I wanted Heinz to take over from me, but you've alienated him too. That gets under my skin, I grant you.'

'Superintendent Keller deserves the credit for that, not me.'

'Well, whoever it was, you certainly recruited anyone you could get hold of. For once, you didn't do a bad job. I could have handled Messer – and you, with one hand behind my back – but fighting the entire CID is another matter. I may be down but I'm not out. Some day, months or years hence, I'll be back on top. Who cares what you've destroyed with the help of this man Keller? It needn't be final. Fortunately, we live in a world where money talks.'

'You're back on the subject of money. I was referring to a human being – Helga.'

'Helga,' Plattner echoed. His eyes were shut now, and he was smiling. 'What does anyone really know about me? I was in love with beauty and symmetry, even as a youngster. Human beauty, architectural beauty – not many people have a feeling for it these days. I've always been lonely, at heart.'

'What about Helga?' Harald demanded, leaning forward with his right hand on the briefcase. 'What did you do to her?'

Plattner's smile congealed. His lips barely moved as he said in a toneless voice: 'I'm a loving man – always have been. I loved my wife, who died. I loved my daughter's youth and exuberance, which you destroyed. I loved Heinz's vitality, his restless urge to do something – anything.'

'And Helga?' Harald said fiercely. 'You misused her – you drove her to suicide.'

Plattner limply raised his two gnarled hands as though parrying the charge. 'I always detested you and your feverish imagination. No one becomes a drunk by accident. You dare sit in judgement on me – you, of all people? It wasn't I who misused Helga, it was you. You neglected her, disillusioned her, spurned her trust and

248

affection. I tried to give her love – love! For the last time, keep your foul insinuations to yourself.'

'The responsibility for her death is yours alone,' Harald said, unmoved. He opened the briefcase and felt for the automatic inside.

'Be reasonable. Who could prove such a thing?'

'I could,' said a calm, businesslike voice in the background. It was Keller.

'Come away with me.' Joachim Jonas's feigned optimism didn't conceal the desperate urgency in his voice. 'Grab every piece of paper you can lay hands on – anything we can convert into cash.'

Eva-Maria Wagnersberger, every inch the chairman's private secretary, eyed him coolly. 'What's in it for me?'

'My love,' Jonas declared with a flourish. 'Wedding-ring thrown in – you can even have it in writing if you like. That's worth something, isn't it?'

'Peanuts,' said Eva-Maria, 'compared with my latest offer from the old man.'

Plattner's offer consisted of an irrevocable contract of employment worth DM36,000 per annum and adjustable to conform with rises in the cost of living. Having helped him to make millions of marks, she was to be repaid in tens of thousands. It was a meagre return, but security had its attractions.

'But what about our relationship, Eva?'

'How much is that worth, in hard cash?'

Heinz had driven Keller and Anton to Plattner's Tegernsee villa in the borrowed sports car. Keller spent most of the trip briefing himself on the villa's location, its immediate surroundings and interior lay-out. Finally he said:

'Heinz, you go round to the back of the house and get in from the terrace. Concentrate on your father's briefcase. Anton and I will make a normal entrance via the front door, though I may have to use the skeleton key I've borrowed from the department. Let's hope we're in time.'

They were.

Heinz paused just inside the french windows. Keller, accompanied by Anton, walked into the room. They closed in on Plattner, slowly and gingerly. The figures on the black-and-white chequered floor of the great hall might have been pieces in a game of human chess. Plattner rose and stared at Keller.

'So it's you,' he said resignedly. 'You and that damned dog.' He glanced at Anton, who had sat down and was regarding him intently. 'I thought I'd seen everything.'

Monologue delivered by Detective-Superintendent Braun to cronies at his regular table in the Bürgerbräu beer cellar and recorded for Keller's benefit by Detective-Inspector Feldmann:

Far be it from me to knock members of my own profession, but our police marksmen didn't exactly shine during that bank raid in Prinzregentenstrasse, when the thieves took hostages. They held off too long.

It wouldn't have happened if I'd been in charge. I'd have stationed myself alongside the marksmen with a pair of binoculars and given the order to fire at will. Disabling shots aimed straight at the hand holding the tommy-gun. If the bastard had caught one in the chest or belly, that would have been his hard luck.

Shoot fast, shoot straight, and hit the target, that's what matters. You can't treat villains like frustrated gentlemen. If you do, it's an invitation to murder. What if some innocent person did get killed in the process? Very regrettable and not to be dismissed as an operational blunder, but it wasn't a police bullet that did the real damage.

These things happen all the time, but in side streets, behind drawn curtains or in the thick of rush-hour traffic – not in front of a thousand spectators, under spotlights and with a dozen crime reporters in attendance. Not in a party atmosphere, with snacks supplied by Käfer's.

Small wonder people make such a fuss about security, but the only way they'll get it is via the police. It's time they realized that, including the mealy-mouthed liberals who use the police as scapegoats and blame the victim rather than the murderer.

'So you think,' Keller said, 'that some crimes are immune to the law. If so, you're mistaken.'

'Are you threatening me?'

'No, just setting you straight.'

Keller was now sitting at one end of the long refectory table, which dominated the room, with Plattner facing him at the other end and Anton, growling and straining at the leash, beside him. Harald had abandoned his pistol-laden briefcase and was leaning against an ornate baroque cabinet.

'I'm sick of being harassed by the police,' Plattner burst out.

'I'm sure you are.' Keller gave a thin smile. 'I'm familiar with Superintendent Braun's methods. He's going to give you a lot of trouble.'

'I don't propose to sit back and take it.'

'I know,' Keller told him. 'I'm aware that you're taking steps to dispose of your Munich company – in other words, sell out. You're negotiating with Duhr, and Duhr seems willing to buy. How much is he offering, thirty million?'

'Forty,' Plattner said, not without pride. He glanced at Harald and Heinz, but they didn't look at him.

'Added to your private fortune, which is estimated at twenty million, that gives you sixty million to play with. Not a bad little stake.'

Plattner turned to the man who was still his son-in-law. 'Look, Harald, you know the firm's worth a lot more than that. You can take over the chairmanship if you like. I'll treble your directors' fees and give you a decent slice of the equity.'

'What happened to Helga?' Harald asked.

Plattner raised his right hand, slowly, beseechingly, as if the movement hurt him. 'I'm even prepared to give a written guarantee, legally attested, that Heinz will inherit the firm on my death. It's still one of the biggest construction companies in this part of the world. What do you say, Heinz?'

'The same as Father. I also want to know what happened to Helga.'

Keller shifted in his chair. 'I can supply a few details.'

'You bastard!' Plattner's voice rose to an uncontrolled bellow. 'Keep out of this. Haven't you done enough damage already? Is there no end to your interference?'

'Oh, yes,' Keller said calmly as he smoothed Anton's bristling fur, 'the end is in sight.'

'You're a bureaucrat!' Plattner roared. 'A pathetic nobody who carries out other people's instructions. I'm a self-made man and proud of it – an empire-builder!'

'It all depends on your point of view,' Keller said indulgently. 'From where I stand, you're the husband of a woman who died in suspicious circumstances, the father of a putative daughter with whom you committed incest or, at best, acts of gross indecency involving a minor, and the father-in-law of a man whom you hated and persecuted. You tried to monopolize your grandson and failed, so you concentrated on your granddaughter instead. With fatal results.'

'This is outrageous!' Plattner shouted. 'Not only outrageous but ludicrous! What gives you the right to rummage around in my private life?'

'A man's private life,' said Keller, 'can be an interminable series of torments which warp his mind and turn him into an agent of destruction – yet the law cannot touch him. It was so in your case, until Helga died.'

Plattner shook his head like a wounded bull. 'Stop threatening me, you fool. Keep your platitudes to yourself!'

'Helga's death,' Keller continued gravely, 'moved me. I've seen many thousands of dead bodies in my time, but I'll never forget how she looked – so young, so sad and helpless.'

Harald and Heinz gazed at Keller as if they were seeing him for the first time. Plattner stared fixedly into space. He opened his mouth and shut it without saying a word. Anton tugged violently at his lead.

From one moment to the next, Keller's voice became crisp and unemotional. 'I employed the services of a forensic scientist. He found some traces of wool on her underclothes. They were structurally distinctive.'

'And you call that evidence?' Plattner revived perceptibly. 'Textile manufacturers turn out cloth by the mile.'

'That's not the point, Herr Plattner. Our micro-analyst conducted his experiment in reverse as well – counter-verification, we call it – and the system paid off. He was able to detect and identify minute pieces of fluff from Helga's underclothes on a pair of trousers belonging to you.'

'You're bluffing!' Plattner said thickly. 'Anyway, how did you get hold of my clothes? Did you steal them – have them stolen?'

'Give me credit for a little ingenuity and initiative,' said Keller. 'And don't be misled by your mistaken belief that I'm a policeman. I retired today, so that makes me a private citizen. It also leaves me plenty of time to devote to you. I've a host of friends in the force who'll be only too glad to help me earn my fee as a private investigator.'

Harald looked at Heinz. 'In that case we may as well go.'

'As soon as you like,' Heinz said. 'This place smells – I need some fresh air, badly. Are you coming, Herr Keller?'

'In a minute or two. As soon as I've tied up a few loose ends.'

Confidential report based on unofficial notes. Detective Chief Superintendent Dürrenmaier to the Commissioner of Police:

1. Sale of Plattner Construction to Clemens Duhr virtually completed. Deal hammered out at the Tegernsee villa, final negotiations in Marbella, where Plattner owns sizeable plots of land and is planning to build hotels. Financial arrangements handled via the Swiss Banking Corporation in Lugano, where Eva-Maria Wagnersberger has just acquired a two-roomed apartment.

2. Jonas. Left Munich for Hamburg, then Frankfurt. No new job in the building industry. Has obviously been black-listed by Duhr, doubtless by private arrangement with Plattner. Obtained a position with a real estate company in Frankfurt but was dismissed a week later. Has since vanished without trace.

3. Hilde Fein. Has left on a world tour with Melanie Weber. SAS booking. Nothing of note to report.

4. Henri Messer, attorney-at-law. His latest acquisition is Feininger, who has retained him to defend in any future criminal proceedings. Messer is clearly trying to influence Feininger politically. The latter's sudden and spectacular advocacy of tenants' rights has made headlines – even the Mayor is showing signs of alarm at all this purposeful activity.

5. Have instructed Det.-Supt Braun – after a confidential chat with Det.-Insp. Feldmann – to concentrate on Penatsch from now on. Case almost complete. Arrest imminent.

Paul Plattner rose with an effort. 'How did it come to this, Keller? How much are they paying you? What sort of a price did they put on my head?'

'A high one,' Keller told him earnestly. 'At least, I think so. The fee is sitting here beside me.'

Plattner's eyes widened in disbelief. 'That miserable hound? You can't be serious! I meant to have the beast poisoned but I never got round to it – the damned thing was always snarling at me. Anyone would think it knew, all the time . . .'

Statements concerning the dog Anton.

1. Proprietor of The Dog-House, Malthäserpassage, Munich:

. . . was offered a most peculiar dog of indeterminate breed, slightly under giant poodle size . . . probably born mid-1966 . . . brought to me by an old man from the Sunset Estate district . . . said he couldn't afford to keep it . . . asked thirty and I gave him ten . . . christened the dog Anton and displayed him in the shop window . . . really, a most extraordinary-looking creature . . . bought only two days later by a Herr Plattner, for two hundred marks . . .

2. From Helga Fein's diary:

. . . presented with a dog by Grandfather, a dear creature. Mother was furious, called him a smelly mongrel any decent person would be ashamed to be seen with. Heinz christened him the Gorgeous Beast and Daddy took no notice of him, not at first . . .

3. Harald Fein, in conversation:

I can't recall exactly when it happened or how, but one day when I was feeling even more depressed than usual Anton jumped on to my lap and settled down as though he'd taken root there. From then on he never left my side.

He stayed with me even when I was admitted to a drying-out home for alcoholics. I insisted on his company and, after a lot of humming and hawing, they consented. Anton's manifestations of sympathy were persistent and unmistakable. He only had to sit there and gaze at me with those big brown eyes of his, and I got the feeling that I owed him a great deal of affection.

One thing I'm certain of. I didn't adopt him – he adopted me. Not permanently, though.

'That dog,' Plattner said to Keller, 'which I acquired so unsuspectingly, has turned out to be an instrument of the devil. Damned mongrel! I'm sure it helped to destroy my daughter's family life.'

Keller smiled. 'Or showed up the destruction that was already there. Anton has his role in life and he performs it with exceptional singlemindedness, quite instinctively and to great effect – that's another reason why I'm fond of him. Well, now I feel I've earned him.'

A small party had gathered in the restaurant of Munich's Riem Airport: Hermann Abendroth and Heinz Fein, Detective-Superintendent Keller (retd) and his dog Anton.

They had come to say goodbye. Harald was booked on the daily flight to New York. He had been invited to do some architectural research in California and give lectures there. After that he was going to Rio for the same purpose. Later, he intended to settle in Italian Switzerland. 'My life has been a series of wasted opportunities,' he had told Keller a few days earlier. 'There's a lot to learn and I don't feel too old to start again.'

He looked surprised as he stared around at the people who had come to see him off.

'And I always thought I was alone in the world,' he said happily.

Hermann Abendroth blew his nose hard. 'A friend always has friends.'

'Speaking for myself,' Heinz said, 'I didn't choose you as a father, but I'm your son just the same.' He paused. 'And glad to be, lately.'

Harald walked over to Keller, gripped his hand and shook it without speaking. Then he knelt down beside Anton and held him close. The dog leant against him heavily, tail wagging.

'Keller,' Harald said, 'if it weren't for you I couldn't bring myself to leave Anton behind. We're the only two people who love this splendid creature as he deserves to be loved.'

Keller smiled down at him. 'Because we're experts on the human capacity for good and evil. Dogs can sense such things. Anton has always known what it is to lead a dog's life – never abandoning hope of being loved unreservedly in spite of everything. Many people have never experienced such a hope and lots of them are forced to bury it still-born. They go on living, but what a life!'